HAWK

Peter Smalley was born in Melbourne, Australia, and hails from a seafaring family. After an early career in advertising he became a screenwriter, broadcaster, and novelist. He lives in London with his wife, Clytie.

Praise for Peter Smalley

'... salute a new master of the sea. Smalley is intending to appropriate the capacious mantle of the late Patrick O'Brian and, on the strength of this book, it should prove a snug fit. Smalley has written a real page-turner, engrossing and enthralling, stuffed with memorable characters. Highly recommended.' *Daily Express*

'Following in the wake of Hornblower and Patrick O Brian . . . there is enough to satisfy the most belligerent armchair warrior: cutlasses, cannibals, as well as a hunt for buried treasure. All this plus good taut writing gets Peter Smalley's series off to a flying start.' *Sunday Telegraph*

'Breathtakingly exciting, magnificent. He captures the stench of brutal conflict in a series of scenes which at once thrill and horrify and which propel readers along at breakneck speed, leaving them gasping for breath. There can be no doubt that *Port Royal* represents storytelling at its very best.' *Daily Express*

PETER SMALLEY
THE
HAWK

arrow books

Published in the United Kingdom by Arrow Books in 2009

1 3 5 7 9 10 8 6 4 2

Copyright © Peter Smalley, 2008

Peter Smalley has asserted his right under the Copyright, Designs and Patents Act, 1988
to be identified as the author of this work.

This novel is a work of fiction. Names and characters are the product of the author's
imagination and any resemblance to actual persons, living or dead, is entirely coincidental

This book is sold subject to the condition that it shall not,
by way of trade or otherwise, be lent, resold, hired out,
or otherwise circulated without the publisher's prior
consent in any form of binding or cover other than that
in which it is published and without a similar condition,
including this condition, being imposed on the
subsequent purchaser

First published in Great Britain in 2008 by
Century

Arrow Books
Random House, 20 Vauxhall Bridge Road,
London SW1V 2SA

www.rbooks.co.uk

Addresses for companies within The Random House Group Limited can be found at:
www.randomhouse.co.uk/offices.htm

The Random House Group Limited Reg. No. 954009

A CIP catalogue record for this book
is available from the British Library

ISBN 9780099513636

The Random House Group Limited supports The Forest Stewardship
Council (FSC), the leading international forest certification organisation. All our
titles that are printed on Greenpeace approved FSC certified paper carry the FSC logo.
Our paper procurement policy can be found at
www.rbooks.co.uk/environment

Typeset by SX Composing DTP, Rayleigh, Essex
Printed in the UK by CPI Bookmarque, Croydon, CR0 4TD

Again for Clytie

FIFE COUNCIL LIBRARIES	
HJ397913	
Askews & Holts	11-Dec-2014
AF	£8.99
GEN	LL

Cutter. A small vessel commonly navigated in the channel of England, furnished with one mast and a straight running bowsprit. Many of these vessels are used on an illicit trade, and others employed by the government to seize them; the latter of which are either under the direction of the Admiralty or Custom-house.

(Falconer's *Dictionary of the Marine*, 1815)

CONTENTS

ONE

1790: Swallow Street, London

Sir Robert Greer looked at himself in his glass, and was frightened.

'Fender! Fender!'

'Sir?' His valet appeared at the door.

'I am unwell. Summon Dr Robards.'

'Unwell, Sir Robert?' Peering at his master. Not five minutes had passed since the valet had fastened the final buttons on his master's coat, turning him gently a little further towards the morning light from the window, and straightened his snowy stock. He had looked very waxy, certainly – but had not complained of feeling ill. 'Is it just come on, sir . . . ?'

'Yes. Yes. Do as I say, man. Dr Robards, at once.' His deep voice a-quiver. He reached a hand for the back of the chair, steadied himself, and sat down. The bumping click as the door of his dressing room swung shut. Fender's footfalls on the stair. Voices. The subdued thud of the great door. A shaft of sun brightened on the floor, and now – a return of the pain.

'Hnnh . . .'

Sir Robert gripped the arm of the chair, the carved mahogany arm. His naturally pallid face was ghastly white, tinged blue about the mouth, his black eyes sunk in his skull. That was what had alarmed him so, when he looked in his glass. His sickly pallor, and his sunken eyes. And now the pain that had woken him this day, as early light crept in discs across the wall, had come back.

Interminable seconds passed as the longcase clock in the corner ticked, and tocked, and ticked. The distant shout of an ostler in the street. Hooves, and passing wheels.

'Where in God's name is Dr Robards –?' The question ending in a hiss of breath. The knuckles tight on the arm of the chair.

At last the sound of a carriage arriving, and the bustle of a person of importance entering the house. A clatter on the stairs as Fender ran on ahead, the creaking of the door, and Fender stood aside.

'Good morning, Sir Robert.' Dr Glendower Robards came in, tall in his black coat, carrying his medical instrument case. He placed it on a second chair, waved Fender out, and approached the patient.

'Thank God you are come, Robards . . . I am not myself . . . hnnh . . .' Dr Robards took the outstretched, clutching hand, and gave reassurance with a squeeze.

'You are in pain, I perceive, Sir Robert. Will you tell me the place, now?' Taking Sir Robert's pulse, and observing its rate against his pocket watch, slipped smoothly from his waistcoat.

Sir Robert pointed to his lower belly with his other hand. 'In my vitals . . . deep in my belly . . .'

'What have you ate, today? You have breakfasted?'

'Nay, I have not. Nothing.'

'Off what did ye dine then, yesternight?' He let go of Sir Robert's wrist, and put away the watch. Adjusted his small frameless oval spectacles, and stared into each of Sir Robert's eyes in turn. 'Hm?'

'Partridge, and a little claret.'

'How little?'

'Eh?' Swallowing, and breathing shallow.

'How little quantity of claret?'

'Very little. A glass only.'

'One glass?'

'Aye.' A further spasm struck, and he hissed, and gripped the chair. 'Damnation . . . ohh . . .'

'We may easily dispose of the pain, in a moment. But first tell me – has it been like this before? Ever before?'

'Yes. Yes. Once or twice before today. But never so bad as this . . . ohh . . .'

'When? Will you tell me exact?'

'For God's sake, Robards. Give me something. Give me some relief.'

'In a moment, Sir Robert. I will not allow you to suffer longer than is entirely necessary. Now then, if you please, when did the pain come?'

'In the morning, once or twice, after I had woke.'

'Early?'

'Aye.'

'Before you had recourse to your piss pot?'

'Yes. I believe so, yes.'

'And was the pain lessened afterward? After ye had passed water?'

'Perhaps it was, a little. But I do not feel pain in my bladder, Robards. Only in my belly.'

'Hm, well. A calculus must pass from the kidney, through the region of your anatomy where you are feeling the spasms. Hm?'

'It is a stone – you think so?'

'Very possibly. Very possibly. Ain't uncommon in gentlemen of your years, Sir Robert.'

'What is the – the treatment?'

'The stone may pass of its own accord. Or it may possibly lodge and remain.'

'Lodge – and remain?'

'In which case, Sir Robert, we must consult the King's own surgeon, Sir Wakefield Bennett.'

'I cannot allow myself to be unwell. I have important business in hand. People that must be pursued, and punished.' Sir Robert drew a determined breath and clasped the arms of his chair as if to rise. A further spasm of pain pinned him in his seat. 'Ohh . . .'

'Do not attempt effortful movement, Sir Robert.' Dr Robards moved to his instrument case. 'I will give you something for the pain.'

'Is it physic?' Shallow, panting breaths.

'It is paregoric elixir, Sir Robert, a liberal measure.' He tipped fat drops of camphorated tincture of opium into a glass, and added water. 'I may prescribe pareira, also.' He handed the glass to his patient. 'Should there be pus in the urine.'

'Pus?' Appalled, clutching the glass.

'You have observed no discoloration of the urine?'

'Nay, none.' Sir Robert drained the glass in one sucking gulp.

'The stream is free-flowing?'

'It is.'

'Hm, that is well.' Taking the empty glass. 'We may perhaps, with good fortune, avoid infection.'

'I wish to put a question. What must I do? What course of action d'ye propose?'

'That is two questions, Sir Robert. In answer to the first, you must practise indolence. As to the second, we must await – developments.'

'Indolence! What nonsense is this? Did not y'hear me? I am engaged on grave matters – '

'Hm. Yes.' Regarding his patient, making a face. 'Grave is the word I fear most, in such a case. I will not like to stand in the rain over yours, and hear the burial service read.'

'Eh?'

'I will like you to be indolent, Sir Robert, if you please. Take broth, and a light diet. No wine. I will leave paregoric to be took at intervals of – let us say – three or four hours. We will wait a week, and if the stone has not yet passed, we will then consult the King's man. Good morning.'

And Dr Robards took up his bag, and quit the house. Sir Robert sat long in his chair, and felt the opium take effect. Felt the pain ease, felt a gradual numbing of his limbs and his senses.

'Indolence,' he said at last. A sigh. If he must be indolent, then he must. His pursuit of Captain William Rennie RN, and Lieutenant James Hayter RN, in the question of treasonable conduct, must lapse for the moment.

'Aye, lapse.' Another breath. 'But not permanent, by God. I will pursue them, and bring the charge home, the moment I am well again. – Fender! Fender!'

'Sir?' At the door.

'I will like to go down to my library. Is there a fire lighted there? Give me your arm, man.'

*

His Majesty's *Hawk* cutter, ten guns, lay at her mooring off the Hard at Portsmouth, immediately south of the dockyard, and some two cables distant from His Majesty's ship *Tamar*, sixty-four, and His Majesty's frigate *Tempest*, thirty-six. *Hawk*'s guns were not yet in her, nor was she provisioned or stored. She had recently been purchased from the small private yard of Thos Varder at Dover, where she had been built to the specification of the Board of Excise, to add to their small fleet, and then commandeered by the Lords Commissioners of the Admiralty in His Majesty's name. She had no guns, and was trimmed only by her ballast of pigs and shingle, but she was a handsome vessel. She was 68 feet long in the lower deck, 51 feet at the keel, 23 feet 6 inches in the beam, and the depth of her hold was a fraction over 10 feet. Her tonnage by builder's measure was 131 and a few ninety-fourths. Her new paint, black along the wales, and her bulwarks red, was reflected in the riding water and emphasized her neat, purposeful lines. Her mast, with topmast and topgallant mast fidded, was tall and slightly raked. That, and her long, flat-sleeved bowsprit, marked her as a revenue ship, able to carry a prodigious spread of canvas both on her square yards and on her steep gaff and long boom. At present her square topsail alone was bent, the yards angled to aid her anchors against the tide. Her commander was absent, as were her midshipmen, her standing officers – boatswain, gunner, carpenter – and her sailing master and steward purser. Indeed, none but her commander had been appointed. A small dockyard crew, assembled by the Master Attendant at the behest of the Admiralty, and the Navy Board, now temporarily manned her. This crew had bent the topsail and mounted an anchor watch.

BOOM.

The noon gun echoed across the harbour, and a flight of black-headed gulls rose wheeling and raucous in alarm, and swooped away towards Gosport across the glinting water.

The Master Attendant Mr Tipping, very florid, stood a little way down the Hard and looked at the *Hawk* from under his shading hand with something like disapproval. To his clerk he said: 'I cannot allow her that mooring very long, with the fleet due.'

'No, sir.' The clerk, nodding.

'*Tamar* must weigh and go up a little, and *Tempest* also. I cannot allow a cutter to occupy that number more than another day or two. It will not answer.'

'No sir.' Shaking his head.

'She don't belong here, unattached. Unmanned, unattached, and God knows where her officers and people may be. I do not. I don't like mystery, and I don't like private ships lying where they oughtn't, Mr Tite.'

'No, sir.'

Mr Tipping looked distractedly at his clerk, frowned down at him, then looked out across the water again. 'I will allow her that number two days more, then I must grow severe. Make a note, Mr Tite.'

'Yes, sir.' Scribbling with his pencil, and following along as Mr Tipping stumped away to the dockyard gates, his wig scattering powder on the shoulder of his coat.

*

'Mr Tipping?'

'Ain't here, sir, just at present.'

'Are not you Mr Tite?'

'I am, sir, yes.' The little clerk, hunched over his desk, saw a well-made young man in the doorway, not in naval dress but with an unmistakably naval bearing; the set of his shoulders, and the placing of his feet a little apart, said that he was a naval officer.

'Were not you the Master Shipwright's clerk, Mr Rundle's clerk . . . ?'

'I was, sir, many a year, but then Mr Rundle passed, d'y'see, and Mr Tipping wanted me – and here I am.'

'Ah.' Nodding. 'I am Lieutenant Hayter, and I – '

'Yes, sir, yes. Mr Tipping did wish to see you most particular urgent, immediate on your coming to Portsmouth.' Laying aside his pen, and rising from his chair.

'Ah. I wished to see the *Hawk* cutter, that I understand – '

'The *Hawk* is here, sir, indeed. Mr Tipping is most desperate anxious that she should weigh and proceed.'

'Weigh and proceed?' Lieutenant James Hayter RN unfastened his cloak and stared at the clerk in the dim light of the Master Attendant's office. 'But I have yet to accept the commission. I have not got my papers, Mr Tite. I wished merely – '

'Oh dear, oh dear. Yes, I see.' A sigh, and he opened and then closed the ledger on his narrow desk, and pushed the inkwell to one side in a tidying motion, and pursed his lips. 'Mr Tipping will be very distressed by that intelligence, I fear. He wished most particular for the *Hawk* to vacate her numbered mooring without further delay.'

'May I see the *Hawk*? Where is the mooring? Is she far out at Spithead, or closer – '

'She is just off the Hard, sir.'

'Is she? Excellent. Then I will go there at once, Mr Tite.' Refastening his brown cloak, and putting on his hat.

'Do you not wish to see Mr Tipping, though? Will I tell him that you – '

But Lieutenant Hayter was already out of the door and striding away across the cobbled dockyard towards the gates, his cloak swirling in the breeze.

He came to the Hard a few minutes after, and strode down the shallow slope towards the water's edge. Boats lay there, and casks, and a group of seamen stood by their barge, smart in their blue jackets and round, beribboned hats, waiting for their officer. James came to a halt, and looked out over the wind-ruffled water. And there he saw the cutter riding at anchor, her topsail angled to the wind, pretty as a picture.

'The *Hawk*,' he murmured.

'Are you for me, sir?' A voice behind him, brisk in tone. James turned.

A short-statured, stooping figure, in an admiral's undress coat and hat. Pale blue eyes, staring cold and direct. Admiral Hollister, Vice-Admiral of the White, commander of the Channel Fleet.

'Well?'

'Sir?' James shook his head a little, entirely at a loss.

'Do not shake y'head at me, sir. Are you our new Third for *Vanquish* – for Captain Repton and myself – or are you not?'

'I am not, sir.'

'Are not you Lieutenant Newell? Lieutenant Rutherford Newell?'

'I am not, sir. I am Lieutenant Hayter, and I – '

'Why are ye not properly dressed, Mr Hayter?'

'I beg your pardon, Admiral, but I am not yet – that is, I am just come to Portsmouth to look at my new ship, and I – '

'New ship?' Admiral Hollister regarded him with a frown,

then: 'Yes, now. Was not your First in the *Expedient* frigate,
under Captain Rennie?'

'I was, sir, but she has paid off, and lies in Ordinary – '

'What is your new ship?'

James pointed. 'The *Hawk* cutter, sir.'

Admiral Hollister shaded his eyes and looked, nodded,
waved away a very young lieutenant who had approached and
now stood waiting, and:

'Yes, I see. Since a cutter is commissioned with only one
lieutenant – she is your first command, hey?'

'That is so, sir. However, I have yet to – '

'Will it aid you to go out to her in my barge, Mr Hayter?
Am perfectly willing to oblige.'

'Well, sir, that is exceeding kind in you, but I am not – '

'Happy to oblige, Mr Hayter.' Over him, nodding
vigorously. 'Most happy to aid a fellow sea officer going into
his first command. Mr Stanway!'

'Sir?' The young lieutenant hurried forward and stood
with his back very straight, his hat correctly off.

'Mr Hayter will join me in my barge. We will take him to
his cutter.' Turning his head to James: 'Tell me her name
again . . . ?'

'She is *Hawk*, sir, ten guns. However, I am – '

'*Hawk*. A felicitous name, for a pretty little bird of prey.
Very good.'

And much against his will – for he had determined merely
to look at the *Hawk* from the shore, and then make his way at
once elsewhere – James clambered into the barge and sat in
the stern sheets with Admiral Hollister. The admiral did his
best to be congenial, and pleasant, as spray flew up from
dipping oars and the barge turned into the wind, by enquiring
after Captain Rennie.

'He is on the beach, sir.' James ducked his head, and
clutched at his hat in the wind.

'He has not got another command?' The blue stare turned
in surprise on James.

'No, sir.'

'That is damned back luck, Mr Hayter. A damned bad business altogether. Their Lordships ought to have applied themselves more assiduous and found something better for a courageous and capable post, that has served the King well, than the wretched low misery of half-pay ashore.'

'I am sure that those are his own sentiments exact, sir.'

'But we had better not damn Their Lordships altogether, hey, Mr Hayter? Perhaps they have got a seventy-four waiting for Captain Rennie at Chatham, or Plymouth, refitting, or undergoing large repair.'

'Perhaps you are right, sir.'

'Hm – but you do not think so, hey? In your heart you do not think so.'

'If I am candid – I do not, sir.'

When the barge reached the *Hawk*, and James had jumped on the cleated side ladder to go aboard, raising his hat in thanks and salute to the admiral, there was no one there on deck. The dockyard artificers who made up the meagre anchor watch were all huddled below in the cramped great cabin, out of the wind.

'Below, there!' James, at the companionway ladder.

An artificer emerged, and slouched up the ladder. He smelled of rum, and a clay pipe was wedged in the side of his mouth. He peered up at James on deck, shading his eyes against the glare.

'Don't you know better than to smoke below?' demanded James.

'The pipe ain't afire, mate. It is fidded in me teeth, permanent, and will not never work loose.'

'Are you a seaman? Who is below there with you?' Hearing other voices.

'No no, mate, we's all artificers out of the yard 'ere. A-lookin' for someone p'tic'lar, was you?'

'No. No, I was not, thank you. I am merely come aboard to look at the ship.' Effortfully polite.

'Ship, izzit? You calls this a ship, does you? Which is very flatterin' of 'er, cert'nly, what is only a piddlin' little sloop, awaitin' on 'er piddlin' bloody off'cer, oo ain't dispose to stir hisself, and r'lieve us of this dooty by takin' command of 'er. If you was a-searchin' for 'im, you will not find 'im 'ere, mate. No, you will fuckin' not.' Swaying a little as the *Hawk* lifted on a passing swell.

'Will you tell me who is in command of your crew?' Vexed now, and beginning to show it.

'Ashore, mate. We was give this dooty ashore. – Has *you* come to r'lieve us? I do 'ope so.'

'No, I have not. At present I am making a brief inspection, that is all.'

'Ohh. Esscuse me, but oo am I aspeakin' to?' Puzzled. 'Noo clerk, izzit, from the Check office?'

'Clerk! I am not a damned clerk! Stand aside now, I wish to go below.'

'There ain't no need of biting off my 'ead.' Removing the pipe now, and bristling. 'If you ain't from the Check, where does you come from? Oo sent you?'

'I am not *sent* by anyone at all! I am offered command of this ship, and you will stand aside!'

'If you *is* an officer, in which I am doubtful – since you has only now said you wasn't – then where is your blue coat, and gold buttons?'

'I am not obliged to explain myself to you!' James was aware that this increasingly intemperate exchange could end poorly for him. He had no papers, he had no warrant, he was not in a blue coat. 'Look here, now.' Assuming a more conciliatory tone. 'The admiral has brought me here, and put me aboard. You see, there is his boat . . .' Pointing. The scolding cry of a gull echoed across the riding water.

'I see no p'tic'lar boat.' Peering a moment. 'There is many boats.'

'Yes, well, he has brought me to the ship, and I will just like to examine her briefly, you know. I will not interfere with your – your work aboard. I will not interrupt you at all. You may pretend I ain't here.'

'Can't do that, look, when 'ere you is stood. I must send someone to the Clerk of the Check, that has give us this dooty, and make sure of your claim.'

'He will know nothing of my being here aboard. I am come of my own volition, d'y'see. To examine the ship.'

'Your own what?' A menacing jerk of the head.

'Look here, now.' Growing resolute. 'I have pointed out the admiral's boat to you. He has brought me to my ship. If you wish to discuss my rank or my duties with anyone at all, it had better be Admiral Hollister. Send a boat by all means, send someone there to *Vanquish*, his flag. In the interim I will look at my ship. Stand aside, if y'please.'

Something in James's tone, some little stiffening of his back and setting of his mouth, told the artificer that no good would come of further dispute, and he shrugged, sighed – and stepped aside.

*

A long line of poplars meandered by the stream that ran secret and quiet through the meadow at the lower end of a broad, undulating slope, a slope crowned on the north by a dense green copse of elm and ash and oak. On the east a flinty path ran down, and James now rode down there on his hired horse. He paused to shade his eyes, half-standing in the stirrups, and saw the house about a mile distant across the meadow, in its own surrounding stand of trees. The day was mild, but the warmth was tempered by a freshening breeze. Gulls floated against high feathery streams of cloud on the wide Anglian sky, coming in from the coast to the north. Norfolk, like so many of the counties of England, could never ignore the sea, James reflected. He lowered himself in the stirrups and cantered on towards the house.

Southcroft House lay just beyond the village of

Middingham off the winding road from Norwich to Fakenham. James had come by the speediest means available to him from Portsmouth – by packet to Dover, thence by a second packet to Great Yarmouth, in a threatening storm that had cleared in great tumbling piles of cloud away out to sea; and from Yarmouth he had come upriver by ferry to Norwich, where he had hired his horse within sight of the castle wall, and taken the road out through Elm Hill. The journey had been arduous, and expensive, much more expensive than he would have liked, but he had felt that the expense must be borne, that the journey was entirely necessary to him. And now he came to Southcroft in the late afternoon, dusty and thirsty and tired.

As he rode up the short drive he found a handsome small red-brick house – smaller than Birch Cottage, his own house in Dorset – with a steep gabled roof, six windows at the front, and the door in a small lowbuilt annexe on the eastern side. Beyond the annexe lay a patch of white, daisy-like flowers, bright against the earth. A plain, plump maid, trimly dressed in apron and cap, answered James's knock.

'Who shall I say, sir?' In answer to his query as to whether or no Captain Rennie was at home.

'I am . . . just say an old shipmate, will you?'

'Old shipmate, sir?' Doubtfully, looking at James's dusty breeches and coat.

'I – I wish to surprise him, d'y'see?'

'Very well, sir.' A brief bob and she retired, leaving James to stand where he was outside, by the iron boot-scraper. He waited, and after a moment glanced again at the flowers, and thought of picking some to discover their scent, then:

'I am very sorry, sir, but Captain Rennie will not allow of anyone he don't know certain to enter the house, sir. "Give the fellow my compliments, and oblige him to state his name" was his very words, sir.' This time she did not bob.

'Oh. Ah. Then – then in course I will.' And he gave his name to the girl.

'Christ's blood – James!' From inside the door a moment
after, then the door was flung wide. 'Is it you? – It is, by God!
Yes, yes, it is! Come in, come in, my dear James! Why did not
ye say at once who y'was, hey? I feel such a damned fool,
leaving you waiting outside like a wretched middy at the door
of the great cabin, ha-ha-ha. Are you well? You look well.'
Guiding him into the library, and at once pouring madeira
from a wide-bottomed decanter.

'A glass of wine, James.' Handing it to him, and raising his
own. 'Your health.'

'Your health, sir.' They drank, and:

'Sit, sit, my dear James. No doubt you are weary after so
long a journey. Jenny! Jenny!'

The maid, at the door: 'Sir?'

'My guest will like an ewer of hot water and a basin,
brought to his room at the top of the stairs. The blue room,
y'have me?'

'Oh, well, you know – I had not thought to stay overnight – ' began James, but was overruled at once.

'The blue room, Jenny. Where is your valise, James? You
have luggage?' As the maid withdrew.

'I have a small bag tied to the saddle of my horse, but I had
thought to go to the inn – '

'No no no, y'will not, unless you wish to wound me, James.
The least I can do is offer you a bed, and a good supper, hey?
You have come far? From Dorset?'

'From Portsmouth – and from Winterborne before that.'

'You are fatigued, no doubt. Let us get you berthed, and
refreshed, and then we'll make an evening of it, eh? By God,
it is right good to see your friendly face again, James. Is
Catherine well? And your boy?'

'They are in excellent health, sir, thank you.'

Not once did he ask James why he had come, and as he was
shown up to his room by the maid, and given hot water, and
made comfortable, James realized that Rennie believed this
was purely a visit born out of friendship and erstwhile

association in a common cause, the reuniting of companion sea officers, both now on the beach.

'We will meet again at seven o'clock, James,' Rennie had said at the foot of the stairs, 'when you are rested and eager for food and conversation. Unless you are hungry now? A wedge of pie? Another glass?'

'No, thank you, sir. You are very kind.'

'At seven, then.' A hand on James's shoulder a moment, a brief pressing of fingers. From such an Englishman as Rennie the sign of great affection.

At seven James descended the stairs, refreshed by a nap, a thorough sluicing, and a change of shirt. The maid had brushed his coat, and now he felt himself presentable as gentleman and guest. Voices in the library made him pause at the door; he had not expected other guests, had wished to talk privately with Captain Rennie – but he went in.

And found Rennie deep in conversation with a man perhaps forty-five or -six, spare except for a comfortably protruding belly beneath his waistcoat, with a pleasant, intelligent, ruddy face and spectacles.

'Ah, James, there you are. Allow me to introduce my neighbour and friend, Mr Rountree.' And he completed the formal introductions. James bowed, the other gentleman bowed, and glasses were filled. A toast was proposed, and drunk, and presently the three of them were seated – rather nearer to the crackling fire than James would have preferred, but Rennie was of the view that a fire should be lighted in a gentleman's library whatever the season.

'We was talking of fear, James, as you came in,' said Rennie, taking a pull of wine.

'Fear, sir? I hope that I have not provoked it, in this pleasant house.' James, with a smile.

'No, indeed, Mr Hayter.' Mr Rountree smiled in return. 'No, indeed. I was telling William about a man I knew years ago, at Norwich. A man that was ever fearful, that was entirely consumed by apprehension. He had a terrible certainty, each time he quit his house, that his head would be beaten in by footpads, or that he would slip on the cobbles of the hill and plummet to extirpation, or that he would be struck by a lightning bolt and instantly braised. The poor fellow could scarce stir abroad for mortal fright.'

'Good heaven, why – '

Mr Rountree raised a hand, deterring interruption. 'Indoors, a dozen prophylactic potions lay at his bedside, within close reach, in case of incipient apoplexy, or fever. A pitcher of water lay at the foot, in case of midnight fire. A great wool scarf entwined his throat, in case of noxious chill.'

'Did not he fear strangulation?' James, lifting an eyebrow.

'Eh?' Rennie.

'From the scarf, sir.'

'He did fear it,' nodded Mr Rountree, 'and kept a handbell by him, in case he should need to raise the alarm. A handbell – and a drum.'

'What was his profession, the fellow?' Rennie, a frown.

'Undertaker.'

'Undertaker! Ha-ha-ha!' Rennie's sudden delighted laugh made him cough.

'That was why he was ever fearful,' said Mr Rountree. 'His duties obliged him, after all, so continually to dwell on the mortality of others that he could not help but reflect on his own, and that became the habit of dread.'

'And did it kill him?' James, again with raised eyebrow.

'Hhhhh – did it kill him!' Rennie coughed and wheezed with laughter. 'Ha-ha-ha, James, ye've always had a way of seeing the absurd side of things. Did it kill him-hhh-hhh-hhh!'

Later, after they had eaten their supper – of fish, and wildfowl, and syllabub, and cheese – and drunk their wine, Rennie became reflective, and talked of his youth:

'Where is that unfeathered boy now, hey? Where his hungry, undiscriminating mind, his wonder and astonishment at the world and all its workings? Where his romantic notions, his ardent fancies? – He is lost. They are gone.' A vinous sigh, and he refilled his glass.

'His heart remains, does it not, sir? In the older, wiser self?'

'Heart, James?'

'A man dare not lose that, else he is lost altogether.'

'Softness, d'y'mean?' Growing severe. 'What business has a sea officer with softness of heart? He makes his decisions out of hard experience and hard instruction. His eye is on his canvas, and his mind on the design of his commission. His heart don't come into it.'

'I didn't mean – '

'He must govern everything of emotion with sound judgement, and practical sense. That is his proper work when he wears a blue coat, and serves the King.'

'Indeed, sir, I would not quarrel with – '

'You above all men should know that, James, good heaven.' A sniff, and he drank off his wine.

Later still Mr Rountree became philosophical, and touched on politics, and the great advances in the present age of enlightenment:

'Who are the great thinkers that have informed the modern scene?'

'Eh?' Rennie, again refilling his glass. 'Who?'

'Hobbes? Locke? Burke? Are not these the men that have taught us to – '

'Burke!' Rennie was now well flown. 'A very dangerous fellow, ain't he? He presumes to know everything about everything. He knows all about the insurrection in France, and approves it!'

'On the contrary, sir, he does not,' began James. 'His views are entirely – '

'Y'find his views congenial?' Rennie turned his fuddled glare on James, and was inclined to be fierce. 'A damned radical Irishman, ain't he?' Mr Rountree perceived his error in having raised the subject, and intervened:

'Ah! Is that the hour?' Making a show of consulting his watch. 'My dear William, I must beg your pardon for having lingered so unconscionable long, and kept you from your bed.'

'Bed? What?' Swinging his head to squint at his other guest.

'It is very late, and I must away.' Pushing his glass from him, and rising.

'Away? Nonsense, it ain't late, not at all.'

'Eleven, you know, eleven o'clock, and I must get to my own bed. It is a mile and more to walk, and I must make an early start tomorrow. I go to Norwich.'

'Ah. Norwich. Ah.' Rennie nodded his head, fuddled but placated. An early start took precedence, always, in a sea officer's mind. When Mr Rountree had put on his cloak and departed with a bow, James too excused himself, knowing that to attempt to introduce the topic on which he wished to consult Captain Rennie was unwise, tonight. It had better wait until morning. And the two sea officers retired.

On the morrow, when James came down to breakfast, he found Rennie already seated at the table in the dining room. Breakfast had been laid out, and a place for the guest. Rennie was drinking hot water, and a whiff of vinegar rose with the steam from his cup. There was no teapot on the table.

'Good morning, sir. You do not drink tea?' James, surprised.

'Ah, good morning, James.' No hint of last night's excess. 'Nay, I am advised by my physician Dr Noble that hot water, with a teaspoon of cider vinegar, is quite the best thing for the digestion in the morning.'

'Ah.' Sitting down. 'And is it?'

'Is it what?'

'The best thing. In the morning.'

'Certainly it is. Certainly. You know that I have always took tea, that I have always drunk it, at any hour. Well well, since I have took up hot water and vinegar, months since, I am altogether improved, and hale.'

'I am glad.' A smile.

'You ought to take it up yourself, James. It purifies the urine, and aids the bowels, it cleanses the mouth, and – ' But now he saw James's smile become a dismayed frown, and relented. 'In course there is coffee, if you will like that instead.'

'Thank you, sir, I would prefer coffee.' Relieved. 'But I did not know that you ever liked it . . .'

'I do not. I never drink the dark troublesome liquor, never. But I know that a gentleman's house ain't quite civilized without it. Jenny! Jenny! Coffee for Mr Hayter, right quick!'

When the maid had brought a tall pot of coffee for James, and filled his cup, Rennie said as she quit the room:

'She would like it if I rang this table bell, you know.' He lifted the little bell, and put it down with a muffled clink. 'She would like me to modify my sea manners, talk quieter and so forth. I fear that I always forget.'

James drank the grateful dark reviving brew, felt its aromatic power clear his head, and presently, as Rennie chopped into a boiled egg:

'Sir, I wonder if I may consult your opinion on an important matter, very important to me? Will you give me some advice?'

'If I can, James.' Digging yolk from the shell. 'Gladly, if I am able.' A benign glance, with slightly bloodshot eyes.

James told him about the *Hawk*. About having been offered her, his first command. About having gone to Portsmouth to look at her. And about his – doubts.

'Doubts!' Rennie dropped his spoon with a clatter. A blob of yolk on the cloth. 'Doubts!'

'Well, I do not like to take her when you are on the beach. It don't seem quite right to accept – '

'Not take her! When I am on the beach! What has my present circumstances to do with it? Christ's blood, James, you damn' fool! You astonish me, altogether astonish me!'

'Please hear me out, will you, sir?'

'Not *accept!*' Shaking his head. 'Not *accept!*'

'I thought that I could not desert you in the question of Sir Robert Greer's pursuit of us – of us, that is to say – concerning our last commission, and the loss of Rabhet.'

'Damnation to that blackguard, James. I am equal to any challenge of his. As are you, yourself. But that is of no importance when ye've been offered your first command. Do not you grasp what it means? Do not you see what honour has been bestowed? You are to be given one of His Majesty's fighting ships! The greatest reward a junior sea officer can hope for! Why, the entire Lieutenants' List yearns, and sighs, and prays for this!' A sniffing breath, and he banged his palms down on the table. 'You must pack your valise, and be on your way. I do not mean to be inhospitable, but there ain't a moment to lose. You must go to London at once, and at once accept. To throw this chance away would be pure folly.' Rising, pushing back his chair. 'Jenny!'

'Sir?' Earnestly, remaining in his seat. 'You did not hear me out.'

'What?' Distractedly. 'Jenny!'

'It is not just a question of the honour, d'y'see. There is – something else.'

'Something else . . . ?' Looking at him.

'I am – I am short of funds.'

'Short of – ' Staring at him now. 'You, James? How so?'

'Well, sir – I have had considerable expenses since we paid off. Heavy outgoings.'

'Had not you saved anything, though, from our earlier little episode?' Rennie was referring to their joint acquisition of several thousands of French money, by an action at sea during their second commission, in the West Indies. 'That is how I am able to afford this house, renting it, you know. Certainly I have not the expense of a family since I – since I lost my dear wife.' He cleared his throat. 'But surely you had some of that gold put aside?'

James, reluctantly and miserably:

'I had indeed. I had put a thousand pound aside for my son, and husbanded the remainder. However – however – I have been obliged to find moneys to pay for a venture.' Lifting his head.

'Venture?' Frowning, waving away the maid, who had come in response to his call. 'Venture? I hope y'do not mean – a *speculation*?'

'Alas. I do.'

'In what?'

'In something of Tom Makepeace's. Not that I blame Tom.' Hastily added. Tom Makepeace had been Second Lieutenant in two of their previous commissions. 'No, I must not blame him. It was my own folly, as much as his.'

'But, good God, what was it that has lost you everything? I take it you have lost everything?'

'All but my house. I have nothing to live on but my pay, and even that must go to pay off the residual debt.'

'James, James . . .' A deep, sniffing sigh. 'It matters little now, I suppose, what the venture was, but y'may as well tell it to me.' He sat down.

'It is a new kind of paint, to protect the hulls of ships against worm, replacing copper sheath.'

'Replacing copper?'

'We thought – that is, Tom thought and so did I, that this new paint would save the Admiralty, and John Company too, tens of thousands a year in copper, and that it could not fail therefore to gain favourable attention.'

'You mean, it is like white lead?' Frowning.

'No, sir, it is a preparation made from coal tar, mixed with mineral oils, and fixed. It forms into a thick coating that will endure for years at sea. It is quite impervious to corruption, impervious to worm, and repels weed. And it is less than one third the cost of copper sheath.' In spite of himself James's eyes had lit up as he spoke, and he found himself leaning forward in his enthusiasm.

'Ah. Ah.' Rennie nodded, made a face, and: 'May I venture to ask, then, why your venture has failed?' With irony.

'Well – the Navy Board could not be persuaded to conduct fair tests, d'y'see. They – '

Rennie held up a hand. 'When you say "fair tests", what d'y'mean, exact?'

'We – that is, Tom and myself, and the others in the syndicate, we – '

'Syndicate!'

'Naturally, you know, we needed sound investment to begin. We needed ten thousand pound, and formed a syndicate. Well, it was already formed, to say the truth, and Tom and I had an opportunity to come in. We needed ten thousand, and were all obliged to dig deep. And so the money was found. Then we – '

'Again, may I venture to ask: how much did you invest? You yourself?'

'I put up five thousand.'

'Five! – And Tom?'

'He put up five, that came from his late father's estate, but that – '

'So between you, you have put up the entire capital of this *venture*, this *speculation*, and the other members of your syndicate have put up nothing. Hey?'

'When you say it like that, you make it sound a very foolish thing. With respect, sir, the paint itself was anything but foolish. The paint is a wonder, a miraculous invention, and our investment in it was sound, and wholly in the nation's interest.'

'You wished to take no profit yourselves?'

'I did not say that. In course we did wish for a profit. I have a young family, and must look to their welfare.'

'Welfare! How have you assisted their welfare in this, James?'

James bit his tongue, and made himself count to five. 'I admit – that I have been guilty of folly. Our folly, mine and

Tom's, was our belief in the good sense and honourable dealings of Their Lordships and the Navy Board. They have behaved with the direst stupidity and bad faith. They have – '

'You had better say no more, James, along those lines. Not to me. I am a senior post captain, whose every action must display loyalty to Their Lordships, and obedience to their wishes and commands.'

'Oh, very well, sir. As you like. – But you cannot deny that Tom and I have lost all of our money through their reckless obduracy and – '

'Have not I just said that you may not talk like this to me?' Sharply.

'I am sorry.'

Rennie looked at him, and unbent a little. 'Well well, I must not bite off your head when you have come to me for advice.' He paused a moment, then: 'Perhaps you will like to consider a different opinion of Their Lordships, if I give it. Propose the case to yourself thus. Copper is a very great aid to Their Lordships in the preservation of ships. It took long persuasion before His Majesty's government felt obliged to vote through the moneys to pay for it, regular. It took years of persuasion. And now you young fellows come along with your new paint, crying miracle and magic, and let us do away with copper entire, it is so damn' wasteful and costly, and so forth, and expect to be embraced, and rewarded, and fêted up and down Whitehall.'

'I never wished to be fêted – '

'Fêted, and covered in glory, and given knighthoods, or peerages even. But had you considered for one moment what it would mean to remove the work of coppering from the dockyards, whose business it is to build and repair ships? A whole enterprise, a whole industry, would be ruined. Not just the men who smelt and make the copper, and beat it into sheath, but all the artificers who nail it to the hull, and prise it off again in a year or two, to repair or replace it, and attend to the rotted timbers beneath. And not just in the naval dockyards, neither. There are many small private yards engaged in the Navy's business. This is a broad enterprise. There are great contractual obligations to be honoured, made in good faith. The business of coppering is very broad, very large, and many people depend upon it. A great deal of money is involved.'

'Exact! That is why – ' Rennie cut him off with a sharply raised hand.

'A great deal of money!' A breath sucked in, and he shook his head. 'Their Lordships are not fools, you know, James. They know what killing copper would mean. It would mean loss. Pernicious, ruinous, terrible loss for a great many interested parties, and great trouble. Their view – and I cannot say that I do not understand it – their view must surely be, why seek out such trouble . . . where none exists?'

'So our paint is to be condemned out of hand? Even when it answers the question of worm and corruption infinitely better than copper?' Furiously.

'Damnation, James, you force me to condemn your own blockhead stupidity! Will you argue and dispute with Sir Charles Middleton, Navy Controller, the man behind coppering? Will you fight him, that has himself fought tooth and nail to sheath the whole fleet? You, a junior sea officer, against all his power, all the power and might of the Navy Board, that in turn has the full confidence of Their Lordships? Do you want to fight the Royal Navy entire, you bloody fool!'

'Then – then – what *am* I to do?'

'Do! Go to London, without the loss of a moment! Accept your commission, and your first command, with open arms and a glad heart!'

'*How can I*?' burst out James in an agony of frustration. 'How can I accept anything from these men, that have ruined and humiliated me? Hey!'

Rennie laughed, throwing back his head in mirthless disbelief. 'By God, you cannot see, you will not see.'

'See?' Pacing, shaking his head. 'See *what*?'

'You disappoint me, James. For a well-educated, level-headed, perceptive fellow, you're as dull as an ox. They are saying to you – here is your reward.'

'My *reward*?'

'Aye, aye, you fool! They are saying – we could not accept your bloody paint, even had we wished it. However, we know ye've strove at it, and believed in it, and so we will like to compensate you for your trouble. Here is a ship. Here is a commission. Take it, with our blessing.'

James stopped pacing. 'You think that . . . ? Oh, but I could not. No, I cannot.' Setting his mouth in a firm line.

'Christ Jesu. Why *not*?'

'It is bribery.'

'Ahh. That is your objection.'

'It is an honourable one.'

'James, you came to see me here at Norfolk to ask for my advice, did y'not? What did you hope for? What did you hope that I would tell you?'

'Well, sir – '

'Did you hope that I would aid you in your dispute with Their Lordships? Take up your case, like some damned lawyer? – I beg your pardon, your brother is a lawyer, I had forgot.'

'I do not know quite what I had hoped for, to say the truth. I was in a muddle. I wished – I wished to talk to a fellow sea officer, and discover another opinion, I suppose.' He shrugged, and sighed, and looked at Captain Rennie. 'I see now that I must make my own way in this. I had no right to expect – '

'Oh, now, what's this?' Gravely, kindly, changing tack. 'You may not ask anything of an old friend? Pish pish, James. That is nonsense.' He turned away a moment to the window, then:

'How much is the debt?'

'Eh?'

'You said that you had put up five thousand. Was all of it your own capital – or did you borrow against future profit? You spoke of a debt.'

'I borrowed two thousand pound.'

'And the interest on that amount, for one year?'

'Two hundred, I think. Why do you ask?'

'I will let you have it.'

'Good heaven, that is quite out of the question! I could not possibly accept! I did not come here to beg, and I could not possibly accept!' Agitated, very red in the face.

'I will let you have it, on one condition. That you go at once to London, accept your commission, then take the mail coach to Portsmouth direct, and assume command of your cutter.'

James drew a breath, and was about to speak, but instead held the breath in, and strode away down the room. Angrily strode, and stood with his hands clasped behind. Captain Rennie waited, perfectly at his ease. At last:

'I will pay you back. I will pay back every penny, with interest.' James, returning. 'I wish it to be absolutely understood between us.'

'In course, James.' Rennie, mildly. 'It is understood.' He shook James's hand, smiled, and:

'Jenny! Jenny! My guest is in a hurry to be away! Pack his valise and bring it down, then tell the boy to bring his horse! Lively now! He has not a moment to lose!'

*

'Captain Rennie!'

'Good God – Sir Robert.' Rennie stopped in his tracks.

'You are surprised? You had not expected to see me?' Sir Robert Greer brushed the grass with the ferrule of his ebony cane.

'I – I am surprised, I confess.' Rennie looked round for a carriage, and could not see it.

'In course I had never meant to catch you inadvertent. I had never meant to startle nor disconcert you. Nay, my purpose in coming here was merely to reacquaint myself with Norfolk, a county I have found charming on earlier occasions.'

'You know this part of the county?'

'You may imagine my surprise when I discovered that you had taken a house in this very district. I could scarce contain my curiosity to see it.'

'Indeed?'

'A handsome house.' Nodding at it, then: 'I have been unwell. You may have heard something about it?'

'I had not, Sir Robert.'

'Ah. Had you not? I was, though. I was very ill for a time. But now I am quite recovered.'

'I – I am glad.' Politely, his hat off and a little bow.

'Not nearly so glad as am I, I assure you. Yes, I was much cast down, for a time.'

'Indeed?'

'Yes, I had a stone.' A black, menacing stare. 'It had to be cut out of me.'

'Very painful, I should think.'

'The surgeon was quick, very quick. Sir Wakefield Bennett, a most remarkable man, the King's own physician.'

'I have heard the name.'

'So swift was his incision, so quick his removal of the stone, that I scarce felt anything. In course I was given paregoric before, and after too. Within a day or two I was a new man, and now I am strong.' Another black stare. 'Very strong, now.'

'I am glad.' Again politely.

'Are you? I wonder if you are, Captain Rennie. I think that you cannot be glad, altogether. Hey?'

'I do not take your meaning, Sir Robert.' Stiffly.

'Do not you? Ah.' The bloodless lids masked the eyes a moment, then slid back. 'You will discover my meaning

before long, I think.' The black stare seemed to penetrate
Rennie's skin. 'Since I am staying hereabouts, we may very
probably meet again.' He made to turn and depart, then as if
on an afterthought: 'In truth, you would aid me in my
enquiries by granting me an interview – very soon.'

'If you mean, Sir Robert, that you wish to pursue me in the
offence of treason, of which you had wrongly accused me – '

'You had not forgot, then?' Over him, then a glance at
Rennie's house. 'Perhaps, however, you had persuaded
yourself that I would forget. Yes?' The black eyes returned to
Rennie.

'I had not thought anything about it, Sir Robert, until this
moment. Living quiet here in Norfolk as I do, my thoughts
in usual are bent on gentler things, rural and bucolic things.'

'Had persuaded yourself', continued Sir Robert, 'that I
would forget, when I was took ill. Yes, I think that is likely so.'

'Sir Robert, I did not know you was ill. How could I,
therefore, have persuaded myself of anything of the kind?'
With an effort of will Rennie kept his tone conversational,
and mild.

'Ah, yes, yes. You did say that you had heard nothing of my
affliction, yes. Hm. I do not like to doubt the word of an
officer' – he did not say gentleman – 'but again I ask myself,
can this be quite true?'

Rennie sniffed in a deep breath. 'Sir Robert, I am in course
duty-bound to talk to you at any time that is convenient,
except the present. I am to dine nearby, and I will not like to
keep my host waiting.' Briskly putting on his hat.

'Dine? Ah, then I must not keep you. – You do not ride
there, to your host's house?'

'I am going to walk there.'

'Is it far?'

'Middingham.'

'The village? Why, that is where I am staying, myself. Let
us walk there together.'

'Sir Robert, I have no wish to be rude, but you oblige me

to be blunt. Months since, you accused me of treason, wrongly accused me, and made clear your object – to see me hanged. And yet you propose that we walk amiable across the fields, as if we was bosom friends?'

'If not quite that, then civilized men, in least. Conversable men.'

'You think it a matter for jest? To threaten a man with execution, and then to pretend – '

'Jesting was the furthest thing from my mind, Captain Rennie.' Over him, and his gaze again grew menacing. He tapped the ground twice with the ferrule of his cane, and: 'Will tomorrow suit? In the forenoon?'

'As you wish, Sir Robert.' Icily polite.

'Very good. Pray come to me at Middingham Court. You know it?'

'I know the house.'

'Eleven o'clock.' Sir Robert turned away without another word, lifted his cane, and a sociable and pair emerged from behind trees in the middle distance, driven forward by a man in livery.

On the morrow Rennie did go to Middingham Court, even though he had decided in the night to defy Sir Robert – and then abandoned the idea when he rose at first light, having lain sleepless from midnight when he returned from Mr Rountree's dinner.

To reach Middingham Court he was obliged to walk through the village. He made his way along the main street, known as Borrow Walk, a narrow thoroughfare of uneven cobbles winding between little flint-and-brick dwellings and half-timbered houses with leaded windows, and two inns. One of these inns, the Plough, was known to Rennie as an hostelry where uncommonly good cooking could be had, and well-kept ale, for a few pennies. He did not think of that cooking now as he passed the inn, nor did he answer the good morning of the innkeeper, who stood in his leather apron in

the square arched gateway to the stable yard. Rennie did not
see him. He did not hear him. His mind and senses were
closed to all things except what lay ahead at the great house.

Today Rennie was wearing his dress coat and hat, and his
tasselled dress sword. Jenny the maid had brushed and
polished and pressed, and Rennie was confident that he
looked his best. He would be damned if he would allow Sir
Robert Greer to humiliate him. He would remind Sir Robert
that in accusing him he accused a sea officer serving His
Majesty, a senior post captain with an entirely honourable
record of service. He would not be pompous, nor arrogant,
nor harsh and strident in his assertion of these things, but by
God he would be forthright and firm. He would remind Sir
Robert, the bloody fellow, that the Royal Navy was a plain-
speaking service, and that all officers were obliged to . . . but
was this verging on pomposity?

'I will not allow him the satisfaction of finding me
ridiculous. I must be brief in my objections, brief and clear,
and leave it at that.'

He came to the house, which stood back from the road
behind a red-brick wall and a tall iron gate with arms
embossed on an iron shield above. The house was of red
brick, with a steep gabled roof and two mansard windows set
in the tiles. A central chimney boasted five narrow pots.
There were six windows on the upper storey, and five below,
and a door with a stone architrave. The rear bay of the house
lay in the shadows of spreading elms. The drive curved
gracefully away from the gate round a central lawn planted
with low bushy shrubs and trees. It was a handsome, solid-
built old house, grave in its demeanour, composed and
dignified in its setting. Had not he been coming here under
such difficulty Rennie would have admired the house
unreservedly. As things were he felt there was an ominous
atmosphere, a gloomy air about the place, hanging in the
earthy smell of leaves and shrubs, and he could not like it. In
spite of his determination to be forthright and straight-

backed, his heart shrivelled within his breast, and his guts were chilled. He stepped through the gate and along the drive, his shoes crunching the gravel. Went up the single stone step to the door, and knocked.

Presently he was shown into the library, a wide blue room, and left alone. He did not sit down, but paced the room, his hat under his arm. Tall shelves housed hundreds of gold-impressed, leather-bound books. The quiet of the room was made almost sombre by the slow, subdued tick of a longcase clock at the far end. A side window there was tinged green by shrubbery pushing against the glass, as if to break through it. Another window, on the opposite side, overlooked an inner paved court. The day was sunny and mild, but in here the air was chill, and Rennie wished that a fire had been lit. He paced the room, and paused in front of a whole-length portrait of a full-figured, imposing man in the clothes of half a century ago – wide-cut, wide-sleeved plum coat, long, elaborately decorated, green silk waistcoat, white silk stock with jewelled pin, shoulder-touching wig – and with the steady gaze of one entirely aware of his position in the world, and the fullness of his purse. Away down the room the clock whirred, and struck eleven. As the chimes died:

'Captain Rennie, you are punctual.'

Startled, Rennie turned. He had not heard Sir Robert come into the room. The fellow had a way of appearing abruptly in a place as if by some sinister magic.

'Good morning, Sir Robert.'

'Not only punctual, neither – but dressed in your finery.'

'I would not call it finery.' Stiffly.

'Would not you? Then what, I wonder.' Sir Robert was dressed as always in severe black and white.

'It is a dress coat, Sir Robert, the correct coat for an officer of my rank.'

'Your rank, yes. Then I must not call it finery, I expect. That would be to make little of a great institution, a noble service.'

Rennie said nothing to that. He wished Sir Robert to come
to the point of their meeting, so that he could respond. And
now he noticed one small addition to Sir Robert's severe
attire. On the little finger of his left hand he wore today a
silver ring with a distinctive red stone.

'You had thought, I am in no doubt, that this morning I
meant to iterate my accusation of treason against your name.
Yes?'

'Just so, Sir Robert, I had.' Again stiffly.

'Following on our brief conversation of yesterday, you had
thought it. Yes?'

Rennie waited, his back straight, his hat under his arm,
very correct. Let the fellow do his worst.

'Yes?' Sir Robert regarded him with his black stare.

'I am at your disposal, sir.'

'Indeed. Indeed you are.'

Rennie bit his tongue and resolved that he would not suffer
this a minute more. If Sir Robert did not come to his point
then he would bow, put on his hat and stride from the room,
no matter the consequence. He would not bear any more of
this damned nonsense.

'However – you are wrong in your assumption.'

'Wrong, Sir Robert? I do not understand you.'

'I have decided to allow the matter of treason to recede in
my mind. To fade, so to say, into the shadows at the back of
my attention. Aye. There it shall rest – for the moment.'

'I do not – '

'On one condition.' The deep, vibrant voice not raised. Only
a finger raised, in emphasis. 'One condition, Captain Rennie.'

'What is it?'

'It is very simple. Just tell me where it is.'

'Where – it is?'

'Now then, Captain Rennie. Pray do not mimic ignorance.
Pray do not pretend lack of acuity. You know what I mean
very well. You and Lieutenant Hayter between you have
concealed it somewhere safe. *Where is it?*'

'If you mean the great treasure lost at sea by Rashid Bey of Rabhet, then I fear I must disappoint you. It is – lost.'

'You persist in this deception?'

'There is no deception, Sir Robert. The great riches of Rabhet were lost when Rashid Bey set sail from that place in a slow, sagging-off xebec, and was attacked by corsairs. A storm blew up, and the corsairs escaped.'

'I see, very well, you do persist. That is very foolish in you.' Shaking his head.

'The fact that he was enjoined to bring his treasure to England, enjoined by you, Sir Robert, led directly to its loss. Perhaps you will like to consider that.'

'Be silent, sir. If you cannot tell the truth it will be better that you do not say anything.'

Rennie had stood all he could, or would. He sniffed in a furious breath, and jammed on his hat.

'If you will not *listen* to the truth, Sir Robert, I see no profit in this interview – for neither party. Good morning.' He made to leave, but Sir Robert stood in his path.

'You refuse absolutely to tell me where you and Hayter have hid the gold?'

'Christ's blood, will y'not comprehend! It ain't hid, it is lost! Lost irretrievable and for ever!'

'Very well, then I must revive the charge of treason. I shall place you under arrest, and you will be confined.'

'Is there a detachment of marines on duty in this house, Sir Robert?'

'There are no marines here.'

'Or soldiers, perhaps? No? Then how d'ye propose to arrest me, hey? Stand aside now, will you?'

'You threaten *me* with violence, Rennie?'

'On the contrary, you have threatened me. A man that offers threats of molestation and violence to a serving officer had damned well better be prepared to follow such threats with action – else be bested. Stand aside!' And he put his hand on the hilt of his sword.

'You are a very great fool, Rennie, if you think I will allow myself to be bested by you. In the long run you will hang for what you have done today.' The voice still calm, but the black eyes glinting with menace.

'I have done nothing, except defend my honour!' He pushed past Sir Robert to the door of the library, and a moment after banged outside and strode vigorously away from the house towards the gate, his buckled shoes kicking up little sprays of gravel. His demeanour, as he walked through the gate and down into Borrow Walk, was defiant, and vigorous, and angry – but the inner man was hollow with dread.

'In Christ's name, what have I done?' Muttered to himself. 'Good morning to you!' To the innkeeper as he passed the Plough, and a confident wave. By the time he had come to the path across the fields to his house he was shivering, as if the air was frozen around him, as if the high, bird-flecked Anglian sky above was dark with foreboding.

Months ago, many months, on their return from a commission at Rabhet in HM *Expedient* frigate, Sir Robert had briefly effected Rennie's arrest and confinement on a charge of treasonable conduct, arising from the failure of that commission, and the loss of great treasure belonging to the regent of Rabhet, Rashid Bey, at sea. On advice from the Admiralty, Sir Robert had been obliged to release Rennie. Their Lordships, having studied Rennie's journals, logs and other documents, had found no fault with anything Rennie had done. Lieutenant Bradshaw, commander of the cutter *Curlew*, had been lost with his vessel that same commission, and thus could not be held to account at a court martial. Their Lordships, in possession of all the facts, were minded to see Captain Rennie walk free. He was a senior post captain in good standing, a brave sea officer who had done his best against overwhelming odds – one frigate against fleets of corsair ships – and had brought his ship safe home to England. He and Lieutenant Hayter both. There was nothing against either of their names.

The mission – to secure Rabhet as a Mediterranean base
for the Royal Navy, as an aid to the protection of trade with
the Levant in the event of future conflict – Their Lordships
had always thought was a supremely optimistic undertaking,
underpinned by political intrigue, and fraught with local
difficulty. Rabhet, far from Gibraltar, on the eastern coast
of Tunisia, could never adequately be supported. Their
Lordships had not been at all surprised that the commission
had failed; they had declined to provide more than two
ships in what had at first been declared to be a simple convoy
duty. And so Sir Robert had been obliged to accede to their
wish for Rennie's release – but he had not forgotten. Nor
had he ever accepted the loss of the treasure, which he
believed to have been brought to England in *Expedient*, and
concealed.

'And now,' muttered Rennie to himself, 'he will have his
revenge.' He was guilty of nothing in the eyes of the
Admiralty, and indeed their political masters in Parliament.
Sir Robert had been a lone voice in this, and it was he who
had failed – he and his people in the Secret Service Fund.
Honourable and brave sea officers could not be blamed,
when they had fought several fierce sea actions, been
severely mauled, &c. They could not and would not be
blamed. All this went through Rennie's head as he traversed
the wide field, but none of it reassured him. Sir Robert was
a man of great power and influence – behind. Rennie knew
that he intrigued at the deepest levels of administration; it
was rumoured that he had the ear of the King. Their
Lordships at the Admiralty did not absolutely have to obey
him, in course, but neither could they ignore him when he
came to them with particular requests. All of Rennie's three
commissions in *Expedient* had been given to him through
Sir Robert's influence. To have defied Sir Robert at
Middingham, indeed to have threatened him with violence,
was surely:

'The greatest folly of my career . . .' Aloud, as he came in sight of his drive. 'Fatal folly, William Rennie, y'damned wretched blockhead.'

*

Lieutenant Hayter accepted his commission at the Admiralty, where he was interviewed not by the First, Second, or Third Secretary, nor by any of the Lords Commissioners, but by Captain Apley Marles. Captain Marles was a grey-haired, middle-aged officer who had lost the lower part of his left leg at Chesapeake, had once held a seat in Parliament, and was now employed by Their Lordships in a capacity James did not wholly understand.

'I have sometime given advice at the Admiralty Court, you know, but in usual I am myself advised, which advice – so to say – I then communicate.' Standing at the table in a small side downstair office, a single high window behind him, admitting shadowy light.

'I see.' James, politely. He did not see.

'You will be attached official to Admiral Hollister and the Channel Fleet.'

'I have met the admiral.'

'Before you had got your wrote-out commission? Before you came here?' Surprised.

'It was merely in passing, sir.' Disconcerted. 'Probably he will not remember me.'

'In passing – ah. Well, you will be attached to him, but you will be just another cutter, among many such small vessels – schooners, brigs, sloops, and the like. In little, you will not be much noticed, neither as an attached cutter, nor as an absent one.'

'Absent, sir?'

'Aye. You will not be much with the fleet. Not at all, in fact.'

'Then – who must I obey . . . ?'

'You will be given your sailing instructions at Portsmouth.'

'I see. – May I ask, what will be my duties?'

'We will meet again, Mr Hayter, at Portsmouth. Ye'll be given your sailing instructions, and my own particular advice, at a future date. Soon.'

'Thank you, sir. – Erm, may I ask . . . ?'

'Yes?' Leaning on his blackthorn stick, his weight on his good leg, easing the pressure on the shortened limb and peg.

'May I ask . . . why have I been so favoured?'

'Favoured, Lieutenant?' Grey eyes, a deeply lined face. Were those lines a result of the pain of his injury, or merely of ageing? James could not guess.

'You may probably have heard, sir, that I have been accused – myself and Captain Rennie, that was my commanding officer our last three commissions – that we have been accused of – '

'Of treason?' Interrupting, and nodding. 'Accused by Sir Robert Greer? Yes, yes, that intelligence has reached me, in course. You was both exonerated.'

'Indeed, sir. However, I never thought that Sir Robert would desist. Nor had I thought that the matter would be quite so readily forgot by Their Lordships, neither – '

'It ain't forgot, Mr Hayter.'

'Oh.'

'May I tell you something?' Quietly. 'Sit down, will you, a moment?'

James did sit down.

'Sir Charles is a man not without influence, in certain quarters.'

'My father . . . ?'

'Aye, your father. That influence has been sufficient to thwart any further attempt by Sir Robert to – to hamper you.'

'D'y'mean that my father has got me this commission? But he knew nothing of my debts . . .' And now he broke off, not wishing to pursue the vexed question of coal tar paint, and the supposed compensatory reward to him of this commission by Their Lordships.

'Sir Robert was indeed minded to resume and continue his pursuit of you, but – this must be entirely in confidence, you apprehend me? Your father did not wish you to know of it.'

'Oh. Ah.'

'He was able to deflect Sir Robert's intentions successfully, in your case.' James half-expected him, now, to introduce the matter of the paint, and his debts – but he did not. 'Aye, in your case, your father's influence was more than sufficient, and the thing is now settled.'

'When you say "in my case", sir – do you mean: not in Captain Rennie's case?'

'My dealings, you know, are not with Captain Rennie. They are with you, Mr Hayter. I am able to tell you only what bears direct on your new commission.'

'Very good, sir. However, Captain Rennie – '

'Captain Rennie must proceed upon his own course.' Over him, firmly. 'He ain't attached to anything of this. Hm?'

'I do see that, sir. However, I am concerned for his welfare, as you may imagine.' He did not say, I am greatly in his debt.

'As are Their Lordships, and the navy. That is why half-pay is accorded to all sea officers on the beach. Captain Rennie, I believe, lives quite comfortable at Norfolk.'

'He does, sir.'

'Exactly so. Your own duties require your full attention at Portsmouth. *Hawk* must be manned, and provisioned, and her guns and stores took in. I should not delay a single moment, Mr Hayter, if I was you. You have your papers safe folded in your coat?'

'Aye, sir.' Rising.

'Good luck to you, Lieutenant.' Captain Marles shook his hand. 'Godspeed!'

*

'Starboard your helm!'

Hawk heeled to larboard, the wind on her quarter filling

her great fore and aft mainsail so that it bellied taut. The sea swirled, rode hissing along her wales, and boiled aft. Shrouds creaked, halyards, blocks, as she came to her new heading, and:

'Hold her so!' The helmsman on the tiller eased his weight against the long curve, and balanced himself, his feet firm on the decking.

'Starboard battery . . . fire!'

BOOM BOOM BOOM-BOOM   BOOM

Five eighteen-pounder carronades belched flame and smoke, and the timbers shuddered. Smoke and powder grit fumed along the deck. Away to starboard explosions of spray as roundshot struck into the swell, missing the floating target of casks bound together on a makeshift raft. Smoke drifted and sank shadowy over the sea as *Hawk* rushed on.

'Reload your guns! Stand by to go about!'

The deep-hulled, surging little vessel came about and beat into the wind on the port tack, as the guncrews went through the ritual of sponging, loading cartridge, roundshot and wad, ramming, adjusting the elevation, and running out. *Hawk* ran cleanly towards the floating target until it was again within range, then James bellowed:

'Put your helm down! Handsomely now!' and brought his charge through the wind on to the starboard tack once more, and:

'Stand by your guns! – Starboard battery . . . fire!'

The repeated blasting of flame, the rushing balloons of smoke and grit and fragments of flaming wad, and this time the roped casks shattered into splinters, an iron hoop spun looping high, and when the spray settled the raft itself had entirely disappeared.

'Well done, lads! Our smashers have done their work! – Reload!'

Lieutenant Hayter had insisted at the gun wharf on being

supplied with the latest carronades, fitted with loops and bolts instead of trunnions, and mounted on a slide carriage. Because the recoil of these squat guns was relatively short, and they weighed one quarter of the equivalent long gun, they could be fought with very small crews – three men, as opposed to eight or ten men for the longer weapon. His official complement was forty-two souls, but he had added an extra man to his muster book, taking his own steward, instead of relying on one of the boys to serve him; thus *Hawk* had a complement of forty-three. His two midshipmen were Mr Richard Abey, a capable Norfolk boy of fifteen years, with whom he had already sailed two commissions in HM *Expedient* frigate, and Mr Wentworth Holmes, of Devonshire, a youth of seventeen, who would act as second-in-command. His gunner, carpenter, boatswain and steward purser had all been assigned to him, as had his sailing master – warranted second. He had been able to fill his lower deck with good seamen, rated able and ordinary, by interviewing men at the Cockpit Tavern, and had also acquired eleven landmen idlers and boys – included among the idlers was his sailmaker, vital in a cutter, with such a vast spread of canvas. He had his quartermaster and mate, and one final and very important man of his choice. He had been able to obtain as his surgeon Dr Thomas Wing, again a most valued shipmate from *Expedient*. In the scheme of things Dr Wing was entitled to expect a place in another frigate, if not indeed a ship of the line. He had earned such a place. However, he knew that because of his stature – he stood no taller than a boy – he would not likely be so favoured, and had chosen to join Lieutenant Hayter in his cutter, when asked.

'It will be a novel experience for me, in so confined a space. I have become so accustomed these past months to assisting Dr Stroud upon the wide wards of the Haslar again, that any sort of ship will seem confining, and a cutter in particular like being afloat in a seaborne wooden cupboard, or similar receptacle.'

His careful diction, the studied language of the auto-didact – he had begun his medical career as a hospital porter – was not displeasing to James's ear because it was tempered with a dry wit and the wisdom of a man who had seen the worst and harshest of life, and overcome it. The lieutenant and the diminutive doctor were firm friends.

'A wooden receptacle, hey. I hope not a coffin, Thomas.'

'Certainly not that, if I do my work efficient. I will not like to kill seamen, James, only cure their costiveness, and lance their carbuncles.' With a smile. 'What is our intended voyage?'

'Ah. There you have me. Perhaps attached to the fleet, perhaps not. I do not know for certain.'

'Do not know?' In surprise.

And now as evening approached, and the glow of the sun sank into the sea beyond the Needles to the west, Lieutenant Hayter brought his cutter back from the Channel to Spithead. The Master Attendant had long since deprived *Hawk* of her numbered place off the Hard, and now she made her signals and dropped anchor on her designated bearing far out. The ships of the Channel Fleet lay tethered on their hawses all around, the flag *Vanquish* half a league distant.

'Mr Holmes.'

'Sir?' The senior midshipman attended him.

'We will hoist in our boat, if y'please.'

'You do not go ashore, sir?'

'Not tonight.'

'Very good, sir. – Mr Dench! Boatswain, there! We will hoist in the towing boat!'

And as the tackles were deployed, James wondered whether it would not be profitable for him to go ashore again. He had seen his vessel provisioned, her guns, powder and other stores taken in, had seen her trimmed, and in every way got ready for the sea, and had then waited in vain for the arrival of Captain Marles, or his representative, and for his sailing instructions. A few days ago he had sought an interview with the Port Admiral, Admiral Hapgood.

'Don't know anything about you,' Admiral Hapgood had told him. 'You are attached to the Channel Fleet, are y'not?' Contradicting himself. Standing very tall at the window in frock coat.

'So I was given to understand, sir, but I – '

'Given to understand! By whom? What officer, where, and when, gave you such "understanding", hey?' Moving back to his desk, bending over to find a document, his black beetling brow like a threat hanging over the room.

'Well, sir, Captain Marles said so, at the Admiralty, and that – '

'You have come to me before this, have y'not?' Finding the document now, glancing at it.

'Yes, sir, when I first came to take command of the *Hawk* cutter, some few weeks since, and – '

'What did I say to you, then?'

'That you knew nothing about me, sir.' Lamely.

'Yes, yes, I did say so. Because I did not, and do not. Don't know Captain Marles, neither. Is his name on the Navy List? I have not seen it, if it is. Yes, what now?' To a clerk at the door.

'The ladies visiting the *Hanover* seventy-four, that has just come ashore in the launch, sir . . .'

'Yes? Well?'

'Yes, sir. They had wished to visit you, sir, upon their return – if you recall . . . ?'

'Good God, yes, you are right. I did ask them to join me for sherry wine, when they returned. Give me five minutes, Pell, to sluice my face and shift into my dress coat.'

'Yes, sir. – Where shall they wait?'

'Downstairs, Pell, downstairs. I will join them there presently.' The clerk disappeared, and Admiral Hapgood walked into his closet. James was left standing, unsure what he should do. A minute after, as the admiral busied himself in the closet, James quietly left the office, trod quietly down the stairs, glimpsed a room full of pretty women, and quietly let himself out into the daylight, and the saline breeze.

He had subsequently requested an interview with Admiral Hollister, as one of the admiral's commanders, albeit a very junior one. The admiral had granted this request, and had seen him in his quarters aboard *Vanquish*.

'How is Captain Rennie?' Stooping, emerging from his quarter gallery, as James stood quietly waiting, hat under arm.

'I think he is quite well, sir.'

'Not pining, nor wasting away, on the beach?' Going to his desk, lifting the lid of a silver box and taking a very small pinch of snuff.

'I do not think that is in his character, sir.'

'Nay, nor do I.' He sat down, having cleared his nose into his handkerchief with a short sharp blast.

James glanced beneath the lashed-up bulkheads at the splendid hanging silks of the admiral's sleeping cabin to starboard, and at the black-leaded stove, the shelves of books, &c.; at the racks of swords, shelves of silver, and the long gleaming splendour of the dining table beyond – until his attention was recalled.

'But y'did not come to me to talk about Captain Rennie, I think, Mr Hayter.'

'No, indeed, sir. I – I wished to discover my duties.'

'What? Your duties? Your duties, sir, are to hold yourself available, watch by watch, until you are needed. Until you are required. That is every captain's obligation and duty, in the fleet.'

'Yes, sir, thank you.'

'To keep your ship clean, and disciplined, and ready for the sea.'

'Yes, sir. I wonder if you were informed, sir, by Captain Marles at the Admiralty – '

'Apley Marles?'

'Indeed, sir. Captain Apley Marles. He – '

'Lost a leg at Chesapeake, did not he?'

'That is so, sir, I believe. Certainly he has a wooden leg. He had given me to understand – '

'You saw Captain Marles, at the Admiralty?' Puzzled. 'Why?'

'Sir, he gave me to understand that he would come to Portsmouth, and himself give me my instructions, but he – '

'What instructions, pray?' A hard blue stare.

'I do not know, sir, exact. I have asked Admiral Hapgood, and he could not tell me, neither.'

'Happy Hapgood? What has he to do with your attachment to me, pray? Ain't a happy sinew in him, by the by. Only don't allow I said so. What has Captain Marles to do with your attachment here? I do not understand you, Mr Hayter.' Not yet quite severe.

'Sir, if you please, I was told that I was to be attached to you official, but – not in fact.'

'Was you? By the Admiralty? That is a singular curiosity at such a time as this, when we have assembled because of the emergency in North America. – Not in fact?' A little jerk of the head.

'In course – I had thought the same thing, sir,' James nodded in hasty agreement, but the truth was that he had been so caught up in his own dealings of late that he had taken little notice of the crisis – the reason behind the assembling of the fleet of forty ships at Spithead: the capture by Spain of British fur-trading posts on the north-west coast of America, and her claim on the coast entire. He had not thought of himself as caught up in the crisis at all, until this moment.

Admiral Hollister frowned at the young sea officer. 'I will not like to think that my officers was not paying their fullest attention to their obligation, Mr Hayter. All officers attached to me.'

'I – I am very grateful to you, sir, for allowing me to come.' A formal bow.

'You are the *Hawk* cutter, are y'not?' Again the blue stare.

'I am, sir.' His back straight.

'Yes – you came to her in my barge some little time since, I think?'

'I did, sir.'

'Pretty little ship, your *Hawk*. How does she handle? Fast by the wind? Sturdy sea boat, is she?'

'Well, sir, I have not – that is, I have waited day by day, since we provisioned and took in our guns and powder, and – '

'You have not weighed and took her out, even for half a day?' Growing severe.

'I have not, sir – since I was without instruction as to my specific duty.' Shamefaced.

'Then, by God, ye'd better discover how your cutter behaves, do not y'think so, Mr Hayter? You must take her out into the open sea, work her, put her about, exercise your great guns, and so forth. How may you become – you and your people – a capable addition to the fleet, else?'

'I have your permission then, sir?'

'My permission? You have my direct order to weigh and make sail, Mr Hayter, without the loss of a moment. Do not stray far, however. The fleet may be given its sailing instructions at any hour.'

'Thank you, sir. Will the French fleet support the Spanish in this, d'y'think?' Attempting to lift himself in the admiral's opinion.

'I do not know the French need give us pause in anything, at present. Their nation is in – disarray.'

'Their fleet is still considerable in size and strength, ain't it, sir?'

And then the admiral had made clear that the young sea officer had imposed long enough on his time, and his patience. 'I am not a political man, Mr Hayter. I do as I am told by Their Lordships, in the King's name. My concern as a commander is the Spanish fleet, not the French. You will oblige me by working up your cutter and your people, in a short exercise at sea, and then you will return to your mooring. Good morning.'

'Very good, sir.' Very correct, and a swift departure, with his chief question left unanswered: in Christ's name, to whom did he really belong – to the fleet, or to Captain Marles?

The answer did come, on the day following that brief exercise at sea.

*

By design James went ashore, not to enquire yet again at the Port Admiral's office as to the whereabouts of Captain Marles, but to discover what had become of the steward he had put on his books. This man he had recruited at the Cockpit Tavern, requiring him to bring himself and his dunnage to *Hawk*, but no one had come; the steward had disappeared. James wished to find him, and to send a letter to his wife Catherine, and to receive hers, care of the Marine Hotel. He wished also to visit his tailor, Bracewell & Hyde, from whom he had bespoke a new coat, waistcoat, breeches, and a dozen shirts. He could not afford them, but Portsmouth tailors were accustomed to wait for their payment, since many sea officers were long away from England. He was emerging from the Marine Hotel with two letters from Catherine in his pocket, and about to make his way to his tailor, when from across the street:

'Hayter!'

James turned in the direction of the voice, but saw no one he knew in the jostling crowds – with the fleet assembling Portsmouth was crammed with urgent humanity – and after a moment he went on his way, but again the voice, louder this time:

'You there, Mr Hayter!'

This was an unmistakably naval summons, and again James paused and turned. A figure stumped towards him, apparently indifferent to the clopping, wheel-rumbling traffic, was twice nearly struck, then gained the safety of the pavement. Captain Marles, and his peg.

'Hhh! Portsmouth ain't London – it is ten times as dangerous!' A little out of breath, brushing dusty chaff from his coat. 'Those damned draymen have no regard for safety!'

'It is the great volume of vehicles, and the comparative narrowness of the High, sir, that make it seem so.' James, his hat off and on. 'Do you wish me to come to the Port Admiral's office?'

'Nay, I do not.' Taking his arm. 'Let us go to the coffee house.'

They walked to the coffee house on the corner, and went in. The gloom of the interior, after the din and glare of the street, was a relief. In here there was not perfect quiet, but the murmur of voices, and the subdued clattering and clinking of crockery, combined with pleasant aromas, were welcoming. The gloom became temperate low light, restful to the eye. At tables round the walls, and at the end, merchants, clerks, a scattering of sea officers, some reading newspapers. The captain and the lieutenant were shown to a table in a corner, and ordered chocolate. Captain Marles at once became confidential, leaning forward.

'I have something to give to you. You must keep it with you, and show it to no one.' He gave James a sealed packet. James looked at the seal and saw to his surprise that it was not an Admiralty impress. A coronet, and initials.

'Am I to break the seal and open the packet, sir?'

'When our chocolate has come – then y'may open it.'

They waited until the pot of chocolate had been brought to the table, and the girl had laid out their cups. When she had gone:

'Very well, Mr Hayter.' Pushing the chocolate pot aside. 'Y'may break the seal, and open the packet.' Nodding. 'Go ahead.'

James laid the packet on the table, his back to the room, and

broke the seal. In the packet were two documents, one a letter.
James opened out the letter and at once saw a signature:

Chatham

and a smaller version of the seal, done with a ring.

'The Earl of Chatham?' James stared at the signature. 'The
First Lord?' And looked at Captain Marles in astonishment.
'Read it, read it.' Nodding again.

And James read:

To: Lieutenant James Hayter RN
        Commanding HM *Hawk* cutter –
        to be given into his hand at Portsmouth

Sir,

According to the detailed Instructions that shall be
given to you together with this Letter, by Captain Apley
Marles RN, you will use your best endeavours to take the
privately owned cutter *Lark*, that frequents the English
Channel for the purpose of landing Contraband goods, &
having took that Vessel bring her without the loss of a
moment to Portsmouth, or failing that place to Weymouth, or Plymouth, should either of those Ports prove
more convenient & necessary to your purpose of capture.

The master of said cutter, believed to be one Sedley
Ward, shall be arrested at all cost, and all other persons
aboard with him, and brought into your ship; he shall
then be brought ashore under close escort. His capture
is as vital to your purpose as the taking of his ship.

On no account, therefore, is *Lark* to be sunk, burnt or
destroyed, nor Captain Ward killed. They must be took.

5th June 1790

Chatham

James now slipped from the packet the second document, unfolded it, and read his detailed instructions. These included lists of dates and times when *Lark* would likely appear, based on observations made over several months by masters of three separate cutters in the service of the Board of Excise, none of whom had been able to match *Lark* in speed and handling. Also included was an accurate description of *Lark*, drawings, sail plan, and probable armament. There was a list of ports in France where *Lark* would take in her contraband goods, and a list of places along the southern coast of England where she was thought to have made landfall. James read through everything, noting the admonition 'Hereof nor you, nor any of you, may fail, as you will answer the contrary at your peril'. And at last looked up from the documents, into Captain Marles's steady gaze. 'You are lucky in that letter, Mr Hayter.'

'Lucky, sir? Yes, indeed, if you mean – '

'I mean that the First Lord is notorious apt to forget to sign his letters, nor any of his official utterances. We are often in despair at the Admiralty. You have been favoured.' A half-smile.

'May I ask a question, sir?'

'In course you may.' Pouring chocolate, now quite cold.

'How am I to detach myself from the Channel Fleet, sir, now assembled?'

'You will not.' A slight, dismissive gesture.

'Ah.' James sipped cold chocolate, made a face and set the cup down. He wiped his lips. 'May I ask: if the fleet is ordered to sea against Spain, and my duties – that I am eager to pursue, very eager, as you may imagine – if my duties hold me here in England, what then?'

'The thing will be managed, Mr Hayter.' The half-smile. 'This chocolate is abominable.' He held up his hand, and the girl returned. 'We will like a fresh pot of chocolate. Hot, if y'please.' He gave the girl a coin. She bobbed, took away the offending pot, and Captain Marles:

'Aye, it will be so arranged that your vessel will not take station, that is all.'

'Ah. – D'y'mean that I am to weigh and make sail, if so ordered, but not put to sea? With respect, sir, each ship must make her signals to the flag, and – '

'Yes, yes,' interrupting, 'do not trouble yourself, Mr Hayter. These are little things, minor details. You are attached to the fleet official, but by the documents lying at your elbow you are released.'

'Thank you, I do see that, sir. However, Admiral Hollister has told me – '

'Admiral Hollister? He spoke to you?'

'Well, yes. I – I went aboard his flag.' James lifted his head.

'What caused you to do that, pray, without instruction?' The half-smile now wholly absent.

'It was at his invitation.' Quickly.

'Hm. Why did he so invite you, I wonder? What prompted him?'

'Sir, again with respect, I do not think you quite under-stand my difficulty. By Admiral Hollister's spoken opinion to me, I am attached to him. On his orders I have already put to sea to exercise my great guns. I am presently at a mooring at Spithead in plain view of his flag, and my cutter is absolutely at his disposal. Can you not see, it is to him that I must look, because his authority overrides and overrules these documents – to all practical purpose?'

'Nonsense.' Curtly. 'Those documents bear the signature and seal of the First Lord. Do not you suppose that – '

'Forgive me, but that is not an Admiralty seal, is it?'

'What? It is the Earl of Chatham's seal, and he is the First Lord. D'you doubt his authority, sir?'

'No, sir.' James was uncomfortable.

'Do you?'

'In course I do not, sir.'

'Very well. Admiral Hollister, in commanding the Channel Fleet, does not, however, command the Royal Navy entire, does he? Their Lordships have that honour. The First Lord. Hey?'

'I am in no doubt of that, sir.'

'Well, then?' Captain Marles sat back in his chair impatiently. The fresh chocolate arrived, and there was a brief lull in the conversation while the girl set the pot on the table and replaced their cups. When she had gone, James tried again:

'Sir, in course I am obliged to follow these instructions.' Tapping the documents with a finger. 'You have given them to me, and they are signed by the First Lord.' A brief pause, then: 'Have I your authority, sir, to show them to Admiral Hollister, should he require me to explain – repair aboard his flag and explain – why I have declined to obey his direct order to the fleet to put to sea?'

'You have not.' Pouring chocolate, and drinking.

'You do not give it?'

'I do not.'

James gave a reluctant shrug, and composed his face into a polite, reluctant grimace. 'Then, sir, you put me in a pretty near impossible fix. I cannot, I fear, lie on both tacks at once, starboard and larboard. It must be one or t'other.'

The half-smile now returned, and became nearly a full smile. 'Yes, you put it nicely, Mr Hayter, I confess. Justly so.' He put down his cup, and refilled it. 'You oblige me to go to Admiral Hollister myself. It is some little time since I was aboard a ship of any rate, leave alone a first. I shall look forward to it.' He picked up the two letters, returned them to their packet, and put the packet away in his coat. 'I must take these with me, to show the admiral the signature and seal, should that become necessary – the signature and seal, and nothing more. Pray return to your cutter, Mr Hayter. I will send word to you.'

'Very good, sir.'

And Captain Marles paid their bill.

*

Lieutenant Hayter remained aboard *Hawk*, far out at her mooring, and no word came to him from Captain Marles. He waited three days, during which time he exercised his great guns, but did not fire them. His supply of gunpowder was limited to the allowance designated by the Ordnance, since he could not – like richer commanders – buy extra powder from private contractors. Beside, he was at his mooring among great numbers of ships. He exercised his great guns in a punishing continuum of several hours each day, until he felt that his guncrews, and his people altogether, were efficient in the business of bringing a ship of war into such a condition that would allow her to fight her weight of metal against any opposing cutter, schooner, or even a brig sloop. In other words, he would be more than a match for the *Lark*.

On the fourth morning, James decided that he must again go ashore. His steward had not yet been found, and he meant to find him. He would also seek out Captain Marles.

'I cannot wait upon Captain Marles's good intentions for ever,' he told himself, and called for the boat to be hoisted out, the mast stepped, and the sail bent.

He tacked through the assembled ships of the line, and ran in to the Hard. From the Hard he made his way to the Cockpit Tavern, and there enquired.

'Has a man called Butt shown himself?'

'Butt? Don't know no one of that name, sir.' The innkeeper, sucking his teeth.

'Plentiful Butt?'

'Ohh. Plenty. Yes. Yes, we knows Plenty.'

'Well, has he been here? This last day or two?'

'No, sir.' With certainty.

'When did you last see him?' He paid for a mug of ale. 'Will you drink something, landlord?'

'That is right kind in you, sir, I will.' He drew off a measure of brandy, and sucked down half.

'You have not seen him recent?'

'He will only come here when he is flush, d'y'see. You might try at the Drawbridge Tavern.'

'At the Point? Good God, that is the worst den of scoundrels in Portsmouth.'

'Aye, sir, I will not dispute that. Not that Plenty is a scoundrel. It's just they will allow him a bed there, when he ain't flush.' He sucked down the rest of his brandy. 'At one time I would oblige him here – but he could not never pay me, and I must pay my own rent, look.'

'Indeed. Thank you, I will enquire at the Drawbridge.' He drank a mouthful of ale, left a further shilling on the counter, and went to the Marine Hotel in the High.

'I will like to see Captain Marles.'

'Captain Marles? Oh. Will you wait here please, sir?'

James waited, and presently was shown into a small private room at the rear, where he was greeted by a lieutenant-colonel of marines.

'You asked for Captain Marles?'

'I did. Is he here?' Puzzled.

'Evidently you have not heard . . .' Looking at James closely.

'Heard what?'

'Captain Marles is dead.'

'Christ's blood . . .' Shocked. 'I had no notion that he was ill.'

'He was not ill. Captain Marles has been murdered. He was found late last night in an alley off Broad Street in the Point.'

'Murdered? In God's name – how?'

'His throat was cut.' The marine officer leaned over the square table that stood against the wall, took up a quill pen, dipped it in the small silver well, and: 'May I have your name, Lieutenant?'

'Yes. Certainly. I am Lieutenant James Hayter RN, commanding the *Hawk* cutter, ten guns.'

The officer made a mark on a list, and laid the pen aside. 'You had business with Captain Marles? This morning?'

'Yes – yes.' Distractedly. 'The Point, you say? What in God's name was he doing there, at night?'

'You know the district?'

'It is notorious.'

'What was your business with Captain Marles?'

'Eh? Oh – Admiralty business.' His hand at the back of his neck. 'What a dreadful thing . . . a dreadful thing.' He turned away distractedly.

'If you please, Lieutenant – what was that business, exact?'

Turning to look at him: 'Well, Colonel . . . I am not at liberty to divulge it. Admiralty business, of a confidential nature.'

'You will divulge it to me, if you please. I am charged with the investigation of all of the circumstances surrounding the captain's death.'

'Then you must enquire at the Admiralty, you know, Colonel. I cannot help you. I may not. – Had Captain Marles any family, d'y'know? A wife?'

'He was widowed, I believe. I must ask you again – insist – that you tell me your business with him, Mr Hayter. It may have a bearing on what has happened.'

'How so?'

'The captain's coat had been torn open at an inner pocket. An empty packet, which had itself been torn open, lay beside the corpse. It is thought documents was removed from the packet. In his effects, found in his bedroom, Captain Marles left a list of names, including your own, and that of Admiral Hollister. Do you happen to know if those stolen documents related to your business with him? Had you had sight of them?'

'Aye, I did have sight of them.'

'It is nearly certain that he was killed for those documents, Lieutenant.'

'Yes, yes, your assumption is correct, I think.' Nodding. 'How very shocking.'

'Well?'

James looked at him, then made his back straight. 'All I am able to tell you, Colonel, is that the business upon which poor Captain Marles and I were engaged was under the direct instruction of the First Lord himself. The documents bore his signature and seal.'

'I see.' Gravely. 'Then I must go to Admiral Hollister.'

'He can tell you nothing.'

'What? Nothing? How d'y'know that?'

'Because he was not party to the business. Captain Marles merely sought the admiral's consent to my release from the Channel Fleet. I am not even certain that he had visited the admiral before – this sad event. In truth I think that probably he had not, else the admiral would have done so.'

'Done so?'

'Forgive me, I am a little distracted. Would have released me, d'y'see. If Captain Marles had asked him.'

'Yes, I am not quite clear. Why should Admiral Hollister release you – supposing Captain Marles had seen him – without he was told the reason?'

'Captain Marles was acting in the name of the First Lord. Not even so powerful a sea officer as Admiral Hollister may gainsay that authority, I think.' A thought came to him now, and he drew in a sharp breath. 'The documents! If Captain Marles had not had his interview with Admiral Hollister, then without the documents I am . . . I must go to London!'

'Nay, Lieutenant, you must remain at Portsmouth until I have concluded my inquiries.'

'Why? I am not material to your inquiry, when I have been living aboard my cutter, far out at Spithead, these last three days. By the by, Colonel, should not such inquiry be conducted by the local magistrate and his constables?'

'The magistrate is conducting his own inquiry.' The colonel looked at James, and frowned. 'However, he has not sufficient runners to be effective in such a matter. The Marines and the Royal Navy, acting together, will be a better instrument. You will aid me by remaining here.'

'Sir, I must go to London without delay. I must obtain new documents, restoring my authority to act as instructed. Without them I am powerless to proceed.'

'I know nothing of that, since you will tell me nothing. You will remain at Portsmouth, if y'please.'

James effortfully kept his temper, and made no reply.

'D'you hear me, Lieutenant?' Growing severe.

'Very good, sir.' A brief bow, and James put on his hat and turned to quit the room.

'I have not given you leave to go.'

'You wish me to remain in this room, sir? Remain in Portsmouth, in this room?'

'Do not be impertinent, Mr Hayter.' A warning glare.

'I am very sorry, sir.' Icily.

The marine officer sighed, and put the list into a leather fold. 'Look here, Hayter, we must not be at odds in this. A good man has been killed, and we must discover why, and by whom. We will go together to Admiral Hollister, first of all, and obtain your release from him. Agreed?'

'Very good, sir.' His bearing less rigid.

'I am remiss, I have not introduced myself. I am Lieutenant-Colonel Brian Macklin of the corps of Marines. Will you shake hands?'

They shook hands, and James managed to relax his grim facial expression.

'To say the truth, the local magistrate is not what I would describe as the sharpest sword in Portsmouth. You apprehend me?' Colonel Macklin put the fold in his pocket.

'In short, he is a dullard?'

'You apprehend me. You came ashore in your own boat?'

'I did, sir. The boat lies at the Hard.'

'I will fetch my cloak.'

James knew that he must humour Colonel Macklin, must go with him to Admiral Hollister in *Vanquish*. He knew that to demur further, and then attempt to leave Portsmouth, would in all likelihood prompt Colonel Macklin into placing him under close arrest. As they made their way to the Hard, and then walked across and down the gentle slope toward the water:

'No, I must go to *Vanquish*, and as soon as I am able thereafter go to London, by the fast mail coach.' To himself. He would seek out the only person known to him at the Admiralty, the Third Secretary Mr Soames. Soames might probably be able to help him obtain further documents – if not from the First Lord, then at least from some other high official – so that he could begin his pursuit of the *Lark* cutter and her master Sedley Ward. Ward was almost certainly behind the murder of Captain Marles.

James, in sea boots, pushed the twelve-foot jollyboat out, and helped Colonel Macklin aboard, who had clearly expected a much larger boat, a launch or pinnace, with a proper boat's crew. James hoisted the single sail, and brought the boat to the wind. The little craft pitched and heeled, the sail taut in the stiff onshore breeze.

'Aye, almost certainly he is,' repeated James to himself.

'Certainly?' Colonel Macklin gripped the gunwale with white knuckles. 'You think we will certainly capsize?'

James had spoken aloud, without knowing it. And now he did say aloud: 'No, sir, no. We are quite safe.'

'I am not much at sea, you know. My duties have kept me altogether ashore of late. Oh!' As a wave smacked in under the boat's bow, and splintered in drenching shards over the two occupants.

The single loose-footed lugsail was not ideal for beating close-hauled by the wind, but James managed both sheets and tiller with ease. He enjoyed this direct, spray-flying form of sailing, and had quickly learned the jollyboat's foibles, and how to master them.

'Tacking!' he called now, and Colonel Macklin was obliged to duck low beneath the swinging foot and leech, clutching at his hat, as James brought the boat through the wind.

Presently they came to *Vanquish*, and were hailed from the deck:

'Boat ahoy! Who are you?'

And James, with a little swelling of pride in his breast, was able as commander of a commissioned vessel to make the traditional reply:

'*Hawk*!'

'Come aboard!'

*

'Ah, Lieutenant Hayter. I know why you have come, I think.'

The Third Secretary Mr Soames rose from his desk, but did not come forward, nor proffer his hand in greeting. He remained where he was, his hand extended merely to indicate a chair.

'I must thank you for receiving me so prompt, Mr Soames.' James sat down on the very plain chair, and put his hat beneath it.

'Under the circumstances I could hardly do otherwise.' Mr Soames resumed his seat, and tucked a fine linen handkerchief into his sleeve. A waft of cologne on the slightly stale air. 'The death of Captain Marles has been wretched inconvenient to us – and to you, I am in no doubt.'

'Inconvenient?' The word came rushing out, harsher and more hostile than he had intended.

'More than inconvenient, indeed.' A brief puckering of the mouth. 'A great nuisance.'

James opened his mouth, then shut it again before angry remonstrance could crash out into the room. He counted to five.

'I – I have come because I need to have replaced the instructions Captain Marles brought to me at Portsmouth, but did not give to me.'

'You never saw them?' Surprised.

'I did see them, but they – that is, Captain Marles did not give them into my possession.'

'Then it's true that they was removed from his coat at the time of the attack?'

'We believe so, yes.'

'We?'

'Lieutenant-Colonel Macklin of the Marines, that is inquiring into the captain's death – his murder.'

'Murder, yes.' Another brief puckering, and the trace of a grimace. 'Yes, an ugly word.'

'I do not know a better one. A more convenient one.'

'You have not considered, I expect, that this was not deliberate murder?'

'Not delib— . . . Christ's blood, his throat was cut!'

'Was it? Was it? That I did not know.' He lifted the handkerchief to his nose a moment, then returned it to his sleeve. 'Yes, what I had meant to suggest to you, Lieutenant, was that the assault – though murderous – was merely one of opportunity, not design. You frown.'

'Surely it is obvious, Mr Soames! I beg your pardon, I did not mean to shout. But surely it is absolutely clear, ain't it? The inner pocket of his coat was torn out, the packet removed and torn apart, and the papers took.'

'Yes?'

'Yes!'

'Mm, yes. It had not occurred to you that the footpad, in such a place as the Point – notorious, I think, at Portsmouth – was merely seeking money? He saw a gentleman alone at night in an alley, supposed that the gentleman had gold money upon his person, and made his assault.'

'In truth that explication had not occurred to me, no. I find it, with respect, entirely improbable.'

'Do you? Ah.' Mr Soames sat impassive, and allowed a moment to pass. 'In course you are entitled to your view.'

'My view! I beg your pardon. Sir, my very strong sense of the thing is that Captain Ward was behind it, that he is now in possession of our plan of capture, and that we must devise a new stratagem. That is why I have come, for new instructions.'

'Sedley Ward, d'y'mean?'

'Aye, Captain Sedley Ward, of the *Lark* cutter.'

'Not Ward, I think.' Shaking his head. 'Word has reached us from Barbados that Sedley Ward died there two month ago, of the fever. He was second officer of a schooner there, thought to be a slaver. He had not been master of the *Lark* for a twelvemonth.'

'When did this intelligence come?'

'Yesternight, in a letter. The papers took from Captain Marles have been destroyed, to a certainty. Torn up, or flung into the harbour, or burned – as worthless. Sedley Ward is dead, and we do not know who commands the *Lark*. But whoever he is, he does not know of our plan. Fair copies were made of your instructions. You shall have those, when further copies have been done. Come here at noon tomorrow, and the papers will be ready for you.'

'I – very good, sir.'

'The impediment is the loss of Captain Marles. He is not easily replaced as your immediate superior. You will have to proceed on your own initiative, for the moment.'

'May I prevail upon you, Mr Soames, to advise me – should I need advice?'

'My dear Lieutenant Hayter, I cannot possibly advise you. I do not decide, I am not party to decision, nor direction. I am a servant of Their Lordships.'

'I wonder . . .'

'Yes?'

'I wonder if I might be permitted to call on the – the assistance of another officer?'

'Another officer? D'y'mean, in the same role as the late Captain Marles?'

'I do. I had thought – '

'You do not mean . . . you cannot mean . . . Captain Rennie?' Mr Soames had lost his air of detachment.

'He has been my commanding officer in three commissions, and he would – '

'No!' Mr Soames half-stood, then as if collecting himself
sat down again, and: 'Such a suggestion is wholly without
merit – it simply don't bear examination.' The handkerchief
again to his nose. 'It cannot be considered at all.'

'But why not?'

'Why *not*? Why *not*?' All of Mr Soames's detached
decorum, his aloof, cologne-scented calm, had vanished on
the stale air. 'Captain Rennie is an officer that has a question
beside his name. In course, he has been exonerated of any
charges against him, all charges was dissolved and dispensed
with, but there remains in association with his name a very
distinct question.'

'What is the nature of this "question"? If Sir Robert
Greer – '

'No. No.' Very firmly, raising a hand. 'I am not at liberty
to discuss it.'

'Then why – forgive me, Mr Soames – but why bring this
into the conversation? I have the highest regard for Captain
Rennie, and any question raised by Sir Robert, or anyone – '

'Young *man*! – Lieutenant Hayter.' The handkerchief.
'Hm. I did not mean to raise my voice.' The handkerchief
again pressed to his nose, then returned to his sleeve. 'If I was
you, I should collect my papers from the clerk tomorrow,
proceed to Portsmouth, and there take up my duties. I should
put entirely from my mind *all other things*. And now, if you
will forgive me, there is many pressing matters in need of my
attention. I trust that you will have a pleasant journey. Good
day.'

And so on the morrow, carrying his new papers, James
returned to Portsmouth – his head alive with questions, and
puzzles, and vexatious troubling doubts.

TWO

Captain Rennie, to his surprise, had heard nothing more from Sir Robert Greer, and nothing more of him. Rennie did not enquire at Middingham Court. He did not know the family, had never met them; they were called Rushton. It was the maid Jenny – who was in effect Rennie's housekeeper, so completely had she assumed control of his domestic arrangements – who informed him of Sir Robert's departure.

'I heard from one of them at the Court that the grand gent has took himself off, and not a moment too soon, she said, very demanding he was of all the staff there, and not a shilling by way of a thank-you, neither, when he left.'

Rennie had never met the family, but he knew that Sir Henry Rushton had six daughters, all of them still on his hands. The innkeeper at the Plough, Silas Wright, who knew everything in the village, about everybody:

'Old Sir Henry is in despair that he ain't produced a heir, and has not got none of his daughters off his hands neither, and the youngest already seventeen. His eldest girl is twenty-five. If she ain't wed at twenty-five, who will have her now, in Norfolk? Lasses here is wed by sixteen, look. I do not say gentry does, mind, but girls is girls, whichever their rank, and young men do not want old maids, they do not.'

'What about old men, hey?' Rennie had asked in jest. 'Perhaps I should try my luck, Mr Wright.'

'I should not do that, sir.' Tapping his nose. 'If you don't mind a word to the wise.'

'Oh?'

'Ain't a bonny one among 'em.'

'Plain fillies, hey?'

'Fillies?' Lowering his voice. 'Moos is the word, I b'lieve. Bovine critchers, Captain Rennie. Steer clear, I should.'

Rennie had not been arrested nor in any way inconvenienced by Sir Robert, but he determined that it would be as well, however, not to sit waiting at home in Norfolk. Was it not possible that Sir Robert was contriving and conceiving and conspiring against him? Might not Sir Robert probably return quite soon, with a detachment of marines and a warrant of apprehension?

Rennie decided to go to Portsmouth. He would take rooms at the Marine Hotel for a week or two. If Lieutenant Hayter was still at Portsmouth, in his cutter, perhaps they could meet. Perhaps James would invite him to go on board. Rennie could give him advice, if he sought it. Only if he did; it would not do to presume. In course, thought Rennie, he would have to be discreet. He would not call on the Port Admiral, nor in any other way advertise his presence. He would not, after all, come to Portsmouth in any official capacity. He was not commissioned. He would not wish to be seen in any sense to be interfering in the business of the Channel Fleet, at a time of emergency. No, he would arrive at Portsmouth merely as a private gentleman, a private visitor minding his own business.

He instructed Jenny to pack his bag, and to look after things while he was gone. To pay the boy who looked after his horse and cleaned the stable; to pay the man who came from the village to tend the garden, &c., &c. He would be gone a fortnight or three weeks, a month at the outside. If – by chance – Sir Robert Greer should call, she was to say that Captain Rennie was away on personal business – in London.

He departed.

Rennie might have gone to London by the same route that James had come to Norfolk, by sea, but he did not. He determined to go by road. He could have hired a post-chaise, at great expense, to take him all the way to London, and then on to Portsmouth. Instead he went by turnpike coach. The mail coach travelled daily to London from Norwich, with an overnight stop at an inn at Sudbury. Rennie paid thirty shillings for an inside seat.

On the coach door was emblazoned the slogan *The London Flyer* in elaborate red and gold script on a green ground. The bodywork of the coach was green, with flashes of gold, the wheels were green with red spokes. The coachman wore a great green travelling cape, and a broad green tricorne. The six horses sported gleaming decorated harness.

'It is all very splendid,' muttered Rennie to himself as he prepared to board the coach in St Stephen's Street, the castle wall behind. 'But does it reflect their efficacy of service?' He climbed in and settled in his facing window seat, for which he had paid an extra five shillings. He noted with approval that the leather seats were upholstered, and that the vehicle gave a little on its springs as each passenger ascended. 'We shall not be rattled and bounced to death, in least.' Politely, to the lady seating herself opposite. She made no reply, but employed her vinaigrette, and closed her eyes. She was a handsome woman, thought Rennie, in her bonnet and waisted blue dress. 'However, she contrives to look ten years younger than her years.' Not aloud.

Towards evening, in open country between Bury and Sudbury, near to a hamlet called Capling Street, the coach came to a sudden sliding, shuddering halt. Rennie had been dozing, and woke with a start.

'What? Are we upset?'

'Nay, sir, I think not.' An elderly gentleman. 'I believe we are – '

The *crack* of a pistol shot. The lady opposite Rennie gasped, and looked out of the window in alarm. Consternation among all of the passengers. And now a shout in the road ahead.

'Stay still now! Very still!' Echoing on the crisp evening air.

The sound of hooves, a single horse on the metal of the road. 'Make no resistance, and you will not be harmed!'

The lady transferred her alarmed gaze from the window to Rennie, and instinctively he felt that he must offer her his protection.

'Never fear, madam.' Quietly to her. She glanced again out of the window, and then looked anxiously at Rennie, as if for reassurance. 'Never fear . . .' He was not wearing his sword, and now regretted it, but he was carrying two loaded pocket pistols. He leaned to the window, thrust down the glass, and cautiously peered out. There was just enough daylight remaining for him to make out a large horse, and a caped figure. A horse pistol was pointed at the coachman, who was out of Rennie's line of sight. The figure urged the horse forward, pointing the long pistol, and in the glow of the newly lit side lantern his face was revealed, pale, with hooded eyes and a narrow nose under a thwartwise hat. He motioned with the pistol, leaning forward in the saddle, and Rennie saw the coachman descend from his driving perch. A second, shorter figure appeared now, that of a youth or a small man, also in black. The youth pushed the coachman towards the rear of the coach, and the pair passed the window. Rennie drew back his head until they had passed, then cautiously thrust it out again. The black-cloaked highwayman dismounted, and came towards the rear of the coach, leading his horse. The horse stumbled on a flint, and for a moment the man's attention was diverted, and he turned his head.

Rennie acted. He flung open the door, leapt to the road, and drew one of his pistols from his coat. The man turned from his horse, saw Rennie, and thought to lift his own pistol, now half-lowered.

'Nay, do not attempt – '

Crack. The highwayman fired, lifting the long barrel in a jerk, and the heavy ball sang by Rennie's head, struck the half-open coach door, and smashed it back with a splintering thud on its hinges. Screams and gasps from within.

Rennie fired in answer, his pistol aimed. *Crack*. The ball struck the man in the temple, his hat flew off and there was a fountaining spurt of blood. His head lolled to the side and his body collapsed. The black cloak billowed and was snatched down by his falling weight. His horse shied away. Rennie turned swiftly, tried to pull the second pistol from the pocket of his coat – and was struck a stunning blow to the side of his head.

He staggered, lifted a hand, and felt a second savage blow to his forearm.

'Damn . . . your . . . blood . . .' he mumbled in dazed fear, and fell to the road. He saw a figure loom over him, got his pistol clear, and fired point-blank into his assailant's body. *Crump*. The shot muffled in cloth. For a long moment nothing happened. Then the blackness of the figure diminished, fell back, became a tottering shape of cloak and breeches and riding boots, gave a cry – pitiful and anguished – and slumped.

'Good God, he is only a child . . .'

Rennie stumbled to his feet, dropped the pistol in the road, and went to the boy, who now lay motionless. He pulled aside the draping cloak, and found – not a boy, but a young woman, quite dead, her dark hair loosed from a red ribbon in a spreading fan.

'Christ Jesu . . .' Whispered.

He had shot her through the heart.

There was inevitable concomitant flurry and inquiry and nuisance after the incident. An agent of the coaching company, the London Flyer Limited, was summoned from Sudbury, the local magistrate was informed, a local physician pronounced the corpses dead, and Rennie was obliged to furnish his explanation of the event firstly to the magistrate, and subsequently to his clerk, &c., &c.

The lady in the blue dress, who put up at the same inn at Sudbury, was a widow, Rennie learned – a Mrs Townend.

She was travelling to London to visit her sister.

'We are all in your debt tonight, Captain Rennie,' she said to him. 'You were uncommon brave.'

'Well, I . . . I have had experience of this before, ma'am.'

'Before?'

'Aye, a year since, journeying with another officer to Portsmouth. Our roads in England, in this age of frequent travel, are not yet suitable safe, I fear. It is a thing the coaching companies must address.'

'D'y'mean armed men, to protect us?'

'I think so, ma'am.'

'We had you, tonight.'

Her late husband, it came out in subsequent conversation, had been a sea officer – Captain Arthur Townend RN. Rennie thought he could recall his name on the List, from several years ago.

'He has been dead these seven years, Captain Rennie. He died at sea, and was buried at sea.'

'I am sorry.'

'It is long past, I no longer feel a pang when I think of it, nor even when I talk of it. Only a little passing regret. You think me harsh? You think me callous?' Looking at him over her chocolate cup as they waited for their rooms to be made ready.

'Nay, madam, I do not. I have lost my own dear wife, and know intimately what such loss means. It is a private thing, and each of us that has known it must find his own way through.'

She inclined her head with a grave half-smile. 'You are a man of understanding, Captain Rennie.'

'I hope that I am, ma'am.'

'And may I say it again – a very brave one?' A further smile.

Praise to his face was in usual disconcerting to Rennie, but in the case of the blue widow he felt a little glow. He had meant to pursue – was that quite the word? – had meant to discover the lady's address at Norwich, so that he might call on her at some future time. He was not sure when, nor even why. To press his attentions upon her? But she had eluded him, when the coach reached London the following day. He was again delayed by company agents, and failed to see Mrs Townend depart the Angel Inn, and deeply regretted it. Rennie thought then, before he secured his seat on the coach to Portsmouth, that he would be a damned fool if he did not attempt to find her, and indeed press his attentions on her. She was a very handsome woman, and she had smiled at him.

Rennie arrived at Portsmouth in a very subdued condition. He had always intended to come there quietly and discreetly, but the dark event on the road, and all of the consequent exigencies of magistrate and clerk and agent, had quite cast him down – in spite of Mrs Townend's kind efforts to lift him. By the time he came to the Marine Hotel, and enquired about a room, his bag lying by his legs, he was almost too self-effacing and diffident in the bustling busyness of the place to make himself heard. Presently he succeeded, and:

'I fear we are very full up at present, sir.' The clerk. 'If you had stayed with us before, there may be . . . I did not quite hear the name, sir.'

A party of young women, escorted by a captain of Marines, made the space loud a moment as they moved towards the dining room, just as Rennie said who he was to the clerk.

'I am very sorry, sir . . . will you just say your name again?'

'Rennie. Hm. William Rennie.'

'And – have you stayed with us before, sir?' Opening the book.

'Yes.'

A finger flicking through the book, moving down a list of names:

'Ahh, yess. Yess, of course. Captain William Rennie, RN!' Triumphantly tapping the list.

'Hush, hush – if you please.' Rennie glanced round.

'I do beg your pardon, Captain Rennie.' Clearly this called

for discretion, and he lowered his voice accordingly, and waited.

'Now then.' Rennie leaned forward. 'I do not wish . . . it is most important that I should have quiet, that I should be quiet, d'y'see. That is – if you are able to find room for me, at such a busy time.'

'Oh, yes, sir. We do keep rooms available for valued guests, indeed.'

'I am not here on naval business. I am here privately. Quietly. I do not wish to be disturbed.'

'Just as you say, sir. – If you was wanting the same rooms as what you took previous, well . . .'

'Yes. No. Quieter rooms, towards the rear, if you have them. I do not wish my presence known.'

'Very well, sir.' Riffling through another book. 'We have a room – not rooms – overlooking the stable yard, at the rear. If that would suit . . . ?'

'Yes, yes, admirable.' Nodding, again glancing round. He saw no one he knew, among the officers and young persons making their way through to the public rooms, and was reassured.

'Very well, sir. If you would very kindly write your name . . .' Dipping quill pen in ink, and offering the pen to Rennie.

Rennie wrote his name. The clerk scattered powder from the pounce box, and summoned a boy to carry Rennie's bag. 'Second floor, back, last room on the left. Sharp now.'

Rennie followed the boy.

'Good God, it's Rennie, ain't it! William Rennie!'

In dread Rennie pretended not to hear, but felt his arm grasped from behind, and was obliged to turn. He saw a tall, confident sea officer, in dress coat, his dark hair greying at the temples, and recognized him. Captain Richard Langton RN.

'Langton. I did not know it was you, else I – '

'Are you with the fleet? What is your ship?'

'Nay, I am on the beach. I am only here privately, you know, a private visit.'

'On the beach? You? That is damned bad luck.' With genuine sympathy, although of course he had already known that Rennie was without a commission, from the List.

'And you, Langton? Have you still got *Tamar*?' Contriving to be polite.

'Nay, I have not, I have got the *Hanover*, seventy-four.'

'A ship of the line, hey? That is well, that is well. My congratulations. You deserve it.'

'I don't know that I do, you know.' A laugh. 'But I have got her, anyway.'

Rennie sensed that Captain Langton was about to invite him to the ship, and quickly:

'Will you forgive me if I go to my room, Langton? I am rather tired. A long journey.'

'In course, m'dear fellow. Perhaps we could meet tomorrow? I am ashore nearly every day, even to sleep, since we have not yet had our sailing instructions. Or we could dine aboard . . .'

'By all means.' Rennie nodded and smiled, and left it at that. He was pleased to have seen his old friend, but convivial dinners, naval reminiscences, &c., were not what he could at present welcome. He would find an excuse, and make it. The only person he wished to see was James Hayter, and tomorrow he would – discreetly – seek him out.

He climbed the stairs.

'Thank you.' He gave a coin to the boy who had carried his bag to the door of the room.

The boy touched his forehead, and said: 'Does you wish the maid to turn down your bed, sir?'

'No no, thank you. I shall rest quiet through the afternoon, lying on the covers.'

'Was you wishing her to turn it down – later?'

Had the boy smirked at him? Had the scut winked, good God? Rennie peered at him, and detected nothing untoward.

Perhaps he had mistook the boy's expression, in the dim light of the passage. Perhaps he had misinterpreted the boy's questions.

'Later? Nay, I think not. I am used to a seafaring life, you know, and am able to manage such things for myself.'

'As you like, sir.'

'I may perhaps wish to dine in my room. I will ring.'

'Will I say so downstair, sir? That you wishes to dine?'

Rennie saw now that what he had thought was a wink was a little twitch of one side of the boy's face, brought on by earnest enquiry.

'Thank you, I will ring.' He gave the boy another silver penny, and went in. Presently he lay down.

When he woke, his valise still strapped up on the floor where he had left it, it was already nearly dark. Until a minute had passed he did not know where he was. For those sixty seconds he lay in utter confusion, looking at the dim square of the window, snuffing the smell of candle wax and hearing from below the scraping of hooves on cobbles.

'What is this place?' Muttered aloud. 'Where the devil am I?'

He sat up, and saw his valise, and remembered. He reached for the candle-holder on the cabinet, and was about to strike a light when there came a sharp tapping at his door.

'Captain Rennie!' A man's voice.

Who could know his whereabouts? Who knew he was at Portsmouth, leave alone in this hotel? An agent of Sir Robert Greer's? But how? Surely Langton had not –

'Captain Rennie!' The rat-tat-tat repeated.

'Who – who is it?'

'May I speak to you please, sir?'

'Oh. Yes. – Yes, about my dinner.' Swinging numb legs off the bed, stumbling pins and needles to the door, shoeless. He opened the door – and was confronted by a pistol and a masked face. The pistol was cocked with a menacing click, the sharpened flint poised in the dim light of the passage.

'Step back, if y'please.' The voice lowered, and now with a sharp edge.

Rennie stepped back, slipped on one of his cast-off shoes, and nearly fell. At once the pistol was thrust at his head, as his assailant followed him into the room, and:

'None of that! No sudden, artful movement, or I will take your life!'

'I – I slipped.' Fearfully, still a little dazed by sleep. 'What d'y'want of me? My purse?'

'Not your purse, nothing at all – excepting intelligence.'

'Who are you? Do you come from – '

'I will ask. You will answer.' The pistol steady. 'You mind me?'

'Very well. If I can answer . . .'

'You will. Sit on the bed.'

Rennie did so, and wished that he had a pistol handy, or his sword. His pistols were in his coat, hanging over the chair in the corner, and his sword was at home in Norfolk.

'Answer me straight out. Where is Lieutenant Hayter? Does he come to you tonight?'

'Eh? Tonight?' Trying to place the voice, of an educated man. He could not.

'Well?'

'Lieutenant Hayter, so far as I'm aware, is attached to the Channel Fleet. You had better ask at the Port Admiral's office, I expect.'

'He ain't attached to the fleet, Captain Rennie, as you know well. He is attached to you.'

'Attached to me? You are grossly misinformed, sir. He is not.'

The pistol thrust into Rennie's throat. He flinched. 'Do not prevaricate, Captain Rennie. I do not care about your life. I will take it in a breath, if you do not assist me.'

Rennie smelled burned powder. The pistol had been fired not long since, and the smell chilled him.

'I – I will try to assist you, if I am able. But you are mistook

about me. I know nothing of Lieutenant Hayter's whereabouts. I am come to Portsmouth as a private visitor.'

'Private visitor!' With contempt. 'Is that what they call it,
in London? Is that what they have told you to say?'

'In London? Who in London?'

'How many cutters are under your command?'

'Eh? Good God, I am not commissioned. No cutters at all.
None.'

A jerk of the muzzle against Rennie's larynx. He coughed,
beginning to choke.

'I will ask you again. How many cutters, and where do they
lie?'

'How can I answer . . . cehhgh . . . when you stop my
wind . . . ?'

The pistol was withdrawn an inch, and Rennie got his
breath, his mind whirling. He opened his mouth to speak.

Rap-rap-rap. 'Captain Rennie, sir?' The boy's voice.

Rennie's masked assailant brought a finger up, a warning
finger, and whispered: 'Send him away.'

Rap-rap-rap. 'Captain Rennie, is you awake, sir?'

Rennie, *sotto voce*: 'It is my dinner. He will not go away until
I have took in the tray.'

A savage whisper: 'Send him away!' The pistol brushed
Rennie's ear.

'Will you leave the tray outside the door? Thank you.'
Rennie, calling.

'I ain't got no tray, sir. I has come to arst what you will like
for your dinner.'

'There is a confusion,' whispered Rennie. 'He has not
brought me what I ordered. I must go to the door, or he will
persist . . .'

'Very well, but do not open the door wider than a crack.
Say you ain't hungry. Send him away.' The muzzle of the
pistol again flicked at Rennie's ear. 'Remember, I do not care
about your life.'

Rennie cautiously slipped off the bed, and moved to the

door, aware always of the pistol pointed at his head from behind. He opened the door two inches, and saw the boy waiting in the subdued glow of a candle.

'I – I have decided . . .' Jerking his eyes in a frantic sideways glance, several times, in an attempt to alert the boy to his predicament. '. . . erm, I have decided that I ain't desperate hungry, after all.' More jerking movements of his eyes, and his eyebrows up and down.

'Not hungry, sir?' The boy peered at him, puzzled by Rennie's demeanour, and lifted the candle-holder.

'Nay, I am very tired . . . desperate tired.' The eyes.

The boy's face twitched, and he frowned a little. 'As you like, sir . . .'

'Here, I will give you a penny for your trouble.' Rennie fumbled in his fob pocket, and felt the pistol at the back of his neck. 'Oh . . . I have not got any money about me. I am most desperate sorry.' Again the eyes. He closed the door.

The glow of the candle under the door faded as the boy went away. Rennie turned back into the room, and tried to make out his assailant's size. He was not a large man, but looked wiry strong, thought Rennie. Could he distract the fellow, wrench the pistol from his grasp, and turn the weapon on him? The masked man seemed to read his thoughts, even in near darkness.

'Do not think of attack, Captain Rennie.' With quiet menace. 'Not while I have this cocked in my hand.' He motioned Rennie to return to the bed. Rennie obeyed.

'Would it not be easier if we had a light?' he ventured.

'It would not, thank you. Now I will like – '

'What if the boy should return? What then? He is – '

'I will ask. You will answer. Do not make me iterate that instruction.' The mask began to slip on his face, and he adjusted it with a gloved hand. 'You will tell me, please, where you are to meet Lieutenant Hayter. Here, or aboard his vessel?'

Rennie was silent a moment, then cleared his throat. 'Sir –

I have no wish to disappoint you, when you hold a loaded pistol at my head. But I must earnestly insist, you are under a misapprehension. Please!' As the pistol was once again thrust into his face. 'For God's sake, now. Will y'not listen to me. If you have come from Sir Robert Greer, then I – '

'Sir Robert Who-is-he?' Withdrawing the muzzle a fraction.

'Sir Robert Greer . . . ? You do not know him?'

'I have never heard the name. Do not attempt to distract me, I warn you.' Again thrusting the pistol.

Rennie had had more than enough of this bullying, hectoring nonsense, and he took a deep, quiet breath.

'Well? Where d'you meet Lieutenant Hayter! Tell me!'

'I am, I fear, unable to help you at all.' Deliberately meek, deliberately defensive, with a little shrug – to provoke his opponent. He succeeded. The muzzle of the pistol was advanced towards Rennie's chin, and in that moment Rennie thrust up a hand, grasped the muzzle and wrenched it aside, and kicked with all his strength into the fellow's crotch. Felt his foot connect, and heard a gasp of pain. Rennie continued the wrenching motion, and felt the pistol loosen in the other's grip, and come into his position. He wrenched it free, reversed its direction, and as his erstwhile assailant sank to his knees with a groan, pointed it down at his head.

'Take off that bloody mask!'

A groan. Rennie reached down, and tore the mask off. The man collapsed on the floor, and lay doubled up, his face hidden. Another groan.

'Aye, I am glad it is painful, you damned blackguard. Only let me find my shoes, and I will repeat it. Show me your face!'

But the hapless man gave a retch, writhed over and fell on his back in a dead faint. Rennie stood over him a moment, then put the pistol on the cabinet, struck a light and lit his candle. He held the candle over the prostrate figure, and examined the face. He saw a clean-shaven man, even-featured, of about thirty years. A man unknown to him.

Presently the man coughed, turned his head a little, coughed again, and came to himself. His face contorted with pain, and he clutched at his testicles.

'Now then . . .' Rennie leaned over him. 'Who the devil are you, hey?'

The man sucked in a breath, stared up at Rennie, and was silently defiant.

'Why have you come here? Why d'you ask me these questions about Lieutenant Hayter? Who sent you?'

The man turned his head away, and attempted to sit up.

'Stay down on the floor, damn you.' Rennie aimed the pistol. 'Stay there, and answer me.'

The man coughed, appeared to sag with pain, then leapt to his feet and flung himself at Rennie, knocking him off balance. Rennie fell back against the bed, and the man swung a fierce blow at his head with his clenched fist. Rennie rolled away, pushed himself off the bed, and as the man came at him again, fiercely, and caught him a blow to the neck, Rennie smashed the barrel of the pistol as hard as he could into the man's arm, then across the side of his head. The flintlock broke and skidded across the floor, and powder from the pan scattered. The man gave a coughing grunt, slumped, his head bouncing off the side of the bed, and fell prostrate and senseless.

'Damned wretch . . .' Rennie got his breath, and dropped the pistol on the cabinet.

Rennie summoned the boy, gave him a shilling, and required him to find two strong men – porters or stable hands – and bring them to the room.

'Say to them that they will be handsome rewarded, in gold.'

The two men came, stable hands from the yard behind, and Rennie explained:

'This fellow attempted to rob me at pistol point.' Stepping aside to allow them to see the prostrate figure. 'I have over-powered him, but I need to have him took out of the hotel. I do not want the runners informed, nor the magistrate. I am here privately, and I want no upset, nor attention drawn to me. You have me?'

'Yes, sir.'

'Aye, sir.'

'He is to be took away concealed in a cart, or a barrow – whatever means you have to hand – and left at a place far from here. I will in course make it worth your while. A golden guinea.'

'Each?' The taller hand.

'Eh?' Rennie regarded him a moment, then: 'Yes, very well. A guinea each. For which payment you are to carry out your task – and keep silent. Will you give me your solemn oath?'

'It is give, sir.' The taller.

Rennie looked at the shorter, stockier man, who: 'Oh, aye.'

'Say it. Give me your oath.'

'I do, sir. Solemn oath.' Touching his forehead.

'Very well.' Standing back. 'There he is. Take him out.'

'When shall we get our payment, sir?'

'When you have done it.'

The taller man looked at his shorter companion, sucked his teeth, and: 'I think we will like to have half now, sir, by your leave.'

'Aye.' The shorter man.

'Oh, very well. Here is a guinea between you.' Opening his purse and finding the coin. He held it up, but did not yet pass it over. 'Remember! Absolute discretion, now. Go very quiet. Not a word breathed to a living soul.' He gave them the guinea.

The two men lifted the unconscious man and carried him out, their way lighted along the passage by the boy with his candle. A door opened to a rear stair. Creaks and muffled thuds as they carried their burden down the narrow stair and away. Presently the sound of wheels scraping over cobbles below.

Rennie let out a breath – he had not been aware that he was holding it in – and found that he was thoroughly done up. He found his shoes and put them on the chair, and then was too tired to undress. He lay down on the bed, and fell into a fitful doze.

In the morning Captain Rennie changed his hotel. He liked the Marine, had stayed there happily in the past, but the incident in the night had greatly dismayed and unsettled him, and he wished to become wholly anonymous, and to reassess his position. Having to fend off three armed assailants in the space of a few days, and having been obliged to shoot two of them dead – one of them a young woman – had taxed his endurance to the limit, and made him uneasy and fearful.

'If I don't go careful I shall become like Rountree's undertaker, good God.' But even this determined attempt at jocularity, directed at his face in the shaving glass, did not cheer him.

Troubled thoughts continued to run in his head as he moved from the Marine Hotel to the substantial old Mary Rose Inn at the corner of St Thomas Street. A further thought came to him as he went in at the door:

'I must disappoint Langton, that is a good fellow, a decent fellow. He will wonder what has become of me, and no doubt think me ill-mannered in not taking him up on his offer of dinner.'

He gave his name to the clerk as: 'Mr Birch, of Dorsetshire.' He was not in naval dress, and since all the best rooms were occupied again had to accept a very small one at the rear, but he had disguised his presence, and was content. Sitting on the hard narrow bed he said to himself:

'Langton must wait. Today I will seek out James, very discreet, and discover what that blackguard at the Marine Hotel meant by his questions. Aye – this damned bed is uncommon firm – I must discover from James what is afoot. If he will tell me. If he will oblige me.'

He fell silent, and thought of his house at Middingham, of the quiet life he had grown used to there, his pleasant easy routine, his understated clothes, his agreeable diet, his every comfort attended to by his servant girl Jenny. Every comfort – excepting one. A little sigh, and he lifted his head.

'In course I had much rather be at sea, I had much rather have a ship under my legs,' he told himself briskly, coming out of his brief reverie with a slapping of palms on thighs. 'But my condition of life at Norfolk – was I a landlubber by nature – could not be better, I think. Nay, it is very pleasant there – was I a lawn-loving, pond-gazing fellow, wandering tranquil among shrubs.'

Captain Rennie found Lieutenant Hayter, not as he had expected by assiduous discreet enquiry as to the location of the *Hawk* cutter, and the whereabouts of her commander – but by chance. He found him at Bracewell & Hyde, trying on his new coat. Rennie happened to glance in at the window as he passed by, and caught sight of his friend inside. He went in, to the sharp jingling of the above-door bell.

Mr Bracewell's assistant, that was not Mr Hyde – Mr Hyde had sold the business to Mr Bracewell long since, and then had died – came forward with a professional smile, recognizing the naval look when he saw it, in spite of the civilian dress, and:

'Sea officer, sir? In need of new – '

'Nay nay, thank you, ye may strike that measuring tape.'

The sound of that familiar voice caused James Hayter to turn from the long glass.

'Good heaven, it is you, sir. Here in Portsmouth.' A happy thought. 'You have got a ship! You have got a commission!'

'Nay, I have not, James.' They shook hands, James in his half-made coat, one sleeve attached, and the back marked with chalk. 'I came to find you, to say the truth.'

'From the Admiralty? They have changed their minds, then?' James as Mr Bracewell waited.

'Eh? No. No, I am here privately. What made you think I had come from the – '

'Give me one moment, sir, if you please.' James nodded, touched his forearm, and returned to Mr Bracewell at the glass. He shrugged out of the new coat, handed it to Mr Bracewell, and retrieved his old coat from a chair. He slipped it on. 'Thank you, Bracewell, I shall return tomorrow, or very soon after.' To Rennie: 'And now, shall we stroll a little way, sir, and talk?'

'I should like very much to talk, James. That is why I have come to Portsmouth, you know. In that hope.'

They went out into the busy street, and walked – at Rennie's urging – away from the press of people, and the traffic and noise, along Battery Road to the fortifications, the castle away to the east against the sky. Rennie walked with his plain hat jammed well down on his head, nearly hiding his face.

'I had myself hoped – half-hoped, anyway – that you would come, sir.' James, as they came to the wall.

'Eh? Had you?' A sideways glance. 'You surprise me, James. Twice in five minutes you have surprised me.'

And the two officers talked. James about his commission, his duties, the murder of Captain Marles – he held nothing back – and Rennie about Sir Robert Greer, his flight from Norfolk, the incident on the road and the intruder at the Marine Hotel, with his questions about James – he held nothing back, in turn.

'I am living under the name Birch, at the Mary Rose.'

'Birch?'

'Aye, you notice the choice of name. Mr Birch of Dorsetshire. I hope y'don't mind me using the name of your house, James.'

James laughed. 'In course I do not, sir. I am flattered. Catherine would be flattered, I am in no doubt.'

A moment of quiet now between the two men, in the echoing cries of gulls, and the distant crack-crack of mallets aboard a moored frigate. The church clock struck the quarter-hour. Clouds slowly drifted, unfurling on the wide blue sky. The moment was significant for both men. Both men knew that if it passed unseized their immediate convergence – here, today, upon the great stone wall – would cease at once, and their lives in the service drift wide apart, perhaps never to converge again. The Royal Navy was by its nature deep and wide in its purpose and duty; oceans and continents could divide and separate its officers over long months and years in pursuit of that purpose, in compliance with that duty; if they let the moment pass, a great deal might be lost. They did not let it pass.

James took a breath. 'I have need of a senior officer to give me assistance, sir, to advise me as Captain Marles would have done in a commission I do not yet wholly understand. It cannot be official, since the Admiralty I know will not sanction a replacement – but I wish it.'

'I am your man.'

And so it was settled, very simply, there on the stone wall, with a handshake.

*

'I thought it best to sail on the evening tide.'

'Not at first light?'

'No, sir. I wish to be at sea, waiting for her, at first light.'

The two officers stood aft of the pumps on the diminutive quarterdeck of *Hawk*, one of them in the uniform of undress coat and hat, the other in plain frock coat and plain dark hat.

Lieutenant Hayter – in uniform – continued: 'We must try to make an interception at sea, I think, rather than attempt to take her when she stands in to put her cargo ashore.'

'Ain't that when she will be the more open to being took, though? When she is vulnerable?'

'From all I hear, *Lark* can never be thought to be vulnerable, sir. At sea I can outgun her with my smashers, and – '

'Forgive me, James, but how d'y'know that?'

'Because I have ninety pound weight of iron broadsides, sir, and *Lark* – '

'She may well have the same, mayn't she? Hey?'

'No, sir. No, I do not think so. A fast cutter like the *Lark* will carry four-pounders, probably. Six-pounders, at the highest. Even if she carried eight six-pounders in each battery, her weight of metal broadside could only be a little more than half of my own.'

'Was not your instructions to take the *Lark*, though? Take her, and never damage her at all? How will you manage that, I wonder, if you go at her smashing with ninety-pound broadsides? Hey?'

James had given Rennie all the information he had thus far himself been given, and had told him his proposed strategy. Rennie did not like the strategy. He felt that the *Lark* would be nearly impossible to intercept at sea, fleet as she was; that she could run up from France as quick as be damned, and likely not even be sighted; that she would be taken, if she could be found, only when close in to shore, in a bay or cove, and her pursuer upward of her, with the wind gage, cutting her off. But he had not felt himself able to say so, direct – until now. And even now he could only demur, politely demur, and say why. He could not countermand an order given by a commanding officer at sea. In spite of his rank of senior post captain he was rated as nothing and nobody here aboard the *Hawk*, not even as supernumerary, since he was not listed on the ship's books. Officially he did not exist.

And yet James had asked for his assistance, his advice, his opinion – had not he? Could not a senior post make a suggestion or two, in least? He opened his mouth again, but at that moment James stepped close to the tiller and said to the helmsman:

'Luff and touch her, Alden Knott, will you. I will like her a point closer, if she will answer.'

'Aye, sir.'

The helmsman put his weight on the tiller and brought the cutter a fraction closer to the wind, so that she heeled to larboard, on the point of sails a-quiver, but not beyond it, cutting sweet and true into the westerly wind, the sea hissing in a froth of lace along her wales and tumbling in on itself astern in the glow of the light. Presently James judged that they had run far enough on their starboard tack, and:

'Stand by to tack ship!' Striding to the weather rail he nearly knocked Rennie down, and there was a moment of embarrassment between them. Both men apologized, a little too quickly, and each stood aside. James did not mind that Rennie was on deck – indeed had felt obliged to invite him there – but he sincerely wished and hoped that Rennie would have the good sense, and the common courtesy, to keep out of his way. Rennie in turn wished to keep out of that way, but James was such an energetic commander, forever striding this way and that, looking aloft at his canvas, going to the weather rail, then to the lee, asking his helmsman how she lay, &c., &c., that in truth the senior man did not know where he should place himself to be out of the way. Should he go below? He asked the question.

'No. No, indeed, sir. I would not wish it. It is damned cramped below, and the air gets stale so quick. You are better off on deck, snuffing the wind.'

Both men knew that the real question had not been answered, had not in fact been properly put. Should Rennie be giving advice at all, about anything, unless he was particularly asked? A big sea rolled heavily in, smacked under *Hawk*'s flat-sleeved bowsprit and bluff bow, and sent both men reaching to clap on to a back stay. The helmsman allowed her to sag off a little as she rode the wave, and Rennie drew breath to say something – and had to bite his tongue. To himself:

'Nay, I must not say a word. I must not say anything about the handling of the ship, good God.' And even as he thought it, James spoke:

'She is sagging off, Alden, bring her back now.'

'Aye, sir.'

James and his people brought the cutter through the wind and on to the other tack, so that now she heeled steadily to starboard, heading west-north-west into the wind, the coast away to starboard in occasional faint glimmerings of light. They sailed on, through the night.

They did not sight the *Lark* by hammocks up, when *Hawk* lay south in the Channel between St Alban's Head and Portland Bill. Rennie did not expect to see her. James had only half-expected it himself, their first foray into the open sea. They went below to breakfast.

'I hope you do not take it wrong – if I make suggestions,' said Rennie at breakfast, which they took together in the cramped little great cabin.

'Nay, in course I do not take it wrong.' James drank coffee. He did not eat. His guts had troubled him in the night, the sea chopping and disturbed, with a deep wind-enhanced swell as they had run close-hauled, tack on tack, heading west, then had come about and gone large, boarding long, in long sweeps. He had insisted on keeping guncrews on deck, fifteen men to man the weather guns, crossing the deck as their course dictated, and the weather side became the lee. This deployment, and the constant requirement of hands to make sail, haul, trim, sheet home, had tested his people to the full, and now they were tired. James had given the order to stand down, and a further order that a measure of grog was to be issued with their oats, to be taken unwatered by those who wished it.

'Is that wise, d'y'think?' Rennie had blurted, when James gave the instruction to his steward purser.

James had frowned, glanced at Rennie and said, not quite curtly: 'They have earned it. I have tested them, and they have earned it.'

Rennie, knowing his error even as he spoke, had nodded and said nothing more.

As they finished breakfast a small vessel was sighted to the south. They went on deck, and Lieutenant Hayter put his helm down and ran towards the sighted ship. She was a cutter.

'Can it be her?' Half to himself. 'Can that be the *Lark*?' Aloud, lowering his glass: 'Mr Holmes! Where the devil is Mr Holmes?' Glancing about. His senior mid was not on deck. He had been on deck at the beginning of the watch. What in Christ's name· did he mean by absenting himself? 'Mr Dench!' To the boatswain, who came aft from the waist. 'Mr Dench, where is Mr Holmes, if y'please?'

'I ain't seen him since two bells, sir.'

Three bells was now struck at the belfry by the companionway hatch.

'What! He has not been seen for half an hour! Christ's blood, Mr Dench, this will not do at sea!'

'No, sir. I will find him – '

'We will beat to quarters, Mr Dench, and clear the ship for action!'

A whack of wind as the call was sounded, and a further passing sea rode heavily under the keel. James steadied himself as hands thudded along the deck to their places, and *Hawk* ran on.

Mr Holmes could not be found, and presently the reason became apparent. Dr Wing came on deck, bracing himself as the wind flung itself into his face. Clutching at his hat:

'I must tell you, James – '

'Now then, Doctor, why have you come on deck? Your place is below, at quarters.' Ducking his head as spray showered over the quarterdeck. 'And you must address me as "sir", you know.'

'Yes, in course, how foolish of me to forget. But I must tell you – Ah, good morning, Captain Rennie.'

'Doctor.' A polite nod, standing well away.

'Yes, I must tell you that Mr Holmes has been took ill.' To James, formally.

'Ill? D'y'mean he is puking, Doctor? That don't excuse his absenting himself from the deck. We must all suffer seasickness from time to time.' Severely.

'It is not seasickness, I fear.' Gravely.

'What d'y'mean?'

'I mean that he is very seriously ill. I fear there is a rupture of the bowel. He is in great pain, and cannot stand.'

'Cannot you do something for him, Thomas?'

'At sea? No.'

'Not at sea, you say?' Glancing away at the other cutter.

'No, sir. No, we must get him on dry land, right quick. He must be got into the Haslar. That may be his only chance.'

'Only chance?' Jerking his head round to look hard at Thomas Wing. 'You are saying that he may die?'

'I am.'

James took a breath, glanced again at the other cutter, and: 'Then we have no choice. Very good, thank you, Doctor.' Raising his voice. 'Mr Dench! We will stand down!' To the helmsman: 'Put your helm up now, and we will run before, due east.'

The call, and the men at quarters stood down from their guns, the ship came off the wind, veered east handsomely, reefs were let out, and her great-bellied mainsail filled with the following wind.

Below, Mr Wentworth Holmes, senior midshipman, lay livid and staring in his hanging cot, his fair hair darkened with sweat and clinging to his scalp. He did not speak, he did not cry out. He lay silent and still, his whole being consumed by pain.

Away to the south-west the mystery cutter kept to her course, dipping a little on the swell, her mast heeling tall and graceful and her pennant streaming as she ran close-hauled.

*

When Mr Midshipman Holmes had been taken in a fainting condition into the Haslar Hospital at Gosport, accompanied there by Dr Wing, Lieutenant Hayter came on to the Mary Rose Inn at Thomas Street, and asked for Mr Birch. Soon he and Rennie were able to converse, in the privacy of Rennie's little room, Rennie perched on his narrow bed, and James on a stool.

'What of the young man?'

'Holmes? I do not know. Thomas Wing looked very dark, I thought, as the boy was took in.'

'Yes, yes – the boy looked very poorly when I left you to come on here. He may die. Hm. Had you thought of a replacement?'

'Eh? No, I had not, not yet. It is too precipitate early to think of that.'

'Hm. It is never too soon to make provision you know, James. Anything may – '

'– happen at sea.' Finishing for him. 'Yes, you are right. But I will not like to anticipate the worst outcome just yet.' A breath, and: 'I am nearly certain it was the *Lark* we sighted. You saw her raked mast? Her prodigious spread of canvas? Her lines, and speed?'

'I saw a pretty enough cutter, at a league and more distance, making fair headway in the English Channel into a stiffish topsail breeze, James. I do not say outright she was not the *Lark*, but I reckoned her at about sixty or seventy tons, no more. The *Lark* is a bigger, heavier sea boat than that, is she not?'

'I could not judge her size and weight exact, at a league and more.'

'No no, in course y'could not. Hm. Mm. – Forgive me, James, but I feel that I must speak up, now that we are again ashore. You do not object?'

'I do not, sir.'

'Well well, to be blunt I do not see how you may take such a vessel as the *Lark* in the Channel, nor anywhere along the coast – smasher broadsides or no – by yourself. I ask myself this: why was you not assigned another cutter to aid you, two cutters, three? If this vessel you seek is so damned important, or so damned inimical to the nation's interest, that the First Lord takes it upon himself to become involved – why are not you commanding a squadron of cutters, or indeed of brigs, or ship sloops. Hey?'

'I do not know the answers to those questions, sir. I had hoped to rely on Captain Marles to guide me, as you know, and – '

'Had you considered the possibility that Sir Robert may be involved in this?'

'Sir Robert Greer? Involve himself in my commission in *Hawk*? Surely you thought I had been given the commission by Their Lordships, as a kind of reward, compensating me for my losses in the tar paint scheme – had you not?'

'Well, I had thought that, but now I have changed my mind, because – '

'Sir, I have discovered that my father was behind my getting a new commission.'

'Your father? Then he must know all the facts of the thing. Have you asked him what – '

'No, sir, no. I do not mean my father asked for me to be given the *Hawk*. I think he used his influence to have his son considered for a new commission, that is all. The *Hawk* was to be acquired for a purpose, taken over from the Excise, that had built her for themselves in a private yard at Dover. That purpose, that duty, was given to me when my name was put forward.'

'Then who was that fellow came to me at the Marine Hotel, and demanded at pistol point to know what I knew about you, about this command, how many ships we had, and so forth?'

'Surely he cannot have come from Sir Robert, though. Else Sir Robert must know of your presence here in Portsmouth, that you have took great pains to conceal.'

'Aye, you are right. – Unless Sir Robert sent those high-waymen to follow me on the road, and – '

'Sir, really you know – I do not think that probable.'

'Eh?' Sharply.

'I do not mean to suggest . . .' James found himself awkward on the little stool, as if he were once again a schoolboy engaged in fanciful discussion late at night, in hushed tones, in a small, cold study room, by the light of a single shielded candle-flame. 'I would never think you were guilty of extravagant notions, sir, but I don't see how Sir Robert could likely be the culprit, there. Nor do I think that Sir Robert had a hand in the death – the murder – of Captain Marles.'

'I never said that he did.' Indignant now. 'Good God.'

'Very good, sir, you did not.' James got up from the uncomfortable stool. 'I must go to the Marine Hotel, and discover whether or no Colonel Macklin has made headway with his inquiry. And I must try again to find that wretch of a steward, that I paid a pound to in wages, in order to secure his employment. Then I had better return to *Hawk*, I expect.'

'You return to *Hawk* tonight? Why not spend the night ashore, James, and I'll give you supper here at the Mary Rose – '

'No, sir. No, it is kind in you, but I must think of my duty – of what may become of Mr Holmes.'

Captain Rennie was not unaware of a returning friction between them, and wondered at the cause. Lieutenant Hayter, for his part, was entirely aware of the cause. He was having second thoughts. He was having doubts. Was it wise to have asked his erstwhile commander to go aboard *Hawk* at all? How could they remain on amiable terms, when a man of Rennie's temperament, and experience – used to commanding men, to being Lieutenant Hayter's superior – was in the nature of things bound to begin to assert himself as if he was still in that position? And then, in course, there was the fact of the debt – the two hundred pound debt.

'Will you like me to come aboard on the morrow, James?'

'I must study the recorded movements of the *Lark*, the dates, tides, and so forth, and decide whether I should again attempt to take her. Perhaps she will not likely appear again for a time. Perhaps not before a fortnight, or a month, even . . . if it was the *Lark* we sighted.'

'You do not wish me to go aboard.' Rennie's voice was cold and beginning hostile.

'No, sir, in course I do not mean that, nor anything like. You are welcome in *Hawk* at any time. But where is the sense in your living cramped aboard, living deprived of all comfort – to no immediate purpose?' A little smiling sigh, and a brief shrug, to make Rennie believe him.

'You will not weigh without me, James?' Lifting his head to stare at Lieutenant Hayter very direct. 'You will not dash off sudden and leave me behind?'

'Nay, I will not. There is nothing further from my mind.'

James returned to the Marine Hotel and found – not Colonel Macklin, but Catherine, waiting for him on a chair in the parlour, off the public lobby. A clerk directed him to her, when James gave his name and asked for Colonel Macklin. He went to her at once.

'My darling, you are here.'

'I am here.' They embraced, and he kissed her, tasted chocolate on her lips, and felt himself dissolving into that taste, and the scent of her, her bodily warmth and sweetness. And yet again was astonished by her beauty – of which in usual she was quite unconscious – that made him whenever he saw her after an absence into a heart-thudding boy, near breathless in her presence. A long moment, he released her, and:

'You stay here at Portsmouth? My love, why did you not say you were coming here, in your letters?'

'I did say so, in my last letter. Did you not read it? Oh, James.' Pretending hurt.

'Yes, yes, in course I have read it.' Hastily. 'In truth, my darling, I have been close occupied with many things, and – '

'You did not read my last letter – written so fond?'

'I may not have read it with the attention I ought.' Looking at her, and now he saw that she was teasing him, and took her in his arms again, and kissed her as a lover. At length:

'You have engaged rooms? Where is our son?'

'He is at Melton.'

'At Melton, ah.' His father's house, near Shaftesbury in Dorset. 'Perhaps that is well, when I have so much to say to you . . .'

'You do not wish to see your son?' Reproving him with a smile.

'In course I wish to see him – but not now. Now I wish to see his mother.'

'Look, I am here.'

'In private. I wish to see her altogether in private.' Holding her.

'There is a gentleman . . .'

'What?' Kissing her, pushing his face in her hair and neck, drinking her in.

'James.' Gently disengaging herself. 'My dear, there is a gentleman at the door.'

'What? Who . . . ?' Reluctantly turning.

'My dear Hayter, do forgive me. I will not intrude now.' And an embarrassed Colonel Macklin, getting red at his own neck, began to turn away from the door of the parlour.

'Nay, nay, Colonel . . .' James frowned an apology to Catherine, and stood away from her a little.

'Nay, I had left my name with the clerk, asking for you, and I must not inconvenience you now. May I present you to my wife? Colonel Macklin that is investigating – a matter.'

The formalities; Colonel Macklin made a leg; Catherine acknowledged him with a polite smile.

'Colonel, will you allow me one moment more?' As the colonel stepped away, James turned to Catherine. 'Are you stopping here, my love?'

'Yes, here at the hotel.'

'Then you have engaged rooms. How on earth did you manage it? Portsmouth is full to bursting.'

'I was persuasive, James. We have got a very small suite – at the rear – very private.'

'But . . . how can we afford it?'

'I will tell you all my news when you have conducted your business with the colonel. You must not keep him waiting.' She gave him the number of the suite, kissed his cheek, and retired by a rear door.

'What news, sir?' James, a moment after, as the colonel came back into the parlour, the lobby and public rooms beyond a-swirl with a large party of people, the sound of their voices hubbub and din. 'Have we made progress, at all?'

'We have, a little. But I don't want to keep you from your charming wife . . .'

'Nay, nay . . . I shall be with her soon. What is the progress?'

'One of the stolen documents has been found.'

'From the packet?'

'Aye. Discarded in a gutter not far from where the captain was attacked. The letter – it was a letter – was much fouled and nearly indecipherable, but for the seal and signature, which identified it.'

'And from this you deduce . . . ?'

'That the motive cause of the assault was not the theft of the documents. These was incidental. The real motive was money. Gold, that an officer might have carried in his purse.'

'But what the devil was Captain Marles about, late at night in the Point?'

'The district is notorious, ain't it? There is your answer.'

'Notor— Ah. Yes. You think that he had visited an harlot there?'

'Almost certainly, don't you think so? And was waylaid, and his throat cut, coincidental.'

'So that is the finish of our inquiry, sir?'

'In course I will write an account of it, a report, you know. The magistrate will wish to pursue the matter, I am in no doubt, but for myself I can see no purpose in further investigation. Captain Marles was simply unlucky, having satisfied his lust, and there's an end to it. Hey?'

James joined Catherine in their suite, and had many questions to ask – but did not ask them at once.

An hour passed, and another hour – and then he did ask them.

'Your mother has been very kind.' Catherine in answer, her hair spread on the pillow.

'Yes, she is very kind, always. She dotes on the boy.'

'I do not mean just that she will always like us to stay with her at Melton. I mean that she has been generous. She has given me the means to come here.'

'Ah.' Propping himself on an elbow to gaze at her.

'More than that, you know.' A smile.

'More than what?' Sitting up. 'How d'y'mean?'

'She knew of your financial difficulty, and – '

'She knew! How did she know? I did not wish her to know, neither she nor my father was to know anything about it! Surely you did not – '

'Darling, darling, my love. I have said nothing. She knew, that is all. Mothers often do know these things, do not they?'

'Damnation, I don't know. Has she said anything to my father, I wonder. My mother may have been in sympathy with you, and given you a few guineas to come to me, but by God my father would be wholly unforgiving if ever he discovered my folly.'

'He has not, I know that he has not. Lady Hayter has kept it from him.'

'Ah. Well.'

'And she has done more. A great deal more, James.' Another smile. Answered by a frown.

'Done more?'

'Nay, do not frown.' Smoothing his brow with her fingers.

'Then tell me what it is. I do not like all this female mystery.'

'She has paid your debt.'

'What?' Staring at her.

'Yes, she has paid it off, altogether. And she has given us the residue, five hundred pound.'

'Paid out my debt?' Staring round the bedchamber, then again at his wife, in a whirling confusion of thoughts and emotions. 'Residue? What residue? I do not understand.'

'She has sold a parcel of land at Leicestershire, that under her marriage settlement remained hers, and some farms. She had always meant to leave the land to you, knowing that you would get nothing from Melton on your father's death. It will not affect her income greatly, so she decided in the goodness of her heart to make you this gift now, and clear you of all anxieties.'

*

'Mr Birch . . .'

Rennie sat alone in the dining room at the Mary Rose, eating his dinner. He drank off his wine.

'Mr Birch . . . may I join you a moment?'

Rennie became aware of a figure in front of his table. He frowned and looked up, and saw Lieutenant Hayter.

'James! There you are. At first I did not recall my other name, you know. Sit, sit, my dear fellow. I had thought you was returned to *Hawk* by this.' Glancing at the longcase clock by the door at the end of the room. It was seven o'clock.

'No, sir. Catherine has come, she is here at Portsmouth.' Sitting down.

'Catherine? Why did not you bring her with you to supper? I will always like to see your beautiful wife.'

'She is resting, at present.'

'What will you like to eat?' Looking round for the servant girl.

'Nay, nothing, thank you. I return to the Marine Hotel to dine with Catherine there.'

'Oh.' Disappointed.

'In course, we shall dine together very soon, but I wish to deal with another matter now, sir, if I may.'

'Another matter?' Looking at him. 'You are going to weigh without me, is that the fact of it?'

'No, sir, no indeed.' A breath. 'It is the matter of my debt to you. The draft you gave me for two hundred pound, drawn on your bank.'

'Surely they have not refused – '

'Nothing like that, nothing like that. No – I will like to return it to you. I have no need of it, now.' He took the folded draft from his coat, and put it on the table by Rennie's dish of roasted meat.

'No need of it?' Rennie peered at him.

'I am most grateful to you, sir, very grateful, and I thank you with all my heart for your kindness, when I was in grave difficulty.'

'No *need* of it? What has – '

'My difficulty has been – settled.'

'Settled. Ah.' Raising his eyebrows, making a face. 'Ah.'

'I am most grateful for your kindness, and will never forget it.'

'Ah. Hm.' Touching the draft, opening it, folding it again, and leaving it there by his plate. 'You are certain? Entirely certain?'

'I am, sir, thank you. All is settled.'

'Very good. Hm.' A sniff. 'Well well, let us drink a glass of wine to acknowledge your good fortune, James. Hey?'

'That is kind in you, sir, but I must return to the Marine Hotel – to Catherine.'

'Will you not drink one glass with me, James?' Injured.

'Forgive me, I am remiss. Certainly I will, sir, thank you.' Seating himself again – he had got up on his legs.

Rennie nodded, signalled, and the servant girl came. 'Another bottle of the claret. Best claret, you mind me?'

'Yes, sir.'

'And another glass for my guest.'

The girl bobbed, and retired.

'A pretty girl,' said Rennie. 'Broad in the beam, but pretty. But you will not like to think of servant girls, James, when you have Catherine, hey?'

'No.' A smile.

'No. Bachelors, however, and widowers . . . well, we notice such creatures.'

'I expect so.'

'I met a very handsome woman . . . recent.'

'Did you, sir? Is she here? At Portsmouth?'

'No no. No, it was – we travelled in the same coach, you know, to London. Her name is Mrs Townend. She is a naval widow . . .' Looking into the distance in his head, a musing look.

'And will you meet her again, sir?'

'Eh?' Returning to the present. 'No, I shouldn't think so. I expect she is well fixed in her life, and has no need of fellows like me. One post captain dead is enough, I reckon, for her. She will not like another – alive, but on the beach – making himself a nuisance.'

'You said she was handsome, though . . .'

Their wine came, and glasses were filled. 'I did, I did. She is handsome, James. But the fellow y'see before you ain't, and knows he ain't. Well well, we will not drink to handsome widows, but to good fortune.'

'To good fortune.'

Two days passed, during which Lieutenant Hayter – staying ashore with his wife at the Marine Hotel – twice visited his senior midshipman Mr Holmes at the Haslar. On the first occasion he learned that Dr Wing had decided, in consultation with Dr Stroud, that to operate was essential in order to attempt the restoration of the ruptured bowel, else Mr Holmes would die. On the second occasion Lieutenant Hayter learned of the death of young Holmes, before the surgery could be done. Dr Wing was greatly disturbed.

'Good heaven, he was only a boy. What business has a boy dying? What a waste of life, entirely and utterly a waste! Where is the sense in it?'

'I am surprised that you talk like this, Thomas.' James and Dr Wing had come out of the hospital to get a sniff of fresh air. 'As if the poor fellow had willed his own death.'

'In course he did not! In course he did not!' A furious sigh. 'It is just misfortune, villainous misfortune. There is no blame can be attached to anyone.'

'Not even the Almighty?'

With quiet vehemence: 'That wretch has enough to answer for, without I blame him for this.'

'Wretch?'

'Aye. I do not much hold with the notion of a benign and loving Creator, ordering all life according to his own design. If there is such a creature at all, he strikes me as a petulant, destructive, cruel, intemperate fellow, a foul and bloody-fingered tyrant. But I fear I do not think that there is such a creature, neither in the heavens nor anywhere in the universe.' A glance. 'Do I shock you, James?'

'Nay, you don't. I am of the same opinion exact.' They walked on a few steps on the gravelled path, towards the gates. 'I must write to the boy's family. His mother will take it hard.'

'You know the family?'

'No, I do not. But I know that all mothers, everywhere, will weep for a dead son, Thomas. That is a universal truth.'

'Yes.' Quietly.

'I must think of his replacement.'

'So soon?'

'It is never too soon to think of efficient working at sea,
Thomas. That is my duty as commanding officer. If I did not
think of it I should be a damned poor one.' Speaking harshly
to hide his own gloom, aware that he had contradicted his
own opinion of only a few days ago, and was airing that of his
erstwhile commander.

Thomas Wing made a face, nodded, and: 'Yes, I expect you
are right. You return to *Hawk*?'

'At once. I am out of her too long.'

'I will come with you.'

James called at the Marine Hotel to say goodbye to
Catherine, and sent a message to Mr Birch at the Mary Rose
Inn to join him at the Hard without the loss of a moment.
When Captain Rennie came to the Hard all three men
embarked in the jollyboat, and returned to their ship.

As they came aboard to Mr Dench's call, James had
reached his decision.

'Mr Abey!'

'Sir?' Attending.

'Mr Abey, you will be my new senior mid. We will
apply for a junior to aid you, but in the interim you'll
choose the brightest and ablest boy from among the
volunteers to act as your second. Ye'll have to apply a good
deal of close instruction, and knock common sense and
seamanship into his head, and teach him quarterdeck
manners. Can y'do it?'

'Oh, certainly! I mean, yes, sir.'

'Very good.' Turning away aft.

'May I ask news of Mr Holmes, sir?'

'He is dead.'

'Oh. I am – I am very sorry, sir.'

'Indeed. We are all sorry. Mr Dench!'

'I am here, sir.'

'We will weigh at once, if y'please.' Striding to the tafferel.

The call, and: 'Stand by to weigh! Hands to make sail!
Cheerly now!'

And presently HM *Hawk* cutter, ten, put to sea into a steady westerly breeze.

*

Daylight still, at two bells of the second dog watch, and *Hawk* standing to the south-west, the wind abating and the swell gentler. At an early supper in the cramped great cabin, in which neither officer could stand erect, Lieutenant Hayter confided in Captain Rennie.

'To say the truth I have been so confused and discomfited since I was first informed I was to have this command, that I had nearly decided it was nonsense.'

'Nonsense, James? By the by, I do not mean to be ungrateful, but is this really your best wine?'

'It's a claret. It's what I could afford when we provisioned.'

'Claret? You think?' Sipping, frowning. 'Well well . . .'

'I was not greatly particular about my store of wine, sir. I had other things was occupying my attention.'

'Yes, in course, I do not mean – I do not wish to give offence. But I hope you will allow me, when next we go ashore, to introduce into the ship a case or two of best claret, from the Marine Hotel cellars. Or even the Mary Rose cellars, that are tolerable.'

'As you wish, sir.'

Rennie saw that he had interrupted his friend's train of thought, and caused him more discomfort, instead of helping to allay it.

'You said you was confused . . . ?'

'Yes, yes – I was. Everything about this command suggested it, don't you think so?' Without waiting for a response: 'Look at the facts. The master of the *Lark* ain't her master, after all, he is dead, a thousand leagues distant, and has never been aboard her since a twelvemonth. Contrary to what was suggested my commission came to me because my father wished it, not because Their Lordships thought to

reward me when first they took *Hawk* away from the Excise
and brought her to Portsmouth. Then Captain Marles, that
was to guide and advise me, had his throat cut and the
pertinent documents stole. Documents not strictly and
properly issued by Their Lordships, but given under Earl
Chatham's private seal, instructing me to take a vessel and her
people – for what purpose? I was not vouchsafed the reason.
Like edible fungus I was kept in the dark, and fed upon
manure. Made into a mushroom!'

'You was never a mushroom, James.'

'Ain't I, though? I have thought more than once these last
few hours, since young Holmes's death – that I should resign
my commission.'

'What? Resign!' Very severe.

'Yes, resign it, because it was a damned foolish nonsense of
a duty, incapable of success, or any kind of adequate result.
Why should I not return to a quiet life at Winterborne, a
quiet pleasant family life? However . . .'

'Yes? However?'

'I am a sea officer.'

'Aye.' A nod.

'A commissioned sea officer, in his first command.'

'You are.' A further nod.

'Whatever I may think of my instructions, it is my
obligation to carry them out. Or in least make my best
attempt. Further, I am free of financial burden, and have you
with me, sir. Taken together these things are a blessing, and
I am a lucky man.'

'Cutter approaching, sir.' Mr Abey, at the door.

'Cutter! Where away?' James, jumping up and bumping his
head.

'On our larboard quarter, sir, tacking up from the south-
east in light airs. I believe her to be an Excise cutter, sir. Her
signal halyard says she wishes to speak.'

'I will come on deck at once.' Stooping, buckling on his
sword.

'May I come with you, James?' Rennie got up on his legs.

'Yes yes, by all means. You have no sword?'

'Nay, it is at home in Norfolk.'

'Take one from the rack.' Indicating a low rack above the lockers, with two blades.

'Surely we will not need swords to speak to an Excise vessel, James – '

'As you wish. But I am not altogether sure of anything in this commission, and I do not trust a vessel that comes at me as dusk falls. I will like my sword at my side if this is some damned piratical smuggler's trick!'

Rennie shrugged, took up a sword, and they went on deck. She was the Excise Board cutter *Pipistrel*, a twelve-gun four-pounder, tall-masted, carrying a great quantity of number six canvas. She came up on *Hawk* very smart, even in light airs, and hove to, as *Hawk* had already done. Her master was Commander Renfrew Carr, and he came to *Hawk* by boat, with one of his two mates. He had thirty-two souls aboard. When James saw Commander Carr's blue Excise coat, and his bluff, confident, officerlike demeanour, he thought that nothing could be amiss, and invited him below to the great cabin. But first impressions can be misleading, as James soon discovered.

'I have no steward at present, and must make do with a servant boy. Will you drink a glass of something, Commander?'

'Thank you, no.' Laying his hat on the table. 'Look here, Hayter, I must talk pretty direct to you, I think. – Who is this fellow?' Noticing Rennie for the first time.

'Who am I? I am – ' Rennie began indignantly, but James, over him:

'This is Mr Birch, that is assisting me.' They sat down. 'How may I be of assistance to you?'

'May I speak in front of him, though?'

'You may, indeed. He is, so to say, my right hand. You said that you wished to be direct? Pray proceed.' Affably enough.

Rennie sat bristling on one of the lockers at the side, and banged his sword back in the rack.

Commander Carr took a breath, pursed his lips in a none too friendly fashion, and: 'Y'have been advised, have not you, to take the *Lark*? Take her, and bring her in, with all hands?'

'Where have you heard this?'

'Allow me to say that I have heard it, and I must always say to you – '

'Before y'do, pray allow me to say something. I do not know the – *Lark*, is it? – I have never seen her, and do not know her. You are misinformed, Commander.'

'Nay, I am not. I know very well that she is your intended prize, and I am obliged to say – '

'Commander, I will not like you to call me a liar in my own ship, you know.' James smiled at him, and spoke quietly, but there was menace in every syllable.

'Liar? I have not called you a liar.'

'Haven't you? Ah. Then we are not at odds.'

'I do not wish to be at odds with the Royal Navy. I wish merely to say that it cannot be part of the navy's duties to trouble itself with minor matters in coastal waters – Excise matters.'

'Whatever the Royal Navy's duties may be, and my own duties within that service, I think that they cannot be the concern of the Excise Board, can they?'

Commander Carr's face darkened a little, and his mouth became a line. 'Do not make a nuisance in these waters, sir, that is my advice. Do not blunder off course and take my wind. The *Lark* belongs to me, d'y'see. She is my prize. Mine.'

'Prize, sir?' Raising an eyebrow. 'You are not attached to the Royal Navy, are you? We are not at war, are we? On neither count, therefore, could you fairly expect to take prizes – could you?'

'Do not attempt to blackguard me, sir. Stay clear of my patrols, and leave the *Lark* alone. Leave her to me. D'y'hear?'

'What is your weight of metal broadside, Commander?'

'Eh?'

'Twenty-four pound, at a guess? Six four-pounders per side?'

'What of it?'

'I am ninety pound. Five eighteen-pound smashers per side. I will not like to mention *matchwood* – except in passing.'

'You wish to threaten me, damn you? You, a sea officer RN, when you are on your oath to defend your country and your King?'

'I have not threatened you, Commander. You may be sure that if I had, you would by now be floundering in your own wreckage. And since we are dispensing advice between us, mine to you is this: return to your own quarterdeck, make sail, and stand well away. I am minded to exercise my great guns, directly. Good evening.'

And when Commander Carr had gone into his boat, grim and silent, Rennie said: 'Attempt to blackguard him? Fffff. The fellow has done that by himself, out of his own mouth.'

'Oh, I don't know.' James, musingly. 'Perhaps I should feel the same, was I in his place. The Excise, after all, is obliged to take smugglers, seize their vessels and so forth. I have heard – in fact I know – that in seizing certain vessels with valuable contraband, part or all is retained by officers as their unofficial due. They may not take these vessels as prizes, official, but in effect that is what happens.'

'Surely the Excise Board takes possession of such vessels, don't it?'

'If it is aware of them, if it is informed. Smuggling vessels may easily be spirited away, I think, re-rigged, painted over, disguised. They are not great ships, but only cutters, most of them.'

'Well well, it is a damned disgrace, James. That fellow Carr is a damned disgrace to his blue coat.'

'Is he, though? The Royal Navy does the same in war, exact – don't it? Is that a disgrace?'

'It ain't the same thing, not at all. They are enemy ships, prizes of war, and we must declare them down to the last cask and nail to the Admiralty Court. We are not at war, at present, and smugglers cannot be considered enemies, good God.'

'Not quite, I expect, but the morals of it are the same.'

'No no, smugglers are merely rogues, that is all. Rogues bringing in such goods that people will like to smoke, or drink, without being obliged to pay the unconscionable taxes the government wishes to impose.'

'Unconscionable, sir? Do we not serve the same government? Are we not duty bound ourselves to intercept smugglers?'

'One smuggler. The *Lark*.'

'But if by chance we came upon another, or more than one, we would be obliged to attempt to stop them, would not we?'

'Yes, yes, in course you are right. Hm. – I resent having to pay tax on my brandy. Only a damn fool would not resent it.'

'Have not you just contradicted yourself, sir?'

'What?'

'You have said that Commander Carr was a disgrace for wishing to gain from his activity, and yet you approve of the other activity behind it – the smugglers' trade.'

'It ain't the same, it ain't the same!' Indignant. 'Carr is a thief and a scoundrel!'

'And smugglers? What are they?'

'Rogues, miscreants, knaves, nothing more. Nothing vicious.'

'Ah.'

'You disagree?'

'It could not matter less what I think, I expect. My task is to take the *Lark* if I can – and if I can, I will. Commander Carr had better keep his distance, whatever his motive, else I shall be obliged to remind him of the very great disparity between us.'

'Aye, we are sea officers in an honourable duty, and he is a blackguard wretch.'

'No, sir. Weight of metal, simple weight of metal.' And he walked aft to the rail. 'Mr Abey, we will get under way, if y'please.'

Pipistrel retired east, tall and graceful in the gathering darkness, shaking out reefs, and *Hawk* continued sou'-west, to where James – by reason of the pattern of dates, tides, and times of sighting, &c., contained in his detailed instructions – believed that he must lie in wait for the *Lark*. Captain Rennie he knew thought different. Captain Rennie believed that *Hawk* should stand in, hug the shore, and wait there for their prey, 'like a lion crouching in the jungle grass'.

'I don't know that jungles are grassy,' James said to himself. 'Nor am I a lion. I am a bird of prey, as old Holly said, circling and circling in light airs, waiting my opportunity to fall swift on the *Lark*'s neck.'

James remained on deck long after dark, long after Captain Rennie had retired to his narrow screened corner of the cabin, and his hammock – having no hanging cot. While Rennie slept James allowed his mind to disengage from the immediate, and to ponder questions that came to him sinewy and shadowy, coiling about his head, out of the flowing night. How the devil did Commander Carr know specifically about the *Lark*, if he was only a 'cise officer, sweeping the Channel for any and all smugglers? How did he know that *Hawk* had been assigned to find and take her, when that was supposed to be a secret? And evidently he knew that the cargo *Lark* carried was of great value, and thus wished to take her for himself – but how did he know that? And:

'He was headed east as we made sail, but will he stay on that course?' Under his breath, treading the little quarterdeck. 'Will he not double back, and dog me?'

Presently he decided something, and:

'You there, boy!'

'I am Michael Wallace, sir, that Mr Abey has chose to be

his junior acting mid.' A stocky lad of thirteen attending, hat off.

'Chose? When? Why was not I informed?'

'He – he did not like to disturb you, sir, when you was pacing so intent.'

'Ah. Ah. Very good, Mr . . . ?'

'Wallace, sir.'

'Aye, Mr Wallace. We will douse our stern light, and our masthead light, also. I will like to be invisible this night.'

THREE

Doctor Bell stepped down from his gig and went up the shallow steps and in at the door, between the great stone urns that flanked the entrance in the Palladian façade. He had been here before to Kingshill House, at the time Lady Kenton was in residence. That lady had long since sold the house and departed. Dr Bell's present patient was Sir Robert Greer, who had bought the house from her; Sir Robert had been his patient for some little time, until now merely on occasions of minor indisposition. Today was different. Today Sir Robert was ill. Dr Bell knew that he had been under a physician in London, Dr Robards, for a stone. Had been operated on by the King's own physician, Sir Wakefield Bennett, and the stone removed. And now, down here, he was again suffering. When Dr Bell was shown into the sickroom – the large green-silk-canopied French bed was the one Lady Kenton herself had slept in – he saw a man very gaunt, very reduced and weakened. Sir Robert had ever been pale, but now he was deathly livid. The voice, in usual deep and vibrant, was now a reedy groan.

'Doctor . . . I need you today . . . I need . . . elixir . . .'

'Good morning, Sir Robert.' Attending at the bedside, laying down his bag.

'I had a stone, you know . . . and it was removed . . . cut out of mhh . . .' Attempting to sit up.

'Do not tax yourself, Sir Robert. I will ask a question or two. A nod, or brief shake of the head, will suffice in answer.'

'I wish to say . . . hhh . . .' A quivering nod. 'I wish to tell you . . .'

'Nay, sir. Lie quiet, now.' Settling him on the pillows, and taking his pulse. As he counted Dr Bell noted the slight rattle at the end of each breath. Unless he was mistook – this man was dying.

His hand now firmly grasped, with fingers surprisingly strong. And the black eyes held his.

'Y'think me already dead, d'y'not?'

'Nay, Sir Robert. Calm yourself.' Releasing himself from the fierce grip.

'Let me . . . assure you . . . I am nothing of the kind . . . I am going to *live* d'y'hear! . . . I shall . . . hhh . . . I . . . shall outlive you . . . and all of them!'

'No doubt you will, Sir Robert. But you are not well now, sir, and you must be quiet – still and quiet, so that I may examine you.' He lifted the covers.

'Nay, I do not wish it! . . . hhh . . . I do not wish hht . . .' A feeble wrench at the covers, all his strength dissipated. 'Give me a paregoric . . .'

Dr Bell, firmly: 'Sir Robert, you have called me to your bedside, and I will not do my duty by you as my patient if I do not examine you. Cannot do it, indeed.'

'Ohh . . . ohh, very well . . . do it, then . . .' And he allowed the covers again to be lifted from his person, his nightshirt lifted, and he submitted to indignity.

'Is there pain – here?' Dr Bell, pressing the lower abdomen.

'Hnnnh! Damn you, Bell . . .' Panting.

'There is pain. And – here?' Pressing again, higher up.

'No . . . only where ye pressed before . . . there! Hnnh! Aye, that is where I feel it, low in my vitals . . . and now I want paregoric . . .'

'How long since you opened your bowels, Sir Robert?'

'That is the least . . . of my concern . . . I cannot recall.'

'Try to recall, will you? It is pertinent.'

'Some few days . . .'

'Several days? A week, perhaps?'

'Perhaps . . . I do not recall.'

'And your appetite?'

'Appetite! I have none . . . none.'

'You have not ate? Since how long, Sir Robert?'

'Two days . . . three . . . and then only gruel.'

'You make water readily?'

'There is . . . no difficulty there.'

'Hm. Hm. I think it very probably a case of costiveness.' His small oval spectacles gleamed briefly as he straightened up by the bed. He removed them, polished them on a white kerchief, turned reflectively to the window. His patient watched him with anxiety.

'Nothing . . . nothing more?'

Dr Bell replaced his spectacles, turned back with a professional smile and: 'Probably nothing more.' He did not believe what he said. He said it because he did not like to alarm his patient. He did not wish to say, straight out: 'There is probably a growth in the bowel, and very likely you will be dead in a fortnight.' That was too harsh. That was too abrupt and cruel. So instead he had said something reassuring, and he followed it with:

'And now I will allow you paregoric elixir, Sir Robert.'

'Eh? Now? Now, you will give me elixir? Should not you give me a purgative?'

'On the morrow, on the morrow. For now – it will be better to soothe the discomfort, reduce the pain in the lower abdomen, and the like. Hm?'

'Well . . . if you think so . . .' And he lay back exhausted and waxy on the pillow.

A few minutes after, having left his patient, Dr Bell spoke to the housekeeper in the kitchen.

'Mrs Reese, I will call again tomorrow in the forenoon. If he will take it give him broth, nothing solid for the moment. And a spoon measure of this physic, that I shall leave with you.' Handing her a phial of paregoric.

'I shall give it to his manservant. He don't like me to go to the bedchamber. He will not allow it.'

When the doctor had quit the house, Sir Robert called to his bedchamber his man of business, Mr Purvis. Mr Purvis had been attached to his household since Sir Robert had acquired Kingshill, several years before. He was a man wholly unlike Sir Robert in looks, manner, character – he was rubicund, and stout, and did not care about his appearance, the cut of his coat, the buckles on his shoes, &c. – and yet he was astute and businesslike in his own provincial way, and a stickler for detail. Sir Robert trusted him. He smelled of cheese, and port wine, and the foxiness of unwashed parts of himself, but he was absolutely to be trusted because he was a man without ambition or imagination.

'I will like to dictate something to you, Purvis.' Pushing back fatigue and weakness with a deep effort of will.

'Very well, Sir Robert.' He brought a chair, and took from the pocket of his coat his book of incidental accounts, turned leaves and found a blank page. Sighed, shook snuff on his fist, sniffed, sniffed again, and settled himself with his pencil. 'I am here, sir.'

'I am going to dictate to you my last will and testament.'

'Good God. That is, that is – are you sure?'

'In course I am sure. Do not stare so, Purvis. I am not yet dead. It is a precaution only. If on the morrow, as I fully intend, I am restored – ye may put this aside. Do not destroy it, though.'

'As you like, Sir Robert, as you declare and wish. – I am here, sir.' Pencil over the page.

And Sir Robert dictated his wishes.

Later, when Mr Purvis had left him, Sir Robert swallowed not paregoric, but two blue pills, that he had concealed in his bedlinen. These blue pills had been given him long ago by Dr Robards in London, and he had eschewed them then – but had kept them aside for just such an eventuality as this. They would either cure him, or kill him. He did not wish – he would not allow himself – to be made to suffer days of further agony and despair.

As night fell the blue pills began to have their effect, and Sir Robert was convulsed. Fender, his manservant, came hurrying in alarm –

'I – I will fetch Dr Bell, sir.'

– but was made immobile by a peremptory bark:

'Ye'll do no such thing-eeennhh! Do nothing, damn y-eeegh! Go away! Hnnngh! Away, man!'

Fender hesitated, alarmed and appalled by the poor writhing creature half crouched by the bed – and then retired, cowed by further agonized barks. Retired to the foot of the stairs, where he and the housekeeper Mrs Reese – worrying at her apron, cocking her capped head – stood in hushed consternation, listening.

*

Hawk heeled over on the starboard tack, and sheets and braces were hauled tight on cleats. As she came just so, the moon broke through a silvery patch of cloud ahead, and rode staring on the black night. The moon was full, and so bright that the whole of the sea around the slipping, slanting vessel glittered and crawled with reflected light. Her wake flashed and tumbled, became living lace, and swirled sloping far astern.

Mr Wallace the acting mid, sent aloft, answered the quarterdeck:

'No sail in sight, sir!' and was ordered down, his newly issued long glass strapped safe on his back.

James handed him his silver flask. 'Take a nip of this, Mr Wallace.'

'Thank you, sir.' The boy sucked half a mouthful of rum, swallowed, coughed, and felt the spirit burn down and warm him.

'We are in an empty sea, hey?'

'Aye, sir!' He handed the flask to James, who took it and sucked down a mouthful or two, then put the flask away in his coat.

'In least that bla— that 'cise cutter ain't following. I was afraid that she would.'

'*Pipistrel*, d'y'mean, sir? I did not see her.'

'Nay, she has gone to her bed elsewhere, I expect. That is well. The last thing we need is her company, on this nor any other night.'

Four bells of the middle watch, and the moon at its staring height over the trucktop of the mast, *Hawk* patrolling on the larboard tack to the south, at that extreme of a quadrant James had determined on his charts was the likely part of the Channel that *Lark* would traverse in attempting to make landfall on the south coast.

'D-e-e-e-ck! Sail of ship to the east! On our larboard quarter!'

James had kept a lookout aloft all the night, and now he bellowed from the quarterdeck:

'What ship is she! How many masts?'

'A single mast, sir! She is a cutter!'

'By God, that is the *Lark*, or I am a Hollander talking Dutch.' James leapt up into the weather shrouds, his glass at his back, and climbed nimbly hand over hand into the top, then swarmed up the Jacob's ladder to the crosstrees. The lookout made room for him on the yard, and James unshipped his glass, focused, and found the vessel, far to the east, a dark shape and a sail against the glittering crawl of the sea.

'She is a cutter, right enough.' Muttering, then to the lookout: 'Can y'make out any colours, Logan Barker?'

'No, sir.' Peering a long moment, then lowering his own glass. 'She is too far from us, I reckon.'

'Aye. Too far, for the present. We must alter that, hey?'

'Sir?'

'We must come about, and chase her down. She heads north.'

'Shall I remain here, sir, or return to the deck?'

'Stay at your post. I will like to hear her every move, as soon as she makes it. Change of course, crowding on of sail, anything. At once, d'y'hear me?'

'Aye, sir.'

James nodded, peered a last time at the distant cutter, slung his glass on his back, clapped on to a stay, and plunged to the deck. As his feet touched the planking:

'Mr Dench! Mr Abey! All hands on deck!'

Running feet. A scramble of bodies. Shouts and curses. Captain Rennie, his nightcap perched atop his sparse hair, came on deck and along the lee rail to where James stood by the helmsman at the tiller.

'May I join you, James? What is afoot?'

'Indeed, indeed y'may, sir. We are about to give chase. Mr Dench!'

'Here I am, sir.' Attending, shrugging into his jacket.

'We will come about and head east-nor'-east. As soon as we are on the new heading, we will beat to quarters.'

'Aye, sir.' He raised his call, and the piercing notes sounded along the deck.

Presently, as *Hawk* swung east with the wind, and ran large on the starboard tack, her guncrews assembled by their squat charges, cartridge boxes were brought up, and sand scattered.

'It is the *Lark*, James? You are sure?' Rennie, attempting to focus his glass.

'If she runs, she is the *Lark*.'

'Might not she be *Pipistrel*, patrolling like ourselves?' Half to himself – but the question irked *Hawk*'s commander, who frowned. Frowned, but made no reply.

Hawk swept on, steady and true and fast, her speed reaching nine knots with the light following breeze. James ordered stunsails bent, and her speed increased to ten knots.

The distant cutter, as yet unidentified, remained steady on her own course, heading north toward the English coast.

Thirty minutes passed, and now *Hawk* was less than half a league from her quarry. The lookout hailed the deck:

'Cutter changing course, sir! She heads sou'-east, crowding on sail!'

'Very well! Keep a sharp eye!' And James gave the order to alter course. *Hawk* swung on to the larboard tack, and began to bear down on the fleeing shape, quickly narrowing the gap between them. Another glass, and they had gained on her again. She was painted black, her sails were dun and drab, and she wore no colours, not even a pennant. She was ported for eight guns per side, and her runs were run out.

'Four-pounders, I think,' said James, his glass to his eye. 'Sixes, at most.'

'She is a big cutter, James.' Rennie, his own glass fixed to his eye. 'Bigger than *Hawk*, but not so wieldy, I think. Nor quite so swift, else she would have outrun us.'

'Since she wears no colours in English waters we will give her a gun. Mr Abey!' He gave the order.

'Aye, sir. A swivel?'

'Be damned to swivels, Richard. We will fire our number one larboard carronade, and let the ball strike as near to her as y'please.'

'Very good, sir.'

The order passed and the lanyard pulled. A flash of powder under flint, and the gun spoke.

BOOM

The whistling rush of the shot, and a white column of spray on the swell half a cable off the cutter's starboard bow.

A moment, then a stutter of flashes along the cutter's starboard wales, and a nearly instant:

BOOM-BANG   BANG-BANG-BANG-BOOM BOOM-BOOM

Hawk's helmsman was lifted in a writhing arc off the deck and flung bodily against the lee rail, torn asunder in a spray of blood. James felt his hat snatched off his skull, and his scalp singed. Heard cracks and splintering thuds forrard. Saw rigging whipped and torn. Saw his gaff snap, sag, dangle. Was thrown off his legs by a snaking rope, fell hard and painful on the deck – and heard dreadful screams. The deck shuddered under him. He pulled himself up, blood streaming from his neck, his head singing.

'Larboard battery! FIRE FIRE FIRE!'

A stunned, lagging moment, then:

BOOM   BOOM   BOOM-BOOM

James stumbled to the rail, and saw that all but one of his carronade roundshot had fallen wide. That one shot had struck the tafferel of the mystery cutter, and done only minor damage.

'Reload your guns! Reload!' Richard Abey's voice, in the waist. James turned groggily, glanced down at his shirt, and saw his whole left side soaked in blood, and his breeches spattered. He clutched at his neck, and felt the jagged end of a splinter. Tried to pull it free, felt a piercing jab of pain, and desisted. And now more screams, rending, desperate, horrible, rang across the deck – his deck, his ship, his people. Smoke drifted, and the sulphur stink of powder.

Captain Rennie, in a crouch, half-covered by a drape of torn canvas: 'They are firing grape and roundshot in alternate guns, the bloody villains.' He scrambled nearer James, and reverted to the formal language of the quarterdeck. 'You are hurt, Mr Hayter. Ye'd better go below to Dr Wing.'

'No, no, I am all right. It is a scratch on my neck, nothing more.' He turned, drew breath, and succumbed to a sudden wave of dizziness. Clutched at the rail, missed his grip, fell in a slewing tangle of arms and legs and lay still.

Hawk, her helm untended, her mainsail slumped and unfit to harness the wind, lost way, fell off, and wallowed on the swell.

Captain Rennie stood up, flung remnants of canvas aside, and bellowed:

'I am assuming command! Boatswain, there!'

No answer. More tortured screams from the waist, and forrard.

'Boatswain!'

Mr Abey came aft, his face laced with blood, his coat torn. He was limping. 'The boatswain is dead, sir. He was struck in the chest with grape, and fell.'

'We must get Mr Hayter below, as soon as we are able. Where is the sailing master?'

'I – I do not know, sir.' His voice cracking with shock. 'We have took an awful pounding forrard.'

'We must reload, and take the fight to the enemy, damn his blood. I will take the helm. You will take charge of the gunnery.'

But now in the moonlight they saw the black cutter swing smartly through the wind, mainsail haul, and come back at *Hawk* with a dreadful certainty of purpose. She bore down on the stricken vessel on the starboard tack, and let fly a further broadside. Flashes, thunderous detonations, smoke – and shattering damage.

In a few seconds – slammed, battered, splinters flying the whole length of her – *Hawk* was further crippled, and a dozen men now lay dead and dying on her deck.

Rennie rose again from a defensive crouch, felt himself gingerly all over, found no impediment, and saw the black cutter running away to the north in a coiling trail of powder smoke, virtually unscathed. Stared after her in wonder, fear, and rage, and muttered – to anyone and no one:

'That ain't the *Lark*. That is bloody Beelzebub . . .'

Cloud slid silent across the moon, became a ragged silver-edged screen, then snuffed out the light entire.

*

Dr Bell stood at the bedside, and observed with baffled disbelief the strewn evidence of his patient's returned appetite. Sir Robert, propped up by cushions and pillows, was pale still, but no longer waxy. He pushed aside an empty dish on which a curled rind of bacon lay, and traces of egg yolk. He wiped his lips with his broad napkin, added the pits of various fruits to the empty dish, and reached for the tall coffee pot on the cabinet. By the pot lay a plate covered in toast crumbs and a half-consumed roll of butter. Having filled his coffee cup, Sir Robert briskly rang a silver table bell, and his manservant appeared.

'Hot water, Fender, and razor. I wish to rise.'

'Rise, Sir Robert?' Dr Bell, raising his eyebrows. 'Are you sure that – '

'In course I am sure, my dear Doctor.' A penetrating black glance. 'Your diagnosis was perfectly correct.'

'Correct, Sir Robert . . . ?'

'You said it was costiveness, and that was indeed the truth of it.'

'Ah. Was it? Ah.'

'I will not quite admit that you have cured me. However, you made up my mind for me. Costiveness, you said, and from that verdict has emerged the solution.'

'Ah. – Yes?'

'Indeed. A difficult, expulsive episode. Several such episodes, overnight. And now here you see me, restored.'

'You – you took a purgative, Sir Robert?'

'I did, Doctor.'

'But – I did not give it you. I did not prescribe it.'

'Nay, y'did not.' Throwing off the covers.

'Then – then how – '

'I had it by me.' A bleak smile, and he swung his legs round, and carefully stood up. 'And now I need trouble you no further, I think. Pray send your bill to me, will you? Good morning, Dr Bell.'

The doctor bowed, and retreated to the door.

'Fender! Ah, there you are, man. Have you brought my small looking glass?'

'I have it with me, sir.'

Sir Robert beckoned his valet impatiently. The servant brought a large ewer of hot water and poured it into the basin in a cloud of steam. From his apron he produced a small oval looking glass, and a razor, and placed them next to the basin. Sir Robert waved away steam, and peered at his reflection in the glass. He was gravely silent, then:

'If I am to face the world, Fender, I must improve upon this.'

'I should not fret, sir. When a gentleman is fresh-shaved he is always a new man, I find.'

'Do you? Do you, indeed?'

'Oh yes, sir.'

'You have brushed my clothes?'

'Everything is ready, sir, as always.'

'My shoes?'

'And your shoes, sir, yes.'

'Tell me something, Fender, will you now? – Have you at any time . . . been married?'

'Married, sir? Oh, no. Certainly not.'

'You have never . . . contemplated that condition of life?'

'Never, sir.'

'You have never felt yourself drawn to a person of the . . . to a female person?'

His servant regarded him blank-faced, drew breath, but felt himself unable to answer without embarrassment.

'Oh, come. We are grown-up men. Let us not pretend. Young men – all men – are attracted to women, are not they?'

Fender cleared his throat politely. 'Will you wish me to shave you, sir, this morning? Or will you like to shave yourself?'

'I shall do it myself, thankee.' A black glance. 'Y'may go.'

'Thank you, sir.' Fender bowed, and retired. To Mrs

Reese, downstairs, he said: 'I ain't never seen him like this, I ain't. There is something strange a-going on in his head. He talked of women, for God's sake. At his time of life.'

'It is the purgative I believe has caused it, it has discommoded him,' said Mrs Reese. 'He has ate two full breakfasts, that never in usual took more than coffee, in the forenoon.'

'But *women*? At his age?'

Mrs Reese pursed her lips, and glanced at the valet. 'Gentlemen ain't dead, you know, until they are dead. That is entirely certain.'

*

Lieutenant Hayter woke in his cot in a small, nearly bare room at the Haslar Hospital. For a moment or two he believed that he was in his bed at the Marine Hotel at Portsmouth, and that his wife Catherine had gone into the annexe, perhaps to admit a maid with a tray. And now he heard a manservant address him.

'Mr Birch will be up directly, sir.'

'Mr Who-is-it?'

'Mr Birch, sir, that has come to see you reg'lar these past sev'ral days, he has.'

'Why should he do that, I wonder? In my bedroom?' James sat up, and found himself oddly stiff in his movements. His head ached. Had he drunk too much wine last evening? The manservant was not dressed as he should be, thought James, peering at him.

'I think you has forgot where it is you presently lie, sir. In an upper room at the Haslar.'

'What? Where is my wife? – Catherine!'

'Here is Mr Birch now, sir.' The man withdrew, and Captain Rennie came into the room, dressed in coat, waistcoat and breeches of plain civilian cut.

'Good God, it is you, sir . . .' Surprised, bewildered, James raised a hand to his neck, and felt there a heavy bandage. He stared round the room, and the reality of his circumstances bore in upon him.

'Am I ill? Am I injured? What has happened?'

And Captain Rennie told him. He told him all of it – or nearly all – and when he had finished, James asked:

'Where is she moored, did y'say?'

'She ain't moored, James. Nay, she is presently in a slip at a private yard at Bucklers Hard. Blewitt's. She is to be surveyed there, as I understand it.'

'D'y'mean – repaired?'

'There is doubt, James, I fear, as to that.'

James frowned at him, and the manservant – the hospital orderly – returned to the whitewashed room and threw open the uncurtained window. Rennie waited until the man had gone out.

'The surveyor has been sent from Portsmouth Yard, a quarterman appointed by the Clerk of the Check. He will make his report in a day or two, and then . . .'

'Yes . . . and then?'

'It will be determined whether or no she can be saved, or must be broke up.'

James's mouth came open a little as he stared at Rennie, then: 'Broke *up*?'

'James – it would be as well for ye to seek out an advocate.'

'Eh?'

'If she is broke up, or sold out of the service – there will likely be a court martial.'

'Good God.' James looked at the opened window, felt the breeze on his face, smelled the sea. 'I – I could be dismissed the service.'

'Nay, James, never think that. Even was you found wanting – '

'Found guilty, you mean.' Darkly.

'Even if the court found against you, I do not think Their Lordships would be disposed to be harsh. Under the circumstances, they could well decide to make little of the court's findings.'

'Circumstances?' An unsmiling laugh. 'The circumstances are that I was bested, sir, at sea, my cutter battered very heavy, and many of my people killed and wounded.'

'Certainly, but I ask this. Will Their Lordships like to acknowledge openly that such an action was fought? In home waters? When we are not at war? When everything of this commission has been dealt with quietly, half-concealed, in the shadows? When the First Lord himself signed your instructions, and yet revealed very little of what lay behind this enterprise?'

James was silent.

'Naturally, given that you are confined here at the Haslar, I would in usual seek out an advocate in your behalf, but my own circumstances make that impossible. I am not here official. So far as the navy is concerned I am at home in Norfolk. When we brought *Hawk* in I straightway left her, and retreated into my private self. All that I have learned since has come from Dr Wing's intelligence, and from young Richard Abey.'

James glanced at him, and remained silent a moment longer, then:

'Are the wounded men cared for?'

'Indeed, they are well cared for. And the dead was decently buried.'

'That is well.' A breath. 'Where is Catherine?'

'Catherine has gone home to Dorset, has not she, before we sailed? You wish her to return?'

Another breath, deeper and more resolute. 'I wish to get out of this damned cot, and out of this place altogether.' Throwing off the covers, and making to rise. 'There is much to be done if I am to save myself, and my ship.' He began to unbutton and throw off his nightshirt.

'Now then, Mr Hayter.' A voice from the doorway, and Dr Stroud came in, accompanied by the diminutive figure of

Dr Wing. 'You will do very well to stay where ye are, if y'please.' The two medical men advanced and gently, deliberately, their faces brooking no demur, pushed their patient back on his cot, and drew up the covers round him.

'You are not yet ready to leave us,' said Dr Stroud. Iron-grey hair cut close to his scalp gave his long, strong face a severe appearance. His spectacles reflected the light from the window as he turned and nodded to Rennie. 'Captain Rennie, good day t'ye. What have you said to excite my patient so?'

'I have said nothing.' Rennie, stoutly. 'Nothing above news of his wife.'

'Ah, his wife.'

'And, Doctor – please to call me "Mr Birch" as we agreed, hey?' Rennie was not going to allow himself to be put in his place in a naval setting, even by so eminent a physician as Stroud.

'Ah yes, in course, Mr Birch.' A further inclination of his head, a hint of irony. 'We must not unmask you, not for a moment – even in private.'

'I do not think you quite understand the gravity of my position.' Rennie, bristling. 'It ain't a matter for jest – '

'Nor is the condition of my patient, sir.' Severely, and then he countered that severity with a brief smile. 'We are all concerned for him.'

'Indeed.'

'And should his wife be brought to him, d'y'think?'

'Why not ask the patient himself?' said James now. 'He is here in the room, ain't he?'

'In course he is, in course you are,' said Dr Stroud. 'Do you wish it, Mr Hayter?'

'No, thank you, unless I am permitted to leave the hospital. I will not like to receive her here.'

'I don't think that will be advisable, you know,' said Dr Wing, moving round the bed to stand on the other side. He took James's pulse, nodded once to Dr Stroud, and asked James to put out his tongue.

'Eh? Why ain't it advisable? I am nearly hale again.'

'Tongue – if you please.'

James sighed, and put out his tongue. Dr Wing peered at it, made a face, and shook his head. 'Costive, I should say. What say you, Doctor?' Dr Stroud leaned, peered, and made a face of his own.

'Costive,' he said. 'And he must be bled, don't you think so?'

'Now then, look here,' began James in alarm. 'I will not like to be bled, merely because I am confined to this damned place, d'y'hear? Why am I not to be permitted to rise and dress, in least, and take the air? Where the devil are my clothes?' To Dr Wing, accusingly.

'Your shirt had to be cut off, and your waistcoat, that was very bloody. Your breeches, I fear, are similarly irrecoverable. It was not simply the large splinter in your neck, that came within half an inch of killing you, but other splinters that had penetrated the cloth up and down your person. Blood leaked from you in alarming quantity. You nearly died of that, leave aside the splintered wood. Had I not come to you when I did, I think we would not now be engaged in this happy conversation.'

'Ah.'

'Instead, we three here would have been required to stand beside your open grave, and listen to the gloomy tones of a clergyman, as he – '

'Yes, yes, very well, I understand you, Thomas. Thank you. I am – I am very much obliged to you for saving my life.'

'Never think of it. It is my proper work. Captain Rennie – that is, Mr Birch – will ye like to wait outside sir, or will you stay and observe?'

'Observe?'

'While I bleed the patient. Some men find it a matter of indifference. No doubt you are such a one, sir, since you have often to my knowledge witnessed dreadful blood-letting at sea, and terrible injury. You are welcome to stay at my side – '

'Nay, nay, thankee, Dr Wing.' Hastily. 'I – I shall go out. I am in need of a little air, myself.'

When Rennie had stepped out of the room, Dr Wing said to James: 'Perhaps, after all, I will not bleed you, James. That is, if you will undertake to remain quietly here in your cot a day or two longer.'

And then James did agree, acknowledging that Dr Wing would not oblige him to be obedient simply out of a desire to impose his will, but on sound medical grounds alone. Dr Stroud now departed, saying that he must attend on his many other patients, among them several of Lieutenant Hayter's people.

'There is a young ordinary seaman who will lose a leg, I fear. We must have it off this day, else lose the poor fellow himself to gangrene.'

When he had gone, leaving James to think on those parting words, Dr Wing began to change the dressing on his neck. James allowed him to work, and then to examine his other bodily wounds, apply salve, and strap them up. When he was done, James thanked him, and:

'Thomas, you are aware certainly of my difficulty. The longer I am detained here, the shorter grows the time I will have to restore my good name. My cutter is to be surveyed for damage, and very possibly condemned.'

'So I had heard from young Mr Abey.' Nodding.

'Either condemned, or sold out of the service. I need to discover the way to prevent such a calamity, Thomas. If she is broke up it is the same as losing her at sea, and I shall face a court martial, and the end of my career.'

'What can I do to help?'

'You can persuade Dr Stroud to release me.'

'Nay, James, you have just now agreed that we detain you here for good sound medical reason.' Beginning to be agitated, and vexed.

'Yes, yes, so I did. But I wonder – if I did rise today, and got myself dressed, and went out into the air, and the world, and walked about a little, and perhaps took a ferry a short distance, and so forth . . . would I die, d'y'think?'

'I do not think you would *die*, exact. You would likely set yourself back, however. You would likely make my care of you infinitely harder, and longer, if your wounds should begin to bleed, or grow infected.'

'Indeed . . . but you do not think I would die?'

'Not at once, in least.' Reluctantly, with a vexed little grimace.

'Very good, thank you, Thomas. Will you ask Captain Rennie to come to me, as you go out?'

*

They came to the slip at Bucklers Hard in Captain Rennie's hired ferry; he, Lieutenant Hayter and young Richard Abey. On the way there, as the ferrymen bent their backs at the oars:

'I had to slip away, sir.' Richard Abey glanced back towards Portsmouth. 'We are all quartered at the marine barracks, and – '

'Quartered at the barracks?' James. 'Why?'

'I think an official from the Admiralty has arranged it, sir. All of us that was not wounded in the action. Excepting Dr Wing, in course. And you, sir.' Nodding to Rennie.

'An official? D'y'know who?'

'An elderly gentleman, in a rather old coat – though his linen is very fine – '

'Soames, by God.' James and Rennie exchanged a glance.

'I do not know his name, sir. I have only seen him once, at the gate, speaking to the guards.'

James and Rennie exchanged another glance, and James gave a little grimace.

And now they had come ashore below the slip, the wide estuary of the river narrowing as it wound away north into the countryside under the broad, gull-tilting sky. *Hawk* lay before them, mast unstepped, heeled a little, showing her smashed rail and splintered wales and ports. A sad sight. James and Rennie stepped out toward the line of low yard buildings, and Abey followed them, picking his way through mud, pools of congealed tar, and loose ends of timber. A row of cottages stood to the right, smoke curling from the chimneys on the breeze. The smells of the yard wafted on that breeze: tar, fresh adzed timber, rope, horse dung. Mr Blewitt, the proprietor, emerged from the lower shed, donning an old-fashioned tricorne hat. A big, heavy-set man, surprising light on his feet, he lit a jutting pipe, puffed blue smoke, and came forward. He had already guessed that his visitors' business was with the broken cutter, and not with the brig building higher up. He noted that none of the men approaching him was in naval dress, and:

'So now, which of you is Mr Tickell?'

'Eh? Tickell?' James.

'The quarterman that I was informed was to be sent down to me from the Check. Is none of ye himself?'

'Nay, we are not from the Clerk of the Check, sir.' Rennie. 'This is – '

'I am Lieutenant Hayter, commander of the *Hawk*.' Nodding toward her.

'Oh. Ah. And Mr Tickell ain't with you? Joseph Tickell?'

'Nay, he ain't. I am Ca— I am Mr Birch, assisting the lieutenant.' Rennie frowned at his near mistake.

'Mr Birch. Who is the squirt, then?' Puffing, glancing at Abey, who drew himself up, and:

'Squirt! I am – '

'This is Mr Abey, my second-in-command.' James, smoothly. 'And you are Mr Blewitt, I think.'

'I am, sir.' Lifting his hat.

James lifted his own hat, and at once came to business. 'What is her condition?'

'Well now, that in truth ain't for me to say, is it? That is for Mr Tickell to say, when he – '

'In plain language, if y'please.' James, over him.

'In plain language, eh?' Removing the pipe from his mouth, and scratching his ear with the stem. 'Well then, she is broke, sir.'

'You mean – she is to be broke up?'

'Again, look . . . that ain't my say-so. That is for Mr Tickell, when he – '

'Yes yes, Mr Tickell. But between you and me, Mr Blewitt. Between you and me – what is your own opinion?'

'Well . . .' A face-creasing grimace, and an intake of breath through the teeth. 'Well . . . she *could* be saved, but at very considerable cost . . .'

'How costly?'

Another grimace. 'I fear we are looking at five hundred pound, cutter, large repair.'

'Very well.'

'Eh?' Mr Blewitt nearly dropped his pipe.

'Eh?' said Rennie, at the same moment. They both stared at the lieutenant. Richard Abey gaped in silence.

'Naturally I will like to see lists, and all items annotated clear, down to the last shilling.'

'May I ask – may I ask, sir, whether or no you are engaging me, Redway Blewitt, to undertake this large repair *yourself*?'

'I am.'

'What? James, you cannot mean it!' Rennie, aghast.

'I mean to repair my ship, sir, and take her to sea.' His jaw set.

'You have gone mad.'

'Not at all. If I am to be dismissed the service, I will undertake the full repair, lease the *Hawk* under private colours, and put to sea. That bloody blackguard that battered me, and her, will encounter us again, by God. And then we shall discover who is master.'

Lieutenant Hayter, Captain Rennie and Mr Midshipman Abey returned to Portsmouth in their hired boat with a storm threatening in the west, and as they came ashore rain began to fall. Rennie paid the ferrymen, and followed his two companions across the Hard. Lightning flashed. Thunder sounded almost at once, thudding and rumbling over the harbour and its ships, and the roofs and spires of the town. The rain grew heavier, billowing on the wind, and obscured the three figures as they ran clutching their hats. Soon they were lost to view.

*

'It is most kind in you, Admiral, to receive me. I had meant to call at your office before this.' Mr Soames waited until Admiral Hapgood had sat down, and then sat down himself, laying aside his hat and cane. 'I was – delayed.'

'Happy to oblige the Admiralty,' said the admiral, with no evident pleasure.

'I am most grateful, indeed.' Tucking his loose kerchief into his sleeve.

'You mentioned there was matters you wished to convey to me, when you came in.'

'I did, Admiral. They concern a – a delicate question.'

'Yes?'

'Yes. I wonder if I might trouble you for a glass of water. My mouth is rather dry, and my throat.'

'Yes, forgive me.' Stung to action by the implied rebuke. 'I am remiss in not having offered you refreshment.' He rang the bell, and presently, as the servant came in:

'Pell, there you are. My guest will like a . . . Mr Soames, perhaps ye'd prefer a glass of something more fortifying? Wine, or brandy?'

'Most kind in you, sir. I should like a glass of sherry, if you have it.'

'Sherry, Pell.' And when the servant had gone: 'And now . . . ?'

'It concerns, the question concerns a vessel, the *Hawk*. Commanded by Lieutenant Hayter.'

'I've heard of that vessel. Cutter, ain't she?'

'A cutter, indeed. There has been an accident at sea involving that cutter, as I understand it.'

'Accident?'

'You have not heard of it? You were not informed?'

'I have not. I was not. What accident? When?' The beetling brows formed into a black frown.

'Ah. Ah.' Mr Soames brought his lace kerchief to his nose briefly, then returned it to his sleeve. 'The *Hawk* cutter is engaged upon duties which have required her putting to sea independent of the fleet. I thought that you – '

'I know nothing of these duties, sir. I know nothing of the *Hawk*. I recollect now that Lieutenant Hayter came to see me, to ask what his duties were. I could not enlighten him. Subsequent to that, his commission, his command, has remained a mystery to me. You should I think ask Admiral Hollister, as to that.'

'Yes. Yes, indeed, perhaps that will be a better course.'

The servant returned with the sherry. When Mr Soames had taken his filled glass, and a sip or two, he nodded in appreciation.

'Excellent sherry.'

'Very good. – Well?'

'Well, Admiral?' Politely raising his eyebrows.

'Do not you wish to tell me anything more?'

'More? – D'y'mean more as to *Hawk*, or Lieutenant Hayter?'

'One or t'other. Nay, both.' The Admiral was not drinking sherry, had not poured himself any from the decanter. 'That is to say, if you please.'

'Yes. Well. Hm.' Returning his glass to the tray. 'I will not intrude longer upon your time, sir. I must proceed with my own pressing duties.' Making to rise.

'Mr Soames! I beg your pardon, I did not intend to discommode you, sir, by shouting at you. However, I will like to hear something more of your duties, your purpose in coming to Portsmouth. Why have you come to me?'

'Admiral, you have been most hospitable, and I have no wish to offend . . . but if you do not know anything of Lieutenant Hayter's duties in *Hawk*, then I fear we cannot assist each other.' Rising from his chair and taking up his cane.

'But why did ye suppose I did have such knowledge? Y'must have had a reason to believe it!'

'You were not acquainted with Captain Marles?'

'Eh? Marles? I know that he had his throat cut.'

'He did.' A sigh. 'An unfortunate end.' Mr Soames took up his hat.

'What the devil d'y'mean by that, sir?'

'I meant nothing, Admiral.' Mildly, a little shake of the head, and he put on his hat. 'Nothing beyond a remark in passing. Has the culprit been apprehended?'

'Don't know, sir. Don't know anything about it. Some officer of marines has took it upon himself to investigate. Don't know him, neither.'

'Ah. Thank you again, Admiral, and good day to you.' He turned towards the door, and paused. 'Oh, yes. I wonder, Admiral, d'y'happen to know – is Sir Robert Greer at home, at Kingshill?'

The admiral did not know, and said so. When Mr Soames had gone, the admiral:

'Pell! Pell! – Yes yes, come in, man, do not cower in the doorway. Go at once to Kingshill House, and discover whether or no Sir Robert Greer is at home. Return immediate to me with the answer.'

'Yes, sir. It is raining, at present. May I wait until – '

'Do not wait! Go at once! Jump, man!' And when Pell had gone out: 'I will be advised, I will be informed, I will know what is being done in Portsmouth, by God, by all persons with RN attached to their names.' Turning to the rain-speckled window, and glaring at the world.

*

Lieutenant Hayter knew that he was expected to return to the Haslar when he had had his little excursion – but he did not return there. Instead he accompanied Captain Rennie to the Mary Rose Inn, where Rennie – perhaps against his better judgement – was able to engage for him a small room at the rear, near to his own. Richard Abey returned to the Marine Barracks. James and Rennie repaired to the latter's room to drink a reviving glass, and James:

'I had meant to ask you, sir, on several occasions during today – how came the *Hawk* to Bucklers Hard? Who brought her there?'

'I am not entirely certain, James. According to young Abey a dockyard crew arrived soon after we had limped in and moored off the Great Basin under cover of darkness. All hands that could walk went ashore, and the wounded was carried. When daylight came *Hawk* evidently had vanished. As you know I came here, and kept myself out of view. Dr Wing attended to the wounded, and had them brought to the Haslar, and the other people was advised to go to the marine barracks.'

'Mr Soames gave that advice, that instruction?'

'I know only what Mr Abey has told us, James. His reported sighting of Soames was the first inkling I had had of his presence here.'

'Very good. I will try to discover more on the morrow.' A sudden dizziness caused James to lean forward, his head in his hands, and his glass fell to the floor.

'Are you going to faint, James?' Anxiously.

'Nay, I am . . . I am quite all right.' Recovering his balance, and sitting upright.

'You are still very weak. You must rest.'

'I am quite well . . .'

'Should not you consider returning to the Haslar, after all?'

'No. No.' Holding up a hand. 'There is much needing my attention. I am determined on my course.'

Rennie saw that he could not persuade his friend to return to the hospital, and tried another tack:

'Will you in least go to bed now, and sleep? You cannot follow any course when you are in a weakened condition, you know.'

'Yes yes, very well, I will go to my cot. Where is my room, exact? I have forgot.'

Rennie guided him there, and when James was safe in his bed, his erstwhile commander sent an urgent letter to Dorset:

My dear Catherine,
    James is ill, here at Portsmouth. He believes himself recovered, but he is not. I think that your presence – if you will come, without delay – will greatly aid him . . . &c., &c.

He said nothing in the letter of his grave doubts as to the wisdom and efficacy of James's plan privately to repair and lease the *Hawk*. He said nothing of the scheme at all. He sent the letter by express post. The letter came to Catherine at Melton House, where she was staying a week or two with her infant son, and as soon as she had received and read it she came to Portsmouth.

During the intervening time of two days, James lay in his bed at the Mary Rose, and Rennie endeavoured to discover the likely outcome of the quarterman's survey of *Hawk* at Bucklers Hard. He was unable to gain that intelligence, since the survey had been further delayed.

Mr Soames kept a close eye on the crew of the *Hawk* at the marine barracks, and made a brief foray to Kingshill, where he called at Kingshill House. He found Sir Robert Greer at home. That gentleman greeted him in his library, before a crackling fire.

'Ain't the day rather warm for a fire, Sir Robert?'

'A gentleman always has a fire in his library, Soames, no matter the season.'

Mr Soames glanced about him at the shelves of embossed books, the wheel barometer, the busts and paintings, the view from the long end window over the sloping lawns and ornamental lake, and as always when he came to Kingshill was approvingly impressed by the quiet grandeur of his surroundings. He came to his point.

'Sir Robert, I wonder if you know of the existence of a vessel, the *Hawk*?'

'*Hawk*? Nay, I think not. Naval vessel, is it? Why d'y'ask?'

'The *Hawk* is indeed a naval vessel, Sir Robert, a cutter. She is commanded by Lieutenant Hayter.'

'Lieutenant James Hayter, formerly of *Expedient*?' The voice more alert.

An inclination of the head. 'Exactly so.'

'Yes, well. I am prevented from noticing the activity of Mr Hayter . . . official.'

'Yes, sir? Ah.' Soames pressed his lace kerchief to his forehead, and neck, and snuffed the sharp cologne with which it was scented, in an attempt to relieve the oppressive heat of the fire.

'Well?' Sir Robert peered at him blackly, acutely.

'You have a continuing interest, I think, in Captain Rennie, have not you?'

'Well?' Again the black glance.

'I think it may be possible that Captain Rennie is here, at Portsmouth.'

'Here! You are *certain*?'

'Nay, I am not. However, I do know that the *Hawk* has been damaged at sea, that she presently lies at Bucklers Hard, and that two gentlemen and a youth went to view her very recent. One of those gentlemen was Lieutenant Hayter, that should have been lying at the Haslar Hospital, gravely injured, and has since disappeared. Another was a midshipman called Richard Abey, that serves with the lieutenant in

Hawk, and is presently quartered at the marine barracks. The third man has been identified as Mr Birch.'

'Birch? I do not know the name.'

'Nor do I, Sir Robert. I believe it to be an assumed name.'

'What? You think that Mr Birch . . . is Captain Rennie?'

'I think it very possible, even probable.'

'This young midshipman – does he know Captain Rennie?'

'He has served under him in *Expedient*.'

'And you have spoke to him, at the barracks? Asked him whether or no the man is Rennie?'

'I have made an attempt to converse with him, but the youth is – how shall I say? – he is not inclined to be forthcoming.'

'You mean he defied you, hey?'

'No, Sir Robert, I would not say that he defied me. I made the attempt to introduce into the conversation the business of *Hawk*'s extensive damage, how it happened, and so forth, and who was with Lieutenant Hayter aboard her. The boy could not remember anything, he said.'

'Eh?' Sharply.

'He said that he had been knocked unconscious by a falling block, at sea, and could remember nothing of the incident.'

'And you did not believe him?'

'Candidly – I did not.'

'Wise in you, Soames.' A moment, his black eyes fixed on the flames of the fire, then: 'What is the Admiralty's interest in this vessel?'

'It is . . . a confidential matter, Sir Robert, of which I know little.' Not quite the truth.

'Confidential? You dare to say that to me, when I have supported you throughout your career? Why have you come to me at all, if you do not trust my discretion? Tell me that!'

'In truth, Sir Robert . . .' employing the scented kerchief again '. . . I think perhaps we may be of service to each other in this. Until now, I have merely facilitated certain documents, and overseen a generality of instruction. I think that perhaps Lieutenant Hayter – and with him Captain Rennie – may have exceeded the instructions. I cannot conceive how the *Hawk* came to be so badly damaged, unless it was by an action at sea. No recent storm of wind, no other aberration of weather, can have caused such damage, since there has been no storm. I will like to find out the truth. You will like to find Captain Rennie. In concert perhaps we may achieve our several aims . . . ?'

Sir Robert stared dark at the Third Secretary, then turned his gaze to the fire once more, and presently:

'It don't matter to me what task the *Hawk* has been given. The purpose of those two officers – Hayter and Rennie both – is to use the *Hawk* for their own ends. They will use it to take the gold, and escape.'

'You think so, Sir Robert?'

'I do. When they returned from Rabhet the gold was in *Expedient*, and they brought it ashore, the entire, vast fortune, and concealed it. Their aim was to wait. Wait until they had cleared their names of any wrongdoing or neglect of duty, and afterward load the gold into another ship, and quietly, secretly, traitorously, make good their escape. The whole plan has been very careful laid, Soames. Lieutenant Hayter's father intervened in his behalf, to obtain this commission for him. Was you aware of that?'

'I was, sir. However, I do not quite – '

'Rennie was to lie low, and as soon as the new ship was ready, join Hayter and set sail.'

'Sail to what place, Sir Robert? To what country?'

'America, of course. There to live out their lives in glorious luxury, on great estates, upon *stolen money*.'

Mr Soames was aware that Sir Robert had attempted to bring a charge of treason against both of these officers, that he had been unable to sustain the charge, and had thus been obliged to see it lapse, and the officers go free. He was also aware that Sir Robert had been struck down by illness, and that Sir Robert felt that this misfortune, as much as – or perhaps more than – any other factor, had prevented him from pursuing Captain Rennie.

Mr Soames did not believe in the Rabhetan gold. He believed that the gold had been lost on the Barbary coast. He thought that Sir Robert's illness had very likely quickened his mind to the belief that the gold was in England, and that his imagination – honed by fancy and suspicion of others in his work for the Secret Service Fund – had produced tenacity of purpose in the matter. Mr Soames did not believe in the gold, but he knew that Sir Robert would be a formidable ally in discovering what had happened to the *Hawk*, and why such obfuscation and mystery now apparently surrounded it.

'Ye've been to Bucklers Hard yourself, Soames?' Sir Robert paced to the fire, turned and came back to where Mr Soames had retreated from the heat, by a small octagonal table.

'Erm . . . no, Sir Robert, I have not.'

'Not! You have not examined the *Hawk*?'

'I have not. I have no knowledge of damage in ships, repair, and so forth.'

'Then how d'y'know the – '

'I have contacts within the Portsmouth Dockyard, you know, and a certain influence there. *Hawk* was brought to Bucklers Hard by artificers and others employed in the Dockyard, and a quarterman appointed to survey her, since there was no place for her at Portsmouth. So far as I have been able to establish, nobody at the Dockyard knows how the *Hawk* came to be damaged. You must understand – since Captain Marles's death, I have been unable to discover very much about the *Hawk* and her duties at all, excepting that she was commissioned to undertake the pursuit of another cutter, a merchant vessel, and her master. That man, it has since emerged, died far away some time since, and had not in fact been master of the cutter for a long time. I have made it my business to try to find out the truth, Sir Robert. I think that you will like to do the same.'

'I will like to be proved right, certainly.' He stared unseeing at the splendid view through the window a moment, then: 'Very well, Soames, we will act in concert.'

When his wife Catherine came to the Mary Rose Inn, Lieutenant Hayter had suffered a relapse, in that he was again greatly weakened by his injuries. The wound at his neck had begun to bleed, and infection had occurred at one of the injuries to his chest, nearly beneath his left arm. He had refused to return to the Haslar, against Captain Rennie's earnest advice, and Dr Wing had been summoned to his bedside. Dr Wing had staunched the leaking wound, and applied a salve and new bandages to the infection lower down. He was there when Catherine arrived, and met her just outside the room, as she reached the top of the stair.

'We have not met previous, Mrs Hayter, but I am an old friend of your husband's – Thomas Wing.' A very little bow. Dr Wing did not love to bow, given his small stature.

'You are Dr Wing? James has told me so much about you . . .' A smile, that faltered. 'Is he – is James very ill?' Glancing anxiously at the closed door.

'He is not mortal ill. Not if he will listen to advice, and allow himself to be took back into the Haslar without delay.'

'What is his condition? Captain Rennie wrote only that he was ill . . .'

'He has been – well, perhaps it will be better if he tells you himself, Mrs Hayter. I will leave you together, and return later today.'

Dr Wing went away downstairs, and Catherine opened the door and went into the little bare brown box of a room, ill-lit and fusty-smelling, and saw her husband.

'Catherine, my darling . . .' Tears started in James's eyes, and he attempted to lift himself in the narrow bed, but was defeated.

'Oh, James, my dearest.' Coming at once to the bed. 'Why did you not write to me to say that you were so ill . . . but you are injured.' Looking at the bandages at his neck, and the new bindings half-hidden by his nightshirt.

'Who wrote to you? Was it Captain Rennie?'

'It was. He did.' Touching his face fondly, leaning to kiss him, and tenderly: 'How came you to be so hurt?'

'I was a little damaged at sea, you know.'

'I saw Dr Wing . . . he said that you had been at the Haslar, and that you must return . . .'

'Nay, nay, it is nothing. I am nearly recovered. Nay, my darling, do not cry. No tears for me, I am nearly well again.'

'Oh, James.' Tears fell on her cheeks, and she kissed him again, and touched the bandage at his neck. 'Oh, I cannot bear to see you so . . .'

'Hush, hush . . . I am all right.' Stroking her hair, blinking back his own tears.

Presently she recovered herself, and saw that James was not about to die quite yet, and wiped away her tears, and they fell to talking.

'Will you promise me to return to the Haslar, as Dr Wing has said you must?'

'Must? I do not respond to must, you know.' Not harshly.

'Then I shall ask. Will you return there, and allow Dr Wing to bring you back to health?'

'Thomas may attend me here. Unless I am grievous ill I shall not return to the Haslar.'

'Oh, but James – '

'Although the Haslar is a well-conducted hospital – indeed, there is no better hospital in England – no hospital is a very pleasant nor welcoming place. There are men in the grip of many and several diseases, there are men dying, crying out, there are others so gravely injured they will never again get on their legs and walk about as free men . . . but will live out their poor lives there, in wretchedness. In short, it is a damned miserable place, for all Dr Stroud's ideas of cleanliness, and sweet air. Unless I am absolutely compelled to it I will not like to go there again, my love. Beside – I have much to do, a great deal to do.'

And he told her something of the circumstances of the action at sea; not everything, but enough to show her where he now stood in the eyes of the Admiralty. When he came to tell her of his plan to pay for the repairs to *Hawk* himself, he was met with – if not hostility, then very severe dismay.

'Why should you be obliged to find this money, James?'

'Because she is my ship, and – '

'Surely she is the Admiralty's ship, England's ship, and you are merely her captain, is not that true?'

'Merely? Merely?' Only half-amused.

'I do not mean that you are little in courage, nor in sailing skill. Only that you do not own the *Hawk*, nor even a little part of her. Why then should you be obliged to pay for her repair, when you were only carrying out your orders? Surely that is the responsibility of Their Lordships?'

'My love . . .' He faltered, his face pale, passed a hand across his forehead, then lay back on his pillow. 'I – I am quite done up. It is all the excitement and delight of seeing you.'

'In course, I should not have argued with you. Forgive me, my darling. Do not talk any more, now. Rest, now. I will wait downstairs, in the parlour – '

'Nay . . . stay here with me, stay by me. Will you?'

She kissed him, and sat down, and waited by his side until he drifted into sleep, watching over him.

Presently Captain Rennie tapped at the door, put his head into the room, and saw Catherine there by her sleeping husband. Rennie nodded, smiled in greeting, indicated by gesture that he would not interrupt, and withdrew.

Mrs Townend and her widowed sister Mrs Rodgers – both of them naval widows – arrived by the fast mail coach at Portsmouth, outside the Marine Hotel, very late at night. They had come from Mrs Rodgers's home at Lambeth, in London, to visit her son Lieutenant Wyndham Rodgers, who

was Third in HM *Tempest* frigate, thirty-six, presently
attached to the Channel Fleet. These two ladies had come
not by previous arrangement, and not entirely upon a whim.
They had come because Mrs Rodgers wished to see her son
before he departed on what perhaps would be long foreign
service, and because she and her sister wished for a change of
scene.

Mrs Rodgers's home at Lambeth was a perfectly pleasant,
free-standing brick house, with a walled garden, and she lived
there in decent comfort, but she was not much in society. Her
late husband's career had meant frequent changes of address,
and now she preferred to be settled and serene. She had no
admirers, having determined on a single condition of life
following on her husband's death of fever at Jamaica, during
the late American war. This life, unstrenuous, mild, comfortable, in usual suited her very well, but the arrival of her sister
– her handsomer and livelier sister – had provoked in Mrs
Rodgers a wish for some little fillip to her existence, a
brightening of the afternoon, so to say, and together they had
come to the notion of this excursion to Portsmouth.

When they descended from the coach in the bustle of arrival
– ostlers, coachmen, the stamping and snorting of horses, the
heaving and bumping of baggage – both these ladies were
pleased to be at their destination, and briefly exhilarated by the
cool air coming in off the sea. Soon, very soon, as they came
into the hotel, fatigue set in, and they felt themselves in need
of hot chocolate and the comfort of repose. The night porter
was – they thought – less than helpful to them, given that they
were the only guests coming in so late.

'Chocolate, madam?' In answer to Mrs Rodgers's request.
'Ho, no. Not at this hour of night, no. It is gone midnight,
look, and the kitchen is closed long since.'

'Could not you find some member of the staff awake that
will give us refreshment?'

'I am the only person that is awake, official, madam. I waits
up for the coach by arrangement.'

'Could not you wake someone, then?'

Mrs Rodgers, in dealing with the servant class outside her own home, was inclined to set her lips, and speak in a nearly peremptory tone, her purse clasped firm in her hands before her. It was not altogether a persuasive manner, and she was not persuasive now.

'I am here, madam, to carry your baggage and show you to your rooms. May I ask what is your name, madam – and you, madam?' To Mrs Townend. 'I will gladly light your way, if you will tell me which rooms you has engaged, if you please.'

Mrs Rodgers began to lose confidence, and exchanged a glance with her sister, who now smiled at the porter, and:

'We came away from London in a great rush, and have not engaged rooms. We will like to do so – '

'Not engaged rooms?' The porter gave a heavy, beery sigh, and allowed their bags to sink to the floor beside him. 'Then I fear I cannot be of no service to you ladies. The hotel is full.'

'That is absurd,' began Mrs Rodgers. 'I have stopped at the Marine Hotel many times with my late husband, and there is always a few rooms kept for naval officers – '

'Well, madam, there ain't no rooms tonight, and that is all there is to say.'

'Will you tell me your name?' Mrs Townend interposed, again smiling.

'I am Jacob, madam.'

'Jacob . . .'

'Jacob Slipper, madam, night porter.' Touching his forehead.

'Jacob, here is a guinea.' Giving him the gold coin. 'I am sure that there is a room somewhere in the hotel that you could open for us, with your key, and let us rest there tonight. It will not matter to us if it is a little room, an attic room, even, high under the rafters. We will not notice its condition, however bare and small it may be. We are greatly fatigued, we have travelled all day to come here to Portsmouth, to see my sister's only son before he departs in his ship on foreign service. We have nowhere else to go, late at night. I know that you will help us – two naval widows – at the hotel which has always opened its doors gladly to all persons connected to the Royal Navy.'

'Well, madam . . .' Staring at the gold guinea, scratching his head, and shrugging apologetically. 'I do not know as I am able to find you a room, when there is none to be had . . .'

'Not even a servant room, a maid's room?' Another smile, and Mrs Townend tilted her head on one side a little. 'I entreat you, Jacob. I can see you have a kind heart . . .'

The night porter, thus rewarded and pressed, was obliged to find them a room – very high under the roof, up a narrow, steep stair – and the two exhausted ladies, supperless but glad of shelter, were able to spend the night in the Marine Hotel after all.

On the morrow they discovered, when they called at the Port Admiral's office, that HMS *Tempest* had already been ordered to sea, and set sail. No detail of her intended duty could be made known to civilians in a time of emergency, not even to relations of sea officers, but Mrs Rodgers was sufficiently well versed in naval matters to know that a frigate sent to sea as a single ship must probably be engaged on reconnaissance, and that *Tempest*, engaged on such a mission, could well be absent some time.

Naturally Mrs Rodgers was disappointed not to have seen her son before his departure, as was Mrs Townend not to have seen her nephew, but both these ladies were entirely sensible of the navy's exigent demands upon sea officers, and of the necessity for naval families to understand and accommodate these demands in turn. No good ever came of bitter lamentation, nor resentment towards Their Lordships, nor forlorn pining for absent sons and husbands. The two ladies accordingly went from the Port Admiral's office to the coffee house, ate a late breakfast, drank chocolate, and thus fortified set about finding themselves rooms and preparing to enjoy their stay in this most naval of port cities.

Catherine Hayter, with the willing help of Dr Wing, had succeeded in persuading her husband to return briefly to the Haslar.

'Very well, I shall go back for a day or two,' he had conceded. 'Only for a day or two, you mind me? I have not struck my colours entire. It is only to aid Thomas, so that he may change my dressings without having to come from the hospital to me. It is for his convenience, not my own.'

'In course, my love, you are very considerate and kind. It is for Dr Wing's sake.'

When she had seen her husband safely settled in his cot at the Haslar, Catherine wrote a note to Mrs Fenway, at Bosham, and sent it by hand.

Mrs Fenway was a gentlewoman known to Lady Hayter, an old friend of hers, who lived in a small pretty house at Bosham, just to the north of Portsmouth on the London road. Lady Hayter had said to Catherine, when her daughter-in-law was obliged to leave in haste to be at James's side:

'Should you need somewhere to stay, my dear, if there is no room where James is lying ill, please to get into touch with Gwendolyn Fenway, who is my oldest and dearest friend. Her husband is master of an Indiaman, and is nearly always absent, and so she is alone in her house. I know that you will like her, and she you. She is excellent kind, and will like to have company. I will write to her.'

At about four o'clock Catherine went to Bosham in a gig, and found the house without trouble. Tattham Grange was indeed a pretty house, with a gabled roof and handsome façade, set well back from the road in a large surrounding garden of tall spreading trees and wide lawns. Everything about it was pleasing to the eye, and Catherine at once felt that she could be at ease there – except that Mrs Fenway was not at home.

'Did your mistress receive my note, that I sent over by hand?' Catherine enquired of the elderly maid who answered the door.

'The mistress is not here, mum. Who shall I say called?'

Catherine told her, and: 'Did not my note arrive?'

'I b'lieve a message did come, mum, yes – but being as the mistress ain't at home . . .' She did not stand aside to allow Catherine to come into the house from under the portico.

'When will Mrs Fenway return? Later today?'

'Oh no, mum. She is gone away out of the district in her carriage.'

'Oh. – When d'you expect her?'

'She visits family in Surrey, I b'lieve, mum. A week at least, I should say.'

'Oh, dear. I had hoped . . . never mind . . . thank you.' And Catherine returned to her gig disconsolate, and was driven back to Portsmouth. On the way the gig was passed by an imposing, well-sprung black carriage, briskly drawn by four black horses. Harness gleamed and jingled. As the carriage passed Catherine caught a glimpse through the window glass of a black-clad figure, chalk-faced, sitting well back in the upholstered interior, hands clasped over the head of a cane. A shaft of sun flashed on a ring, there was the ember spark of a red stone, and then the carriage was gone in a dry spinning rhythm of wheels.

By the time the ostler she had engaged to drive the gig had brought her safely again to St Thomas Street and the Mary Rose Inn, Catherine had consoled herself with the thought that Mrs Fenway's house, pleasant though it was, would not have been convenient – lying as it did so far from the Haslar – and she resigned herself to occupying James's small bare room until he was well enough to leave the hospital. The outing had done her good. She had breathed fresh air, and felt the sun on her face, and all lowering thoughts of James's wounds, and his determination to squander what little capital they possessed on the repair of his cutter, had quite gone out of her head. She met Captain Rennie as she went in. He bowed, and invited her to dine with him.

Catherine hesitated, smiling, then demurely:

'I do not think I can accept, Captain Rennie, when I am alone.'

'Oh. Ah. Hm.' Disconcerted. 'Forgive me, my dear, I – I had not took account of that. In course it would not answer, when you are a married woman, and – and I am not.'

Catherine giggled to herself all the way up the stairs as she thought of this reply.

Later, after she had written a letter to her mother-in-law, and sent it to the post, she reflected that perhaps she had been unkind to Captain Rennie. Under the circumstances there could surely be no impropriety in her dining with an old friend – an entirely respectable, widowed sea officer in middle life – could there? She thought not, and attempted to make amends. However, Captain Rennie was not in the hotel, and Catherine was obliged to dine alone – her earlier sense of well-being quite dissolved.

*

Mr Soames, in a clean shirt and his shoes newly polished, a sprinkling of cologne on a fresh lace kerchief, had been summoned. Yesterday, from under his nose at the marine barracks, *Hawk*'s people had been removed to an address unknown to him, and now he had been summoned – to the Port Admiral's office. He went.

'Ah, there you are, Soames.' Admiral Hapgood made an impatient, beckoning gesture, and Mr Soames noted with displeasure and a twinge of vexed dismay that he was no longer 'Mister'. He came into the room and saw a figure seated beyond the admiral's desk, silhouetted against the light from the window. Mr Soames peered at the figure, and heard a deep, vibrant familiar voice:

'Soames, good morning to you.' The silver-topped ebony cane, the silver-buckled shoes.

'Sir Robert.' Mr Soames came forward and was about to extend his hand, but Sir Robert Greer did not rise from his chair, nor extend his own hand, and Mr Soames instead adjusted the kerchief in his sleeve.

'Since we met last at Kingshill, there have been – developments.'

'D'you mean – ' Soames saw Sir Robert's warning glare, and did not ask his question.

'Developments, and here we are.'

'Indeed, Sir Robert.'

'Sir Robert has matters he wishes to discuss with you, Soames,' said Admiral Hapgood now, anxious to assert his authority on his own ground. 'Matters which I think you wished to discuss with me, on an earlier occasion, but felt constrained by etiquette, and so forth – '

'Yes, thank you, Admiral.' Sir Robert now stood up, and moved to the window, and stood there leaning on his cane.

'Naturally I would wish to aid you, gentlemen, in any way I can,' continued the admiral. 'However, I cannot do so, you know, without I am told what is afoot.'

'Afoot?' The single word delivered with such dry rejecting disdain that the admiral was shocked.

'Hm. Perhaps you will like a glass of sherry, Sir Robert?' Very stiff. 'Before we begin?'

'No, thank you.'

'Brandy, perhaps? Pell!'

'Nothing, thank you.' And as Mr Soames began to say that he would indeed like sherry, Sir Robert, over him: 'And nothing for Mr Soames, neither.'

The admiral's man had appeared, and the admiral made a show of: 'Ah, Pell. Bring sherry, a decanter of sherry.'

'Nay, Admiral, we do not want sherry,' said Sir Robert. 'We will like to be left alone.'

'Hm. I myself wish to drink a glass of sherry,' began the admiral, and was again cut off.

'Y'may take refreshment in another room, Admiral, if y'please,' said Sir Robert. 'I have business in this one.'

'You – you wish to turn me out of my own office?' Admiral Hapgood was further shocked, then he saw his man hovering and waved him away irritably.

'You do not wish for sherry, sir?'

'No no, go *away*.' And when the man had gone, Admiral Hapgood drew a breath through his nose. 'Really, you know, Sir Robert, I do not care to be thrust precipitate out of my own door, when there – '

'Yes yes, in course, I do beg your pardon, Admiral. Will you do me the kindness of allowing me the privacy of your room? Thank you.' A dismissive nod.

Admiral Hapgood made a last attempt to assert his authority. 'Sir Robert, surely you have adequate rooms at Kingshill where you may conduct private business, if that is – '

'This is official business, sir.' Over him, cold and hard, without raising his voice.

'But, good heaven, if it is official business, then I myself must be – '

'You are not party to it.' Curtly.

'Not party to official Admiralty business! What the devil d'y'mean, sir? Hey?'

'Admiral Hapgood. Spain threatens our interests in the Americas. France is governed by a demonic rabble. His Majesty's government, and its instrument the Admiralty, must look to the nation's interests, and take certain measures of precaution. You will not wish, I think, to commit the folly of interruption to such business – will you?'

Admiral Hapgood closed his eyes in a display of contained ire, drew himself up, and: 'I do not perfectly understand why you should require my room to conduct such business, Sir Robert.' Opening his eyes. 'If I may iterate, ye've more than adequate premises not five mile distant. Would not the nation's interests be best – '

'A person is to come to me here at this place. I did not wish him to come to Kingshill, where his arrival would probably have been remarked. Far better that he should come here, unobtrusive, in the general hubbub of a busy port. *Now* d'you apprehend me, sir?'

'As you wish, Sir Robert.' Defeated, Admiral Hapgood retired, black brows thunderous as he went out of his own door and closed it with a barely governed violence. A moment, then a muffled bellow on the stair: 'Pell! Pell, damn you! Where are you when I want you?'

If Sir Robert heard this outburst he gave no indication, but turned again to the window, and:

'You are to return to London, Soames.'

'To London, Sir Robert? Do not you need me here?'

'It ain't what I want, Soames, nor you, neither. I have had a communication, placing in my hands particular facts. I must act upon these facts. You must put the matter of the *Hawk* and her people from your mind entire.'

Mr Soames stared at him. 'Sir Robert, I do not think I am able to do so. If you will recall, it was I that drew the *Hawk* to your attention. Surely I am the person most fitted, therefore – '

'Y'will return to London by the noon coach.' Sir Robert moved to the admiral's desk. 'Please to take this sealed packet with you, and give it into the hand of Sir Philip Stephens, at the Admiralty.'

'The First Secretary. May I know – '

'Y'may not.' Giving him the sealed packet. 'Into his hand, you mark me?'

'Very well, Sir Robert.' Taking the packet.

Sir Robert consulted his silver pocket watch. 'Ye'd better be away to the Marine Hotel at once, Soames. The coach departs in two-and-twenty minutes.'

'Oh, but I have not packed my things, at the barracks – '

'Your baggage will be sent on to you.'

Miserably: 'Sent on? Oh, very well.' He put the sealed packet safe inside his coat, and sighed.

'Forget all about the *Hawk*, Soames, and your little excursion to Portsmouth. Your servant, sir.' The briefest bow, and Sir Robert sat down at the desk and opened his pocket snuffbox.

'Your servant, Sir Robert.' Mr Soames bowed in turn, and quitted the room.

Presently there came into the room unannounced a figure in a large dark boat cloak with a dark hat pulled low over his face. The hat and cloak – when the door was safe shut – were thrown off, revealing a stocky man in his thirties wearing a plain blue frock coat, and cream waistcoat and breeches. His face was pleasant without being handsome, his hair cut close to his head.

'Your Royal – '

'Nay, nay, Sir Robert.' Waving a hand. 'As we agreed, as we agreed, hey?'

'Very good, sir. Mr Hope.' A bow.

'Indeed, Hope is who I am, and what I represent. I see you wear the ring.'

Sir Robert touched the ring, pale fingers straying over the red stone. 'I do wear it, sir. Am honoured to.'

Mr Hope nodded and wandered to the window, taking a pinch of snuff.

'I do not think it advisable for you to stand at the window, sir . . .' Sir Robert, an anxious frown.

'Eh?' In mild surprise.

'In full view, there is always the risk that you – '

'Ah. Ah. Quite right, Sir Robert, quite right.' Stepping away from the window. 'Lord Howe is to take overall command.' Nodding in the direction of the sea. 'Old Holly will not like it, but he ain't the arbiter of what shall be, or not. Eh?'

'No indeed, sir.'

'Hey, now, listen . . .' Mr Hope's manner grew confidential. 'What is the difference between a cockerel, and a cock?'

'I – have no notion . . .'

'One stands up and crows, and t'other stands up and *snows*-hhhhh!'

'Indeed . . . a capital joke, sir.'

'Hhhhh-*snows*-hhhhh!'

'If I may draw your attention to the question of the moment, sir? The business particular to us here, this morning . . . ?'

Everything of Sir Robert's demeanour now would have astonished his earlier interlocutors, Admiral Hapgood and Mr Soames, or indeed most of his acquaintance. He was if not quite obsequious then certainly deferential, very correct, very polite; his care of expression was nearly humble. His guest, sobering:

'Yes, yes, business. We must get down to it, by all means.' A pause, raised eyebrows. 'Have ye by chance a glass of madeira and a biscuit to hand, I wonder? I did not eat breakfast.'

'In course, sir.' Sir Robert went to the door, opened it and called: 'You there – Pell!'

The man came cautiously up the stair, and peered at Sir Robert. 'You wish for – '

'Madeira and biscuits. Knock, and I will take the tray.' He shut the door.

When the tray had been brought, wine was poured, and Mr Hope drank it off in one draught, munched biscuits, and refilled his glass.

'Now then . . .' munching '. . . the *Hawk*.'

*

Several days passed, and the fleet remained in readiness at Spithead, Portsmouth continued crowded to overflowing, and James was permitted by Dr Stroud and Dr Wing to leave the Haslar Hospital, and return to the Mary Rose Inn. On the same morning of his release a letter came to Catherine at the inn, by hand from Mrs Fenway.

My dear Mrs Hayter,

How very sorry I was – when I read your letter upon my return from Haslemere – not to have been at home when you called, a week since, and were in need of assistance. Lady Hayter is my very great friend, and I will like to make amends for my absence.

Will you and dear James come to me at once at Tattham Grange, and stay with me here as long as you please? I do hope that yr husband is greatly improved in his health, but even if he is not, everything that could be wished for is at your disposal here – fresh air, a wide garden, plentiful food – to restore him to his usual self. You will be most welcome indeed.

May I expect you today, without fail?

Gwendolyn Fenway

*

'And you are resolved on this course?'

'I am, sir.'

'I cannot dissuade you, in light of the very great difficulties you face?'

'You cannot.'

'Not least of them that you will be obliged to find new guns, and pay for them, above the repair?'

'You cannot.'

'Very well.'

'I shall proceed alone. There is no need of anyone else. I am quite alone in this endeavour, and alone I mean to bring it to conclusion.'

'Well well, I will say nothing more, except – '

'Nay, do not say it, if you please. My mind is made up.'

'I was only going to say – '

'Sir, I beg you, do *not*.'

' – going to say – '

'No! *No!*'

' – that I am still your man.'

'Eh?'

'I am still your man.'

'You would risk everything – your whole career – to stand with me in this?'

'I gave you my word, James.'

This exchange took place in the garden at Tattham Grange, beneath a spreading tree, the sunlit lawn and flowering shrubs a scent-drifting backdrop. James and Rennie sat in the shade, James with a rug over his knees – in spite of the balmy warmth of the air – and Rennie with his face turned into a patch of sun. James was yet a little pale from his sojourn at the Haslar, and a little thin. A bumble-bee wove between them, and swerved away on its meandering flight. A long moment, then James, quietly:

'You know that I would never hold you to such a promise, when everything has altered since it was made.'

'I do not alter, my dear friend.'

James saw the garden as a blur for a moment, and felt his throat constrict. He brought his kerchief from his pocket, and blew his nose. Then, clearing his throat: 'The air is cool, do not you find. I have a slight chill.'

'It is cool, a little.' Knowing it was not.

The sound of bees, and the chee-chee of a coaltit on the soft air. And now a voice, an enquiring voice, careful of breaking into a private conversation:

'Gentlemen, I hope I do not disturb you?'

Mrs Fenway approached, under a wide hat. She was a handsome woman in middle life, full-figured but not plump, with nothing artificial in her manner or appearance. When he had first come to the house to see James, Captain Rennie had liked her instantly, and now as he saw her, smiling at them as she walked towards the shaded spot where they sat, he found himself aware of her – charms. He rose and bowed. James made to rise, but Mrs Fenway:

'Do not get up, my dear James. I have brought you a letter, just come. Bertha has gone into the village, so I have brought it myself.' She held it out to him.

'That is very kind, Mrs Fenway.' James took the letter from her hand, recognizing the seal.

Rennie also recognized it, and said to Mrs Fenway: 'Will you show me your garden, Mrs Fenway? I shall very much like to see it, with so charming a guide.'

She smiled at him, saw that her younger guest should be left alone to read his letter, that this was what Captain Rennie meant, and: 'In course, I shall be delighted, on such a lovely day.' They fell into step, and moved away down the path. Mrs Fenway laughed at something Captain Rennie said, turning her head towards him under her hat, and presently they disappeared from view.

James broke the seal, and unfolded his letter.

FOUR

The wind veered between due west and west-sou'west, mild in temperature but not in strength. The wind was brisk, and the sea getting rough. Spray was flung up and across the deck in hanging fans, and exploded under the bow. On the fall the living sea slid curling along the lee rail, rode over the deck, swirling and sucking at the gun carriages, and poured streaming away through the scuppers on the lift. The foot of each headsail streamed and dripped, the flat-steeved bowsprit streamed, the vessel shuddered and shook, and now the order came.

'We will take another reef in the mainsail, Mr Dumbleton!' Shouted against the wind.

The sailing master Garvey Dumbleton repeated the instruction, seamen jumped, and *Hawk* grew tractable, her bellied mainsail now harnessing the wind more efficiently. Lieutenant Hayter was satisfied. To the helmsman at the tiller:

'Keep your luff. Hold her just so.' And he trod to the weather rail. 'Mr Abey!'

'Sir?' His senior mid, attending.

'Pass the word for the carpenter, if y'please.'

'Aye, sir.' Lifting his hat, going forrard.

The carpenter came on deck. 'You wished to see me, sir?'

'Aye, Mr Hepple. What depth of water in the well?'

'Remarkable little, sir. A few inches only. Blewitt's has done us proud the large repair. Everything fitted true, and caulked and sealed admirable. She is a sturdy sea boat again.'

'Very good, thank you. There is one other thing . . .'

'Yes, sir?' A hand to a stay as *Hawk* pitched through a swell.

'Yes, hm. I will like a very small partition built below. I know there ain't room for a quarter gallery in a cutter, in course. But I will like a light bulkhead, and a canvas door that I can close or draw. I have made this sketch in pencil . . .' Giving his carpenter a page from his notebook.

'Yes, sir, I see what you wish for . . .' Examining the sketch, scratching the back of his head.

'You are doubtful, Mr Hepple.' Frowning at him.

'No, sir, no . . . only there is so little room for me to place such a bulkhead. If I may make a suggestion?'

'Yes, yes – by all means.'

'If you was wishing for simple privacy, I could rig up a metal rail at the deck head, and run a canvas screen in a half-circle round the space, that could be handed and tied off when not in use.' Pulling his own pencil from behind his ear, and making his own quick sketch on the page.

'Ah, yes. Yes, I see.' James peered, nodded, grimaced. 'It would make for complete privacy, with only a canvas screen?'

'Oh, indeed, sir. Rigged full length, in a half-circle, from the rail, it will answer right well.'

'Very good, Mr Hepple. Make it so.'

The screen had become a necessity, since he was obliged to share his great cabin with an official guest these next few days. The guest, presently below, was to be known in the ship as Mr Hope. Lieutenant Hayter knew that he was not Mr Hope, but a sea officer of royal blood, with whom he was obliged to share his cabin, and who must be treated as if he were a person of minor importance, sent to him as a supernumerary observer. The reason for this subterfuge had been made apparent to him, and he understood it – but it did not make him comfortable.

'Will not you like the great cabin to yourself, sir?' he had offered, when his guest first came aboard.

'No thankee, Mr Hayter. I am like you a sea officer, and

have learned naval ways from a boy – how to share, and be
civil together, and not to mind cramped quarters below. I will
gladly share, if you will have me?'

'Am honoured, sir.' Bowing.

'Good, good. And none of this bowing and scraping and
such. To your people I am plain Mr Hope, civilian-dressed,
come to observe.'

'Very good, sir.' Stung by the accusation of 'scraping', but
hiding it.

'And by the by, Mr Hayter – never think I am here to
examine your seamanship and shiphandling and the like.
That ain't any part of my purpose.'

'Thank you, sir.' A polite nod.

'We rendezvous with *Pipistrel* at sea, I think?'

'That is my design, sir.'

'Commander Carr, Excise Board, hey? Acquainted with
this officer, are ye?'

'I am, sir. We have met.'

'Well?' A keen stare – a naval stare.

'Well – I think that Commander Carr is very likely a
competent officer.'

'In short, y'don't like the fellow.'

'I would not wish to malign – '

'Don't like him, but ye'll serve alongside him, in the
nation's interest. Yes?'

'I shall always like to serve the King, sir.'

'Ha! The King! Indeed, indeed. Well said, sir.'

And now as he trod his very small quarterdeck, the wind in
his face, and his cutter beating close-hauled on the starboard
tack, James reflected on all that had occurred over these past
few busy weeks.

The letter that had come to him at Tattham Grange,
bearing an Admiralty seal, had not – as he had at once begun
to think when Mrs Fenway gave it into his hand – been the
communication to him of his ruin, his court martial and ruin,
but a much happier document. The First Secretary, Sir Philip

Stephens, begged to inform him of the decision of Their Lordships, in consideration of a report from the Navy Board, itself hinging upon the survey carried out by Jacob Tickell, quarterman, Portsmouth Dockyard. HM *Hawk* cutter, ten guns, was to undergo large repair at Blewitt's private yard at Bucklers Hard. As soon as that should be completed *Hawk* was to continue her commission. Certain conditions would henceforth attach to that commission:

Lieutenant Hayter RN, commanding HM *Hawk* cutter, 10, shall act in concert with Commander Carr of HM Excise Board, commanding the *Pipistrel* cutter, in attempting to take the *Lark* cutter and her master.

Additional aid & counsel will be offered to both Lt Hayter and Commander Carr by Sir Robert Greer, in his capacity as adviser to His Majesty's Government, & friend in this Duty.

In view of the loss of Captain Apley Marles RN, attached beforehand to this Duty, it was thought advantageous to appoint Capt. W. Rennie RN, senior post captain, to take Capt. Marles's place – given that Capt Rennie & Lt Hayter had served together previous, in three successful commissions in HM frigate *Expedient*, 36, presently in Ordinary. However, several attempts to get into touch with Capt Rennie at his home in Norfolk having failed, it has been decided to afford another person that opportunity, & accordingly Their Lordships have appointed Mr C. Hope Esq. as a friend to the officers herein described.

No mention was made in the letter of the circumstances surrounding the damage to *Hawk*, nor of the action in which that damage had been sustained. The import of the letter was that this was a new beginning for *Hawk* and her commander, with everything ahead.

James had attempted at once to have Captain Rennie

appointed to the position given to Mr Hope – a person
unknown to James, and apparently not a sea officer – that is, he
had been about to attempt it when Rennie himself declared:

'No, James, no.'

'Eh? You do not wish – '

'Hear me out, will ye now?'

'Certainly . . .'

'Listen, now – if it came out that I had been at Portsmouth
all the time, living as Birch, then in all probability it would
come out that I was aboard *Hawk* when she was damaged, and
that I had took command.'

'*You* took command, sir?' James stared at him. 'You never
told me that. I thought that the sailing master had – '

'Nay, he did not. All was confusion on deck, very bloody
and bad. I am a sea officer of long experience. I thought it my
duty, given the condition of the ship, and the very great injury
to her people – to you, James – I simply thought it my duty to
assume command . . . as a matter in course.'

'Yes, I see.' Quietly.

'However, if it ever came out that I had done so – with no
commission, under an assumed name, not listed on the books
– well well . . .'

'. . . we should likely both be court-martialled, and dismissed the service.'

'Just so, James.' A nod. 'Had you undertook the thing
privately, repairing and taking *Hawk* to sea under your own
colours, so to say, then there would have been no scrutiny of
your people, and I would gladly have joined you again, but
now . . .'

'Could not you return to Norfolk, recover the letters sent
by the Admiralty, and respond – saying that you had been
staying with friends a few weeks?'

'Nay, James, it is too late.'

'Very well, sir.' A resigned sigh. 'Then I fear I must leave
you ashore, and accept Mr Hope. Have you heard of this
fellow Hope?'

'I have not.'

'He is a mystery.'

And so the mysterious Mr Hope had come into the *Hawk*. He arrived in a boat that at once pulled away, and jumped below – swathed in a great cloak, his hat pulled down – in a great hurry, but in such an agile way that James at once sensed that here was a fellow with salt water in his veins. James followed him below.

'Mr Hope, sir, at your service!' Sweeping off the cloak and hat and flinging them down on a locker – with some little difficulty, since the deckhead lay so close over his stooping neck. James, bending into the great cabin, had stared nearly open-mouthed, and blurted:

'Good God! I – I mean, I beg your pardon, sir –' There followed the exchange about the sharing of quarters, and the rendezvous with *Pipistrel* and Commander Carr, then Mr Hope continued:

'You wonder why I am come, d'y'not?'

'Well, sir . . . I confess that I do.'

'Naturally, ye do.' He sat down, and James sat down. 'It is the wish of Their Lordships – and the King – that this man be captured.'

'The master of the *Lark*?'

'Aye. I have a particular interest in him, because he has served with me.'

'Served with you, sir? May I know his name? – I know that it is not one Sedley Ward, that died long since.'

'His name is Aidan Faulk, and he served with me as Third in my first command. He then left the service, and went abroad, where he found himself – by design – among certain people who became his friends. He joined their cause. Subsequent to that he found the means to purchase the *Lark* – from Sedley Ward, the smuggler, whose name was used by Their Lordships as a convenience.'

'A convenience, sir?'

'Aye. You were not to be party to the truth – at first.

However, when you came to a sea action with the *Lark*, and was bested, and nearly killed, it was decided that I should come to your aid, in view of my – well, my unique position. The government is keenly interested in Mr Faulk. They know him to be not merely a smuggler of goods, but of men. Men inimical to the nation's interest. I may say nothing further at present, excepting that Mr Pitt wishes Faulk took. The Admiralty wishes him took. The King wishes it. And so do I, Mr Hayter. Together we shall do it. What say you?'

Of course James had agreed, wholeheartedly agreed, and had pushed aside all private doubts and questions – flattered, honoured, pleased beyond measure to have been given this second chance in so important an affair. But later, when he came to reflect on those doubts and questions, they began to grow larger in his mind.

He had failed to take the *Lark*. He had been outsailed, outfought, and bested in a fierce action. He had all but lost his own cutter, had come within an inch of losing his life, and had lost a dozen of his people wounded and killed. And yet Their Lordships had not relieved him of his command, nor obliged him to face a court martial; they had seen fit to allow him to continue in his duty, aided now by his exalted, disguised observer. Why? And what was Sir Robert Greer's role in this? How came he to be involved? Had he – in truth – been involved from the beginning? And what of that fellow who came to Captain Rennie's room at the Marine Hotel, put a pistol to his head, and demanded to know about cutters? Was that man Aidan Faulk? Was he?

James had never regarded himself as a political fellow. He had little knowledge of party politics, and the machinations of power in London. Naturally, as an educated man and the son of a prominent family, he was aware of such things. It was simply that he did not regard them. The great men of the day – Burke, Pitt, Fox – were great in a way entirely detached from the life of a practical sea officer. James was aware that Edmund Burke abominated what had happened in France, and that Mr Fox did not. He knew the long history of conflict between England and France, and that if the fleet presently assembled went to war with the Spanish fleet then the French were bound by treaty to support their Iberian ally. Beyond these broad facts he did not venture. He saw his duty in narrower terms: he must follow his instructions, harness the wind, and seek out the *Lark*; he must take her, and her master, and deliver them up. However, however . . . he could not prevent, nor wholly ignore, the rising of doubts in his mind . . . could he?

His new boatswain Mr Love approached, and hovered, hat off.

'Yes, Mr Love?'

'Your pardon for disturbing you, sir. You wished me to remind you as to the shrouds, and tar.'

'Shrouds? Ah, yes.' And they began a technical discussion about Stockholm tar, and its use. Presently, the boatswain satisfied, James cleared his wind, strode aft, and:

'Mr Abey!'

'Sir?'

'We will come over on the larboard tack, if y'please.'

'Very good, sir. – Stand by to tack ship! Put your helm hard down!'

The cutter's head through the eye, headsails aflap, and then she leaned tall on the port tack, mainsail bellying taut, stays and halyards sharp against the sky, and her pennant streaming aft, and began to run again fast and true close-hauled.

Presently the lookout called: 'D-e-e-e-e-e-ck! Sail one point on the larboard bow!'

Soon they could all see *Pipistrel* as she ran before, growing larger by the moment, towards the rendezvous.

*

'Why, surely – it is Mrs Townend, ain't it?'

'Captain Rennie, here you are at Portsmouth.'

'And here you are, indeed.' His hat off, and he made a leg. 'I did not know you was here, Mrs Townend, else I should have sought you out. How long have you – '

'A month and more, Captain Rennie. My sister Mrs Rodgers and I have taken a small house on the Cambridge Road. Where do you stay?'

'At the Mary Rose Inn.'

They had bumped into each other in the High, Rennie on his way to the coffee house, and Mrs Townend to Paley's the confectioners on the corner of Lombard Street. Captain Rennie was still dressed in plain civilian clothes, and keeping up the pretence of Mr Birch, Lieutenant Hayter having asked him to remain at Portsmouth as his unofficial adviser and friend. Mr Birch could pass unnoticed – a clerk, a merchant – among the massed naval coats and hats of this city. Mrs Townend was in blue, as was her custom, and her very becoming small hat was trimmed with fur. By God, thought Rennie, she was a handsome woman, a more than handsome woman.

'Is Mrs Rodgers's husband a sea officer?' he asked. 'That is why ye've accompanied her to Portsmouth?'

'He was, Captain Rennie. My sister is now a widow, as am I.'

'Two widows at Portsmouth, hey?' He smiled at her, and felt his heart lift when the smile was returned.

'You are not in uniform, Captain Rennie?' A further smile, enquiring.

'Nay, I am here – I am here privately. May I walk with you as far as Paley's?'

'Pray do, Captain Rennie.' The merest hint of the coquette. They fell in step on the crowded pavement. An earlier shower of rain had left the cobbles slippery, and now Mrs Townend nearly lost her footing, and gripped Captain Rennie's arm. He steadied her. It made him feel very manly to support and right her so, and now she rested her hand lightly on his arm as they walked on.

They came to Paley's, the twin bow windows filled with all manner of sugary delights – cakes, sweetmeats, glazed fruit – in elaborate and tempting design and display.

'Will you come in a moment, Captain Rennie? I should like to introduce you to my sister.'

They went inside, through the glass-panelled door, and found a comfortable crowd sitting, standing, milling slowly in the confined space, chatting and drinking chocolate and eating sweetmeats. Captain Rennie did not feel himself quite at home, and began to regret the care with which he had tied his stock; it was uncommon tight, and he was too warm in this press of women and girls. With an effort he kept a smile on his face as he followed Mrs Townend to the rear, where her sister was seated at a small table.

Rennie was duly introduced to Mrs Rodgers – as the brave officer that had saved her sister from highwaymen – was self-deprecating and civil, thought Mrs Rodgers a pretty woman but not near so comely as her sister, declined an invitation to stay and drink chocolate, lingered a moment or two and discovered their address, and made his escape. As he did so, behind an effusion of giggling girls, he was further accosted:

'Rennie, good heaven! I thought that y'must've quit Portsmouth long since!'

Captain Langton, bluff, tall, a smiling frown, in his dress coat.

'Langton . . . ha ha, there you are, dear fellow. I have been away, you know, and have only now returned.'

'No commission, as yet?' Making his face sympathetic.

'No, no . . . oh, d'y'mean my clothes? My uniforms are at Bracewell & Hyde, refurbishing.'

'Ah, ah. You have no dress coat? I had thought to ask ye to dine aboard. In course, you are welcome as you are – '

'Um, um . . . I should be happy to dine, Langton, honoured to dine. Name the day, by all means.'

'Tomorrow, then. My launch will come for you at the Hard at noon.'

'Excellent. Happy. Very good.' Nodding, smiling, lifting a hand.

'Noon, then.' And Captain Langton strode on.

'Damnation.' Rennie, under his breath, and he strode on. 'Why could not I have said to him that I was engaged tomorrow?' He walked on towards the coffee house, changed his mind and turned about, and returned to the Mary Rose Inn. He would write a note to Mrs Townend, asking her permission to call on her tomorrow. If a favourable reply came he would send a message to Langton, excusing himself on the grounds of a previous engagement. That was the better plan.

'Langton will be offended, I am in no doubt,' muttering to himself. 'That cannot be helped.'

No, he could not allow himself to be seen aboard one of His Majesty's ships of the line just at present. Dining in Captain Langton's great cabin, doubtless with many other officers, was not advisable. He must remain absent from Portsmouth so far as the Admiralty was concerned, and available only privately to his close friends. He was and must continue to be Mr Birch, plain Dorsetshire Birch.

He came to the Mary Rose, and was going in when he remembered: 'I had promised James that when he had put to sea I would call on Cathy at Mrs Fenway's, and reassure her – and I have not.' Was she yet at Tattham Grange? Or had she gone home to Dorset? He did not know. He had better go there now, today, else James would think him negligent of his duty.

'Little!' Calling to the landlord. 'Mr Little!'

'Yes, Mr Birch?' Emerging from his snug, wiping biscuit crumbs from his mouth.

'I will like to hire your gig, if y'please.'

Captain Rennie waited out a shower of rain, then drove to Tattham Grange at Bosham. There Mrs Fenway told him that Cathy had gone home.

'I entreated her to stay with me here, and to send for her

little boy – that was her chief reason for going to Dorset, in course – but she could not reconcile herself to staying a moment longer, and so she has gone away this morning. It was selfish in me to expect her to stay on, no doubt, when James has gone to sea, but I do feel her absence very acute. She is such a dear young woman and I have grown very fond of her.'

'Do not distress yourself, my dear Mrs Fenway. James will not be long at sea, I think. It is not foreign service, after all. And when he is again at Spithead, I am certain Cathy will wish to come to him, and that they will be glad to join you here at Tattham, together.'

'A comforting thought. Thank you, Captain Rennie. To be a sailor's wife is a lonely thing, and my husband is away sometimes twelve months together, or longer.'

'Indeed – indeed.'

'You are not married, Captain Rennie?' Then, as she saw a shadow pass over his face: 'Oh, do please forgive me – you are a widower, as you have told me.'

'There is nothing to forgive. I am quite recovered from my loss.'

'I am glad.'

They were drinking tea in the sunny drawing room, and Rennie – having done his duty, and not feeling himself competent to make small talk – was thinking of making his excuses and coming away, when:

'I wonder, Captain Rennie – do you like to dance?'

'Eh? Dance?'

'There is to be a dance at Mrs Caversham's in a few days. She has begged me to bring a party, and – '

'I do not think I know that lady . . .'

'Oh, she is a friend of mine, you know, and I have said to her, My dear I shall do my best. I have not been quite truthful, however, because I cannot bring a party. All the women or girls I might have asked are already engaged for it, to dinners and suppers and the like, and I had thought that I must at last send a note of refusal, since I cannot respectably go alone.'

'Ah. Ah.' In something like dread. Captain Rennie did not love to dance.

'If you were not engaged on that evening, Captain Rennie – '

'What evening is it?'

'Wednesday evening.'

'Wednesday? Well well, you are very kind, but on that day I regret to say I am engaged to – I have another engagement.'

'Oh.' Mrs Fenway looked very prettily wistful and disappointed. 'Oh, could not you break your engagement, Captain Rennie? Surely it cannot be so much fun as a dance – can it?'

'Hm. Hm. It is – it is a naval matter, Mrs Fenway.' A polite little bow. 'It is kind in you to think of me, very kind, but I regret . . .'

As he came away a few minutes after, Rennie said to himself: 'A handsome woman, indeed, but a married one, William Rennie. You don't like to dance, my boy, and dancing there would be damned dangerous sport.' Climbing into his gig. 'Walk on!'

At the Mary Rose he climbed the stairs, turned towards his room, paused at the door, sniffed in a breath through his nose, and resolved his difficulties all at once:

'I cannot continue to be Birch any longer. I cannot continue at Portsmouth at all. I cannot be useful here, in any particular. I shall return to Norfolk.' A nod, another sniff, and he opened the door and went in.

'Mr Birch, is it?'

'Christ Jesu – Sir Robert.'

*

At sea, *Hawk* and *Pipistrel* in line astern, sailing steadily due east, under reefed canvas. Four bells of the second dog watch,

and the scramble and thud on *Hawk*'s deck of hammocks
down. In the great cabin, a supper in the cramped space for
Lieutenant Hayter, Commander Carr, and Mr Hope.
Lieutenant Hayter's new steward Plentiful Butt present –
having been duly entered in the ship's books immediately
prior to sailing – and squeezing his way at a crouch to serve
and remove.

'May I speak wiv you, sir?' An urgent whisper.

'No.' Curtly. 'Fetch along our next course.'

'Sir, if you please, I – '

'Did not you hear me?' Furiously.

'Sir I – ' Plentiful Butt made a dash, reached the door but
failed to pass beyond it, and was violently sick.

'Oh, Good God! You wretched, lubberly . . . go on deck!
Gentlemen, I apologize. – Mr Abey! Mr Abey! – He is . . . my
steward is new.'

'Never think of it, Mr Hayter. We are used to such things
at sea.' Mr Hope, taking a pull of wine.

'You are familiar with the sea, Mr Hope?' Commander
Carr regarded the other guest. 'I had thought you was – '

'A lubberly fellow, like the steward? Hey?' Mr Hope in
return regarded Commander Carr.

'It ain't my business, in course.' Commander Carr waved
his napkin in front of his nose in a vain attempt to disperse the
stench of vomit.

Lieutenant Hayter, at the door, standing aside from the
reeking splatters on the decking. 'Mr Abey, there you are.'

'Yes, sir. Oh . . .'

'Aye. You will find two idlers, and clear this up. At once, if
y'please. And for Christ's sake tell my steward to puke to
leeward, on deck.' As the sounds of further retching reached
them.

'Very good, sir.'

Lieutenant Hayter took up a flask of vinegar from the table
and sprinkled pungently aromatic drops liberally by the door.
Seating himself:

'I am very sorry about this.' A frowning grimace at his two guests. 'Let us continue, by all means.'

'Before we do, Hayter . . .' Commander Carr, a brief, not quite disapproving, glance at Mr Hope.

'Yes?' James waited.

'I think it must be made clear at once, as to which of us is to be in command.'

'It ain't clear to you?' Politely.

'Not at present.' A slight edge in his voice.

'Very good. Allow me to make it clear. I am in command.'

'Ah. You think that, d'you? Allow me, in turn, to make myself – '

'Commander Carr.' Mr Hope, putting down his glass.

'Mr Hope?' An impatient tilt of the head.

'Lieutenant Hayter, as the senior officer present, will be in command.'

'Senior officer! Now, look here, he has only just now took command of his first cutter. I have five years as master of mine.' A frown. 'And pray, what business is this of yours, Mr Hope? Who are you? What – '

'Kindly be quiet.'

'Eh?' Staring at him.

'I am here at the invitation of Their Lordships. This is a naval cutter, sir, and you are an Excise man.'

'You say that with contempt, sir, whoever you are. How dare you presume – '

'I have presumed nothing, Commander Carr. I have merely stated a fact. Nor have I raised my voice. I think it will be better if you lower yours, sir.'

'Well, I'm damned.'

'Nay, sir, you are not. You are a guest in one of His Majesty's ships of war.' Mr Hope raised his glass. 'Speaking of which . . .'

James, taking his cue: 'Aye, aye.' He raised his own glass, and proposed the toast. When the health of the King had been drunk, he said:

'Commander Carr, I have no wish to be in dispute with you. Surely you must understand, the Royal Navy is the senior service. It is my duty, therefore, to take command of this endeavour – '

'What of my duty? Am I to – '

'– else I should be in direct contradiction of Their Lordships' instructions.'

'Yes, instructions. Do not y'suppose that I have my *own*?'

Mr Hope removed from his pocket a small desk seal with a carved handle, and pushed it towards Commander Carr. 'D'y'know what this is, sir?'

'A gentleman's seal.' Stiffly.

'Indeed. Pick it up.' Gesturing. 'Look at it close, if y'please.'

Commander Carr picked up the seal impatiently, and glanced at it. His impatience gave way to a frown, then to a look of astonishment.

'But . . . this is a – '

'Aye, Commander Carr, it is.'

Two boys had appeared at the door with buckets and cloths, and they began the unrewarding task of mopping up.

Commander Carr sat briefly with his mouth open, became aware that it was open, and closed it.

'I – I – am I to understand that this is your own seal, sir?'

'You are. It is.'

'Then, then – I must humbly beg your pardon, Your Royal –'

'Nay, nay, plain Mr Hope, if y'please, Commander Carr. I am here to advise and assist, at Their Lordships' request, mmm . . . in a private capacity.'

'Private, Your . . . Mr Hope?'

'Mm-mm, private. The whole matter is private, in its way, you know. Nothing of this will ever be acknowledged, should questions be asked afterward.'

'Ah. Oh.'

'Mr Abey?' James, to his senior mid, who had reappeared to check on the boys.

'Sir?'

'Will you discover what the cook has achieved in regard to our next remove? Tell him we shall soon starve in the great cabin if we are not fed, will you?'

'Shall I tell him to come to you, sir?'

'No no, Richard. Send only our victuals, tell him, as quick as he likes.'

'Very good, sir.' His hat off and on, and he went forrard. The two boys finished their work, touched their foreheads, and followed. The stink of vomit had now been eradicated, the cabin was redolent of vinegar and lye, and James gave his guests more wine. Soon the cook's mate brought their main dish in a covered kid. James dismissed the man with a jerk of his head, and served his guests himself.

'Let us eat, gentlemen.'

'Indeed, let's.' Mr Hope. 'Thankee, Mr Hayter.' As his plate was filled. 'And when we have ate, let us get down to business.' Glancing at James, and at Commander Carr. 'Our business, here at sea. Hey?'

They ate, Commander Carr not quite at his ease, since he had never before broken bread – leave alone eaten sea pie – with a prince of the blood. All the gusty, blustering wind had been stolen from his sails, and he was almost entirely docile. However, fortified by the rich stew and a further glass of wine:

'You said something, sir, just now. Our business. Our business at sea. May we know your meaning?'

'We are to find and take the *Lark*, gentlemen.'

'Indeed, sir.' Commander Carr, glancing at James. 'The question is – why?'

'So it is, Commander Carr, so it is.' Regarding him. He turned his head and regarded James a moment. 'You know why, do not ye, Mr Hayter?'

'I do, sir.'

'It cannot be simply a matter of her smuggling activity, I assume?' Commander Carr did not get a direct answer to this question. Instead:

'Her master is one Aidan Faulk. Ye've heard that name?'
Mr Hope looked at Commander Carr.

'No, sir.'

'No.' A brief nod, and he wiped his lips with his napkin.
'We will like to interview with Mr Faulk, and discover –
certain intelligence.'

'When you say "we", Mr Hope,' Commander Carr met his
gaze, 'd'y'mean Their Lordships and yourself, sir? Or . . .
others?'

'Oh, Their Lordships certainly have an interest in seeing
him took.' Inclining his head. 'As to others, I will say . . . yes,
there is others wish it. You will ask me again, why. Mr Faulk
is a very resourceful fellow. An educated fellow, that might
be described as a person of independent mind. From
boyhood he loved the sea, and boats. His father had
interests in merchant shipping, and the boy was indulged in
his passion for sailing. He is now possessed of a considerable
private fortune, some of which he used to purchase the *Lark*
from – '

'From Sedley Ward,' James broke in, forgetting for a
moment that Mr Hope's not precisely truthful explication
was for the benefit of Commander Carr, who was not to be
taken fully into their confidence, but employed merely as a
useful ally should they come to action. James bit his lip. Mr
Hope looked at him very direct, and:

'Indeed, from Captain Ward, that has since died in a
tropick place. To continue . . .'

'I beg your pardon, sir.'

'To continue, Mr Faulk did first come to the attention of
your Board, Commander Carr, in regard to his smuggling
activity.'

'We have pursued the *Lark* for some time, sir – without
success. We did not know the name of her master.'

'Smuggling is a long-established practice along these
coasts. The Board of Excise does its duty, and the Board of
Customs. You Revenuers are very assiduous, I am in no

doubt.' A little shrug, a little pushing-out of the lips. 'But we know, do not we, gentlemen – if we are candid – that even the most respectable country priest, even the most upstanding gentleman farmer, ain't above acquirin' his brandy and his cheroots too, free of duty. Hey?'

'I think you are right, Mr Hope.' James smiled.

Commander Carr did not smile. He looked uncomfortable. 'We have had considerable success of late, you know, in taking some of these vessels, and the villains that sail them. It may be that people ashore find it convenient to throw the laws of the land down on the ground and stamp on them, but if they do they behave like villains themselves, by God – ' He paused, aware of eyes on him.

'Pray continue, Commander Carr.' Mr Hope, leaning forward politely.

'Well, no, sir . . . I don't know that I should like to lay down the law, so to say, to a person such as yourself. Please forgive my intemperate language.'

'Nay, Commander Carr, nay. Do not apologize, sir. You are quite right to feel as y'do. Quite right.' A glance at James. 'Ain't he, Mr Hayter?'

'Eh? Oh, yes. Yes, quite right.' Making his face stern. 'It is our sworn duty, all of us together.'

'I have heard – sometimes heard, you know – that high officials in the Revenue do not always know to an ounce and a shilling what becomes of the goods seized. Had you heard anything of that, Commander Carr?'

'I – I do not quite take your meaning, sir.'

'Do not you? Ah. Ah. No doubt I have heard wrong, then.'

'I – I could not say, sir.'

'Well, no matter. Smuggling ain't quite all of our business, anyway, this cruise. Mr Aidan Faulk is our business . . . and his other purpose.'

'Other purpose?' Commander Carr was nettled, and it showed in the flush at his neck.

'To kill good Englishmen such as yourself, Commander,

and Mr Hayter.' As if stating the obvious. 'We must stop him, the fellow, before he does any more damage. We must capture him, and discover . . . who are his accomplices in this enterprise.'

'And – and that is all the intelligence you seek, sir?' Commander Carr glanced briefly at James, then returned his gaze to Mr Hope, who made no reply. Commander Carr was an arrogant man, a man inclined always to want his own way, but he was not a stupid man, and he had begun to believe that he was being told – if not a pack of outright lies, then something very like. However, he felt that he could not say so without discommoding himself. It was very vexing to him, vexing and wounding, that his companions did not wish to take him into their confidence. Looking ahead he could see little benefit to himself in any of this endeavour, even if *Lark* were taken, and he did not like it.

The three at table ate jam roly-poly and drank their coffee, and Mr Hope wondered aloud if he might drink a glass of madeira. Embarrassed, Lieutenant Hayter was obliged to reveal that he carried no madeira aboard, nor port wine neither, nor brandy. Mr Hope smiled tolerantly, and professed indifference:

'It is no hardship to me to live on grog and biscuit, Mr Hayter, never fear. I am used to such things, never fear. I am content.'

James was stung by this remark, but he did not show it. He merely thought that his eminent guest might have been a little less dismissive of his efforts, of what had been, for *Hawk*, as near to a feast as could be managed. His guest now leaned forward, nodding and blinking, drew breath theatrically, and enquired:

'Gentlemen, have you heard the tale of the maid that tried to milk the bull? No? I will tell it you!'

Presently the two cutters hove to, Commander Carr returned to *Pipistrel* in his boat, and on the *Hawk*'s quarterdeck Lieutenant Hayter called to his sailing master:

'Mr Dumbleton, we will get under way, if y'please, and come about directly. Set me a course west-sou'-west, and let us crack on.'

'Aye, sir, west-sou'-west.'

The two cutters would now separate and diverge, and patrol the lanes calculated to be those most likely frequented by the *Lark*, at this time. Should one or other encounter her, a red rocket was to be fired at once, and rendezvous made with all speed.

Mr Hope joined Lieutenant Hayter on deck as *Hawk* came about and heeled into the westerly wind on the starboard tack. He lit a cheroot. An ember from the glowing tip wandered on the wind across the deck, and bounced off a carronade.

'He will never be easy took, you know, even when we are two cutters to his one.' Quietly, at James's shoulder.

'I know it only too well, sir. I have a scar at my neck and several others up and down my body to remind me.'

'But he must be took. He must be took and brought ashore.'

Something in his tone – of urgency, or even of fear – made James turn and look at Mr Hope. In the glow of his cheroot Mr Hope's face betrayed nothing. Smoke slipped from the corner of his mouth, and flew away over the wake.

*

A shower of rain, passing across the harbour from Gosport to Portsmouth, had left the cobbles shining in the light from the windows of the inn, and lifted from the street and the walls of the buildings a clammy odour of distemper, and old bricks, and moss. Two men emerged from the door of the inn into the yard at the rear, fastened their cloaks against the evening chill, and climbed into their hired gig. The older man took the reins, and drove out of the yard into the street, and away out of the town. Sir Robert Greer and Captain Rennie were driving to the White Hart post inn, where they would dine in a private room.

Half an hour later they were in that room, and Sir Robert, removing his cloak, indicated the chair on the far side of the small table. Rennie removed his own cloak, and sat down.

'I am glad we are to have this opportunity to dine, Captain Rennie.' Sir Robert glanced round the room, and pulled out his chair with a sharp squeak of wood against the plain boards of the floor. The room was sparsely furnished, not quite mean in appearance, with white walls, a narrow grate at the far end, and standing irons. Their light came from a pair of candles on the table, on which Sir Robert had caused to be placed a linen cloth.

'Naturally', seating himself with a momentary caution of movement, 'I should have asked you to dine at Kingshill, in other circumstances.' A brief quaver in the deep timbre of his voice as he pulled up his chair under him. 'But my house is watched.' A final little exhalation of breath as he took up his napkin.

'Watched, Sir Robert?' Rennie, warily, unwilling to be his companion's friend. 'By whom?'

'Enemies.'

Rennie waited a moment for elaboration. None came, and he took up his own napkin, and spread it. Presently, when Sir Robert had rung the table bell, Rennie sniffed in a breath and:

'I have been at Portsmouth on private business, Sir Robert. I was on the point of returning to Norfolk when you found me. If y'have decided to press the charge of treason – '

'I have not. I do not wish it.' The black eyes met Rennie's gaze, and Rennie noted – not with compassion or sympathy, only with surprise – that Sir Robert now in the candle glow looked older and thinner and less substantial than when they had last met. 'Nay, I do not.'

'I am glad of that, in least.' Drily.

'There are more dangerous and immediate things claiming my attention, Rennie, as they must now claim yours.'

A porter brought in their first course, a steaming broth, and retired on Sir Robert's nod.

'You are aware, in course, of Lieutenant Hayter's commission.' A statement, not a question. 'That is why ye came to Portsmouth, ain't it?' Breaking a piece of bread.

'On the contrary, Sir Robert. I came here – to see a lady.' With a hint of defiance.

'Eh? A lady? What lady, pray?' Sharply.

'I cannot think that is your affair, you know, Sir Robert.' Mildly enough, but with an added stare.

'She knows nothing of the commission? Of your involvement?'

'Allow me to iterate, I am here private. The lady could hardly, therefore – '

'Pish pish, Captain Rennie!' A return of the old authority and menace. 'Let us have no idle pretence between us. You go about as Mr Birch.' His spoon poised over the broth. 'Why?'

A little shrug, determined not to be browbeaten. Let the fellow do his worst.

'A man came to you in your room at the Marine Hotel, some little time since. Yes?'

Rennie looked at him, and put down his own spoon. How much did Sir Robert know? What was his purpose?

'A man that you fought with and overpowered, and later caused to have carried away from the hotel by two yardmen, under cover of night. Yes?'

Rennie waited, and said nothing. Clearly Sir Robert had informants at every level in Portsmouth.

'Yes?'

'I repeat, I came to see a lady. She is a Mrs Townend, a naval widow of Norfolk, that has took a house on the Cambridge Road. She is living there with her sister.'

'Then why d'y'call yourself Birch? Why d'y'skulk about in civilian clothes, if you have come to woo a naval widow? Hey!' Banging down his spoon beside the bowl. Broth shivered, slopped.

Rennie allowed a further moment to pass, then:

'Sir Robert, I think that you must tell me, if you will be so good, what it is you want of me. I do not at present hold a commission, but I am in course as willing as you are to serve the King. Admonition and rebuke will not bring us to our design – will they?'

This calm request and unbending tone had their effect. Sir Robert made a face, picked up his spoon and addressed his broth. Presently:

'Very well, Rennie, very well. I will not pursue you as to Birch. I do not care about Birch, and ladies in the Cambridge Road. What d'y'know of a vessel, the *Lark*?'

'I know that Lieutenant Hayter's duty is to pursue her, and take her. A smuggling cutter, ain't she?' Lifting his eyebrows in polite enquiry.

'What did you convey to the fellow that came to your rooms at the Marine Hotel? What did y'tell him about Mr Hayter?'

'I told him nothing, Sir Robert.'

'With a pistol at your head?'

'His pistol was not long pointed at my head, you know. My foot went in his testicles right quick, and the pistol became mine. I have it yet.'

'Had you any notion who the man was, when you had him carried off in the night?'

'None.'

'Very well. His name is Aidan Faulk. Perhaps y'may have seen his name on the Lieutenants' List.'

'He is a sea officer?' Surprised.

'Was. He has left the service.'

'In what circumstances?'

'That is immaterial. It is his present activity concerns us. Ye've had sight of Lieutenant Hayter's instructions?'

'Well well . . . I have.' Rennie saw no point in pretending otherwise, now.

'Then you know of my own duty in this matter, and will

understand the importance Their Lordships and the government attach to the taking of the *Lark*.'

'Clearly they attach high importance to it, Sir Robert.'

'You also know that Their Lordships wished you to assist Lieutenant Hayter in the same capacity realized by Captain Marles, before his untimely death – but could not discover your whereabouts.'

'I am aware of it, yes.' Rennie now attempted – lamely attempted, because his heart was not in it – to explain the complicated circumstances surrounding his arrival in Portsmouth, and to offer excuse for his conduct. Sir Robert cut him short.

'We will put all of that aside, Rennie, until a later time. For now, in the immediate, we must bury all difference, and work in concert. Yes?' The penetrating black stare.

'As you wish, Sir Robert.' A sniff, and a little sigh of relief and resignation. He would submit, and do as he was told.

'Very good. Now then, Aidan Faulk had intelligence that you was in Portsmouth, else he could not have found you at the Marine Hotel.'

'Sir Robert, how did you know of his visit to me? Who told you he put a pistol to my head?'

'I was able to put questions to one of the yardmen you bribed to take Faulk away. He saw the pistol, and put two and two together to produce four.'

'Ah. May I ask – how did you come to put your questions to the yardman? Surely he did not make himself known to you – '

'There is no mystery nor subterfuge.' Impatiently. 'You gave those men a guinea each, Rennie, did not you? To such men a gold guinea is a week in liquor, and liquor loosens tongues.'

A brief smile, a nod. 'My compliments to you, Sir Robert, on your many overhearing spies, at Portsmouth.'

If Sir Robert did not quite care for that remark he did not show it. A black glance, and:

'I wish you to make Aidan Faulk believe that you have information for him.'

'Eh? How am I to make him believe that, good God, when he is at sea?'

'He ain't always at sea, though. He came to you at the Marine Hotel. He comes ashore regular, is my intelligence, and he will come to you again – if you bait your hook rich.'

'But how? I have told you, Sir Robert, I kicked the fellow's privates so damned hard he fell down in a faint. No doubt he woke up very sore, in some foul ditch where the yardmen threw him. I do not think he will likely return to me, you know, under any circumstance at all.'

A brief, emphatic shake of the head. 'You do not know him.'

'I am not his friend, certainly.'

'You do not know his motive, his philosophy, his purpose. He is a very determined man. One little setback will not deflect him, and – '

'Little setback! God damn me, I near killed the poor bugger. If I was him, by God, I would not again venture near the fellow had done that to me, not before old Nick ate snow, at any rate.'

The hint of a smile on the grim face, 'Yes, in spite of your very colourful turn of phrase, Rennie, you are wrong.' The smile gone. 'He will come because what you have to offer will be too valuable to him to ignore.'

Rennie raised his eyebrows, shrugged, and was prepared to listen. Sir Robert continued.

'What I tell you now, Rennie, may be very painful to you, but please to hear me out. – You will be disgraced, and dismissed the service.'

'Dismissed – '

'You will be flung permanently on the beach, without half-pay, without a pension, without support of any kind – and no prospect of further employment, not even in the lowliest merchant brig. In little, you will be ruined.'

*

Captain Rennie was dressed in hastily purchased and slightly ill-fitting full dress uniform, and wearing a sword obtained for him on commission by Bracewell & Hyde. He straightened his stock, took a deep, sniffing breath, and went in at the door past the marine guard. In the day cabin of HMS *Zealous*, seventy-four, there faced him – with unwavering gaze, at the thwartwise dining table – four senior post captains and an admiral, and the judge advocate in his robes of office. One of the posts was Captain Langton, and his usual bluff and benign expression was today absent. His face was nearly expressionless. It was his eyes that betrayed his deep, dismayed disapproval. Rennie, who knew sea officers, saw this at once. Had this been a genuine court martial, he reflected, he would now be feeling bladder-squeezing disquiet at what he read in Captain Langton's look – but today it merely reflected the success of the subterfuge. These stalwart sea officers, grim-faced and correct in their dress coats, knew nothing of the underlying deception. So far as they were concerned the officer before them was to be tried on what they believed was a cogent and serious offence, under the Articles of War.

Rennie was to be charged, under Article Thirty-Three, with 'behaving in a scandalous, infamous, cruel, oppressive, or fraudulent manner, unbecoming the character of an officer'. A charge that, Sir Robert Greer had assured Rennie, would be wholly invented to suit their case; which would, temporarily, until it was reversed at a later hearing, result in his being dismissed the service.

Light glinted and glanced off the riding water outside the stern gallery window, and was reflected on the deckhead. The judge-advocate, a mild, pink-cheeked little man, read out the warrant authorizing the assembling of the court, and then administered the oath. The court president, Rear-Admiral Steer, took the oath last. Rennie lifted his head, playing the part of the accused with what he hoped was a certain dignity and nobility of countenance, and waited for the charge to be read. What followed shocked him to the marrow.

'You, Captain William Rennie RN, are hereby charged, under Article Eighteen of the said Articles of War, concerning the duty of officers and seamen of all ships appointed for convoy and guard of merchant ships, that on or about the – '

'Article Eighteen!' blurted Rennie, ashen-faced. 'But I – I thought that I was to be charged under Article – '

'Silence, sir!' Admiral Steer, very stern. 'You will kindly be silent whilst the charge is read out to you.'

'But there is certainly some mistake.' Rennie leaned forward earnestly. 'I was to have been charged under Article Thirty-Three, and – '

'You will be silent, Captain Rennie!' Admiral Steer, very harsh indeed. 'Else ye'll be removed from this court, and the charge read in your absence.'

'But I – I must protest. I was to have been – '

'D'y'wish me to summon the sergeant of Marines, sir? Do you? Hey!'

'No, sir.' Rennie, utterly bewildered. 'May I be permitted to – '

'Y'may not, sir. Make your back straight, and be quiet.'

'Very good, sir.' And he was silent as the charge was read. The rest of the morning passed in a blur for Rennie. Witnesses were called – seamen and warrant officers and others, none of whom he could remember ever having met, nor served with – who swore to his cowardice and flight in the face of the enemy, when HMS *Expedient*, his former command, had been commissioned on convoy duty on the Barbary shore, and the convoy lost.

The noon gun was fired, the court deliberated, the accused was brought again before them to stand and hear the verdict. He was found guilty, and immediately cashiered.

'Captain Rennie.' Admiral Steer's blue glare was no longer

quite so severe, Rennie thought. It had pity in it, now, and
perhaps even regret.

'Sir?'

'It is my painful duty to say – be gone.'

*

'Sir Robert, I demand to know why I was deceived!' Bursting
into the library at Kingshill.

'You risk coming here, Captain Rennie?' Sir Robert rose
from his chair, and gripped the edge of the desk to steady
himself. 'Did not I say to you that the house was watched?'

'Damnation to that! I demand to know why you led me to
understand I would face only a charge of misconduct, when
what I faced amounted to a capital charge, by God!'

'All right, Fender.' To his anxious servant at the door.

'How will I ever get back into the service, now? The charge
of cowardice in the face of enemy was proved! On spurious
evidence, but proved!' Pacing up and down. 'They will never
reverse that! Why did you do it, for the love of Christ! I
meant to help you with Faulk! I swore that I would follow any
scheme you devised!' Smacking his hat against his leg.

'Captain Rennie, calm yourself.' Sir Robert lowered
himself into his chair. A brief wince.

'Calm myself, y'say! It is very fine and easy for you, damn
your blood, that sit in the shadows and make puppets of us
all!'

'Take care what you say to me, sir, and be calm.'

'I shall damned well be calm when the time is right, and
that ain't now!' Flinging down his hat.

'You must in least endeavour to be temperate. Else how
may I come to explication.'

'Do not you see that by all reason and logic I am ruined!'
Rennie stopped in front of the desk, breathing furiously
through his nose. 'Not in make-believe, neither. Not in let-
us-pretend. In plain bloody – '

'Will you be silent one moment!' Sir Robert stood up, his voice booming down the room.

'Ah-hah! Yes! Now it is you requiring me to be silent!' Rennie was trembling with anger. 'It ain't enough that I should be traduced in the great cabin of a ship of the line, and endure it silent! Now I must endure it silent here! I will not! I will *not*!'

Sir Robert staggered, and again gripped the desk. A moment, a breath, and:

'Pray do not raise your voice to me in my own house.'

'Are you ill, Sir Robert?' Peering at him.

'Nay . . . but perhaps I will sit down again, though. Will you sit down?'

'I will remain on my legs, thankee.' Curtly.

'As you wish.' Sir Robert lowered himself into his chair, and took a moment to compose himself. Then lifted his black gaze, and Rennie saw with a twinge of dismay that it was as pitiless and unrelenting as ever.

'You should not have come here, Rennie. I would have come to you, in due course. Since you are here, you had better have the truth.' A moment, the black stare. 'You was traduced, as you put it, for a reason. I could not be sure of you, else.'

'What? Not sure?'

'You had to be made aware, by being found guilty of an unpardonable offence, that without my particular aid and intervention behind, you would never again serve in the Royal Navy. It could not be sham. It could not be pretence. It must needs be *real*. And now I think that you are aware. Are not you?'

'But I had already said I would help you!' Tears of rage stood in Rennie's eyes. 'I gave you my word!'

The black stare.

'Captain Rennie . . . I do not trust any man that I cannot destroy, if I wish it.'

So there it was, naked and raw. The pure malevolence of the fellow came off him like the stink of scurvy from rotted gums, and seared the air. And nothing for Rennie to do but sniff it in, and bear it.

'For Christ's sake, then . . .' not much above a whisper '. . . what is it you really want?'

'I will like you to provoke a quarrel with your friend Langton.'

'Langton? Why should I quarrel with Captain Langton?'

'He was a member of the court that found against you, and naturally you feel bitter towards him.'

'But I do not. Had I been the member, and Langton the accused, I should have found just as he did – and the others – on the evidence.'

'You feel bitter towards him,' continued Sir Robert, 'and angry. You will say all manner of intemperate things, as if you was in drink. You will say in particular that ye'd be better placed serving France.'

'But that is damned nonsense!'

'Captain Langton will know nothing of our subterfuge, and must learn nothing. He must believe you absolutely. When he objects – as he will – you will challenge him.'

'Challenge! But good God – we shall then be obliged to fight.'

'Exact. A duel will be arranged, seconds appointed, a place and time agreed. You will fail to appear. Langton will win by default.'

'Fail to appear?' Shocked. 'Fail to fight?'

'You are going to say . . . that you will be disgraced. Mm-hm.' A faint, bleak smile. 'You will.'

'Sir Robert, what you propose is very hard. To be cashiered, and then exposed as a coward, on a matter of honour . . . How can I ever show my face again?'

'It will be a very great scandal, indeed . . . and that is everything we wish for – '

'Everything you wish for, perhaps. I do not wish it, not at all. I am coerced.'

'Everything we wish for,' continued Sir Robert, unmoved.

'Aidan Faulk cannot fail to hear of it, and when you make clear – in certain places that I shall list for you – that you are prepared to do anything for money, that you will do anything to injure the Crown, anything to aid France, then Faulk will make his approach, through an intermediary, I am in no doubt.'

'I am glad that you are in no doubt, Sir Robert. I doubt the whole damned business.'

'When he does,' patiently, 'you will give him valuable intelligence, in a letter. He will duly discover its veracity, and worth. And then, Rennie, then he will arrange a meeting with you.'

'In little, you do not ask anything very much of me – do you, Sir Robert?' A sour little shake of his head, and Rennie turned away down the room.

Sir Robert watched him, and his eyes narrowed. Did Rennie mean to defy him, after all? Rennie reached the far end of the room, but he did not go out of the door there, nor even touch the handle. He hesitated, turned and came back. Sir Robert relaxed.

'I think that we will both benefit, Captain Rennie, by a glass of wine. Yes?' As Rennie approached the desk.

'I am no longer a post captain, Sir Robert. You need not call me that, any more.'

'I do so as a courtesy. And as a reminder that in spite of what you are disposed to believe, things will be made right for you in the end.' He rang a bell, and presently his servant Fender appeared. 'Madeira wine, Fender. – That is your preference, ain't it, Rennie?'

'Hemlock, more like.' Staring out of the wide window.

'Madeira, Fender.' The servant withdrew.

Sir Robert took a breath, and: 'Come now, Captain Rennie. There is no need for dark thoughts. You are not alone in this.'

'Not alone? How could I forget your presence, Sir Robert, lurking like a spider at the heart of its web, and I the hapless fly, caught on a thread.'

Sir Robert's face tightened, and his mouth set in a line –
but he said nothing.

Their wine came, but neither man felt disposed to toast the
success of their venture, nor each other. They drank in
silence. Presently Sir Robert opened a leather fold on his
desk, and took out a square of paper.

'I have wrote out the plan, Rennie.'

Rennie put down his glass, wordlessly held out a hand, and
took the sheet.

*

On the appointed day he had primed himself, not merely with
the turbulent lines written out for him by Sir Robert Greer,
but with drink. He reasoned that if he was to achieve the
appearance of drunkenness, then he had better take some
little quantity of drink, so that he was a little flushed and
smelling of liquor when he confronted Captain Langton.
Rennie dressed in his civilian clothes, consumed three glasses
of brandy, then strode down to the coffee house as the noon
gun was fired. He knew that Captain Langton would likely be
there, and he marched in at the door, head high, face florid,
Sir Robert's lines in his head.

Sir Robert had said: 'Begin with the court martial. You feel
that it was unjust. Say so, vehement and bitter. Then when you
see that Langton is present, round on him. Do not hold back.
Attack him reckless, in the most fiery fashion. You have me?'

Rennie sat at a table by himself, banging the chair out and
then thudding it in as he sat down. He decided now to depart
from Sir Robert's script a little – to be inventive. Loudly he
demanded:

'Ain't a fellow able to get attended to in this place? Or is it
too damned grand for that? Hey!' Jerking his head, glaring
about him.

'Sir?' A serving girl with a tray, looking concerned.

'Ah, there y'are. Brandy, right quick!'

'Sir, you must know that we do not serve spirits here. Only wine, if you wish it.'

'Must know! I know nothing of the kind! Brandy!'

'We has no brandy, if you please, sir. Perhaps you will like to go to an inn . . .'

'Oh, very well . . . wine, then. I will like wine. Bring it, bring it. What is your name?'

'Rose, sir.'

'Rose, Rose, I do beg your pardon.' Bowing extravagantly. 'I did not mean to bite off y'head, my dear. Damn' bad manners. My apologies.'

The girl withdrew, and Rennie pretended to see Captain Langton for the first time. He was seated with three other sea officers at a table down the room.

'Ah, there they are! The bloody Royal Navy!'

Langton glanced at him, clearly embarrassed, and at once averted his gaze. One of the other officers turned and glared at Rennie, who continued:

'Damned villainous wretches, all of you! You and your damned tribunals and courts! Justice, in the navy? Christ's blood, y'might as well expect honesty among *thieves*!'

More uneasy glances, a further glare.

'That's right, Langton, cringe! Don't think that I do not see you there, you damned fair-weather friend, you!'

The glaring officer, a stout, square post captain, now stood up and came over to Rennie's table. 'Look here, I think that you'd better desist.' Keeping his voice low, staring at Rennie very direct.

'Desiss! Desiss! Why should I desiss, you damned ninny!'

'What! By God, sir!' Very red in the face.

Rennie leaned forward, grimaced and nodded, and: 'Know what I think? Hey? I think that I should be better off serving in the French navy! Far better! D'y'know why? Because they are all *honourable men*!'

The square post captain drew breath fiercely. 'Captain Rennie, I warn you, you had best leave this place at once.'

'Who the devil are you to give me instruction, damn your blood! I do not obey the likes of you! Nor that damned poltroon *Langton*, sitting there on his arse!' Staring blearily and aggressively at the hapless Captain Langton.

The serving girl brought Rennie's wine, but was followed to the table by the proprietor, who took her elbow and whispered to her to take the wine away. The proprietor, a small, amiable, rotund man with a wisp of hair combed across the shining dome of his head, smiled at Rennie and:

'Good morning to you, sir.'

'What? Oh, good morning.' Jerking his head to squint at the proprietor.

'Supposing you and I discuss it over a splash of something in my own quarters, sir?'

'Discuss what, pray?' Rennie frowned at him.

'Whichever is the difficulty you may be having this morning, sir. Quietly, eh? In my own rooms at the rear, without unpleasantness.'

'Go to the devil.' Rising, and pushing past the proprietor. 'Langton! Do not skulk there, you bloody wretch! I will have an apology from you, sir! Aye, a public apology for my humiliation at your hands!'

Langton flicked him a now ferocious glance, then turned away.

'Nay, nay! That will not do, Langton! Do not turn your miserable back on me, sir!' Advancing on the table. 'Before I take myself off to volunteer my services to France, I will have your apology! Now, if y'please!'

And now Captain Langton stood up, turned to Rennie, and:

'You will get nothing from me! Nothing at all! Be very careful what you say next, sir!'

'Be damned to careful, you bloody lawyer's lickspittle! Apologize, and mean it too!'

'I will not, sir. I will call you out, instead! Well?'

'Ha-ha-*ha*! So I have tickled your testicles at last, eh? You are a man, after all. *Accepted*, sir! I am at your disposal, at the Mary Rose Inn!'

Rennie turned, strode, cannoned into a chair, nearly stumbled – and flung away out of the door into the street. Only when he was in the open air did he allow himself a small, shaky smile. His clothes were soaked through with sweat.

*

Rennie was shown into the library. A new-lit fire crackled in the grate, but the room was chill. The curtains had not yet been drawn. Candles glowed on the desk and in reflecting girandoles on either side of the fireplace. The glow was mirrored in the wheel barometer, and shone dully on the papier-mâché globe by the desk. Beyond great banks of books tall portraits loomed in the reduced light of the far corners. Rennie heard the click of the door, and:

'Good evening, Sir Robert. I hope that I do not disturb you, but there is a – '

'Damnation, Rennie, why have you come here again!' Sir Robert was very vexed, his face waxy as he came forward in the candlelight. 'Did not I say to you, do not come anywhere proximate to Kingshill, nor to me, until the matter is settled?'

'Aye, sir, you did. However, there is a question I must ask – '

'Come away from the window!' Sir Robert jerked the silk rope at the wide window, and drew the curtains. 'Did you confront Langton?'

'I did, sir.'

'And? And?'

'A challenge was issued, and accepted.'

'That is well, that is well. But I wish y'had not come here.'

'I took pains to be unobserved, Sir Robert. I left my gig some little distance outside the gates, and walked in by another path.'

'You do not know these people.' Darkly. 'They are capable

. . . never mind. You will go away from here at once, else you will wreck our design entire.'

'Not before I know the answer to my question, Sir Robert.' Firmly. 'Why is the *Hawk* at sea?'

'What?'

'If our design – your design, Sir Robert – is that I should meet Aidan Faulk ashore, why is Lieutenant Hayter at sea in *Hawk*, aided by a second cutter? For what purpose? When I meet Faulk you will spring your trap, will not you, and take him prisoner?'

'Indeed.' Curtly, a black glance.

'Then I repeat – why is *Hawk* sent to take him at sea, in the *Lark*?'

Sir Robert sighed, motioned to Rennie to sit, then sat down himself at his desk. The longcase clock struck the hour, the chime sounding with a cold resonance through the room.

'There is some little disagreement between the Admiralty and me, about this matter.' Sir Robert, after a moment. 'It is Their Lordships' belief that Faulk can only be took at sea. I do not concur. Lieutenant Hayter's experience, in his last encounter with the *Lark*, was a near disaster. I do not believe that *Hawk* and one additional cutter will produce the outcome Their Lordships desire. There is also the presence of Mr Hope. You know who Hope is?'

'I do not.'

Sir Robert told him, and Rennie was astonished.

'So you apprehend the importance . . .' Sir Robert continued, and he took a pinch of snuff '. . . that Their Lordships place upon this duty, at sea. I am more circumspect, Captain Rennie. I am also more practical.'

'Their Lordships will not like to hear they are not practical men, you know.'

'I do not seek open conflict with Their Lordships, nor any of their connections. I shall not provoke it. Quietly and discreetly I seek an outcome ashore, because it is more practical

than an encounter at sea. I have learned to employ simple
means, practical means, to gain a simple end.'

Rennie thought, but did not say, that Sir Robert's notions
of practical means were uncommon devious, many-layered,
and fraught with difficulty. Instead, he asked:

'Sir Robert, if you and Their Lordships differ in this, how
was you able to persuade them to sanction my court
martial?'

'Ah. Yes.' Sir Robert closed his silver snuffbox, and allowed
his head to tilt a little on one side. 'I told the Prime Minister
it was part of my grand design, and he gave me free rein to
achieve it.'

'You have the ear of the Prime Minister?'

'On occasion, on occasion. Their Lordships did oppose
your court martial, at first. The Prime Minister wrote a letter,
and said a word, and opposition fell away.' A nod. 'And so,
Captain Rennie, we shall achieve our ends together, you and
I. Yes?'

Rennie rose and took up his hat. 'I shall do my best.' A bow.
'Your servant, sir.'

'Your servant.'

*

'Captain Rennie, I have come to ask: who is to be your
second?'

'I have not yet made that decision.'

'Not yet?' The young man seemed surprised. He was Mr
Cornwell, a lieutenant of Marines, and was today in civilian
dress. He had introduced himself to Rennie in the dining
room of the Mary Rose Inn, and requested an immediate
interview. He and Rennie now occupied a private parlour at
the rear.

'Not yet.'

'But the challenger wishes to know when you will be
disposed to make yourself available. He wishes to know

whether or no pistols will be acceptable, where you and he may meet, at what hour, and upon what day. Certainly these things may not be left uncertain very long.'

'No no, you are right, Mr Cornwell.' A nod, a sniff.

'What I mean is, I cannot very well put these things to you direct. I must put them to your second. Ain't that the correct form?'

'Is it? I expect so. If you say so.'

'Captain Rennie . . . you have me at a very great disadvantage. I – I have never acted in this capacity in my life. In truth I wish that you and Captain Langton could find some opportunity for accommodation. A duel is a very wretched thing – do not you think so?'

'Has he required you to say this to me?'

'No, he has not.' A hint of indignation. 'I say it because I believe it to be true, that is all. It ain't right that two senior officers should meet in this dismal way. If I speak out of turn I do so because I do not wish to see life wasted, when a simple apology would end the matter.'

'You mean, that Captain Langton wishes to apologize to me?'

'Nay . . . t'other way about.'

'That I should apologize to him – is that your suggestion?'

'Well, yes.'

'It is a damned poor one, Mr Cornwell. Captain Langton has made the challenge. If he wishes to withdraw it, let him apologize.'

'I do not think that possible, you know. What I mean is, he feels himself the injured party . . .'

'Why did he call me out, if he did not wish to fight?' Rennie raised his eyebrows.

'I have not said that! I hope you do not think that! He is ready to fight, at any time!' Dismayed, and now very irate.

'Very good, Mr Cornwell. I will let you know. That is, that is – my second will, when I have engaged his services.'

'I see. Very well, Captain Rennie—'

'By the by, I am no longer a post captain. I am plain Mr Rennie.'

'Very good, sir. Good day.' Very stiffly Lieutenant Cornwell bowed, put on his hat, and departed.

*

Early morning, a ploughed field, the sun dew-bright on thick bordering grass. Trees on the north. A knot of men, one in the standing-out white of his shirtsleeves, under the spreading shadow of the branches. Captain Langton.

'Christ's blood, where is the fellow?' Low, to Lieutenant Cornwell at his side.

'He ain't here, that is plain.' Equally low, opening the pistol case he carried. Lying neatly with flask and mould were a pair of walnut-stocked, iron-mounted pistols. Each barrel was a heavy octagonal, with a raised sight at the muzzle.

'Are these the rifled pistols, sir?'

'They are, Mr Cornwell. Manton made them for my brother in London, five years since. Rifled barrels, four-tenths calibre, very accurate.' A breath that was half a sigh. 'Where is the bloody man?'

'D'y'know, I hope that he don't come.' Blurted.

'What!' Looking at him sharply.

'What I mean is, would it not be – '

'No, it damned well would not!'

'I beg your pardon, sir, I should not have spoke.'

Captain Langton glanced again at his second, did not respond, and paced to the edge of the field. Paced back.

They waited a further thirty minutes, until it was broad day. Swifts flitted and swooped above the field. A hare fled across the furrows and swerved away behind a clump of brush. In the distance the clacks of jackdaws, echoing on the sky.

Captain Rennie did not come.

FIVE

A choppy day in the Channel, and a gusting, blustery, uncomforting easterly, making *Hawk* pitch as she ran east close-hauled on the larboard tack. Deep-hulled as she was, and a good sturdy sea boat, she was not a large vessel, and pitching produced seasickness. Mr Midshipman Abey was pale at the gills as he stood near to the helmsman at the tiller. He had the deck, and wished he had not. Lieutenant Hayter came on deck, accompanied by Mr Hope.

'Is *Pipistrel* in sight, Mr Abey?'

'No, sir. I have not seen her all the watch.' Consulting his glass-by-glass notes, shielding them with his coat. 'Three brigs and a snow, westward bound, an Indiaman making east a league and more southward of us, fishing vessels . . .'

James nodded with a brief grimace. 'And no *Pipistrel*. Very good, thank you, Mr Abey. How does she lie?'

Richard Abey told him, James looked aloft and forrard, trod from weather to lee and back, and twice brought his glass to his eye to make a brief, quartering sweep. Everything was very damp. Spray exploded under the bow and the lee rail forrard, slewed across the deck, and foamed and slid away through the scuppers. The wind whipped angry spray off the steep, uneasy chop, and drove it in the faces of the watch on the fall. Oilskin weather, boat-cloak weather. James himself wore a pea-jacket, and a blue kerchief tied about his head. He went to the binnacle, peered at it, and strode a little way forrard towards the boat secured on its skids. He came aft, his glass pinned beneath his arm, his hands clasped behind his back.

Mr Hope waited until Lieutenant Hayter approached and stood by his side. Mr Hope was by any measure the senior man, but sea etiquette prevented him from approaching a commanding officer on his quarterdeck unless invited to do so. He thought that the lieutenant had the appearance of a piratical smuggler, but did not say so. Again by convention he waited for James to speak first.

'No sign of her.' James, shaking his head.

'D'y'mean the *Lark*?'

'Nay, I meant *Pipistrel*, Mr Hope. As to the *Lark* – well, we have not sighted anything that even remotely resembled her all the time we have been out. We have kept to our pattern of search, we have been very thorough, and one or t'other of us would have seen her, had she come near to the English coast. Hey?'

'Aye, aye. Unless she slipped by us at night.'

'I do not think that possible, you know. Until today we have had clear weather, fine nights, and as you will recall we patrolled far to the east and south in searching sweeps all through each night, both cutters.'

'Aye, we did. But 'cisemen make these sweeps regular, do not they, and rarely catch a smuggler at night?'

James glanced at him, and strode to the tafferel. Another sweep with his glass. Presently he came forrard to the binnacle, and keeping his voice low:

'Will you give me your candid opinion, Mr Hope?'

'Candid opinion? What d'y'mean, sir?'

'Are we chasing a ghost? A wraith of the waves? A will-o'-the-wisp?' A grim little smile.

'We are chasing the *Lark*.'

'Yes? Are we?'

'You know damned well we are, sir. What can y'mean by these questions, at all?'

'What I mean is, would the *Lark* risk another sea action, against two well-armed cutters, by attempting landfall on the southern coast of England – day or night? Ain't it more like

that she would sail far to the south-west, then double back
and make for – say – the north coast of Cornwall, or Devon,
or even go into the Bristol Channel and make landfall on the
northern coast of Somerset? At Lynmouth, or Minehead?'

'Minehead? I do not know that. I do not think that.'

'Then – then – perhaps she is still in England, and has
never gone away at all. Nor her commander. Had y'thought
of that, Mr Hope?'

'I had not! How long have you harboured such notions
yourself, Mr Hayter?'

James did not reply immediately. He raised his glass and
peered at the horizon from his heaving deck, bracing his feet
apart. Lowered the glass, and:

'Some little time, Mr Hope. They have not sprung at me
all at once, out of the depth of the sea.'

'D'y'propose to act upon these thoughts?'

'I think I should require some advice, and guidance, as to
that.'

'From me?'

'If you will oblige me, sir.'

'Very good. If I was you, sir, I should put it from my mind,
and do my duty as ordered.'

'I have done that these several days, sir – without result.'
Putting his glass under his arm again.

'Are not you provisioned for a fortnight and more? In case
you should have to run south, and double back, and so forth?'

'I am provisioned for a month, sir. I would be prepared to
continue these patrols, these long sweeps – day and night – a
whole month, if I thought they would likely produce the
Lark. I do not now think that probable, I am obliged to – '

'Didn't I just say to you: put doubt from your mind? Hey?
Christ in tears, sir, what business has a sea officer to question
his instructions! What pennant do you fly?'

'It is the common pennant.'

'Not an admiral's, then? Nor a commodore's broad red?'

'In course – no, sir.'

'Exact!' Looking at him very direct. 'Look t'your canvas, sir, and follow your orders. That is my advice. That is my guidance.'

James was now prepared in turn to look very direct at Mr Hope. He did so, and continued:

'That is all quite clear, sir. All according to the book, and so forth. But I wonder if you will give me your opinion?'

'Damn me, I have just done it! Did not y'hear me?'

'Sir, you gave me advice – go by the rules. I ask, will you give me your own private view, one sea officer to another?'

'Private view, sir? The Royal Navy ain't a bawdy house, with a spyhole in the wall. What?'

James tried again. 'Sir, Mr Hope, we are embarked upon a hidden, private quest, are not we? That will never be acknowledged, official? Come sir, I beg you to assist me, if you please, man to man. As an instance, what men is Mr Aidan Faulk bringing with him into England? Or . . . are these men already ashore in England, with Mr Faulk?'

'Nay, they are not, I am certain. I will grant you this. There may be some proceeding ashore, something else behind it all, that we are not party to, at sea.'

'Aha!'

'Do not be so eager, Lieutenant Hayter, to discover sinister underhand motives. D'y'think Their Lordships would send me on an idle errand? I am here because they wish me to aid you in taking Mr Faulk and his cutter. As does Mr Pitt, as does the King himself. I will like to do my duty, sir. Will ye not do yours, quiet and honourable?'

'Mr Hope, if you know more of this than I have been told, more of Mr Faulk than that he was once your junior lieutenant, I beg you most sincerely to tell what it is.' Very earnest and low, standing next to Mr Hope on the canting deck. Mr Hope clapped on to a stay as *Hawk* pitched through a steep swell.

'I can tell you naught else, sir. I cannot and may not, because – '

'Sir, I have come near to death once already in pursuit of this fellow, and I – '

'Cutter, sir!'

'Where away?' James, bringing up his glass.

'A league to the south, on the starboard quarter!'

'Two cutters, sir!' Richard Abey, his own glass focused. 'It is *Pipistrel*, I think, chasing another!'

'By God, has he got her? Has he got the *Lark*?' James braced himself, focusing his own glass. He found the two vessels on the pitching sea, held them a moment, identified *Pipistrel* by her colours, and saw at once that the chase was not the *Lark*. She was smaller and painted a lighter colour – green or grey, with a light band along her wales. A smuggler, almost certainly. He lowered his glass.

'No, that ain't the *Lark*, Mr Abey.'

'Should we join the chase, sir?'

'What is their heading?'

'Due west, I should say, sir. Ah – no – the chased cutter is breaking away to the south.'

James again focused his glass, confirmed Mr Abey's observation, and:

'I see no useful purpose in joining a chase that *Pipistrel* herself will soon abandon. T'other cutter is too fleet of foot, and will soon outrun her, and fly down to hide along the French coast.'

Mr Hope did not quite approve of this development. Gripping James's elbow, forgetting all about quarterdeck manners, he said:

'D'y'think this is quite right, sir? D'y'think you may just let a smuggler go, without even an attempt to apprehend him? Without even beating to quarters?'

James glanced down at the hand on his arm, politely drew his arm free, and once more brought up his glass.

'Yes, as I'd thought, *Pipistrel* is outrun. Carr will chase a little while to save his honour, you know, and then he will desist.'

'Ain't it our duty to take smugglers, Mr Hayter, good heaven? D'y'think the Royal Navy should stand away, sir, from any skirmish that may happen, just because it is a smuggler?'

'Mr Hope,' gently but firmly, 'I think you have forgot yourself, sir.'

'Eh? Eh?' Beginning to be irate. 'D'y'know who I am, sir? Do you?'

'You are my guest, sir, in a civilian coat, on my quarterdeck by invitation. Let us go below, and find a splash of something and a biscuit. It will do us both good.'

And he led the way to the companion hatch.

Their respite was brief. Almost before they had had time to raise a glass in the cramped little great cabin, Richard Abey came below to inform his commanding officer that *Pipistrel* had indeed broken off the chase, had come about, and was now heading nor'-east toward *Hawk*.

'Permission to go about, sir, and sail large to meet her?'

James came on deck, made a face, and at last gave a brief nod.

'Stand by to go about!' Mr Abey; and the boatswain's call rang across the deck.

The reason for James's scowling reluctance was his knowledge that Commander Carr would likely be angry. He would rush to the rendezvous, and would want to know why Lieutenant Hayter had not come to his aid in pursuit of the smuggler. Demand to know. James could not like Commander Carr and Carr could not like him. Hades could freeze solid before they would ever be friends. *Pipistrel* would heave to, and her commander come to *Hawk* in his boat, chopping rough as the sea was, in order to make known his righteous ire. It would be an uncomfortable half an hour for James – even though he was in command, even though he could and would say that his reasons for standing clear of the chase were perfectly sound and sensible. Underlying his reluctance to endure Commander Carr's contumely was his now certain apprehension that this duty, this running ceaselessly about the Channel, day and night, was a sham, an entirely fraudulent enterprise imposed upon him and Commander Carr by conspiring men ashore.

'We are bloody dupes,' under his breath. 'Both of us dupes, only Carr don't know it, and I may not tell him. So I must endure his livid wrath and scarce concealed contempt, the fellow, and be silent.'

'Are you ill, sir?' Richard Abey, peering at him in concern as *Hawk* came pitching through the eye.

'Eh?'

'You – you had such a look of agony, sir . . .'

'Agony be damned, Mr Abey. It is toothache, that is all. – *Sheet that home, there!*' Striding forrard, pointing and shouting at a seaman, very fierce.

Presently *Hawk* hove to, and *Pipistrel* came rushing up and spilled the wind from her sails. James braced himself and prepared to bite his tongue as Commander Carr's boat was lowered, and the two cutters rose uneasily, topsails aback in the Channel wind.

*

'Mrs Townend.' Rennie removed his hat, and bowed. 'My very great pleasure, madam.'

'Oh. Captain Rennie. Yes. Hm.' And Mrs Townend passed on in her bonnet and blue dress, with an embarrassed little grimace of a smile, her parasol held tight.

'That is to be my lot,' reflected Rennie, in his head. He put on his hat. 'I am now an outcast, by all reckoning, everywhere in Portsmouth.' It was wounding to see Mrs Townend – formerly so well disposed to him – turn her back on him in the High Street, but he had agreed to Sir Robert's plan and therefore could not complain when it bore the desired bitter fruit. He wished, however, that Mrs Townend could have

been made immune to his new condition. He did not like to
see dismay and disapproval in her eyes. He did not. An inward
sigh. 'It cannot be helped.'

He walked on down the High to Hatton's Coffee House,
straightened his stock, lifted his head, and went in. Within
moments he was again in the street, having been required to
leave – in fact, ejected. Tables of shocked faces had greeted
him, hostile stares and glares, and the proprietor had guided
him peremptorarily to the door.

'No, sir. No, sir. Not in here, you ain't.'

'Ain't what?' A show of protesting.

'Kindly do not enquire.' Standing aside at the door,
holding it open. 'Never a-gain.'

He tried Paley's. A sudden hush as he came in, made
emphatic by the tick of a single spoon against a dish. There
were not here the same hostile, glaring looks as among the
men at the coffee house, only averted eyes and the faintest
whisper of satin and lace arrayed against him. He glanced
round, a sardonic expression on his face, and sniffed. 'Well
well,' he said, and walked out.

His duty of public humiliation was nearly done. He would
walk along to Bracewell & Hyde, in the hope that at least one
or two, perhaps several, officers would be there, trying on
coats, or buying shirts, and that he would cause suitable out-
rage by going in. He was rewarded beyond expectation, but it
was a painful reward, by God. Captain Langton was there.

As Rennie came in to the clang of the above-door bell Mr
Bracewell came forward, a hand held up, palm out. His tape
measure fell to the floor.

'Nay . . . nay . . .'

Captain Langton saw Rennie and froze, his face rigid with
contempt. A moment, and:

'You, sir? Here, sir? When you could not keep an
appointment at another place?'

'I . . . I was delayed, unavoidable . . .' His faltering voice not
altogether contrived.

'Delayed! On a matter of honour! How dare you remain at Portsmouth, now!'

'I – I am come to see about some new shirts. May not a gentleman ask about shirts, good heaven?'

'Gentleman! Christ's blood!' And he turned away.

Mr Bracewell was very anxious and uncomfortable. 'Now, sir, dear dear . . . do not you feel that it would be better to return at another time?'

'You would welcome me back, at another time? Would ye, Mr Bracewell?'

'I would not wish to give offence. Never that, never that. But you really must *go away now*, sir, if you please. Will you?'

'I will, Mr Bracewell. Thank you.' Rennie gave him a sad little smile and nodded to him, and went out to the mocking clang of the bell. It rang in his ears all the way back to the Mary Rose Inn, and his heart was shrivelled in his breast by what he had been obliged to do this morning. When he came to the inn Mr Little was waiting outside the parlour. In his hand he held an itemized account, newly written in black ink. He coughed, half-apologetic, half-defiant, and:

'I am – I must ask you to settle your bill, sir.'

'Settle my bill, Mr Little? It ain't the end of the week, is it, already?'

'No, sir. Howsoever, I must ask that you settle your bill at once, if you please.' Firmly, meeting Rennie's puzzled gaze. 'I require the room for another gentleman.'

'What! Require the . . . d'y'mean I am to leave the Mary Rose?'

'I do, sir. I has allowed the room to another gentleman, that wishes to occupy it at once.'

'But this is beyond all . . . Mr Little, have I not paid my way here, week by week?'

'I cannot help that, sir. The room is let to another gent, fair and square. You must pack up and depart, right quick.'

'But *why*, Mr Little? What have I done to offend you?'

'You knows all about that, sir, I reckon. You knows very

well. I cannot have my hostelry made mock of, and lose my livelihood, because of one person, look.'

'But you have just told me ye've already rented the damned room to another man! How d'ye square that with losing your livelihood, good God?' With counterfeit fury.

'I cannot help that, I cannot help that. You must pack up your dunnage and clear out quick!'

'You bloody scoundrel! I've half a mind to – '

'Now then! Now then! Don't you raise your voice to me, Captain Rennie! You are a disgrace, and you knows it! Must I call the constable? Must I call for protection against your cowardly violence? Eh?' Retreating to his parlour with an alarmed snarl, and ringing a bell vigorously.

'Very well, very well.' Rennie feigned defeat, and held out his hand for the bill. 'Give it to me, damn you. I shall pay, and get out. I do not wish to live in a nest of rats.'

Twenty minutes later, his valise by his legs outside, Captain Rennie was homeless, friendless, and in spite of himself – so convincingly had he mimicked the bitter poltroon – very nearly overcome by misery.

Rennie found a room at the Drawbridge Inn at the Point, where the landlord Sawley Mallison was tolerant of any and all persons, irrespective of their social standing, providing they could pay, and did not set fire to their beds. Conditions were primitive, but apparently clean. In fact the rooms were infested with beetles and other vermin, and Rennie took care to sprinkle vinegar into the corners, and cologne liberally upon his pillow.

'I cannot abide itching filth,' he muttered as he took his shirts from his valise, looked round for a cupboard or chest of drawers, found nothing, and put them back.

'Christ in tears . . .'

Later, in the taproom, he again feigned drunkenness – as he had at the coffee house several days since – spilled gin, shouted, and fell down. Got up on his legs, and:

'I should be better served in the French Navy! Better served by serving *France*!'

He stumbled out into the night and further into the stinking Point, where he found another tavern, the Pewter, and went in. Here he made a similar spectacle of himself, and again declared himself for France.

'Who will join with me?' he demanded. 'Lan'lord! Brandy for any and ev'ry man that will come with me to France! Where there ain't damned foolish, meek and pus'llanimous bowing-down to those that don't d'serve it, by Chrice! A free, decen', hon'rable people, an hon'rable country, with a navy serving the people!'

'You wishes to go to France, does you, mate?'

A large presence at his elbow.

'I do, sir. Indeed, I do!' Pretending to lurch and squint. 'Will you join with me – '

Thud.

A great knuckled fist flew into his temple and crushed flat his ear with sickening, brain-numbing violence. In the buzzing blur of the air as Rennie fell – a hoarse, scornful voice:

'Let that send you on your way then, you bloody dog!'

He regained consciousness in a place unknown to him, by candlelight.

'You are awake, Captain Rennie?' A figure against the light.

'Who are you . . . ? What is this place . . . ?' Groggily attempting to sit up. Waves of pain flowed round and enveloped his skull. 'Ohh . . .'

'It is a dwelling, sir. You are safe, and among friends.'

'Friends . . . ?'

'Shall we say . . . friends of friends?'

'Ah. Ah.' Lying back against piled pillows. The bed was narrow, but comfortable.

'It is possible – when you are rested and recovered – that as your friends we may very likely be able and willing to do you a service.'

'Service? What d'y'mean? Ohh . . .' as he again attempted to sit up, to see the hovering, shadowy figure silhouetted against the candlelight. Rennie clutched his throbbing head, and felt an egg at his temple. 'Ohh . . .' as he tried to swing his legs to the floor.

'Nay, do not trouble yourself to get on your legs just yet, Captain Rennie.' A restraining hand. 'You have been battered, and knocked senseless. Drink some of this now, will you?' A cup was proffered.

'What is it?' Suspiciously, sinking back on the pillows.

'Tea, sir. A beverage you favour, I think.'

'Ah, tea. Thankee, I do.'

He took the cup and sucked down the grateful brew. Only when he had drained the cup did he reflect: What if the tea was poisoned? But he did not say it aloud.

'Another cup?'

Rennie shook his head, and wished he had not. It nearly fell off.

'Will you like to eat something, Captain Rennie?'

The thought of food repelled him, and:

'Thank you, no. Where is this house? At Portsmouth?'

'Near to Portsmouth, sir.'

'How did I come here?'

'You were brought, Captain Rennie. We brought you, in a carriage. Your friends.'

'Why?'

'Because we wished to aid you. As you may wish to aid us.'

'Aid you? How so? I do not know you.' Peering again at the figure. 'I cannot see your face.'

'No? Perhaps that is well, for the present. Until we are – shall we say? – mutually confident, each in the other. No?'

Rennie thought he could detect a slight accent, the merest hint that this man was not English. Perhaps, in his fuddled condition, he was imagining it.

'You do not trust me, even when you say I am to aid you? You know who I am, sir, but I do not know who you are – or what you may want of me. That ain't a square bargain, hey?'

'Ha-ha, perhaps not.' Neutrally.

'In course, I am greatly in your debt, for rescuing me. I must thank you for your kindness in doing so, and for bringing me here to safety and comfort. May I know your name . . . ?'

'For the moment, I prefer – we prefer – that you should simply know us as friends. Names will come into the bargain later, you see?'

'Nay, I do not. I am a plain-speaking sea officer, sir, and –'

'Captain Rennie.' Iron had come into the voice – not quite menace, but a hardened edge.

'I am here . . .' Politely.

'Captain Rennie – you are not a serving sea officer any more, are you? You have been thrown out of the Royal Navy, have not you?'

'Evidently, you know that I have.'

'You have been disgraced, and then disgraced again. No?'

'I was tried unfair, and unjust. In their eyes I was disgraced. Not in my own.' Defiantly.

'Ah, but you were also involved in an affair of honour. No?'

'I don't know what you mean . . .'

'Do not you?' Again the hard edge. 'I think that you do, sir. You provoked a quarrel, and were subsequently challenged.'

'Ohh – that. That was – it was nothing, a misunderstanding.'

'A misunderstanding! A challenge issued, and accepted, and then not met?'

'I tell you, it was a misunderstanding. I was in my cups, you know, and said things I ought not to've said . . . that is all.' Feigning great embarrassment.

'Ah, yes, I see. Then – perhaps we cannot aid you, after all. You had, as I understood, made certain statements about wishing to leave England, and go elsewhere. No?'

'Well well – I may have done.'

'You no longer wish for this?'

'Well well – perhaps I do wish it.' A sharp breath, and he gripped the other's arm. 'Listen now, I have been poorly treated. Very hard used. I had thought I would always be treated fair and decent by my own service, but I was traduced, and deceived, and spat upon! Aye, that is not too extravagant a description. Spat upon, and kicked, and cursed, like a damned mongrel cur! Well well, we shall see about that, by God!'

'Yes, Captain Rennie? How?'

'I – I may have certain intelligence, that I may be willing to share with certain persons.'

'Intelligence? Yes? What does it concern? How to fight a duel?'

'I thought y'said you was my friend!'

'I thought you were ours. Now – I do not know. If you will not even admit to your mistakes, how can we trust you? How can we know that you will tell us the truth?'

'Listen, that damned duel was not my doing! Captain Langton deliberately provoked me by finding against me at my court martial, and then *he* issued the bloody challenge, as if *he* was the injured man!'

'Why did not you challenge him?'

'Why should I do that, hey? Why should I accommodate him?'

'That is a curious way of looking at the question. No?'

'No.'

A brief silence, then:

'Will you tell me – what is this intelligence you wish to share with us?'

'Ah, well, if we are getting down to cases – I should in course need something in return.'

'Money?'

'Money? You insult me, sir.'

'I do? How very unfortunate. I should not wish to provoke a quarrel. What is it you do wish for, exact?'

'Safe passage elsewhere, and a commission.'

'Do you mean a reward, or a position?'

'Naturally, I seek a position. A commission.'

'For money?'

'Oh, good heaven, this is poor stuff! D'y'wish to make a bargain, or no? Ohh . . .' His head spun horribly, and his stomach lurched in answer. He nearly puked, and was obliged to lie back against the pillows again.

There was no immediate response to this outburst, then a sigh and a shrug, and:

'I do not know. I cannot say, just at present. I must consult with my friends, and then let you know.' The silhouetted figure turned, hat in hand as if to leave, and hesitated. 'Unless . . . unless you were willing now, tonight, to give me some little hint, some little part of the information you hold, as a gesture of good intent. Hm?'

Here at last was the vital moment Sir Robert Greer had anticipated and planned for. The baiting of the hook.

Rennie in turn let out a sigh, a sigh of capitulation. 'Very well.'

The figure put aside the hat, came close to the bed, leaned over it. 'Pray proceed, Captain Rennie . . .' Nothing of iron now in the tone, only carefully restrained eagerness.

'Two cutters presently seek a certain party, in the Channel. They are *Hawk* and *Pipistrel*. They are to be joined very soon by six more, making a squadron of eight, under the command of Lieutenant Hayter RN. The Royal Navy is entirely determined to take this party, and his vessel. The navy will not rest until this has been accomplished.'

'When will these new cutters come to the aid of the others? How soon?'

'Within the week. They are presently being armed with new guns – carronades – and stored with extra powder. They are to be manned by hardened crew, all with experience of sea action, and well able to fight those guns. It will be a formidable force, I fear, against one vessel.'

'How have you come by this information, Captain Rennie? You are a disgraced officer, an officer cast out.'

'Yes, I am disgraced. But as I told you, only in official eyes. I am not without friends in the navy, I am not without connection.'

'There are others in the navy who think as you do?'

'Many.'

'So?' Again that hint of eagerness.

'Aye, many.'

'Thank you, Captain Rennie. Pray return to your inn, and wait there. I will convey this item of intelligence, and we will communicate with you in due course.'

'You wish me to leave at once?'

'When you are rested, when you recovered. A carriage will take you. Ring this bell, when you are quite ready. And now I must leave you. Goodnight.'

'Goodnight. And thank you for your kindness.'

'Nay, sir – thank you for yours.'

*

The Drawbridge Inn at the Point in Portsmouth was a low-built, part-timbered, grimy structure, with lead-mullioned lights and sturdy timber door. It stood as its name suggested immediately adjacent to the wooden bridge spanning the moat between the town side and the island of the Point. The door had been replaced three times, occasioned by raids on the tavern by constables, revenuers and others, in pursuit of miscreants among patrons, or 'clients' as the landlord Sawley Mallison liked to call his guests. It was now a door made of oak – some said oak recovered from a shipyard – studded with heavy nails. There was a cobbled yard at the rear, and a low entrance to one side that led through pantries and the kitchen to the interior. This entrance was in usual barred, and locked.

The taproom was at night blue with tobacco smoke and rumbling with the din of voices. Light came from lanterns hung from beams above, and the atmosphere was not unlike that of the lower deck of a ship of war, with hands piped to their dinner at the messes. Save for the pipe smoke, reflected Captain Rennie as he made his way through the rows of rough tables towards the figure of Sawley Mallison at the rear.

'Mr Mallison.'

'I am 'ere.' Turning his good eye on Rennie. His other eye was walled white. He removed his clay pipe from strong yellow teeth. Grey-flecked hair grew low on his forehead, emphasizing his one clear eye and giving him a distinctly simian appearance. But Sawley Mallison was no slow wit. Here was a man of high acuity and understanding, as Rennie had begun to learn.

'Mr Mallison, I am expecting a letter. I will like it that you inform me the moment it comes.' He fumbled, found a coin, and was about to pass it when a strong hand closed over his, and:

'There ain't need to pay me each time you was wanting a simple service, sir. I looks out for naval men, always.'

'Ah. That is kind in you, Mr Mallison.' Lowering his voice a little. 'I am – I am no longer in that service, however.'

'I knows all about that, Captain Rennie. You was done down, sir. Put your money away, now. I shall send word to 'ee, soon as letter comes.'

'Very good, thankee, Mr Mallison.' Putting the coin away in his pocket, then bringing it out again. 'May I give you a glass of something?'

'Oh, well, now. That I will not resiss, no. Bliss!'

'Sir?' The potboy, pausing with tankards.

'Brandy, Bliss, two glasses, corner table. Sharp.'

The boy nodded, and dodged away between tables, slopping ale. Mallison led the way to a small table in a corner, away from the great seething of the room. They sat down, and Mallison lit his pipe with a taper from the candle. He offered his pouch to Rennie.

'Smoke, sir?'

'I don't, thankee. My vices are tea and alcohol only.' A nod, politely. He was not quite at home in the taproom of the Drawbridge.

'Would you prefer tea now, sir?'

'Nay, Mr Mallison, I will like a splash of something else, at night. Brandy, indeed.' Another nod.

'I knows this ain't your notion of a pleasant place to stop, sir.' Mallison sucked on his pipe, then put it aside. 'But you need never fear while you is under this roof.'

'You are very kind.'

'I knows your surgeon very well, see.'

'My surgeon? Dr Wing, d'y'mean?'

'Aye, Tom Wing is my old friend. He has come 'ere many a time, when one of my clients was poorly. Other surgeons would not like to come 'ere, not in darkness like. When Tom was prenticed over to the Haslar, he would come always, if asked. Many a time he has stopped 'ere a night or two. A gent, is Tom.'

Rennie thought a moment, and did vaguely recall the connection from a previous commission, when Dr Wing's dunnage had been collected from the inn, and brought into the ship. Recalled too, with a pang of shame, that he had pronounced Mallison a scoundrel, and the Drawbridge a place of iniquity.

Their brandy had come, and Mallison poured two glasses. 'Your health, Captain Rennie.'

'Your health, Mr Mallison.'

And as the fiery spirit ran down his throat Rennie felt his own spirits rise a little, for the first time in many days.

The letter came not at night, but in the morning, by an errand boy, who did not wait for a reply, only demanded his penny and was at once gone into the grimy bustle of Broad Street. Rennie read the letter – by invitation – in the landlord's own small parlour, where he drank a pot of strong dark tea.

'Will you take a drop in your tea, sir?' Mallison offered his flask.

'Thankee, no. This is excellent tea, excellent tea.'

'Aye, and I never gives a farthing more for it than I must, neither.' Tapping his broad nose. 'I will leave you to read your letter, sir.'

When Mallison had gone Rennie unfolded the letter, and to the muffled sounds of the landlord cursing his potboy in the taproom beyond, he read:

Dear Colleague,

We wish to know details of new vessels to be employed in pursuit of another. To wit:

Tonnages of each vessel
Rigging & sail plans
Number of guns
Numbers of crew

Exact dates of deployment

Present deployment of vessels already in service

Proposed plan of action should our vessel find herself outrun by the new increased deployment. Take her? Or sink, burn, destroy? Take her master alone? Take her people also, or dispose of them?

Please to respond in writing, and the boy will call again in the forenoon tomorrow.

You must be mindful, dear colleague, that upon your accurate & detailed reply will depend all else, inclusive of yr safe passage to another place.

A friend

Rennie remained indoors at the Drawbridge all the day,

and drafted a careful reply, according to Sir Robert Greer's plan, and with some additional refinements of his own invention. At length he had a suitable text, and wrote it out diligently – as diligently as he would have written one of his formal letters to the Admiralty, at sea.

My dear Friend,

I thank you for your most welcome letter of yesterday's date, and the proposals therein.

I am obliged to say at once, for yr own protection, that I am loth to send all of the details & particulars you require by the hand of a boy.

I will like to bring these particulars to you by my own hand, not merely as a safeguard, to obviate impairment to their delivery by interests inimical to our design; I have, in another distinction, further information I wish to give you, in the form of a most heedful, intricate and safe route of departure, whereby all hazard and difficulty may be put aside.

I send this by the boy, but dare not entrust to his immaturity anything more of my intention & purpose.

In the most earnest hope & expectation that you will look favourable on this proposal, I await yr earliest response.

I will only add that in course I am willing to come to you at any hour, at yr convenience.

I remain, sir, yr most humble & obedient servant,

A colleague

On the morrow Rennie waited at the inn all the morning, and the boy did not come. He waited until the evening, and then ventured out for a breath of air – as relief from the stale and foetid fug of the taproom, and the sparse solitude of his room upstairs – with the earnest injunction that if the boy came there in his absence he was to be detained until Rennie's return.

He walked along the fortifications in the gathering darkness, saw the lights of the Gosport shore, and the riding lights of ships at anchor, and smelled the wind coming off the sea. The evening was unseasonably chill. Rennie shivered, turned up the collar of his coat, and imagined himself on the canting deck of the *Hawk*.

'What will James be thinking, now?' he asked himself. 'Will he wonder at his instructions, his duty? Yes, very probably he will – since he ain't a fool, and will put two and two together when he don't find the *Lark*. He will do his duty, all the same, as I would in his shoes . . .'

He shivered again, hunched into his coat, and walked back to the Point. When he reached the Drawbridge Inn, Sawley Mallison took him aside in the taproom, cupped a hand and in a brandy-wafting husk spoke in Rennie's ear.

'There's a gen'man to see you, sir. Urgent, in the parlour.'

'Who is it? Did not the boy come?'

Mallison shook his head. 'He did not. Gen'man's name is Scott.'

'Scott?' Mystified. 'I know no one of that name . . .' Had the fellow come in the boy's place?

Rennie made his way to the parlour door, and went in. He saw no one, and then heard the door click shut behind him.

'Captain Rennie.'

Rennie turned sharply, and saw a man in a shabby brown coat and breeches, and plain buff stockings and worn shoes. His face was half-hidden beneath a brown hat in the subdued light – until he came forward and removed the hat.

'Good God – Sir Robert!'

'Indeed. Shall we sit down?'

Rennie saw that on Sawley Mallison's little parlour table a tray had been laid, with a jug of wine, glasses, and a plate of biscuits. The fire had been stoked in the grate, and a new candle lighted. They sat down, and now Rennie remembered.

'We have met before in this way, Sir Robert, have not we?'

'Indeed, Rennie, we have. Years since, at the Marine Hotel,

when I had adopted this same disguise in pursuit of my various aims, you came to me there, in a private parlour.'

'Exact, I did.'

Sir Robert poured wine, offered biscuits. 'I will like to know what progress ye've made, and why there has been so great a delay in communication.' The black gaze.

'I am awaiting upon a reply to my letter, sent by hand yesterday.'

'You made a copy of the letter?'

'Ah – no. I had – '

'No copy! Did not I tell you most particular, you must make a fair copy of anything sent? Hey!'

Rennie began to bristle, checked himself, and instead of a snappish reply he said:

'I have kept the original letter, that came to me here.'

'Show it to me.' Putting down the jug and holding out an impatient hand.

Rennie brought the folded letter from his coat, the broken seal catching in the pocket and sending a crumble of red wax on the floor. He gave the letter to Sir Robert, who perused it with a frown.

'Very well. Now then, tell me accurate – line by line – what you have said in reply to this.'

Rennie told him, and Sir Robert listened intently, head cocked on one side. When Rennie had finished:

'Very well. I do not quite like your embellishment about the route of departure, and so forth, but no matter. If it will aid us in arranging a meeting between you and Faulk, then your work will have been done, and our design accomplished.'

'Thank you, Sir Robert.' Inclining his head in what he hoped was not too ironical a manner, damn the fellow. 'However, there may be an impediment . . .'

'Yes?' The gaze.

'When I was brought back here – did I tell you of this? – when I was conveyed from the house where I was took after the brawl in the Pewter Tavern, I was blindfolded, so that I would not know the location of the place – '

'D'y'mean – where Aidan Faulk was? He was there, himself?'

'I do not know that it was Faulk. I could not see his face, Sir Rob—'

'You was at his hiding place! You was took there! And did not contrive to get word to me! Good heaven, Rennie, the wretch might have been took! This whole episode might now have been concluded, and Faulk in chains!'

'Sir Robert,' with great forbearance, 'I was carried there unconscious from the Pewter Inn, and woke very hazy in a low-lit room – '

'Surely y'could have contrived to escape! Surely y'could have sent word! Why do I learn of this only now, tonight?' Sir Robert turned away down the little room, and stood with his hands clenched at his sides. Turned back with a piercing dark furious glare.

'I wonder if I have not chose the wrong man in you, Captain Rennie. The wrong man entire, for this exacting work. You are not a man of high education, nor under-standing, nor enterprise. You are found wanting, in the nation's interest. Timid, faltering, and inept.'

And now Rennie could contain his anger – his furious anger – no longer. All the duties, pressures, requirements and stipulations lately placed upon him, in all their exhausting cost to him, to his very sanity, now welled up and surged in a tide from his breast into his head. Sir Robert came to the table, and opened his mouth to say something more, and Rennie:

'Damn your infernal cruelty and impudence, sir! Nay *nay*! Do not utter a single further syllable, or by God ye'll know the consequence! *D'y'hear me?*'

In spite of himself, of the great inner conviction of his power and position, Sir Robert was given pause by the bitter ferocity of Rennie's outburst. He took a step back, quite involuntarily, and opened his mouth to reassert his authority. Before he could say a single word:

'Did not I say, *do not speak*, damn your blood! You will allow me – by God, you will – to tell you my only proposal as to this affair! I absolve myself from it! Aye, absolve!'

Sir Robert closed bloodless lids over his black eyes, a gesture he had used to great effect in many past circumstances where his authority must needs be imposed upon unruly naval men. Closed them, and raised an imperious hand, and drew a deep breath. However:

'*Hush! Hush, sir!* Do not have the temerity to speak to me, until I allow it! I absolve myself, release myself, find myself at liberty entire! And you may do your worst, sir! Threaten, and condemn, and have me bound in chains, instead of your damned quarry Aidan Faulk! I do not care! I am no longer your slave, your snivelling, complaisant, gutter-low creature! Y'may go to the devil, and may he welcome you with open arms, too, you miserable savage, for you and he are *blood brothers*!'

And Rennie turned away, trembling from head to foot, and flung out of the door of the parlour, thrust, pushed, strode headlong through the crowded taproom, spilling ale, knocking aside chairs, shouldering away larger and stronger men, who fell back from this raging madman and let him whirl away out of the great oak door into the night.

Sir Robert stood silent in the parlour, rooted to the spot a moment, staring at the open door. At last he gathered himself, and:

'That is the consequence of allowing a fool free rein. I will not allow it again.'

Sir Robert put the letter away in his coat, took up his hat, and presently slipped away through the taproom unremarked.

*

When the storm began to blow up Lieutenant Hayter quickly decided to run for shelter, and declared his intention to Mr Hope, who had come on deck.

'I shall run into Weymouth and ride out this weather in the bay.'

'Run?' Over the rising wind.

'It makes little sense to risk *Hawk* now, when *Lark* ain't in these waters.'

'It is out of the question, out of the question.' Mr Hope shook his head vexedly, clapped on to a stay as a frothing sea surged over the deck, and continued: 'This is just the kind of weather *Lark* has waited for, to make her dash. This will be your best opportunity to take her, Mr Hayter, when the energies of her people are wholly occupied in keeping her from broaching to.'

'Energies of –' James looked at him to make sure that he was not being facetious, saw that he was not, and shook his own head. 'Mr Hope, I must consider the energies of my own people, and Commander Carr's. Aye, and their lives, too. I will not like to risk them riding out a fierce Channel storm on the open sea.'

'Pish pish, an ordinary merchant cutter will not have nearly the same number of men in her as a naval cutter. We have forty men, the *Lark* has half that number, and she is a bigger vessel, and therefore harder to handle.'

'Twenty men? To fight all that number of guns? Ho, I think not. I think she will have the same number of men as –'

'I will not argue with you, Mr Hayter.' His voice rising with the wind. 'We will continue the chase.'

'Chase! What bloody chase? We have never seen the *Lark* yet, this cruise!'

'Did not y'hear me, sir!'

'I cannot chase a vessel ain't to be seen!'

'You defy me, sir? Knowing who I am?'

James shook his head again, drew breath, opened his mouth, but before he could speak:

'Knowing what I am capable of, in the question of your future activity in the Royal Navy? Hey? You oblige me to be blunt, sir. Very blunt. We'll continue the chase, Lieutenant Hayter, or by God I'll chase your arse so far inland ye'll never sight the sea again, sir, so long as you live!'

James's blood boiled in his heart, surged searing through his veins, and threatened to flush all self-protective reasoning out of his head. He became aware that the helmsman was looking at him with an astonished expression, which disappeared as soon as James looked directly at the man. But James had seen that expression, and had realized at that moment how intemperate this quarrel had become, how loud and public a dispute, recklessly embarked upon on the quarter-deck of one of His Majesty's fighting ships.

'Mr Abey!'

Richard Abey came from the binnacle, where he had retreated in embarrassed consternation.

'Sir?'

'Starboard tack, heading east-south-east, and a point east!' Cupping his hand as the wind gusted in a stay-whistling howl, and the cutter heeled. 'We will further reduce the mainsail by another reef. Make tight those hanks, Mr Abey.'

'Aye, sir. East-sou'-east, and a point east. Third reef in the mains'l.'

'Mr Hope.'

'I am here.'

'Kindly go below, sir, if you please.'

Mr Hope glanced with grim approval across the deck and briefly aloft as *Hawk* began to run large away from Weymouth, and safety. The chase would continue on the open sea, according to his wishes. He nodded once, did as he was asked, and went below.

When *Hawk* had settled on her new heading, James again summoned Richard Abey.

'Make to *Pipistrel* that she is to come about and hold station astern of me.'

'Aye, sir.'

'And Richard . . .'

'Yes, sir?'

'Foul-weather jackets on deck. We are all going to get very wet and cold, this day.'

'Very good, sir.'

'And lifelines. We will rig lifelines, fore and aft.'

The wind increased in strength through the afternoon watch, and at seven bells, when *Hawk* would soon be obliged to go about and beat into the teeth of the gale, else be driven in on the shore of France, at Dieppe, Lieutenant Hayter was again on deck. The wind was now fierce, bringing with it squalls of rain and a heavy, surging swell. Spray whipped off the waves and smashed across the deck like a hail of canister shot. *Hawk* scudded across the sea, with *Pipistrel* half a mile astern of her.

'Mr Abey!'

'Sir?' Attending, hunched down into his jacket against the scattering spray and rain.

'We must beat into this storm of wind now, on the return leg. Make to *Pipistrel* that we will go about and head west.'

'Aye, sir. Stand by to go about!'

Further shouted orders, the boatswain's call, and seamen ran aloft in the shrouds to shake out the reefs in the topsail. Flags on the signal halyard, snapping and streaming. A boy being sick over the lee rail as *Hawk* pitched, plunged, rolled round on the new heading, and the sea swirled about the boy's feet and legs as he clung there, racked and saturated.

'God damn and blast this miserable cruise,' muttered James to himself. He brought his flask from inside his jacket, and took a pull of burning, lifting, unwatered rum.

By the end of the first dog watch the storm had become so violent that even Mr Hope was obliged to concede that no chase was now possible, and that to seek shelter was perhaps the wisest course. He went up the little companionway ladder and on deck, to seek out Lieutenant Hayter. He found that

James had anticipated him, and was about to give the order. He would attempt to head north to St Helen's Road, and seek shelter there in the lee of the Isle of Wight, beyond the Foreland.

'Would it not be wiser to run east, and go into the Downs?' Mr Hope, shouting over the wind.

'I will not like to sail east, sir. There is too great a risk of going aground at Beachy Head, or Dungeness. I must attempt northing, and shelter at St Helen's.'

An immense sea – freakishly steep and wide – came running at *Hawk* from the west, and just as it reached the cutter she dipped her head, and pitched her flat-steeved bowsprit deep into the wave. Lifelines had been rigged fore and aft, but Mr Hope had not clapped on, and as the heavy surge of water rode along the deck, burying everything under it in a green massy seething, Mr Hope was lifted bodily and flung against the tackle block of the mainsail sheet. His head smacked against the block with a nasty thud, he tumbled slackly away under the great boom, was washed against the lee rail, and sucked face down forrard as the sea retreated.

'Christ Jesu!' James clung to the lifeline, kept his head above the wave, found his feet and lurched across the deck to where Mr Hope lay senseless, one hand caught under him, the other flung half across the rail, water sluicing in a sluggish swirl away.

'Bring her head up! Keep your luff!' Bellowed at the helmsman, himself half-drowned.

James knelt, heaved, got Mr Hope into a half-sitting position, and with great effort got his shoulder beneath one of his arms, and lifted him up. The movement caused Mr Hope to spew a great gush of water over James, and to cough and gasp. His head lolled, he groaned, but was still a dead weight. A further sea – lesser than the first, but still considerable – now flooded aft, and water poured down the companion hatch. The wind roared mad in the rigging, and buffeted the deck.

Mr Abey emerged from the companion and fought his way on deck, streaming and hatless, and at once saw his commander's need. Together they got Mr Hope below, where everything was very wet. Dr Wing was summoned, and in the cramped, lurching, confined space attended to their guest. James again went on deck, accompanied by Midshipman Abey. Michael Wallace, the junior mid already on duty, was very green about the nose and mouth, but was on his legs.

'Mr Wallace!' James, shouting over the wind.

'Sir?' Bravely lifting up his head.

'Make to *Pipistrel* that she is to form up close astern.'

'If you please, sir, I cannot see *Pipistrel*.' Over the wind.

'What?' Looking at him, then away astern.

'She is not there, sir.'

James braced himself at the tafferel, and stared hard astern on the rise of the sea. The boy was right. There was no sign of *Pipistrel*. He waited, and the following rise looked again for the Excise cutter, briefly bringing up his glass to sweep. He found nothing but the heaving, rolling sea. *Pipistrel*, plainly in sight not half a glass since, had vanished.

'By God, it was that tremendous sea . . .' Muttered to himself. 'Unless he has run east.' James jumped forrard and into the shrouds, hooked an arm through and swept with his glass. There was no sign of *Pipistrel* away to the east, neither, only the tumbling, spray-billowing wilderness of the storm.

'She has foundered.'

He descended to the deck. In these conditions there was no hope of picking up survivors. There would be no survivors. The only hope now was that *Hawk* herself could be saved.

'Stand by to tack ship!'

*

Rennie had walked for several miles in and about Portsmouth after storming out of the Drawbridge Inn, striding along, head bent, oblivious of streets, fortifications, towers, the

Dockyard; of people, time, circumstances. In his head and breast were turmoil and rage, and a dark, desperate melancholy that burgeoned and swelled until it subsumed all else of his mood, and became his humour entire.

'What is my life?' repeated again and again as he tramped heedlessly over cobble and stone and chaff-strewn flint. And answered himself again and again – unconsciously aloud, believing it was all in his head:

'My life is all a waste. It is nothing. I have lost everything a man might value, everything he might esteem, and love. What is my life? I lost my one chance of happiness when my dear wife was took from me. I lost my ship. I lost my career. I will never get back these things. My life itself is lost, except in animate activity – and that is nothing, it is only mechanical. My life is nothing, a hollow, dismal list of nothings and nothingness, a purser's book of nothings, by God. – What is my *life*? *Nothing!*'

'Are you quite well, sir?'

'What?' Startled.

'Are you quite yourself?' A constable, peering at him, lantern raised.

'What?'

Rennie had paused at the corner of a narrow alley and a larger street. He had no idea where he was.

'You was speaking quite loud, sir. Only I did not see your companion, like.'

'Companion? I am alone.'

'Yes, sir. Yes.' Nodding. 'I see that, now.' A discreet sniff. 'Took drink tonight, sir, has you?'

'Drink? What?' Stepping back from the lantern. 'I am alone, walking alone, and perfectly sober. What d'y'want of me? Hey?'

The constable heard the tone of authority in these retorts, and knew that he was dealing with an officer.

'Nay, sir, I do not want nothing at all. Only – please to talk less ve-hement, if you will be so good, eh?'

'What? I am sober, and silent.'

'Yes, sir. Only this is the Cambridge Road, very peaceful at night. Was you seeking a partic'lar place? A partic'lar address?'

'Cambridge Road? Is it? Ah. Well well, in fact I was. I am seeking an address. I am going to number – number fifty-four.' Recalling Mrs Townend's address.

'Very good, sir.' Turning and pointing. 'You will need to turn to your right, and pro-ceed a little way along. You will endeavour to be quiet as you go, will not you, sir?'

'In course I will, in course I will, good heaven.'

'Thank you, sir. I will say goodnight.'

'Goodnight to you.' Rennie nodded, grimaced politely as the constable held up the lantern to light his way, and turned right into the Cambridge Road.

Presently he found number fifty-four, an end-of-terrace house, not very wide but three storeys high. A glimmer of light at one of the windows. Should he knock at the door? What o'clock was it? He took his watch from his pocket and peered at it in the darkness, but could not properly see the face. The bell of a church clock answered his question. Nine o'clock.

'Nine o'clock? Nine o'clock at night? Nay, that is too late to call. I cannot call on a lady, uninvited, at such an hour.'

And he knocked. There was no answer. He waited, and then knocked again, and now a servant girl answered the door. She held up the stub of a candle in its holder, just as a voice called from within:

'Who is it, Aggy?'

Rennie recognized the voice of Mrs Townend's sister, Mrs Rodgers.

'Yes, sir?' The maid, very timid, holding the candle and staring at him askance.

'I am – will you say to Mrs Townend, if she is at home, that Captain Rennie would very much like to speak to her? Say to her that I am aware of the lateness of the hour, and – and so forth – but that it is a matter of great importance.'

'Aggy . . . ?' The same voice, again calling.

The girl bobbed in something like confusion, shut the door, and Rennie was left standing on the upper step outside. Muffled voices inside, and he waited, grew apprehensive, and then self-accusing.

'You damned fool!' To himself. 'You bloody fool. She will not see you, at night. Why did y'knock at her door at all? How can she admit you, when she thinks you are a coward?'

The door opened, and he lifted his head. The servant girl stood aside, and: 'Please will you come in, sir?'

A moment after he was in a pretty, small drawing room, with a fire burning in the grate, and a lamp throwing a glow over the table and two chairs, and an embroidered screen to one side of the fire. Mrs Townend was alone in the room as he came in, and now she came forward, and Rennie saw with a little lurch of emotion that she was smiling.

'Captain Rennie, you are welcome.'

'Mrs Townend, it is – I am so very grateful that you felt able to admit me, at such a late – '

'You would not have come unless on a matter of urgency – as you said to Agatha, just now.'

'No. No, indeed. You are quite right.' Feeling himself wretchedly awkward. Why in God's name had he come? He bowed to her.

'Will not you sit down, Captain Rennie?' Stepping back nearer the fire, and sitting down.

'You are very kind.' He stepped to the other chair and sat down.

'May I offer you refreshment? Coffee?'

'Thank you, no. I – I wished to – '

'A glass of madeira?'

'Nothing, thank you. I wished to tell you, Mrs Townend, that I am not a coward.'

'Oh. Oh. I had thought that you were about to say – pray

continue, Captain Rennie.' Mrs Townend appeared disconcerted, and Rennie was further embarrassed. He stumbled
on, wishing that he had accepted the offer of madeira.

'Hm. Perhaps you will have heard rumours in Portsmouth
that I was called out. And that subsequent, when I had
accepted the challenge, I did not meet my obligation, I did
not meet Capt—'

'No! Captain Rennie, I beg you, do not mention any name
to me. I wish to know nothing of this affair.' Greatly
discomforted.

'As you wish, madam.' Inclining his head. 'May I
continue?'

A troubled little smile. 'Captain Rennie, I had thought you
would seek to – had I known you would talk of this other
affair, well . . .'

'I am very sorry. I wished only – '

Over him: 'I had thought you was come to me on another
matter. I see now that I was wrong.'

'Nay, Mrs Townend, do not accuse yourself of wrongdoing in my presence. I will never like to countenance that.'

And now she looked at him, a deep, startled, intimate gaze.
Rennie felt obliged to meet it, and to say something more.

'I had – I had only come to offer explication *incidental*,
d'y'see? So that you would not continue to feel harshly
toward me, when I needed your help.'

'Help?' Further startled.

'Aye, madam. I am in great need of your assistance this
night. May I ask . . .'

'Yes, Captain Rennie?' Very soft.

'May I avail myself of that glass of madeira, offered a
moment since?'

'Oh. Yes.' Again disconcerted, ringing the table bell. 'Yes,
in course you may.'

The wine was brought to him, and to his relief Mrs
Townend took a glass herself. He knew now what he would
say to her. If she refused, as she almost certainly would, then

he would take his leave, saying that he understood perfectly, &c., &c.

'Mrs Townend, I have fled my lodging, and am sought high and low by evil men. I have nowhere to go. I wished to take a room in your house, where no one would think to look for me. Naturally, I will pay handsome – '

'Stop, please stop, Captain Rennie.'

Very good, thought Rennie, she has been so affronted by this absurd request that she will now show me the door, and the whole stupid episode will be over. He held up his hand, nodded, and:

'In course, I understand you. It was a most foolish and ignoble request.' Making to rise.

'Nay, it was not, it was not. The only thing foolish was to offer payment. I would not think of accepting money in aiding you, dear Captain Rennie.'

'Eh? Oh.'

'I have – I have not told you all of the truth, Captain Rennie.'

'Oh.' Quite out of his depth, now. 'Ah.'

'Nay, I have been remiss. I thought you had come here tonight to – nay, I cannot speak of it now. All I would wish to say is that I was ashamed of myself when we met in the High Street, and I turned away from you. I confess that I half-believed the rumours that were flying about. Then when I came home here I thought of what you did on the road at night, in the coach, of how you saved us all from a cowardly and violent attack, risked your life to save us, and I was doubly ashamed. I knew that you were not and could not be a coward, and that some unhappy circumstance which you had not the power to alter had caused the scandal.'

'You are very kind.'

'Captain Rennie, will you excuse me a moment? There is something I must say to my sister. You will not go away?'

'I will not, if you do not wish is.'

'I do not wish it.'

She left him, and he drank his wine. The fire crackled, and he was aware all at once of a tremendous fatigue, as if his whole body was drained of energy. He stifled a yawn. Presently Mrs Townend returned.

'It is all arranged, dear Captain Rennie. You are to stay here with us – ' Mrs Townend paused, and stared. Captain Rennie was fast asleep in his chair, the nearly empty glass of wine tipped to one side in his hand.

When Rennie woke he remembered coming upstairs and being left alone with a candle-holder in a plain small bedroom at the rear of the house. He was vexed with himself for having fallen asleep downstairs, and for having been too tired to resist when Mrs Townend and her sister declared him their guest. The maid had guided him to his room, he had lain down on the narrow bed and at once fallen asleep. The candle now guttered in the holder, and he heard the church clock strike – one, two, three, four. At sea, eight bells of the middle watch.

He sat up and leaned against the wall in the flickering semi-darkness. At home in Norfolk he had a clock by his bed that chimed in imitation of a ship's bell – ting-ting, ting-ting. He thought of his house, of the stretching peace there in the wide Norfolk countryside, under the bird-turning sky. Of his maid Jenny busying herself day by day, keeping the house clean and pleasant. He had left money to settle household bills, and so forth, to pay the boy and the man who came in to tend the garden. All would be well at Middingham, until his return. Aye, his return. When would that be? His thoughts turned sourly on his present circumstance.

'What the devil have I done by coming here to this house? By fleeing the Drawbridge? By defying Greer, the fellow? I cannot stay here, good God. Skulking, hiding, peering from behind the petticoats of respectable women. I must return and face my obligation, my duty. However damned unpleasant it may be, however wretched and discommoding, I must do my duty as undertaken and agreed.'

He nodded, nodded again, and swung his legs off the bed. A further thought came to him:

'Supposing that Sir Robert don't want me, any more? What if he has decided that I am of no further use to him in pursuit of Faulk? Would it not be entirely justified in him to think me a weak-willed, impetuous, petulant, reckless bloody fool, that ain't to be regarded at all, nor trusted, in anything? Could he be blamed for making another arrangement altogether?'

Rennie sat very still on the edge of the bed, and thought everything through with dull, relentless logic. If Sir Robert thought this of him, and had now abandoned him, then he would never get back his career, never be restored as post captain, never again have a commissioned ship under his legs. He would remain in fact – as he had until now been merely in imitation – an outcast, driven from all of ordered, decent, rank-observing life, never to be admitted again.

'Christ Jesu . . .' Whispered.

A mist of disadvantage seemed to surround everything in his life, a swirling mist that was thickening into a dense fog of despair. A deep sigh, and: 'This will not do, William Rennie,' he admonished himself. And now the sense of something else began quite abruptly to assert itself – the instinct of self-preservation, piercing the fog like a bright shaft of light.

Rennie stood up and strode to the little window, pushed it open and snuffed in a breath of night air, and was restored.

'I will go home to Norfolk, to Southcroft House, and arrange my affairs. It will not take more than a day or two, and then I shall depart. Aye.'

He found a ewer and basin on a stand by the window, dashed cold water in his face, and washed out his mouth – as if to cleanse it of all foolish, self-pitying talk.

'Home to Norfolk, and away – to America. I am not known there, and will introduce myself as Captain Birch, and offer myself to merchant owners, at Boston. Aye, that is the solution, William, my boy. That is how to fight clear of this frightful, lowering, foul-smelling mess ye've allowed y'self to be bullied into. Go to America, and make a new start!'

*

'*Pipistrel* lost?' Admiral Hapgood looked at Lieutenant Hayter with an expression of baffled disapproval. 'She is an Excise cutter, ain't she?'

'She was, sir, yes.'

'Then why d'you inform me of her loss? Why do not you inform the Excise Board?'

'Since she was aiding me, sir, in my duty as a sea officer in the Royal Navy, I thought it best to inform you, the Port Admiral, and – '

'How d'y'know she is lost?'

'We were patrolling together in the Channel when the storm of wind blew in from the west, and we lost sight of her.'

'Yes yes, but how d'y'know she is *lost*, though, hey? How d'y'know she did not make for another port, and that she ain't there now? Dover, as an instance?'

'I do not think that possible, sir. *Pipistrel* was close by us in *Hawk* when – '

'Yes yes, when the wind came up. Did you heave to, and send a boat?'

'Indeed no, sir. Conditions – '

'No? Y'did not? Why not, if you thought she was foundering?'

'Well, sir, we did not see her founder – we simply observed that she was gone from her position. Beside, the conditions was very severe. We could not heave to, nor lower a boat, without great risk to *Hawk* herself.'

'You say "we" very frequent, Mr Hayter. Are not you commander of *Hawk*? Ain't the sole responsibility of command your own?'

'That is so, sir. However – '

'No no no no. Not "however", if y'please. Are you in command of the *Hawk* cutter, or are you not?'

'I am, sir.'

'Then why d'y'insist on this "we-we-we" foolishness? Do not attempt to conceal blame behind others, sir, when the blame is entirely your own.'

'Blame! I am not aware that I am to blame, in anything.'

'Did not you just now tell me, sir, that ye had *lost the bloody Pipistrel*! Then you are to *blame* for it!'

'Sir. Admiral Hapgood. I will not like to contradict you, sir, but *Pipistrel* was lost by the action of the storm, not by any action of my own.'

'Then who is "*we*"?' With glaring triumph. 'Hey?'

In his agitation and anger at this flood of unmerited accusation, James grew incautious, and:

'My adviser and friend this commission is Mr Hope.'

'Ahh – Mr Hope. And who is he, pray? What is his rank and duty in *Hawk*?'

'He – he has no rank, official. He advises me.'

'What? He is a passenger? A supernumerary? A gentleman idler? What?'

A sharp rap at the door, just as James opened his mouth to reply, and Mr Hope came into the room, a bandage swathed about his head. Admiral Hapgood looked at him sharply, prepared to rebuke – then recognition flooded and transformed his face.

'Good heaven – Your Royal High—'

'Nay, I am not. Not today, not at present. I am Mr Hope, Admiral.'

'*You* are, sir? *You* are Lieutenant Hayter's adviser?'

'Indeed. And in havin' advised Mr Hayter to come here today, I think perhaps I was mistook, after all. I will like you to notice nothing of what has been said here in this room today. Nothing of the *Pipistrel*, nothing of me. In fact, we was never here at all. You apprehend me?'

'As you wish, sir.' Now more than ever baffled, his beetling brows up and down. 'As you wish.'

'Am obliged.' Assuming a grave expression. 'Now then, supposin' Ireland was a large great backside, pointed at England. What would we find in the vital position? Hey?'

'I – I hope that you will tell us, sir.' Admiral Hapgood.

'Cork!'

'Cork . . . ?'

'Hhhhh – Cork! A bung stopper, in Ireland's arse! Hhhhh!'

'Ah. Ha-ha. Indeed.' Admiral Hapgood, politely, a dreadful half-smile.

'Come, Hayter, we cannot dally here, makin' jokes. Good day t'ye, Admiral.' Mr Hope paused at the door. 'And you mind me, we was never here.'

'Very good, sir.' A bow, as Mr Hope put on his hat over the bandage, and stumped away down the stair. James followed him.

Coming away from the Port Admiral's office, the hat pulled low over his face, James attending close by his side, Mr Hope gripped James's arm, and:

'We'll go to Greer, now. He will know what to do. We should never have gone to Admiral Hapgood to report the loss. I should never have agreed to that, you know.' Forgetting that the idea had been altogether his own. 'We must have a new stratagem.'

'Ain't Kingshill watched, though? Is it wise for us to go there, sir, d'y'think?'

'D'y'presume to advise me, now, Mr Hayter? Ain't it t'other way about?'

'Very good, sir.' Obediently, with an inward shrug, thinking: 'I do not care, now. It is a damned underhand, ill-favoured, misbegotten shambles, careless of careers, careless of life. All I want is to be rid of it, right quick.'

They hired a gig – rather, James hired a gig, while Mr Hope waited – and drove to Kingshill. Mr Hope waited outside in the gig, and James went up the shallow steps at the entrance, between imposing urns, and knocked at the door. Presently he returned to the gig, shaking his head.

'Sir Robert ain't here, sir. We had better go away at once, else we shall be seen by those observing the house.'

'D'y'believe there are such observers, do you?' Mr Hope looked away across the grounds.

'Sir Robert has often said so, and surely he is in a position to – '

'Candidly, I do not.' Over him. 'It is my belief they are a contrivance of Sir Robert's, for his own purpose. He is a great fellow for deception, and concealment, and danger-in-the-shadows, ain't he? It is at the heart of his understanding, and mode of life. It is the greater part of his power and influence.'

'I expect you are right, sir.' Neutrally, climbing into the gig.

'However, it don't influence me.' Getting out of the gig, and flexing a leg. 'I am of a mind to drink something stronger than fresh air, and eat a biscuit. We'll go in, and enquire.'

'Go in, sir? Sir Robert – '

'Go in, and wait.' Glancing up at the sky, holding out a hand. 'It is coming on to rain, Mr Hayter, and I will not like to get wet.'

The day was fine and sunny, with not a cloud in sight.

They went in, were politely if bemusedly received by Sir Robert's staff, and given refreshment in the library.

'Sir Robert don't do himself 'tall bad, hey?' Mr Hope strolled round the room, peered at a book or two, looked up and down at portraits, came to the window and stared out over the lake. He strolled to the desk, glanced idly at papers, sat down on a chair, got up again. 'Not wanting in comfort, here.'

'No, sir.' James stood quietly by the broad mantel, holding an unsipped glass of wine.

Mr Hope refilled his glass at the tray, stoppered the decanter, and:

'D'y'think Admiral Hapgood will keep his gob shut?'

'You ask my opinion, sir?' Surprised.

'I do, Mr Hayter.'

'Then – I think it very likely he will.'

'Very good.' A pull of wine. 'And we should say nothing to Sir Robert, neither.'

'Not tell him that *Pipistrel* is lost?'

'Oh, we must tell him that, certainly. No, I meant – say nothing of going to the Port Admiral.'

James knew very well that that was what he had meant, but chose to make Mr Hope uncomfortable.

'Deceive him?'

'It is not deceit, it is not deceit, good heaven. – I don't know why we went to Admiral Hapgood, now. I was persuaded against my better instinct.'

'Persuaded, sir?'

'We went together, did not we? It was damned folly. What bloody business is it of Hapgood's? He ain't party to our business. No no, Mr Hayter, next time you must endeavour to be circumspect.'

'I do not quite understand you, Mr Hope.' A frown, holding his glass halfway to his lips.

'Never mind, never mind.' Drinking off his wine.

James put down his glass untouched, and leaned against the mantel. The room was cool, almost chill. No fire crackled in the grate today. A moment or two, and:

'On reflection, sir, I do not know that I am altogether confident . . .'

'Eh? Confident?'

'That Admiral Hapgood will say nothing. As Port Admiral he may well decide he must make a written account of what was said to him, and – '

'Lieutenant Hayter! You will do well not to entertain fantasy aloud, sir! I will hear no more of bloody Admiral Hapgood, when failure in our duty stares at us malignant! D'y'apprehend me!'

'Very good, sir.'

And so their waited for Sir Robert, James having taken out his bitter discontent on Mr Hope by these several sharp thrusts. Conversation ceased, and they were left with the slow ticking of the longcase clock.

SIX

Captain Rennie, having made his decision to go away, to leave everything behind and go away for good – first by going to Norfolk to settle his private affairs, then by taking ship for America – had still been resolved to do so when at nearly dawn his bedroom door was opened. In alarm, believing himself discovered, he made to defend himself, and:

'Captain Rennie?' Mrs Townend's voice, in the shadowy darkness.

'Oh, Mrs Townend, you startled me, madam.'

'I did not mean to, dear Captain Rennie. I wished – I wished only to convey to you . . .'

She came forward to the bed, and Rennie saw that she was in her nightdress, her hair very fetching in a blue ribbon. She looked vulnerable, shapely, and entirely feminine.

'Mrs Townend, you are – you are in my bedroom.'

'Yes. Yes, I am here quite deliberate.' Softly. 'I wished you to know, certainly and beyond – '

'Madam, I am not quite prepared for this.' His voice curiously unsteady, and hoarse.

'Nor am I in truth, dear William. It has just – happened, that is all.'

'Happened?'

'There is no use in pretending, when we have both been wed, and know what life is, dearest.' Coming very close to him. 'Is there nothing you wish to say to me?'

'I? Say?' Hoarsely.

She touched his hand now, took it in both of her own small,

warm, trembling hands. Before he could think, calmly, resolutely, sensibly about his condition of life, and all that he had decided and planned, he was drawn into a soft, intimate maelstrom of lips, and hands at his head and neck, and yielding flesh against his harder self. Until he himself helplessly yielded, and they sank down on the bed together, and presently, fervently, became one.

Dawn came, and the room slowly filled with light, and a waft of air came from the window over the pillow. Soon, as the reality of the world beyond filtered into the room with the broadening day, they began to talk.

Their voices rose and fell, became passionate and even vehement in exchange, but were always subdued by the need for decorum in a shared house. Rennie revealed his plan to go away to America, and much of the underlying cause of this extreme design. Mrs Townend was tearful and practical in turn. They declared their love for each other, and Rennie was deflected from his intended course, dissuaded of the need to go away, and persuaded instead that he must stay – not only to make the best of things, but to improve upon them, upon all of the life that lay ahead for them both.

'I must go to Sir Robert, and make an ultimatum.' Rennie, sitting up at last, pulling on his shirt.

'Will it not be best, my love, to make – a suggestion?'

'I must be firm with him, you know. He is not a man to be influenced by polite supplication.'

'Nay, in course . . . but will not he be better persuaded by sound reason, argued forthright and decent, by a sea officer?'

'Well well – put like that . . .' He leaned and kissed her. 'You are right.'

And so as the morning grew late Captain Rennie – feeling his life, his whole being and way of seeing the world transformed – had set out from the house in Cambridge Road towards Kingshill.

He came to the house careless of Sir Robert's watching

enemies, in a gig, saw another gig waiting and was puzzled – and went in at the entrance.

'Sir Robert ain't at home, sir.' Fender, the servant.

'Ah. Perhaps I will wait – if I may?'

'You may as well, sir. Nearly the whole world is a-doing it already.'

'Eh?'

'Just step in the library, sir, and you will discover my meaning.'

Rennie went in there and found Lieutenant Hayter and Mr Hope.

In the hour following there came in turn recrimination, indignation, detailed and surprising revelation, and at last the united determination of three sea officers to face down Sir Robert Greer, when he deigned to appear. They would demand that he allow them all of the intelligence, all of the facts of this vexing, taxing, troubling matter, before they set foot outside Kingshill again. Never again would they permit themselves to be made party to half-truth, obfuscation, and hidden motive. They wished to know all of the truth about Aidan Faulk, what he was about, and why he was sought.

'The Royal Navy is nothing if not a plain-speaking service, gentlemen.' Mr Hope, refilling his glass. 'We must have plain answers in response to plain questions, and Sir Robert is the only man can properly provide them. We are in accord?'

They drank on it, and thus fortified settled themselves to wait.

Sir Robert Greer did not return.

They waited all day, with undiminished purpose but increasing pessimism, Rennie and James talking together, Mr Hope, fumy with wine, sprawled dozing on a sofa. At dusk he roused himself, and at first did not know where he was. As he began to come wholly awake, there was a commotion in the depth of the house, the alarmed shrieks of the housekeeper, and then the door of the library was banged open.

'What the devil . . . ?' Mr Hope rose from the sofa as James and Rennie came forward from the desk. Several figures strode into the room, two of them manhandling the struggling Fender, whom they had gagged. The leading figure wore a blue coat. As Mr Hope stared at him blearily:

'Mr Scott? Is it?'

'Scott? Who is Scott? And who the fucking hell are you, sir?'

'I am Major Braithwaite, of His Majesty's Board of Customs – sir. If you are not Mr Scott – which of you two gentlemen is?' Turning to Rennie and James.

'I am Lieutenant Hayter RN,' said James.

'And I am William Rennie.'

'Come, gentlemen, one of you is Scott. This is his house, and here you are inside it.'

Mr Hope, recovering his composure: 'You are mistook, Major Braithwaite, you know. This is Sir Robert Greer's house, and we are his guests. That poor fellow your men have apprehended . . .' glancing at the struggling Fender as he was taken away '. . . is his manservant. Sir Robert will not like it, on his return, when he discovers you have mistreated members of his household.'

'The man was obstructive, and violent. He was restrained. Now then, gentlemen – if you please, let us have no more obstructive behaviour from yourselves. Which of you is Mr Scott? I may say that in course you will not be manhandled, if you give yourself up quietly.'

Mr Hope glanced at Rennie and James, and became wholly naval in his manner: 'Major Braithwaite, you overreach y'self, sir. You are in the wrong house, and ye've got the wrong men. Stand off now, or know the consequence!' Confronting him squarely, feet planted apart, hands behind his back.

'Bluster will not aid you, Mr Scott. I am placing you under arrest. Smethers!'

'Sir?' One of the men that had manhandled Fender, returning to the room.

'You will escort Mr Scott outside to the – '

'Damn your blood, sir!' Mr Hope stepped to James's side, and drew James's sword from the scabbard with a ringing hiss. He moved toward Major Braithwaite, the sword pointed, and: 'You attempt anything against me, and I will run you through! D'y'hear me!'

'Mr Scott, sir, this is most unwise in you – '

Smethers was joined by another man, and they began to advance. Rennie now produced from his coat a pocket pistol, which he cocked and aimed at Smethers.

'You damned fools! Do not y'know that you are about to arrest His – '

'Be quiet, Rennie!' Mr Hope. 'There is a mistake here. Let us not add to the confusion.'

Another man now entered the library, a young officer, brisk and upright in a blue coat. Shutting the door behind him: 'Major Braithwaite, sir, we have discovered forty-one casks of brandy in one of the outbuildings, and a great quantity of tobacco leaf – oh . . .'

'Did y'say brandy?' Mr Hope, to the young officer. He lowered the sword.

'I did.' Glancing from his commanding officer to Mr Hope and back, unsure quite what he had walked in on.

'And tobacco, y'said?'

'I did.' Noting the pistol in Rennie's hand, which Rennie now uncocked.

'In an outbuilding, in the grounds of this house?'

'Yes.'

'What in God's name is going on?'

'We had hoped that you would like to tell us, Mr Scott.' Major Braithwaite. 'All right, Lucas. Examine all of the buildings, break down doors if necessary, and make a full list of everything y'find, will you?'

'You – you do not need my assistance here, sir?' Glancing again at the sword, and the pistol.

'I do not, thank you. Everything is in hand.'

'Very good, sir.' The young officer retired, doubtful but obedient, followed by the two underlings. The click of the door behind them.

'Put up the sword, Mr Scott.' Major Braithwaite sighed, raising his eyebrows. 'The evidence is plainly there, sir, ain't it?'

Mr Hope passed the sword to James with a nod of thanks, and James sheathed it. 'The evidence, as you call it – ' began Mr Hope, but was interrupted by Rennie, who addressed the major:

'May I ask – have you a likeness of this Mr Scott you seek?'

'Eh? Likeness?' Major Braithwaite frowned at him.

'A sketch, a portrait drawing of him.'

'Nay, I haven't.' Curtly.

'He has been described to you, then?'

'Described?' Harshly.

'D'y'know what he *looks like*, sir?'

'In course I do, when he is standing before me!'

Rennie, with exaggerated patience: 'My dear Major Braithwaite. This is *not* Mr Scott. This is Mr Hope, known to me and to Lieutenant Hayter. We three are here to meet Sir Robert *Greer*, in whose library we, and you, are presently standing. You have made – a *mistake*!'

'Aye!' Mr Hope, emphatically.

'There is no mistake in those outbuildings.' The major's eye had begun to gleam, and there was a new hardness in the line of his mouth. 'Contraband, sir. Forty casks of it!'

'We know nothing of contraband, at all.' Mr Hope gave a confident grimace, and nodded. 'Nor, I am entirely certain, does Sir Robert. If you have found these things, they have been hid without his knowledge, by this fellow Scott. A large house, set far from the road, in extending grounds, and many outbuildings, barns and the like – it is the ideal place for concealing such things, without the hapless owner of the estate knowin' anything about it.'

'I will not be dissuaded by idle argument of this kind, sir. And you may draw swords, aim pistols, and so forth – but the house is surrounded by men. I have only to say the word, and you will be took by force. All of you.' Looking at each in turn. 'Let us have no bloodshed now, if you please.'

The sounds of hooves and wheels without, a further commotion, a door banged, and a deep, angry voice echoing through the house. The library door rattled, and Sir Robert Greer strode in.

'What is the meaning of this disgusting invasion of my house? Who are you?' Glaring at Major Braithwaite. Then: 'Good God, Rennie, it is you. And Lieutenant Hayter. And . . . Mr Hope.' His anger becoming surprise.

'Sir Robert, may I present Major Braithwaite, of the Board of Customs? He – joined us, whilst we was waiting on you.' Mr Hope, coming forward urbanely. 'Major Braithwaite, Sir Robert Greer.'

'Sir Robert.' Major Braithwaite bowed.

'Major Braithwaite.' Sir Robert gave him the briefest of nods. From outside distant shouts, and the stamping and snorting of horses. Sir Robert glanced away, then: 'What brings you to Kingshill, sir? Why have you and your men intruded on my privacy? Where are my servants?'

'Sir Robert, I must say to you at once that a great quantity of contraband goods has been discovered on your property.'

'Contraband? Here?' With polite contempt, drawling the words.

'Aye, sir. Here. We have strong reason to believe that a man named Scott lives here, and – '

'Scott, did y'say?' A frown, looking at the others. Rennie did not meet his gaze.

'Aye, that is the information in my possession. I am certain that – '

'And the contraband is – where, exact? In the house?'

'No, sir. Not in the house itself. In an outbuilding – '

'What outbuilding? In which direction?'

'I required my men to search the buildings to the west of the house – '

'You are aware, I trust, that the many outbuildings beyond the house, on the western side, attach to a neighbouring property? Yes?'

Major Braithwaite began, nearly imperceptibly, to lose confidence. 'You – you are saying they are not your buildings?'

Sir Robert moved to his desk, laying aside his hat and stick. He took a pinch of snuff from the silver box on the desk, and:

'Mm. Mm. The neighbouring property, as I thought y'would have ascertained beforehand, Major Braithwaite . . .' a black glance '. . . is derelict. The house has been empty these many years, and the sheds, greenhouses, an aviary, and so forth, mouldering and decaying, lie contiguous with my own land. They are nothing to do with Kingshill – excepting in proximity – nor with me.' He rang a table bell. 'Where are my servants? I hope that your men have not disturbed them?'

'They – a man was restrained, that was very violent when we first entered the house. And the woman has been locked in the kitchen.'

'You have *locked up* my servants?'

'Sir Robert, I can only – I must discover the facts as to the question of those buildings, sir. If you will excuse me – '

'I will not, sir. I will *not*. You will oblige me by explaining yourself.'

'Sir Robert, I have my duty to undertake, and I – '

'Your duty is to invade the homes of your betters, is it?' Lifting his head and staring blackly, bleakly at the major. 'Out of addled, contemptible, snarling underdog spite? *Hey!*'

'Sir Robert, I will not allow myself to be deflected from my – '

'Ye'll be deflected, sir, by God. Ye'll be flayed alive, if I have the power to do it. *Be silent, sir!*' As Major Braithwaite again attempted to speak. 'You have thrust yourself, clumsy, barbarous and inept, upon wrong intelligence, and eagerly believed falsehood, into my house, my domain, my world. And you will pay the price.'

'If I was mistook, I will in due course apologize.' Major Braithwaite, bravely, his own head now lifted. 'However, I must say to you that Mr Scott has been followed here on several occasions, and seen to enter the rear of the house, at night. There can be no error in this. My source is of the highest integrity and honesty.'

'And who is this – source?'

'I cannot tell you his name.'

'Hah! In course you cannot! This – Scott – whoever he is, has been seen going into the neighbouring property, where ye have found your contraband. The house there, the derelict, empty house, ain't dissimilar in proportion and look to Kingshill. They was built in the same year, I believe. Your *source* has followed your *villain* to that house, in darkness, and you, Major Braithwaite, have come to *this* house in *error*.'

'I do not think so, with respect. My informant named this house very distinct. Kingshill. Kingshill House.'

'Hm.' Another pinch of snuff. 'Hm.' He leaned over the desk, took a sheet of paper and wrote a quick note. He scattered a little powder from the pounce box on the paper, and folded it.

'Lieutenant Hayter, you are in uniform. May I trouble you to drive down to the Marine Barracks at Portsmouth in your gig – that is your gig outside? – and give this note into the hand of the commanding officer. Say to him that the matter is urgent, will you?'

'Very good, Sir Robert.' Taking the note.

'Wait a moment, if you please.' The major, still brave enough to assert himself. 'I do not wish anyone to leave this house, until all the facts have been understood.'

'Am I under arrest?' James, very direct.

'I can order your arrest, if you push me to it.' Defiantly. 'What is in that note?' He held out his hand.

'I will not reveal the contents of a private – '

'That's all right, Mr Hayter.' Sir Robert, now quite calm. 'I will tell the major myself. The note is a request for a party of Marines to attend me at my house, to protect me from assault. It is a long-standing arrangement. I assure you, Major Braithwaite, that if your men in any wise impair the action of the Marines, they will be shot and killed. Evidently you do not know who I am. You do not know how and where I am connected. You do not understand my position at the heart of power and influence. But perhaps you *begin* to see what you have done, sir, in smashing into my house at night? You have disturbed and intruded upon the business of the nation, you have damaged the nation's interest, and you have insulted me.'

Major Braithwaite, for all his courage, was beginning to falter. He opened his mouth to speak, and was cut off:

'Call off your dogs, Major. Call them off, and go away, and there will be no need for Lieutenant Hayter to drive to Portsmouth.'

'I – I cannot simply ignore the evidence, Sir Robert, in the contraband goods. Nor the person of Mr Scott.'

'Major Braithwaite, I am trying to help you. You are an officer in His Majesty's service. I too serve His Majesty. Cannot you grasp that we believe in and serve the same cause?'

'I do not know what to believe.'

'Then I fear that I cannot help you, after all.' Very cold, with an air of dark, dismissive finality. 'Lieutenant Hayter, pray proceed.'

Major Braithwaite stood frowning and irresolute a moment, and glanced once or twice at Sir Robert, as if trying to read the thoughts behind that black unrelenting stare. James put away the note in an inner pocket and prepared to leave the room. Major Braithwaite stepped in front of him with a little shake of his head, then turned to Sir Robert and:

'Very well, very well – I will summon my men from the search, and go away as you ask.'

'I am glad.'

'However . . .'

Sir Robert continued to stare at him, with a slight interrogative lifting of his head. 'However . . .?'

'I must return on the morrow, and continue the search in daylight, when we are better able to see what we are about.'

'I for one will not interrupt your endeavours – if you leave me alone. Will you do that?'

'I do not wish to come again to this house, if you will give me your solemn oath that the man Scott is not here, and has never been here.'

'You have it.'

'Thank you, Sir Robert. I will say goodnight.' A brief bow, and he left the room. Presently there were more shouts, repeated in the distance, the sound of many feet outside, a door slammed, then there was silence.

Broken by a knock at the library door.

'Yes?' Sir Robert, calling from his desk, where he had sat down, looking suddenly exhausted and frail. They all looked towards the door as it was opened. Fender, one eye bruised black and swollen, a cut on his cheek, and the sleeve of his coat torn.

'They has gone, sir.'

'All of them?'

'There is none of them left in the house, sir, thank God.'

'What of the greenhouses?'

'I do not know that, sir.'

'Then look, Fender, look there at once.' Urgently.

'Yes, sir.'

'No – wait. You are hurt. Is Mrs Reece herself? Ask her to tend to your wounds. Y'may go.'

'Thank you, sir.' Fender retired, closing the door.

'Lieutenant Hayter.' Sir Robert was now waxy and ill-looking. He stood up shakily, and shakily clutched the edge of his desk to prevent himself from falling to the floor.

'Sir Robert?'

'Will you come with me to look at the outbuildings?'

'I will gladly walk over there, sir, but I do not think you are strong enough to go out again tonight. I will go alone, with a light. What do you wish me to discover? Whether or no they left a guard?'

'I will go with you, James.' Rennie, moving to his side.

'Nay, Rennie, y'will not!' Sir Robert, gripping the desk, turned his black stare on Rennie, and made it malevolent. 'You are no longer part of my world, nor my interests. You absented y'self from your duty to me, you snarled contempt and vituperation, baring your teeth, and ran away! Do not attempt to come sidling back, sir, like a cringing, guilty, tail-turned-under cur.'

Rennie was very shocked. 'But I – I had come here willing to treat, to start fresh, and to offer my services in any new plan we all of us might devise together to capture Aidan Faulk.'

'We! All of us! New plan – ! Hnnh . . .' A shaft of pain ran through Sir Robert, and his fingers clutching the desk whitened at the knuckles. 'Oh-dear-God . . . hnnh . . .'

James ran to the door, jerked it open, and: 'Fender! Fender!' Finding no response, James hurried away towards the kitchen, his boots echoing on the stone floor. 'We must fetch a doctor!'

Sir Robert now fell into the chair at his desk, and lay back in it, one hand clutching at his belly and the other gripping the arm of the chair like a white claw.

'Is there nothing I can do for you, Sir Robert?' Mr Hope, anxiously bending over the stricken man. 'A glass of brandy?'

'No . . . hhh-no . . . it is a spasm . . .'

A brief shudder, and Sir Robert appeared to sink into himself. His grip on the arm of the chair slackened, and his hand fell loose.

'Good God – is he dead?' Rennie, peering at him.

Mr Hope felt at Sir Robert's neck. His fingers fumbled with shirt and stock, then:

'His pulse is there. It is faint, but it is there.' With relief.

James came back, the library door swinging half-shut behind him. He looked energetic, but distracted, glancing back at the door, then at the slumped form in the chair.

'Fender has gone to fetch the doctor. I let him have our gig. I would have gone myself, but he would not hear of it. He is very loyal to his master. Is Sir Robert . . . ?'

'He is unconscious, but alive.' Mr Hope, loosening the stock further.

From outside the sound of hooves and wheels moving briskly away, and fading on the air. James glanced again toward the library door, and:

'I fear there may indeed be men left on guard at the outbuildings.'

'What is that to us?' Mr Hope straightened and stepped back from the desk, and went to the tray on a small table at the side. 'That need not concern us here at Kingshill.'

James exchanged a glance with Rennie, who made a face.

'What Lieutenant Hayter means, sir, is that – well well, although he denied any knowledge of Scott, Sir Robert was not quite telling the truth, d'y'see.'

'Eh?' Pausing with decanter in one hand, stopper in the other.

'As a matter of fact – Sir Robert is Scott.'

'Nay, do not jest. This is not a time for jesting – '

'Captain Rennie does not jest, sir. Sir Robert has many interests, as we had already discussed before his return, and in pursuit of some of them he assumes the disguise of Mr Scott.' James, in earnest support.

'Then – you think all that about brandy and tobacco in greenhouses is true?'

'I cannot be sure of that, sir. However, we must assume that Sir Robert – as Scott – has attracted the attention of the Board of Customs officer, inadvertent, and they have made this foray tonight to what they believe is Scott's house.'

'D'y'mean that as Scott – he is a smuggler? Is that what y'mean?'

'I do not believe it is quite so straightforward, sir.' Again glancing at Rennie. Rennie read that glance, nodded, and:

'I am in no doubt, sir, that Sir Robert is involved in subterfuge of many kinds, connected with the pursuit of Aidan Faulk. Perhaps – without informing us – he has made connections in the world of smugglers, and smuggling, in order to – '

'But that is nonsense, Captain Rennie.' Mr Hope, severely. 'Why should he conceal such an activity from us? Ain't we all in pursuit of the same thing?'

'I beg your pardon, sir, but I must again remind you of what we have discussed here this day. I fear that you do not fully understand what Sir Robert is capable of, in his various capacities. You have heard, in course, of the Secret Service Fund?'

'Naturally.' A hint of acerbity.

'Perhaps you may think that it is still used for political bribes by the Prime Minister . . . ?'

'Do not be foolish, Rennie. D'y'think I am unaware of Sir Robert's capabilities, his *capacities*, as you so prettily put it? I know full well what he does, and why. He works behind, often in secret, and he is a man of considerable weight. What I do not and cannot understand is why he should wish to hoodwink us – his friends.'

'Well, sir, well . . .' Rennie was careful of his words. 'Had you not considered – in view of our earlier discussion – that Sir Robert does not always confide fully in his friends . . . because he does not in fact trust *anyone*?'

'Eh? Now that is damned nonsense. In course he trusts the Prime Minister, how could he not? He trusts Their Lordships. I know for a fact that he trusts me. He did me a little service a year or two since, and I marked that service by the gift of a ring.'

'I have seen the ring,' said Rennie. 'But you know, sir, your

gift of a ring does not necessarily mean that he has placed his
trust in you entire, in return. We agreed earlier, did not we,
that – '

'The ring certainly marked a friendship.' Stoutly.

'Forgive me, sir – how well d'y'really know Sir Robert? He
is your intimate friend, would you say?'

'The service I spoke of just now . . . concerned a lady. A
young lady that sought to be troublesome, you know, to make
difficulties for me. Sir Robert put the matter straight in the
most understanding, confidential, gentlemanly way. I think I
may say that Sir Robert and I established a mutual trust of the
most sympathetic kind. Yes, I think I may say we know each
other intimately well, as men of understanding.'

'Then I must say nothing more about your friend, sir.' A
sniff, looking away.

'Don't be a bloody fool, Rennie. If y'have something to say,
speak plain. We are sea officers, ain't we, after all?'

'Very good, sir. With respect, I do not believe you may
have your cake and eat it too. Either Sir Robert is your friend
in whom you have complete trust, or he is a duplicitous fellow
that will not hesitate to deceive his intimates as it suits him.
He cannot be both. Can he?'

'That is very harsh, Rennie – very harsh.' Mr Hope walked
down the room a little way, holding a glass of wine. He
paused, turned, came back and stood looking at the slumped
figure in the chair behind the desk. At last, with a glance at
Lieutenant Hayter, he asked Rennie:

'What d'y'propose?'

Rennie let out a long-held-in breath. 'I propose that we
leave Sir Robert as comfortable as we can make him, out of
common decency of feeling – carry him to that sofa – and let
the doctor attend to him presently. And then that we go on
our way. Altogether our own way – in everything.'

*

'My dear, I must leave this house for the present, and return to the Point.' Rennie held Mrs Townend's hand as he told her, and she nodded.

'You have agreed to obey Sir Robert Greer. I am glad.'

'Nay, I have not.' Withdrawing his hand. 'I will never again consent to such a course.'

Rennie could hear plates clattering in the kitchen to the rear. He wondered where Mrs Townend's sister was. Listening, concealed behind the door?

Mrs Townend sensed the rebuke in the withdrawal of his hand, felt a qualm, and attempted to restore the contact by taking his hand in her own. 'But I thought you had decided to be his friend again . . . ?'

'No. No, I had not.'

'Will not you stay here again tonight?'

'I cannot. I must return to the Drawbridge Inn at once.'

'William, you have not forgot what we arranged between us, for our future . . . ?'

'Eh? No no, in course I have not. However, I must tell you that –'

'Will not you call me Sylvia, as I have asked you to?' Again attempting to take his hand in hers. Her very anxiety, her gazing into his eyes and feeling for his hand, made Rennie nervous, and inclined to withdraw. He simply could not allow pleading of this kind to impinge on his urgent design.

'My dear. Sylvia. Please not to make my task more onerous –' Then, seeing her distress at this adjective: 'Nay, I did not mean onerous. I meant, I meant that just now, my dear, I must give all my thought and energy to the task ahead. It will not help me, you know, if you cling – '

'Cling? You think me clinging?' Hurt and offended. 'I have no wish to impede you, sir, by clinging.' Withdrawing her own hand now, and raising a lace handkerchief to her mouth. 'If that is what you think of me, then – '

'Nay, nay – I do not.' Rennie felt himself increasingly at a loss. 'In course I do not, good heaven.'

'Then why say such a thing to me?'

'My dear. My dear, please. I am not a man for niceties of language, I fear. If I have offended you, forgive me. Will you?' Tilting his head, peering at her.

She glanced at him, then turned her gaze away in continued reproach.

'Will you not forgive me? Sylvia?'

Clattering dishes. The sound, from the road outside, of a dog barking as it ran after a wheeled vehicle. Rennie heard these distracting, intruding sounds, and:

'Dearest, I am in a rush, just now. I must go.'

'Go, then.' Beginning to be tearful.

'Oh, dear.' A sigh. 'I am very sorry if I have said anything untoward – '

'Must you go immediate? At once?' Tearfully.

'I fear I must, you know. It is most important that I – '

'Am I not important to you? I will like you to tell me, William, if I am not.' The handkerchief.

'In course you are. In course you are.' And in desperation and haste he kissed her full on the lips, held her to him a moment, and was gone.

'Oh, William . . .'

He did not dare turn back for fear of further entreaties, further desire for evidence of his affection. Why could not women grasp the need for action in men, good God? Why must they blind everything with tears, and the need for tenderness?

'Because that is their nature,' Rennie told himself as he hurried away from the house, pulling down his hat on his head. 'They cannot help it.'

Rennie found Sawley Mallison in the taproom at the Drawbridge Inn. He did not greet Rennie, but gave him a morose wall-eyed glance, and when Rennie asked a question replied:

'What is the matter, you asks?' Mallison sucked at his pipe, shook it out irritably and threw it into the grate, where it smashed into white fragments. 'That damned villain Scott, that come here seeking y'self, sir.'

'What has he done?'

'I don't know what he has done outside of here, but the revenuers come breakin' down my door, and heaving my sticks about, banging down in my cellar, banging out in my yard, turning the whole bloody premises upside down – all in the ques' for Scott, they says!'

'Oh, dear. I am very sorry indeed. I had no idea they would come here. In truth I had no idea that Mr Scott would come here, in search of me, and cause me such upset . . .'

'Well, they did come, izzen it? They come, and they made theirself a bloody horrible nuisance, Captain Rennie. "Where is the brandy? Where is the brandy?" Shouting at the top of their fucking voices, frightening my lad fit to piss hisself. "Where is your associate Scott?" A-hiding up his own arse, I told them. Why don't you look there, hey?'

'You said that?' Raising his eyebrows.

'And more beside.' Frowning darkly, then allowing a grimace to crease his face. 'Hhh-hhh-hhh – I said: Why don't you hixamine your own arses, and make certain he ain't hid there? Hhh-hhh, they did not like that, they did not, hhh-hhh-hhh, fucking trulls.'

'You did not lose anything by it, I hope?' Rennie looked round quickly for evidence of damage. 'No casks smashed, nor the like?'

'I ain't such a lackwit that I keep my spirits where they could find them, Captain Rennie. Nay, I knows how to conceal, how to dis-guise my goods. All they was able to find was casks of ale, and a bucket of fish-heads stinkin' ripe, that drove them off the scent right quick.'

'Well then, nothing very calamitous has happened, has it? All is well?' Anxiously.

'Nothing? I was disturbed. My place of business was disturbed and invaded. And unless I am mistook, they will return and disturb me again, Captain Rennie.'

'Then in course I will go away. I would not wish to bring further trouble here.'

Mallison protested. 'I do not blame y'self, sir. I would never do that. I blame Scott, that come here.' Protested, but was inwardly relieved by Rennie's reply.

'He came here only because of me. If I go away, he will not come here again, and the Customs men will lose interest in the Drawbridge.'

'Well, sir – if you is entirely sure? It is only I do not like revenue men a-breakin' down my door . . .'

'Yes yes, I am determined to go.'

'Then I will not hinder you in your intentions, Captain Rennie. The boy will fetch down your dunnage, when you are ready for him.'

'Thank you.' He turned away towards the stair.

'Ho, yes, by the by – a letter come for you, by hand.'

He found the sealed letter, and held it out. Rennie came back.

'Who brought it?' Taking the letter.

'The same boy as come previous.'

'When did he bring it? Today?'

'This morning, sir.'

'Thankee, Mr Mallison. I shall send down directly.'

And he went upstairs to his room. He had half expected to find his own belongings scattered and flung about, but found nothing disturbed. He sat on the narrow cot, broke the seal and read:

Go to Bucklers Hard, where you will find a ferryman. Go into his boat, and do not resist when you are blindfolded. The meeting you desire cannot take place upon the shore. We must find ourselves together at sea. Eight o'clock tomorrow, if you please. The ferryman will wait one glass only, at the lower slip.

Do not fail us.

A friend

Rennie went to the Marine barracks, where Lieutenant Hayter and Mr Hope were temporarily accommodated, with the *Hawk*'s people. He found James alone in the officers' quarters, up a narrow stair at the end of a corridor.

'Mr Hope has had to go to Gosport.' James, rising from his chair, putting aside his book.

'Gosport? D'y'mean to the Haslar?'

'Yes, sir. His bandaged head, and copious wine, have undone him. He is stricken with severe headache, crippled with it. He had to be carried into the boat.'

Rennie nodded, and: 'Then at last we are free of all impediment in this affair.'

'Eh?'

'Sir Robert is absent by reason of illness, and now so is Mr Hope. They was always holding us back, James.' He showed James the letter.

'You intend to keep this appointment, sir?' Reading the letter.

'Yes yes, in course I do.' Pacing to the narrow window, which overlooked the barracks yard.

'Let me understand you. Without even informing Sir Robert?'

'How can I inform a man that is lying deathly ill, hey?' Rennie, turning from the window, raised his eyebrows at James. 'So far as I am concerned, Sir Robert bloody Greer ain't a party to this any more.'

'Nor Mr Hope?'

'Nor Mr Hope, James. Good God, why are you so timid all on a sudden? We agreed before we came away from Kingshill that we should proceed on – '

'Yes, I know. I know we did, sir.' Over him. 'Proceed on our own course, and so forth. But surely we cannot defy Their Lordships altogether? In least, I do not think I can.'

'Well well, you make the distinction between us. You are a serving sea officer, and I am not.'

'I meant no disrespect, sir – '

'Good God, James, do not we know each other well enough to preclude all talk of "disrespect"? That ain't the question.'

'Then – forgive me – what is the question, sir? I am commissioned to undertake – '

'Pish pish, James, this ain't a regular commission, and we both know it. There is nothing regular about it, in any distinction. We must act according to circumstances, if we are to succeed. That letter you hold in your hand will lead me direct to Aidan Faulk.'

'Perhaps, but if you go away in that damned boat from Bucklers Hard, who is to say you will not be held against your will? You may be took away from England for ever. I cannot be – '

'James, James – in the past we have always prevailed when we faced our enemies together, just the two of us. This is our opportunity to do so again!'

'I don't quite see where I come into it. Where shall I be, tonight, when you go alone to Bucklers Hard?'

'Ah. Now then.' Rennie held up a finger, and told James his plan.

*

Rennie came down to the lower slip at Bucklers Hard in darkness, making his way through timber and mud by the light of a hand lantern. He had come to Beaulieu Water much earlier, in a fishing boat, and come ashore south of Mr Blewitt's yard. He had made his way to the cottage rows beyond the yard, and had given an old woman in one of the cottages a shilling so that he could sit in her parlour by the fire – the day was overcast and damp – and wait.

Now in darkness and beginning mist he could make out a figure at the water's edge, and the dim outline of a boat. The night smelled of the sea, of tidal mud, and the tar and timber of the shipyard. A dog barked in the cottage rows, as if to lift its spirits. Rennie approached the figure, holding his lantern up.

'You are waiting for me, I think.'

The figure turned, peering at Rennie in the lantern glow.

'Who are you?' The voice harsh, almost hostile. An unshaven face.

'I am Rennie. William Rennie.'

'Douse that glim, will ye? D'y'want us to be took?'

'Who would take us here? We are all alone.' But he shut off the light.

'Come on, then. There is no time to lose.' The ferryman strode to the boat, shoved off and stepped in, all in the one easy movement, and Rennie was left to follow. He stumbled on tide-greasy slip timbers, nearly lost his footing, and clambered into the boat, wet to his knees. The boat heeled under his weight.

'Don't upset the boat, for Chrice sake. I thought you was a seaman.' Growled.

'I am,' Rennie said defensively, seating himself on a thwart, bracing his wet feet. 'I have been at sea all my life.'

'Then show it. Take up them oars, and I will steer.'

'You mean that I am to row?' Astonished.

'If you wishes us to catch this tide.'

'But I am an officer.'

'Lissen, there is no officers in this boat, mate, only boat's crew.'

'One thing puzzles me. Will you enlighten me? Why have I not been blindfolded?'

'Enlighten, y'said? Allow me to endarken you.' The ferryman handed Rennie a strip of dark cloth. 'Put that over your eyes, and tie it behind.'

Rennie did as he was told and tied the cloth round his head, shutting off his sight.

'Is it tied secure?' The ferryman. 'Can you see anything?'

'Yes, it is tied. And no, I cannot see.'

'Nothing at all?'

'Nothing, I assure you.' A hint of impatience.

The ferryman aimed a sudden darting blow at Rennie's head, but Rennie did not flinch. The ferryman was satisfied.

'Get them oars to pass, now.'

Rennie fumbled and found the oars, fitted them into the thole pins, pulled blindly to larboard with one oar, and felt the boat swinging round to head into open water. The rippling suck of the oar, a waft of air off the sea, and a dank swirl of mist. Rennie felt the moisture on his face.

'Give way!' The ferryman, now at the tiller.

And for the first time in many years William Rennie bent his back to row a boat. Within ten minutes he was soaked in sweat and aching in every limb and sinew, his back a curved blade of pure pain, his breath on fire in his throat.

'Give way, there! We has a long journey tonight!'

'Damn your blood, you wretch!' Under his burning breath.

In twenty minutes they were sliding down the estuary toward the open sea, carried along on the ebb, and Rennie could sense swirling mist all round them. Another twenty, and by now he had begun to get his second wind.

'How much further?' he asked.

'I will tell you when we are near.'

'Near to the *Lark*?'

'Do not keep asking me.'

Rennie ceased rowing, and rested on the oars. He did not like the tone of the ferryman's reply. It was avoiding, and duplicitous. 'Listen now, either hhh you tell me that it *is* the *Lark* we are going out to, or I will hhh allow us to drift.'

'You give way there, you idle bugger!' But the ferryman's bluster was not entirely convincing. 'We be going where we's supposed to go, see.'

Rennie's increasing doubt was now sharper even than the pain in his back, and had descended prickling and spiking into his guts. 'I will not give way until you tell me this: are we going out to meet the *Lark*, or are we not?'

'I am only doing what I was *told* to do.' A note of angry

defiance entering the gruff voice. 'Bring the man Rennie from Bucklers Hard, wivout fail. For Chrice sakes give way, will you!'

'How much did they pay you?'

'That is nothing to you.'

'They paid you to bring me in your boat to them without fail, and to make sure that I was at the oars, blindfolded, and you at the helm, so you could keep your eye on me all the way. Yes?'

The ferryman was silent.

'They forgot that a sea officer of long experience would wish to ask certain questions. That he would not just obey orders blindly, so to say. Hey!'

'I am only doing what I was told to do.' Sullenly now.

'Paid to do! How much?' Barking out the words, trying to assume the authority of a post captain, in spite of the blindfold and his apparently helpless position.

'I have been paid adequate.'

'I will double it, whatever it was, if you will tell me the truth! Where do we go?'

'I dare not do anything against them – '

'Not even for double what they gave for your loyalty?'

'They ain't men to cross, I knows that. I do not wish for a knife in my guts.'

'Then we will drift. I will not row any more.' Determined not to proceed until he was certain that the *Lark* was their design, since the plan he and James had devised could only succeed if this were so.

The plan was for Rennie to go in the ferryman's boat to the *Lark*, and when they approached the cutter, overpower the ferryman. Rennie would then fire off the red rocket that he had brought with him to Bucklers Hard, and slung inside his coat. James would be waiting at sea in the *Hawk*, standing off. As soon as he saw the rocket on the night sky he would fly to the place, and attack, while Rennie kept clear in the boat. Attack and take the *Lark*, and Aidan Faulk. The strongest part of this scheme was the element of surprise. The weakest part – of many weak parts pointed out by James when Rennie first put the scheme into words – was that *Hawk* might be far away from the *Lark* when Rennie fired the rocket, and thus unable to prevent her escape. Or Rennie's capture, or worse.

'The only surprise to them would be your rocket, sir,' James had said. 'If I am far distant I will have no advantage at all.'

'Well well, it is a risk worth taking, don't you think so?'

'Supposing they blow the boat out of the water, to prevent you firing further rockets?'

'But I will have only one rocket with me.'

'They will not probably know that in *Lark*, sir – will they?'

'You make difficulty where none exists, James.' Rennie had begun to grow irate, and impatient.

James was disinclined to be deflected:

'Even if they did know it, they could well decide to smash you to splinters out of vengeance. Could not they?'

'I do not think so, I do not think so. They will be thrown absolutely into confusion. It will not occur to them to fire on me in a damned little boat.'

At length Rennie – by virtue of his greater years, authority and experience, and his passionately expressed wish to see Aidan Faulk took and the whole affair concluded – had persuaded James to agree to the plan, in spite of his grave doubts, and even graver misgivings. They had calculated roughly where the *Lark* might lie, waiting for the boat, and decided where *Hawk* should lie accordingly. But it had all been guesses. The whole thing hung upon guesses.

And now here in the boat on the open water, with the clammy menace of the night all about him, and the cold, rippling tide, Rennie had begun horribly to doubt those guesses, and to fear that it was not after all the *Lark* for which they were bound, but another vessel, a larger ship altogether, hidden far offshore in the slow swirling fog. He felt the boat sway as the ferryman stood. Rennie sensed his anger.

'Lissen, now . . . you 'ear this?' The ferryman's voice, then a further rustle of movement and a metallic click. 'You knows that sound?'

Rennie lifted a hand to snatch off his blindfold, and felt cold metal at his throat.

'Ho, no. You do not require to see what is in my 'and. It is a pistol, cocked. Which I shall not 'esitate to pull the trigger of it, if you continue in dis'bedience. Give way!'

Rennie lowered his hand, sighed, then took up the oars and did as he was told. He would have to bide his time, and carry the plan through whether or no they were headed for the *Lark*. He felt the movement of the boat as the ferryman returned to his tiller and resumed his seat, and heard the subdued, ratcheted click as the hammer of the pistol was carefully lowered. Rennie bent his aching back, and rowed on.

SEVEN

A rolling bank of fog off the coast, and *Hawk* standing away in the lightest of airs on the larboard tack. The cutter showed no lights, according to the plan Lieutenant Hayter had agreed with Rennie. No lights, no bells at the turning of the glass, no stamping of feet, shouting in the top or at the falls as sails were trimmed. No undue noise below, at the Brodie stove, or at the messes. Hammocks down had been accomplished with nearly unnatural quiet. Even the issuing of grog – in usual accompanied by jokes and laughter – had been done with preternatural solemnity. Lieutenant Hayter had been fiercely in earnest about the need for silence, and his people had seen it in his eye, and the set of his mouth, heard it resonating in his voice as he enjoined and instructed them before they weighed at Portsmouth:

'Never be in doubt, we must be quiet – or fail. I will not like to fail. I will not allow it. Our business tonight is to *prevail*. Are you with me in this?'

'Aye sir.'

'Aye.'

'We are with you, sir.'

'And what are we called?'

'We are Hawks.'

'I cannot quite hear you. Do not fear to speak out, now. It is your last opportunity. What are we called?'

'Hawks! We are Hawks!' Roaring together.

'Very good. – Mr Love!'

'Sir?'

'Stand by to weigh and make sail!'

And now *Hawk* came over on the starboard tack, and slid silent to the west-sou'-west. All her carronades were double-shotted at full allowance, and her swivels loaded with canister. The fog floated and slowly rolled, eddying before puffs of breeze through the shrouds and ratlines and yards, through stays and halyards and blocks.

'Shall we find out our speed, sir?' Richard Abey, very quietly, by James's side.

'Very well, Mr Abey, thank you. I should estimate not above three knots, but we may as well discover it as near exact as may be possible.' Whispering.

'Aye, sir.' His hat quietly off and on in the feathery dark. Presently: 'Two knots and a half, sir.'

'Thankee, Richard. We will remain on this tack half a glass, then go about.'

The rippling wash of the sea, and the splash of a fish half a cable to starboard. All sounds both muffled and oddly echoing in the engulfing mist, as if the wide expanse of the sea were artificially enclosed beyond the vessel by a great unseen wall.

James waited in vain for the glow of the rocket, suffusing the mist away to the south. No sign came. There was no glow, no pink-diffused bursting of stars. He waited, and presently:

'Where the devil is the signal?'

'Is it the *Lark*, sir?' Richard Abey, thinking James had seen something.

'Nay – I do not know what has happened.' Half to himself, shaking his head. 'The boat should have worked near to the *Lark* by now, and fired the rocket to give us her bearing.'

'Are we to attack her, sir?'

'Our task is to take her, Richard. Take her, and her master.'

'Is Captain Rennie aboard her?'

'He is in the boat. In least, he ought to be in the damned boat.' A deep breath, and he let it out – and made his decision.

'We will go about, Richard. Say so to Mr Love – very quiet, now.'

Hawk came about, silently, and the helmsman at the tiller steered her toward the place James thought and felt the *Lark* must be, to the south-east. He could not wait longer. There was little enough wind now, the merest zephyr in the wafting fog, and *Hawk* was seriously delayed in her approach. Her shrouds and stays dripped with moisture as she drifted through the laden air, her canvas hanging nearly limp. James ordered men to the sweeps.

'Cheerly now, lads! But quietly, too.' A fierce, hoarse whisper.

Nearly a glass, and by now James was deeply dismayed. No hint of a boat, or of the *Lark*. The man in the chains with the lead sent back his soundings by a boy, to be whispered in James's ear. Likewise the lookout in the bow, standing and peering into the mist. James paced from windward to lee and back, tearing his hat from his head. Peered into the dense darkness, desperate for the merest glimmer of light, the smallest sign, anything.

At last the mist lifted, abruptly lifted, became threadbare – and cleared. The open, darkly glistening sea, the broad swell stretching away on all sides – and nothing more. No *Lark*. No boat.

James lifted a hand to the back of his neck, his hat at his side in his other hand, flapped hard against his thigh.

'Christ's blood . . .' To himself. '. . . I am a blind fool. I did not *see* the bloody rocket in the mist, it was too thick. And in course as soon as it was fired, they did not tarry. They made sail at once.'

'Sir?' Richard Abey.

'Why should they wait?' A quick glance at his mid, keeping his voice instinctively low. 'They have took Captain Rennie, and run! Oh, why did I allow the foolish man to persuade me!'

'Sir?' Abey again, risking his commander's wrath.

'Well?'

'Should we – should we not chase, sir?'

'Aye, Richard, aye . . . but *where*? That is the question!' Dashing his hat to the deck.

James stalked aft, paused, stalked forrard. Midshipman Abey dared say nothing further, and stood well clear of his commanding officer, mutely waiting. James retrieved his hat, brushed moisture from it with his sleeve. Breathed forcefully through his nose, as if to force a decision from himself. He lifted his head, and saw the lookout's boy approaching.

'Light ahead, sir!' Urgently whispering.

'Thank God!' Urgently whispered in turn, peering ahead. 'Where away?'

'Away to starboard, sir. About half a league distant.'

James brought his short night glass from his coat, and found the light. Focused the refracting lens. And saw that it was a stern light, its glow faintly illuminating the tafferel not of a cutter, but of a much larger vessel.

'Nay – nay – that ain't the *Lark*.' Lowering his glass with a sigh. 'That is a ship.' He shook the head, then raised the glass – from habit raised it – and attempted to make out the name of the ship in the subdued glow of the light, enhanced by the lens. Saw a boom, vangs, a spanker, and chase ports, and surmised that here was a small single-decker, a small frigate – what the French called a corvette. Lowered the glass. Frowned.

'Why is she hove to, I wonder, at night?'

'The fog, sir.' Richard Abey, thinking he had been asked a direct question.

'The fog has lifted, though.' Distractedly, and again he brought up the glass, peered a moment, lowered it. 'Who is she?'

'Perhaps she is a smuggler, sir, waiting for just these conditions – the fog dispersed – so that she may steal inshore.'

'Nay, Richard, she is too large a vessel for a smuggler – and a smuggler would surely use the cover of a mist to creep close in.'

But again he raised his night glass, and caught in the lens the image of several men crowding upon the quarterdeck of the corvette, their faces illuminated a moment in the light of the opened binnacle. One of those faces produced in him a sharp intake of breath, and:

'By God, that is the captain!'

'The captain of the vessel, sir?'

'Captain Rennie! They have got him a prisoner there aboard her!'

The binnacle light was now shut off, but not before James saw in his sensitive, enhancing lens that Rennie's chalk-white face was streaked with blood, and that he was supported in a half-fainting condition between two of the men.

'Mr Abey! Mr Love!' His fiercest whisper. They attended on him.

'We will hoist out the boat, as quiet as mice, now. Boat's crew to muffle thole pins. I will go into the boat myself. Richard, you will remain and take the conn in my absence. Should I not return within one glass and a half – forty-five minutes – you are to assume command of *Hawk* and make for Portsmouth. Mr Love, I want five extra men, your strongest and stoutest. You and they will come with us in the boat. Every man to be armed. – You there, boy.' To the lookout's boy.

'Aye, sir?'

'Find the cook and ask him to provide you with a can of blacklead from the stove. We must all blacken our faces. – Quiet there!' A furious husk as a fid was dropped forrard with a dull clatter.

*

In the boat James settled himself in the stern sheets with Mr Love, his face blackened. As the boat's crew gave way, he began to feel distinctly odd – and then felt a return of the debilitating weakness of body and spirit that had followed on his wounding in the action against the *Lark*: a wave of nausea washed through him, rising from his swirling guts into his swimming head. He attempted to stand, and found he could not keep his legs. He lurched, gripped the gunwale, attempted to steady himself and to fight off dizziness, but to no avail. He slumped forward on the thwart with a groan.

As a child James had been inclined to walk in his sleep, an affliction that greatly alarmed his mother, who feared that he could march blithely out of his bedroom window and plummet to his death. Bars were fixed at the window, until his father Sir Charles saw them there, and heatedly objected:

'I will not have the boy imprisoned in the house! Are we living at the Clink, good heaven? Nay, nay, I will not allow it. The bars are to be removed at once.'

'But you know that he walks asleep.'

'Madam, it will not do. The boy ain't a madman. Only madmen are confined so.'

'But surely, dearest, it is – '

'Did not y'hear me, madam! – Knox! Knox!' To his butler. 'Summon Tobias Hodge, Knox, and ask him to bring his tools. I have a job for him.'

And so the bars had been duly and patiently removed by Tobias Hodge, the estate carpenter – who had patiently installed them at Lady Hayter's request – and James left to his troubled dreams without their protection. Nor was his door to be locked at night.

'The boy must be let alone,' his father had said. 'Certainly it is true that Nature protects the somnambule, and thus we need have no fear.'

'I have never heard of that, dearest. Where is that wrote?' Lady Hayter had felt obliged to be defiant and vigilant in defence of her son's safety. Sir Charles had not been swayed.

'The King's own physician has said it, madam. I do not presume to know better.'

And there the matter had rested – even though James had not.

On one occasion he had waked to find himself in a field, in dense mist, just at the grey glimmering of dawn, bemused but not at first frightened. Until a monstrous shape loomed out of the vapour, dark and terrible, thudding, growing huge.

'Oh, help! Help me!' Backing away from the awful shape, that breathed in rushing snorts, a dragon, a behemoth, come to crush out his life.

'He-e-e-e-elp!'

But there was no help. He was alone in the field, trapped in the mist, as the great creature inexorably advanced, tall, lumbering, towering over him as he stumbled backwards and fell. He had opened his mouth to scream again, sucked in a lungful of cold morning air . . . and found himself staring up at a curious shire horse, that stood peering down at him in equine surprise. Its mild eye rolled a little as James sat up, and it took a backward step, snorted, twitched a little, then lumbered away, trailing whorls and eddies of vapour, and was lost.

This memory was in James's head as he found himself gripped under the arms, and helped into a seated position again, in the boat. As he had in the misted field he sucked in a lungful of cold air – sea air – and came back into himself, and the watery present.

'Are you quite well, sir?' An anxious Mr Love, whispering at his side. The coxswain also peering at him anxiously.

'Yes, yes, I am perfectly hale.' He murmured it with confidence, remembering to keep his voice down, and stood up in the stern sheets to give the declaration emphasis. Blood drained from his head.

'Very good, sir.' Doubt remained in his subdued voice, and James heard it, dimly.

'Have ye a flask, Mr Love? I have forgot mine.'

Mr Love passed James his flask, and James took a pull of neat spirit, swallowed, coughed, and handed the flask back. And noticed now that they were not moving, that the double-banked boat's crew rested on their oars.

'Why have we ceased rowing?' To Mr Love.

'We wished to know if you was unwell, sir. It did not seem right to proceed if you – '

'But I am not unwell, Mr Love.' To the crew: 'Give way, there!' in a hoarse whisper. The men at once began rowing again, quietly and in a steady rhythm, the padded thole pins muffling the oars.

'Sir?' Mr Love, persisting. 'It was not just your health, sir – only the fog has come on again.'

James, fighting off a further wave of dizziness, sat down without properly hearing this last.

'Eh? What'd y'say, Mr Love?' Blowing out a breath, sniffing in another, peering away into the darkness. 'Where the devil is the ship?'

'The fog has drifted in again. But we are headed correct, sir, to find her. She is hove-to.'

'Damnation to that. We must go careful, else fall upon her without warning and give ourselves away. – Lay on your oars, there!'

And the boat again drifted to a stop on the wide sea. Soon they were altogether enveloped in the dense, rolling bank.

*

'Well, then, Captain Rennie, you have had your "breath of air" on deck, as you wished. And now it is time for you to pay for it, with information.'

'I have told you – told you all I know.' With an effort, since his wrists were again bound with twine behind him, and his ankles bound. He was again kneeling on the forrard platform of the orlop in the corvette, in the glow of lanterns. The place was narrow, the timbers hard under his knees. On either side, cramped storerooms and lockers. The stink of the bilges in this French ship was repellent to him, but his tormentors seemed scarcely to notice it. Their concentration was wholly upon him.

'Come now, Captain Rennie.' The same slightly accented voice, the same man he had encountered before, when he had been seized in the inn at Portsmouth and taken to the house outside. The same softly persuasive tone, now utterly menacing. 'Come now, if you had told us everything, and we knew that to be true, why should we continue to press you, hm?'

'Press me? Is that what you call this damned torment?' The last word exhaled in an exhausted huff. Torture was exhausting. His head pained him savagely, as if the back of his skull had been split to the brain pan, the wound gaping and burning in the foul air. He closed his eyes and tried to pray. The pain in his head, in his wrist, and in his kidneys – where his relentless interlocutor had struck him repeatedly – precluded prayer. No words of supplication would come.

'Do not *sleep*, Captain Rennie.' Rennie felt his head jerked up by his sparse hair, the roots nearly torn out. Again the fiend's voice:

'Wake *up*, if you please. Wake, and answer me. Why did you overpower the boatman?'

Rennie dragged open his eyelids.

'Your clumsy pretence of loyalty to our cause has lowered you in my estimation – you know? *Abbaissez! Imbécile!*' All softness gone. 'What did you throw overboard, from the boat?'

'You are mistook . . .' His head sagged as the fellow let go. 'The boatman attacked me. He tried to strike me with the boat's anchor, and it fell . . .'

At any and all cost he must not admit the truth. That he had torn free his blindfold, knocked the boatman senseless in a sudden lunging attack with an oar, and then attempted to fire the rocket. That the rocket – damp with his sweat and with seawater soaked through his coat – had failed to ignite, and that he had been forced to throw it over the side when the boatman regained his senses and grappled with him.

'*Ecoutez-moi*, *Capitaine* Rennie.' Bending to Rennie's

bloody ear, his breath on the torn flesh. 'Do not attempt to deceive me again. And do not repeat that nonsense about disguising the *Lark* as a vessel of the Royal Navy. Was that Sir Robert Greer's plan? His plan to capture us?'

'No . . . no, that is my own plan, I tell you. It has nothing to do with Greer. Greer is my enemy, my persecutor. He wishes me destroyed – and I him! That is why I wish for a commission in the French Navy!' Again the huffing exhausted breath as he tried to convince them and placate them. He closed his eyes again, in futility. It was hopeless, was it not?

'I said – do not fall *asleep*!' A piercing pain in Rennie's side as he was kicked in the ribs.

'Oh Christ!' Not aloud, but screaming inside his battered skull. 'Oh, Christ Jesu, save and protect me!' The pain seared through his ribs and burned into his spine. He nearly fell forward on his face. All that sustained him now was the one small spark of hope that was still alive within him. Would James in *Hawk* find him – by a miracle find him? He dare not allow that spark to go out.

*

The boat swung quiet and smooth, with hardly a ripple, and bumped gently against the ship's side. Mist swirled.

'Make fast!' James's whisper.

The man standing in the bow found a protuberance – a stunsail boom – and tied off the painter. They had approached at a greatly reduced rate – fifteen – and had found the ship by dead reckoning, or quickened luck, where they had hoped to find her, exact, looming black out of the fog.

'Oars!' Whispered. The oars were quietly brought inboard and boated, James raised a hand, cocked his head, listened. Misty, droplet-ticking hush. The washing immensity of the surrounding sea caught in a great bell-glass of silence. James waited, and was on the point of ordering his men to board, when the stretching silence was broken.

From beyond the corvette, on her far side, a muted hail, and the ripple of sweeps. 'Another damned vessel approaches!' James, urgently whispering to Mr Love.

'I hear it, sir. Who can it be?'

'I'll wager my warrant of commission it is the *Lark*. That is why this ship is hove-to. She waits so *Lark* may come to her.'

'Then – if we remain alongside, we shall be discovered.'

'Nay, I don't think so. *Lark* will likely send her own boat, and approach on t'other side. We shall remain where we are, alone on this side.'

'But if *Lark* should not approach on the far side? If she should approach on this, sir . . . ?'

'Then we are lost.' James, simply. 'We must take that risk. We have no choice in the matter.'

'Then, when the *Lark* and this ship have conducted their business – then we will board, sir?'

'Nay, if we are to board at all it had better be at once, when all attention on deck is on the *Lark*.'

But this proposal was at once exploded by the thudding of feet and general activity on the deck above. It became clear that the corvette was about to get under way.

'What are we to do, sir?' Mr Love was increasingly apprehensive, as were the boat's crew.

'Do? We will do nothing, Mr Love.'

'Nothing, sir? Will we not be discovered at any moment?'

All this in heated whispers.

'No, I think not.' James, firmly. 'If as I suspect *Lark* merely joins the corvette to form a little squadron and proceed forthwith to France, then we will do very well simply to cut our painter and remain quiet here in our boat, lying low, until they have both made fresh way. Then we will make for *Hawk* at a fast rate, go aboard, and begin the chase.'

'You – you wish to chase them *both*, sir?'

'They have got Captain Rennie.'

*

James, his face blackened still, stood in his working rig beside Richard Abey on *Hawk*'s deck. He had set a course for France, in pursuit of the corvette and the *Lark* – now out of sight – and had again ordered sweeps deployed. The wind was very light, scarcely more than a stirring of the air, and patches of mist drifted and slowly rolled over the quiet black swell. The sweeps were a steady, rinsing pulse above the wash of the sea along the wales, and the creaking and sighing of timbers. A sailing vessel at sea has many small voices, whispering, muttering, sighing, all uttering the same message of intent: I drive, I swim, I am alive. James heard these voices, and was in harmony with them. They whispered and quietly sang in his ears, flowed in his blood as it streamed through his veins.

'Two knots and a half, sir.' Richard Abey with the half-minute glass.

'Very good, Mr Abey, thank you. We will lift the rate, if y'please. I want three knots – four, if we are able. But no chanting, no singing to the rhythm. We must remain silent.'

'Aye, sir.'

The instruction passed by a boy, his face blackened, his feet pattering on the deck. The pulse of the sweeps presently quickened, the grunting breath of the men as they pulled joined the other sounds and became part of the cutter's murmuring voice.

'We will all take our places at the sweeps in turn,' James decided. 'Say so to Mr Love, Richard.'

'Aye, sir.'

'Glass by glass, say to him.'

And soon, as the glass was turned, he and Midshipman Abey took their places at the great oars, with Mr Love, and the cook, relieving spine-weary men, and drove *Hawk* on through the sea. Thomas Wing appeared, demanding in an indignant whisper to know why he had not been called upon to take his turn at a sweep with the others.

'Nay, Doctor – hhh – you are not required on deck – hhh . . .' James, bending his back.

'Is it because I am too small? Hey?'

'In course it is not – hhh . . .'

'Then tell me the reason!'

'Hhh – keep your voice low, for Christ's sake – hhh . . .'

'Then oblige me with an answer, if y'please!' Furiously husking.

'Oh, very well – hhh – take your place . . . relieve Dickens forrard there . . .'

'Thankee, I will.'

Dr Wing duly relieved the seaman at the sweep, and bent his own back. Small as he was in stature he was not lacking in strength; in fact, he was exceptionally powerful, and contrived to pull on the sweep with great vigour. However, he was quite unable to find the correct rhythm, and each of his strokes was out of tempo with the others on his side of the deck. He strove to correct the impediment, which caused his sweep to snag others, but failed utterly to achieve his desire – and was soon obliged to desist.

'Dickens! Worshipful Dickens, resume your place, resume your place!' Mr Love, and the seaman obeyed, taking the sweep wordlessly from the embarrassed doctor, who stepped away, wordless himself, and went shamefaced below.

'Hhh – he will take it hard – hhh . . .' James muttered, half to himself. Presently: 'We will lift the rate again, lads! Never forget, we are in a chase!' Calling in his hoarse husking tone.

The men at the oars renewed their efforts, bending their backs with a will, and *Hawk* slowly increased her speed.

Half a glass, and:

'Sir, I feel a wind on my face.' Richard Abey.

'Aye, so do I.' James turned his face to one side, and felt the zephyr flowing over his sweating cheek and neck, felt it grow in strength, blowing and gusting from the west, felt *Hawk* begin to heel.

'Oars!' he called. And gratefully the weary seamen

feathered and rested on the sweeps. A moment or two after: 'Lay in the sweeps! Hands to make sail!' Abandoning whispers now, and bellowing the commands in carrying quarterdeck.

The great oars were dragged inboard and stowed, and men hurried aloft in the shrouds, took up position at the falls, and *Hawk* busied herself in renewed hope and purpose with harnessing the wind and running before in pursuit of the two vessels ahead, flying toward France.

'Cheerly now, lads! Let us crack on!'

*

Rennie lay in a dead faint in the lantern glow, slumped on the forrard platform of the orlop where he had fallen.

'Damnation!' said Aidan Faulk, holding up a lantern. 'Why have you pressed him so?'

The man who had tortured Rennie shrugged, pushing out his closed lips in a moue. 'I thought that you wished him to be pressed.'

'Hell's fire, what use is he to me, or you, or to our cause, when he lies unconscious?' Sharply.

Faulk had come aboard when *Lark* ran up beneath the corvette's stern, allowing him to clap on to the flung rope ladder, cling there above the sea and mount the twisting strands as *Lark* stood away to take station. His feet and legs had been made very wet, and he was not in best humour when he came below to the orlop. Now he was very angry.

'Did you learn anything at all?' Severely.

'Learn?' Icily, in turn growing irate. 'We did not need to learn that he attacked the boatman, and nearly killed him, and threw something overboard in the struggle. He was seen from the deck.'

'Attacked the boatman? Why . . . ?'

'That is the question I asked, exact. Also – what did he throw into the sea?'

'And he did not answer?' Without waiting for a reply he held the lantern closer to Rennie's supine form, as if proximity of light would bring out the truth. 'It don't make sense . . .'

'*Mais oui*, it makes perfect sense.' The torturer, softly. 'He was never "with us", as you say in English. He meant us harm, I tell you.'

'One man, in a boat? Do not be foolish.' He stared down at Rennie, then quietly: 'Was he not blindfolded by the boatman, as ordered?'

'He tore off the blindfold when he attacked the boatman.'

'Are you certain, entirely certain, that the boatman did not attack him? That Rennie was not simply defending himself?'

'A lookout was posted, and he saw the whole thing. It was just as I have said.'

'Where is the boatman now? I will like to ask him certain questions myself.'

'He has remained unconscious since we hoisted in the boat.'

'Christ's blood, is everyone senseless in this damned ship?' An exasperated sigh. 'Now I cannot talk to either man! I wished most particular to ask Rennie how much the Admiralty knew of my activity, and to pursue an host of other things. Lieutenant Hayter – what has become of him and his cutters? What is the involvement of the elusive Mr Scott?'

'I did ask him these things, naturally. He would tell me nothing, and then – '

'Why did not y'listen to me more careful, damn you? When I said press him, I meant persuade him to speak freely. Pump him, not put the wretched fellow on the rack.' He paused, lifted his head, frowned. 'Wait, though . . . yes . . . I believe I have it, after all.'

'Have it?'

'Aye. Aye. I must apologize for having doubted your logic and suspicions, *monsieur*. They are entirely justified.'

'Thank you, your apology is accepted. You believe now that Rennie meant us harm?'

'I do. The boat was followed.'

'Followed! No, surely we – '

'It was followed, and Rennie was about to make an agreed signal to the shadowing vessel. A light, a pistol shot – and the boatman threw overboard the pistol, or the lantern, during the desperate struggle that ensued when he saw what Rennie intended to do. Your lookout was right in all but that one detail.'

'But we would of course have seen such a vessel, if it was there. We have seen noth—'

'Not if they have been clever. They will have kept their distance in the mist, and even now they may be astern of us, waiting their chance to attack.'

'You believe this?' Doubtfully. 'Frankly – '

'It may be more than one ship – perhaps two, or even three. I am going on deck. There ain't a moment to lose. We will beat to quarters at once.'

'Monsieur Faulk, you forget that this is not the Royal Navy, and that you are not in command of this ship.'

'At once, if you please!'

'If I was you, Monsieur Faulk, I should be careful not to overreach myself, and upset my friends. I should remember what they have done for me.' A hint of menace.

'What you have done for me! If you mean that you have helped me to make a large fortune, may I remind you that I have spent every penny of it in aiding the cause!'

'Ah, yes. Yes. You have not put any of it aside, of course.'

'I haven't time for this bloody foolishness! We must get under way!'

'Perhaps, if you have not put any money aside, then you are the foolish one, no? Perhaps, before you attempt to take command of a ship that is not yours, you should consider this. Your part in the cause is really a very little one. You and I – all of us – are little parts of the whole, and we must not presume to know everything of the grand design.'

'I never have presumed it! I have always done what I was asked, purely out of belief and loyalty to great ideas, to the noble ideals of the revolution. But I am also a practical man, a practical sea officer. If I am right about the boat being followed, and the shadowing ships, we face great danger. Surely you must grasp that I am in the best position to undertake – '

'You are *not* in command here, Monsieur Faulk.' Over him, with cold authority. 'Please return to your own vessel, and leave all questions of strategy and command to us. Yes?'

Aidan Faulk stared hard at the other man, shook his head, then ran up the ladder and went on deck, into the rising wind.

*

Dawn at sea, the grey light broadening over the wind-licked swell, spray flying from the crests, and vestiges of mist rolling and swirling away all round the tall heeling shape of HM *Hawk* cutter, ten guns, sailing large on the starboard tack, the wind three points on her quarter.

'D-e-e-e-e-ck! Two sail of ships to the east!' The lookout in the top.

James jumped into the shrouds, hooked an arm through for steadiness, and focused his glass. Found the sails, a league or more distant across the hazy, wind-tossed sea, the crests foreshortened in the lens.

'They make for Dieppe.' To himself. Jumping down to the deck:

'Mr Love! We will beat to quarters!'

He had not kept the guncrews at quarters in darkness, thinking it unwise to make men weary when they could be at rest. Better that they should fight the guns fresh and alert than that they should come to an action bleary, stiff, and tired. The scattering roll of the drum, the calls, thudding feet, sand strewn in fans across the deck. A lone herring gull floating at the topsail yard, dipping and gliding, his grey and white plumage, the wings black-tipped, coming clearer in the rising light. He saluted *Hawk* with a battle cry – 'quah-quah-quah' on the wind – and heeled away towards England. The rush of sea along the wales, curling up nearly to the rail, and surging away aft in a seething lace of foam. Backstays humming and taut, blocks a-quiver aloft, the pennant flickering long from the trucktop, curling and streaming seventy foot above, and the great standing curve of the mainsail spanking them along at fourteen knots.

James drew in a mist-cold, lung-filling breath, and felt himself alive to the tips of his fingers.

'Starboard battery, Mr Abey!'

'Ready, sir!'

'Very good.'

Hawk dipped her head and yawed a little, and corrected herself with almost no help from the helmsman at her tiller. James smiled, and set his hat a little firmer athwart his head.

'Come on, then.' Murmuring to himself as he raised his glass and peered. 'Now we shall discover who is master, right soon.'

Nothing of this was officially sanctioned, he knew, nothing of it was according to the book, yet he did not feel that what he undertook today, what he meant to undertake – in rescuing Captain Rennie, and bringing him home safe, and besting the other vessels at sea – was in any wise reprehensible, or ill-advised, or wrong.

'On the contrary,' he murmured, 'it is entirely right.'

He had decided on a stratagem during the night. First, he must disable the *Lark*. He must shatter her rudder by raking her stern. He must then contrive to dismast her. Rudderless, unable to make sail, she could not bring her guns to bear. Straightway after he must deal with the corvette. She was ported for at least twenty guns, probably six-pounders. She could well carry other guns – chasers, or carronades, and swivels. Rennie would be kept below, James was in no doubt, and thus would not be in immediate danger during the action. *Hawk*, with her eighteen-pounder carronades, could match the corvette's broadside weight of iron – and better it, too, by thirty pound. In speed of handling, going about, and reloading, *Hawk* also held the advantage.

However, he must in least consider the possibility – probability – that *Hawk* could suffer damage. Should the corvette manage to loose a broadside at *Hawk*, and strike her with even a fraction of the roundshot aimed, severe injury could result. Two or three six-pound roundshot, flying at a thousand feet per second into *Hawk*'s rigging, or striking her mast, gaff, yards, could deliver crippling impairment. He must rely on speed, and the sheer determination of his assault. Again he went over the plan in his head. One broad-side to disable her rudder, a second to dismast her. Then an immediate following attack, even as the guns were reloading, upon the corvette. He summoned Midshipman Abey.

'Sir?' His hat off and on.

'I know that you are tired, having kept the deck all night.'

'I lay down under the boat as you advised, sir, and got an hour or two of sleep.'

'Very good. You are refreshed?'

'I am, sir. And ready for anything asked of me, or ordered.'

'I will like marksmen in the top when we attack the corvette.'

'Aye, sir. How many?'

'Two, Richard. But they are not to carry muskets aloft. They are to carry swivels, and canister. They are to fire down into her waist, and kill men.'

'Aye, sir.' A little subdued.

'That is a very harsh thing for a sea officer to require of his people – we must kill seamen deliberate – but in this action we shall have no choice. We are outnumbered very severe.'

'Yes, sir.'

Glancing away, and taking a quick step or two, then

returning: 'Our first broadsides will in course be roundshot, to smash *Lark*. Reloaded, our broadsides are to be grape.'

'Grape, sir?' Surprised. 'To attack the larger ship?'

'Aye, y'heard me right. I know that I said we would use roundshot throughout the action, with full allowance powder, when I gave you my plan of action yesternight. I have changed my mind.'

'Yes, sir?'

'I will like to employ French tactics against this French ship.' Seeing the youth's puzzled face: 'They will naturally expect from an Englishman roundshot broadsides, first fire.' He shook his head. 'French gunnery method – I believe it is in their fighting instructions – is to deploy grape, firing into the rigging, and firing at guncrew, for maximum damage and injury. Very good, we shall match them. Only we shall fire first, that is the essence of it. Fire first, and bring down on their heads a great tangle of rigging, yards, and canvas on the heads of gravely broken men. Throw them into terrible disarray. Then, our second broadside . . . ?'

'Roundshot, sir?'

'Roundshot, Richard.' A nod. 'Pass the word for the gunner, if y'please. I will like full allowance and *double* shot, our second fire on the corvette. Then we must board her, and find the captain.'

When James had seen the gunner, and given him his instruction, he again fell into reflection. Not only was this stratagem without official sanction, it was very probably – the plan entire – a career-ending matter, should it go badly. England was not at war with France – not yet, at any rate – and to make war on another ship at sea in the peace was in usual described as piracy. If things went wrong, badly wrong, by God he could face court martial, and be cashiered.

'Disgraced.' Aloud.

'Sir?' The helmsman.

'Nay, nothing. I was clearing my wind.' And he coughed and made a performance of clearing his throat. Glanced aloft, and forrard, and asked the usual questions. How did she lie? How did she respond? Received the usual replies: *Hawk* was a fine sturdy sea boat; she sailed true and fast.

'We will ease her a point.'

'Aye, sir.' And it was done.

A few moments told James and the helmsman both that *Hawk* was not appreciably faster, in fact was perhaps a fraction slower, and James gave the order to take back that point, the wind on her quarter, and again she lay fast and true, cutting through the sea.

James summoned the carpenter, and discovered the depth of water in the well – negligible. He strode forrard, and trod the length of his command, and returned. Jumped up into the shrouds, and focused his glass. They had gained. *Hawk* had gained, despite the chased vessels' stunsails and clear determination to outrun the pursuer.

'I mean to prevail this day.' James jumped down on the deck. 'I feel in my marrow that I will.'

The day broadened, and the distance between pursuer and prey narrowed on the sea.

*

The first intimation Lieutenant Hayter received that his stratagem was undone was the divergence of the two vessels ahead. It happened abruptly. The corvette turned away wide to the south; *Lark* ran in a looping sweep to the north.

'Christ's blood,' James, in consternation, 'we must chase one, or t'other. But which?'

He summoned his sailing master, Garvey Dumbleton, and presently made his decision:

'We will smash *Lark* first, and then pursue the corvette. I want you to lay me as close in by the cutter as may be possible.'

'Aye, sir. Ain't Captain Rennie in the . . . ?' Faltering as he saw James's glare.

'What about Captain Rennie?'

'I only meant – that I believed him to be in the corvette, sir.'

'So he is, Mr Dumbleton. I will not like to attack the corvette, however, only to discover *Lark* doubled back and lying under my stern, and her shot raking my own rudder. I must disable *Lark* at once.'

'Very good, sir.'

He did as he was told, and soon *Hawk* was in fleet pursuit of the fleeing *Lark*, the sun gleaming and dazzling from out of the east, from out of the hidden coast of France.

*

The *Hawk* pursued the *Lark*, the bird of prey attempting to fall on the songbird, and gained on her. The lookouts in the top kept the deck constantly informed; one watched the cutter, the other the corvette.

'D-e-e-e-ck! *Lark* coming about!'

'Coming about?' James, bringing up his Dollond glass.

'The corvette continues due south!' The second lookout.

James swung his glass briefly to the south, saw the corvette still in full retreat, and was part relieved, part dismayed. If he did not resolve the question of the *Lark* right quick, the corvette would slip away altogether. Muttering:

'Why does she go so far south? Why don't she swing east for Dieppe?' He swung the glass again to the north, just as the first lookout:

'*Lark* heading due south, sir!'

'South! He sails at us direct?' James lowered the glass a moment, frowning, then: 'Yes, I see. The corvette makes for Le Havre, not Dieppe after all. The *Lark* seeks now to engage us, having lured us away, while the corvette escapes into Le Havre, to take Captain Rennie ashore and into the depths of France, where we cannot hope to rescue him.' Louder, sucking in a breath:

'Mr Dumbleton!'

'Sir?'

'I have changed my mind. We will go about, if y'please, and head south in pursuit of the corvette.'

'Aye, sir! Very good!' His hat off and on, with enthusiasm. 'Mr Love! Stand by to go about!'

James peered again through his glass, braced himself as *Hawk* swung in a swift, heeling arc to head south, and: 'Mr Abey!'

'Sir?' Coming aft from one of the forrard carronades.

'We must outrun the *Lark*, now – if we can. However, if she should gain on us we must turn and fight, at the last possible moment. In that event I will like you to be ready with your larboard battery to fire *as we go about*. You apprehend me?'

'Yes, sir.'

'You will so angle your carronades on their transverse trucks as to bring them to bear when we are yet at an oblique, impossible angle of fire – as *Lark* will read it. You see?'

'I do, sir.' Nodding eagerly.

'Thus you will be able to fire on the *Lark* well before she is able to fire at us, because her long guns cannot be brought to bear. Your purpose, in fact your design entire, is to dismast her.'

'Very good, sir.'

'Smash me her mast, Mr Abey!' This largely for the benefit of the crew, to encourage them.

'I will, sir.'

James put his hand on the youth's shoulder. In a quieter, more confidential tone: 'Now then, Richard, I am depending on you, this day.'

'I will not fail you, sir.' Earnestly.

A nod from James, and the midshipman went forrard, his heart lifted, his whole being filled with the responsibility placed upon him.

Less than half a glass, and:

'*Lark* gaining on us, sir!' From aloft.

James peered, gauged the distance, and gave no command. A few minutes more, and:

'D-e-e-e-ck! *Lark* gaining rapid upon us!'

James again employed his Dollond, nodded once, waited a moment, then:

'Mr Dumbleton! Hard-a-starboard! Mr Abey, larboard battery stand by!'

Moments of creaking, spray flying, heeling change, and as *Hawk* came off the wind on the new heading, her five larboard carronades were trucked at a sharp angle in the ports.

Midshipman Abey waited, poised like a wild animal about to spring – and loosed his battle howl:

'*Larboard battery! Fire! Fire! Fire!*'

BOOM   BOOM-BOOM BOOM BOOM

The great multiple concussion shook the *Hawk* from stem to stern, to the fierce song of rushing ball. Smoke ballooned and eddied across the gritted deck.

At two cables, even at an acute angle, *Lark* was a very considerable target, and three of Richard Abey's roundshot found their mark. One smashed the bowsprit and rendered her headsails useless. Two struck her mast.

A moment of washing quiet as the sound of the guns fled away over the sea. *Lark* appeared to pause, as if uncertain of her purpose. She faltered, still uncertain, and then with a rending rasp her topmast fell, and crashed in a tangle of ropes, yards, and sagging canvas.

A roaring yell of triumph from *Hawk*'s crew, ringing across the water.

'Mr Dumbleton! Mr Love! We will tack ship, and head south!'

'Aye, sir.'

'Very good, sir.'

'Mr Abey! We will reload the larboard battery with grape!'
Hawk swung again to the south, leaving her opponent
smashed and broken, riding the wind-ruffled swell.

By now the corvette was well ahead, her sails getting small
against the sky.

*

The coast of France just visible on the horizon to the south,
and *Hawk*, sailing with the wind one point abaft her starboard
beam, had caught up the corvette, and was nearly within
range. Lieutenant Hayter had preserved his original tactics
intact in his head. His scheme was to attempt to shatter the
corvette's rudder, then to lay in close alongside and rake her
with grape. He would have to risk a potentially devastating
broadside from the corvette's six-pounder great guns, but his
own roundshot – fired at and through the corvette's stern –
would already have wrecked not only her rudder; they would
also, he believed, have battered gun carriages and injured
men, smashing through the stern gallery and all the way
through to her forecastle.

'Aye, it is a great risk, Mr Dumbleton.' In answer to the
sailing master's obvious concern. 'Sea actions always involve
risk, do not they?'

'One broadside of ten guns, sir – even if only half of her
roundshot slammed home – would cripple us entire. We are
only a very little light cutter, after all. Certainly I can lay you
close alongside, but the – '

'Then that is all I ask of you, Mr Dumbleton.' Over him.
'If I am killed I hope that you will raise a glass of good claret
to my memory.' He saw the sailing master's shocked
expression, and at once regretted his flippancy. 'Belay that. It
was a damned foolish thing to say. We all risk our lives today,
and I beg your pardon.'

'Very good, sir.'

The wind steady, and a strong swell running. *Hawk* pitched

steeply, and as she righted herself – twin orange flashes from the corvette's chase ports.

BOOM-BANG

Roundshot rushed the length of *Hawk*'s deck, missing everything except a halyard, which snapped apart as if cut by a giant invisible knife. Shouts of alarm along the deck.

'*Steady!*' bellowed James in his loudest quarterdeck.

A shroud-humming, sea-scudding moment, spray flying, then:

'Starboard your helm! Starboard battery, stand by!'

The heeling turn, and Richard Abey:

'*Starboard battery – fire, fire, fire!*'

Five carronades thudded in sequence, and five eighteen-pound roundshot hissed away across the sea. One went wide and ploughed into a lifting wave in an explosion of spray. Four went home. The corvette's rudder was smashed from its pintles, and dashed in jagged pieces into the sea. The stern gallery imploded with a heavy crunching crack, glass and timber punched inward, and men screamed horribly beyond. The tafferel disappeared, and the chase ports, in a disintegrating blast of timber and iron. Gun carriages tumbled askew. The mizzenmast trembled, the spanker boom swung and fell, vangs, blocks, stays whipped and coiled and snarled over the side.

More screams. Sea-shadowing, drifting smoke. The singing wind.

'Mr Dumbleton! Lay me alongside her!'

Hawk close in by the corvette, to starboard of the half-crippled ship. And now came the corvette's reply. Six guncrews had survived of the ten in the starboard battery, and they fired almost as one.

The flashes of the guns were so close, and the concussive thuds, that the shock waves buffeted men on *Hawk*'s deck, even as the six-pound roundshot slammed into her side. She took the full crushing force of that flying metal, shuddered her whole length, and James knew at once that she had suffered grave wounds. The sea swirled over her deck, her larboard rail smashed away, the hammocks gone, and two of her larboard carronades. Men lay bloody and broken, with pulped limbs and torn heads. Some cried out for their mothers. Others moaned. A powder boy stood breathless and unable to move, his chalk-white face streaked with blood, his eyes staring in terror.

The stink of burned powder, and burned flesh. The stink of terror emptied bowels. The stink of death.

James picked himself up off the deck, deafened, half-blinded by smoke, and:

'*Larboard battery! Fire! Fire! Fire!*'

BOOM   BOOM-BOOM

A storm of grapeshot across the corvette's deck, clipping, cutting, smashing, thudding. One of the hailing shots smashed off a man's hand at the wrist as he raised it to his head. Another punched a hole through a man's chest, spraying his lungs and half of his shattered spine out through the back of his shirt. The overall effect of those three rounds of grape was calamitous to the corvette's people, and to the ship herself. Over half of her guncrews were dead or shot down and dying. The roundshot had done frightful damage, and now the grape had smashed and mangled what remained.

'Marksmen in the tops!' James bellowed. 'Shoot into her waist! Shoot to kill! Shoot to kill!' All compunction gone. No sympathy left for the seamen in the corvette, that were his mortal enemies, now.

Crack!   Crack!

from aloft.

And now Midshipman Abey's voice, striving for steadiness:

'Re-lo-o-o-o-oad!'

'Belay that, Richard!' James. 'We will board her, and find Captain Rennie! Boarding party to the forecastle! Mr Love! Grappling irons on deck!'

Crack!   Crack!

again from the tops. The shots smacking into motionless flesh on the corvette's deck.

'*Cease firing! Cease firing!*'

The moans and cries of the dying on both vessels. The whipping of the wind. The lifting slap and slop of the sea along the wales. Dr Wing on deck, his face set, his eyes fixed on the first man he reached, who lay on his back with blood bubbling from his mouth, and sucking and bubbling from a hole in his side.

'We will leave you to do your best for them, Doctor.' James, a hand to Wing's shoulder as he passed him, going forrard.

*

They found Rennie shackled in the corvette's orlop, in the noisome bedlam of injured and dying men that the sweat-soaked, bloody-armed ship's surgeon was attending to. Mallet and chisel were brought from the carpenter's store, and the shackles broken off. Rennie was conscious, but dazed and parched and greatly reduced by his ordeal. Blood had dried on his scalp and face, and lay congealed in a ring at his neck and shirt.

Lieutenant Hayter and Mr Dumbleton helped Rennie up the ladder and on deck, where the sea air revived him a little. He turned his face to the wind, and saw the devastation all round.

'By God, what a very bloody action, James. What is the damage to *Hawk*?' Glancing towards the cutter.

'Very considerable, sir. We must get aboard, right quick. I fear other French ships may come to investigate. The French coast lies to the south, quite near.'

Rennie peered briefly in that direction, then stared round him again at the scene of destruction.

'You have done all this damage to the ship yourself? Just *Hawk*?'

'Aye, sir, we have. It was the carronades. Damned good smashers, those carronades.'

'And the *Lark*?'

'We left her part dismasted to the north. Come, sir, if you please. We have not a moment to lose.' Helping Rennie across the bloody, grit-strewn deck through a tangle of fallen rigging and canvas, and slumped bodies. As they stepped across and down into *Hawk*, Rennie supported by his rescuers, he asked:

'What of Aidan Faulk? You took him out of *Lark*?'

'Eh? No, sir, we did not. Have a care as we step down off the rail, now.' Helping him.

'Then where is Faulk?'

'I have not the smallest notion, sir. – Mr Abey! Mr Love! Stand by to disengage and make sail!'

Rennie held James's arm. 'You do not know?' Urgently.

'My concern was to find you, sir, and bring you home safe to England.'

Activity now all round them on the damaged cutter's deck. James had stepped aft to get a clear overview of his command: his rigging, canvas, guns, and people. Rennie followed.

'Do not think me ungrateful, James. I prayed for you to come, even when I was unable to fire the damned rocket. And I thank God y'did come – thank you indeed, with all my –'

'Did not fire the rocket!'

'Nay, I could not. It was soaked through, and quite useless. I threw it overboard.'

'Good God.' James stared at him, then gave a wild chuckle. 'Ha-ha-ha! Did not fire it! Then luck was with us both this day, by Christ! No wonder we was able to steal up so close to her!'

'Eh! Steal up?'

'Nay, never mind. Will you go below now, sir? Ask Dr Wing to look you over.'

'Dr Wing will have more important things to occupy him just at present, I think.' Another glance round the bloody deck.

'Please just go below to my cabin, will you? Lie in my hanging cot. Ask the steward to attend you. I must busy myself here on deck, you know.' Kindly enough, but with an urgency of tone that Rennie recognized, and ignored.

'I am very grateful to ye, James. However, I fear that your concern for me – to the neglect of your other duties – may count against you.'

'Count against me? – Mr Love! We will get under way! Mr Dumbleton! Lay me a course for Portsmouth! Cheerly, now!' Moving away from Rennie briskly. Risking censure, Rennie limped after him.

The wind faltered and slewed round the ship, then began after a brief hesitation to blow from a new direction – from the south. James drew in a breath, turning his face to the wind, and was about to issue a further command, when Rennie:

'James, will you not consider returning to the *Lark*? I am nearly certain that Aidan Faulk is aboard her.'

'I have no time for Mr Aidan Bloody Faulk, now. I have done what I set out to do. I have got you back safe. And our luck holds, you see. The wind has changed, and will aid us in getting clear of French waters. I must bring my gravely injured people home to Portsmouth, and the Haslar.'

'I do see that, James. However, I think – '

'Sir! If you please! Will you go below, now!' It was no longer a request, and as *Hawk* broke clear of the damaged corvette, and made sail in the freshening wind, Rennie reluctantly did as he was told.

When James came below himself after the passage of
another glass, having satisfied himself that no French ships
pursued him, and that *Hawk* could sail unimpeded to
Portsmouth, with repairs undertaken that might be managed
at sea, he stepped briefly into the great cabin. He found
Rennie not lying in the hanging cot, but sitting hunched on a
side locker, attempting to transcribe his experiences in one of
James's notebooks. He had washed his face and neck, but was
yet very pale and drawn.

'Sir, surely you are not well enough – '

'I am all right, James, I am all right. My heart was so lifted
by your arrival that I was lifted altogether. I have took the
liberty of drinking some grog, and that has lifted me further.
I am quite buoyed up.'

'I am very glad.' A smile, a nod. 'And now I must look in on
the injured men, and Dr Wing.'

'Before you do, James, before you do – I will like to press
you in the matter of Aidan Faulk, if I may – '

'Aidan Faulk is nothing to me, now.' Over him, curtly, the
smile vanishing. 'I do not care anything about him.'

'Don't care anything about him? Good heaven, James,
ain't your commission altogether about him? Well, ain't it?'
The question itself, and his tone and demeanour, all
contradicting the lieutenant.

James sighed. 'I expect so, official. However, we have long
since abandoned any notion of this commission as a duty
according to what was wrote out in the instructions.
Everything has changed, and I – '

'No, James, no. You will discover, I think, that Their
Lordships will not see it in that light, when you come to write
your despatch, and make your report. "Where is Aidan
Faulk?" they will ask. "What has become of him? You have
fought an action at sea, against a French ship, when we are
not at war. You have smashed that ship, and took much
damage yourself, in pursuit of what aim, sir? If your aim was
not to bring us Aidan Faulk, then what was it, pray?" These

are the questions Their Lordships will ask, will not they? Nay, James, you must return to the *Lark* and make Faulk your prisoner, without the loss of a moment.'

'I am not altogether certain that Aidan Faulk was in the *Lark*, anyway.'

'He was not in the corvette, was he?'

'He was not. We searched among the injured.'

'When I lay in the orlop my captors thought I had fallen senseless under their torture. I was not always senseless. I know that Faulk came into the corvette, and then went out of her again. Where did he go, but to his own vessel? – Will not you think again, James, and return to – '

'And what of my injured people?' Over him, hotly. 'What is to become of them, hey?'

'Dr Wing is the most capable surgeon in the Royal Navy, James. In the short time it will take us to reach the *Lark* he will bring to your injured people all the immediate succour and aid they could ever hope for at the Haslar. If they survive, then they may go to the Haslar upon our return. If not, then they would not have survived in any case.'

James stared at him a long moment, was tempted to say that Rennie was ungrateful, very ungrateful, to press him so harsh – then he saw that Rennie was in all likelihood correct, that Rennie wished only to assist him, warmly assist him, and guide him to a happy outcome.

A nod. 'Very well, sir, we will return briefly to the *Lark*.'

But when the *Hawk* reached the bearing at sea where they had last seen the *Lark*, lying severely damaged, adrift – she was nowhere to be seen.

EIGHT

Mr Hope was yet in a poor condition of health at the Haslar Hospital at Gosport, but Sir Robert Greer had again recovered sufficient to be able to sit up in his bed and receive callers. He was with his physician, the forbearing Dr Bell, and his stout man of business Mr Purvis. Sir Robert had heard the advice of his doctor to remain in bed, and the advice of his man of business about the purchase of a parcel of land nearby; had ignored the one, and agreed with the other; had made it clear to both – as he swung his legs out of bed and gained the chair adjacent – that he expected the arrival almost immediate of another visitor – from London.

'In little, you will like us to retire, Sir Robert?' Dr Bell sighed and closed up his bag. Mr Purvis gathered his sheaves of documents, notes and deeds, and tied them up in a leather fold.

'Gentlemen.' From the chair. 'Good day to ye.'

Mr Purvis went out of the door, but Dr Bell paused there, opened his mouth, and:

'You waste your wind, Doctor, if y'seek to chastise me,' said Sir Robert, before the doctor could speak. 'I know my own capacities, I think, and how to husband them. Good day.'

Dr Bell conceded, nodded, and retired.

Quarter of an hour passed, then Sir Robert's servant Fender tapped at the chamber door, opened it, and announced:

'Mr Soames is here, Sir Robert.'

'Come in, Soames, come in.'

Mr Soames duly came in. His journey overnight from

London had not been comfortable. The express coach had thrown a wheel, the passengers had been violently flung about as the hub struck the road in a shower of sparks, and there had been the delay of two hours until the wheel could be found, and the hub repaired and greased. Soames had sat with the other passengers in a dirty, smelly, ramshackle inn, its doors opened with the utmost reluctance by a surly landlord, who would not give them anything hot to drink. Soames had arrived at Portsmouth tired, hungry and thirsty, in the small hours, had been unable to engage a room, and had sat disconsolate in the parlour at the Marine Hotel until it was time to go to Kingshill.

'Y'had a pleasant journey from London, Soames? Sit down, man, sit down. We don't stand on ceremony here.'

'Thank you, Sir Robert. I am – a little stiff.'

'Stiff? Are you? I wonder how you think I feel, myself, when I have been confined to bed?'

'I hope that you are feeling a little better, Sir Robert.' Pressing his cologne-scented kerchief to his forehead as he sat down.

'Indeed, indeed, much better, thankee. But stiff, by God.' Stretching a leg under his nightshirt. 'Now then, what news?'

'I wonder, Sir Robert, before I begin, if I might prevail upon you to allow me a little refreshment?'

'Eh? Refreshment?' A frown.

'Yes, Sir Robert. I – I have took almost nothing at all since yesterday afternoon.'

Sir Robert gave a sigh of compliance. He rang a table bell, impatiently rang it, and his servant attended.

'Mr Soames will like "refreshment", Fender.'

'Yes, sir.' Turning to Soames. 'What may I bring to you, sir?'

'Eggs. Poached eggs. And toast and butter. And marmalade. And coffee. Nay – chocolate.'

'. . . and chocolate, very good, sir. Anythink else . . .?' Brightly polite.

When the servant had gone out, Sir Robert, his tone still impatient:

'Well, Soames, well?'

'Their Lordships have instructed me – they have instructed me to say – '

'Well? What?'

'That they are not quite entirely satisfied.'

'In course they are not. In course they are not. I am not satisfied myself, when the – '

'I think that what Their Lordships have in their minds, Sir Robert – '

'Yes?'

'Well, sir . . . that they are not quite satisfied . . . with you.' A half-apologetic little grimace.

'With *me*?'

'That is so, Sir Robert. It is the matter of the person Aidan Faulk.'

'Aidan Faulk! What d'you know of Aidan Faulk, Soames?'

'Very little, Sir Robert. I am not party to the affair, except as an official of the Admiralty, doing my duty as instructed. And I hope that you will understand that when I convey Their Lordships' displeasure as to – '

'Displeasure! Is that the word they have employed, exact?'

'I fear that it is, Sir Robert. Exact.'

'Where is the letter? Why have not ye given it into my hand?' Holding out that hand.

'Ah. Hm. There is no letter. Their Lordships – '

'No *letter*! D'y'mean that Their Lordships have entrusted you, a lowly official, with the task of coming here to *me*, in admonition? Is *that* what y'mean?'

'I do not think that I am quite so lowly as all that, Sir Robert, with respect.' Stung to asperity.

'Oh? You are not?' A black glare.

'No, sir, I am not. I am the Third Secretary to the Admiralty Board, serving the King. And your opinion nor estimation of me, personal, ain't the question before us.'

'Us?'

'You, and the Royal Navy, Sir Robert.'

'And d'y'include yourself in "us", Soames?'

'I am caught up in the matter, Sir Robert, not by my own choice – but by duty.' Stiffly.

'Ah. Duty.' Another black gaze, that Mr Soames found very disconcerting, in spite of his determination not to allow himself to be bullied. He raised cologne-scented fabric again to his nose, and heard:

'You have not completed your duty in whole, Soames. You have not been specific as to *why* Their Lordships are not satisfied with me.' With icy precision.

'Very well, Sir Robert. I shall be specific, as instructed.' He paused, drew breath, and turned away a moment, frowning in concentration, then faced Sir Robert and recited from memory.

'Their Lordships require you to produce Aidan Faulk to them, in person, within the passage of one week. They require you to accompany their appointed representative in the matter, Mr Hope. You must also bring with you Lieutenant Hayter RN, that commands HM *Hawk* cutter, and a full, thorough and comprehensive account of all activities conducted in Their Lordships' name, both at sea and ashore, pertaining to this duty. They are exercised and concerned very particular about the activity of two additional persons – Mr Scott, and Mr Birch – recently brought under their notice.'

'Scott? Birch?' Lifting his head uneasily.

'Those were the names given me, Sir Robert, that I was to bring to your attention.'

'One week?' Shaking his head. 'Do not they apprehend? I have been ill. Laid low.' Gripping the arms of the chair. 'I cannot possibly – '

Fender came into the chamber, backing in with a heavy laden tray on which silver gleamed.

'Take that damned muck out of my bedchamber!' Sir Robert's deep voice tremulous with ire. 'Remove it to the library, where Mr Soames may eat it, if he pleases, before he departs.' He said 'eat it' like a curse.

'Yes, sir.' Obediently backing out again.

'Good morning to you, Soames.' Sir Robert took up a book and irritably riffled pages, not looking at his guest.

'Good day, Sir Robert.' Soames moved to the door, and there fired his carefully aimed parting shot:

'You will not forget, will you, Sir Robert? Seven days. If you please.'

Sir Robert shut the book with a snap, and glared at the wall. Mr Soames made a brief formal bow, and followed the servant downstairs.

*

'What was you thinking of, sir?' Sir Robert Greer, chalk-faced and thin, but with great intensity of purpose, fixed Rennie with his piercing black gaze, as if to pin him to a board like a specimen insect.

'I was thinking, Sir Robert – and feeling, indeed – that by carrying through this venture with Lieutenant Hayter, I was at last returned to something like naval duty, sea officer's duty, instead of involving myself in dismal, wretched, ignoble intrigue ashore.'

'Ignoble! What d'y'mean by that, sir?'

'I am not a man for such intrigue, Sir Robert, nor spying, nor going about in disguise in the dead of night. I am a man for action, like my friend Lieutenant Hayter. Hard, honest sea action, gun and gun, and seamanship.'

'Yes yes, very honourable, very admirable.' With heavy sarcasm. 'However, in conducting yourself honourable you engaged a French ship at sea, when we are not at war, and failed utterly in your design.'

'With respect, Sir Robert, I did not engage the ship, I was a prisoner in that ship, and Lieutenant Hayter very courageously effected my rescue – '

'Pish pish, Rennie. You was there, you was party to the business. Let us not play with words.' Turning to Lieutenant Hayter. 'What have you to say for yourself, Mr Hayter? Will not you speak up in your own behalf? You are not Rennie's creature, are you?'

'Captain Rennie has spoke for himself, Sir Robert.' Emphasizing 'Captain'. 'I shall do the same for myself, if you will permit it.'

'Well?' The black stare.

'I undertook, at my own origination, a course of action that I believed – '

'You acted wholly outside your instructions!' Vehemently, over him. 'You flouted them, and threw them aside! And then failed in the task ye'd set y'self, failed absolutely to apprehend and bring to us as prisoner the man Aidan Faulk, that has now escaped, further to aid the insurrectionists in France, who may probably very soon become our enemies!'

Sir Robert turned towards the window, and stood very still and quiet a moment. They had assembled in his library at Kingshill House, and as always in that room a fire burned and crackled in the grate. Today it lent no warmth to the room. The sound of flames consuming logs instead was oddly chilling.

James drew breath, and began again to speak: 'Sir Robert, if you will hear me out, I think that I may be able to persuade you that my actions – '

'Do not you grasp what the insurrection in France may lead to in England, Mr Hayter?' Turning to look right at James. 'Have you no conception, sir?'

'In England, Sir Robert?'

'Aye, in England. It may lead to the predominance in the streets of violent, vengeful, ignorant mobs! The triumph of those mobs over the rule of law, and the mutinous over-throwing of all that we hold sacred!'

'I – I do not think that very likely, Sir Robert, in truth. Surely we have had our revolution in England a century and more since, and long ago settled our pattern of governance –'

'Do not presume to lecture me, Lieutenant! You know nothing of politics, and unrest, and the wickedness of the common people.'

'I know seamen, Sir Robert.' With a hint of defiance. 'They are not wicked men, certainly.'

'Be quiet! You know nothing of life in the lowest streets and dwellings, the filth and hatred and envy that lie there in simmering ferment. You can have no understanding of what may happen should that loathing and viciousness burst forth and prevail, as it has in France.'

'I do not recognize the England you imagine, Sir Robert.'

'Because you are a junior officer, whose business is to manage boats upon the sea, where men obey in daily fear of the lash. Your life ashore has been one of privilege, protected and cosseted behind your father's gates, and now you live in a handsome country house with a silken wife and all the trinkets you desire. You know nothing of the real world!'

'I do not see why you mention my wife, Sir Robert.' Beginning to be more than defiant, now.

'Nay, James . . .' Rennie, whispering beside him.

'You will do well not to upbraid me, sir. You will do very well to listen, and learn hard facts.' With icy menace. The fire crackled behind him, the light of the flames gleaming in the irons. 'If it was not for men like me, pampered young men like you would perish.'

'I do not understand you, Sir Robert.' Curtly.

'Nay . . .' Rennie to James, half under his breath. 'Be careful . . .'

'Do not you? Ahh. Then allow me to inform you. Men like me are the true guardians of this nation, and the King. We understand, better than all of you golden fellows – that have the understanding of mere infants in the dark – how the world is managed. It is managed by sheer ruthlessness of intent, and cold, hard, bright understanding of the nature of mankind. The mass of men are indolent, stupid, feckless and brutish. Was it not for men like me, they would cut your throat, Mr Hayter, as soon as they saw your tailored coat, and the lace of your shirt. Cut your throat, violate your wife, and burn down your fine pretty house.'

'That is the second time you have spoke of my wife.' Bristling.

'Because I wish that you will keep her, and honour her, during a long and contented life. That may not be possible in England, young man, unless you will allow me to know better about politics, and insurrection, and the violent, bloody, brutal consequence if we allow men like Aidan Faulk to betray us, and assist in our downfall. *Now* d'y'begin to see?'

'I will not argue with you, Sir Robert. However, I cannot believe that men like Riqueti, nor l'Abbé d'Espagnac, are vicious brutes. On the contrary, I have met them, and they are civilized and – '

'Riqueti?'

'Honoré-Gabriel Riqueti, Count Mirabeau, Sir Robert. I have known these men – '

'Mirabeau? He is a garrulous, pock-marked scoundrel. The Oath of the Tennis Court, so called, is an abomination.'

'Very well, Sir Robert, that is your view. Even when it is moderate I may not express my own, it seems.'

'You have allowed Aidan Faulk to escape, Mr Hayter!' Very cold and hard. 'Your views don't matter to me, nor to the nation nor the King! You have failed in your duty! That is what matters!'

James stood silent, biting his tongue, breathing through his nose.

'Wait a moment, though . . .' Sir Robert looked away to the window, then back at James. 'Have you failed? Or was this simply an exercise in deception? Hey? A scheme that allowed you to simulate bold action, and at the same instant permit Aidan Faulk to escape!'

'Permit him to escape . . . ?' James stared at him in astonishment.

'Ah, yes. You simulate surprise with great skill, Mr Hayter, but I see beyond your subterfuge! Yes, yes, now I do see! Aidan Faulk is your friend, is not he? You sympathize with his aims, and motives, do not you? The Oath of the Tennis Court? The nobility of the "cause"? Hm? In little, you think him justified in all his actions!'

'I do not, sir. You misjudge and malign me.' Barely able to keep his voice steady.

'Do I, though? I think not, Mr Hayter. All the time during this commission you have deceived us. You and Rennie both. And now you are discovered and exposed.'

Rennie at last responded, his back straight, his gaze steady.

'I must ask you, Sir Robert, what you mean by that. D'y'mean that I have deceived, or that I have been deceived? Which, if y'please? I am not clear.'

'Do not dissimulate, Rennie. I warn you – both of you – that if – '

'Do you mean to suggest that I have deceived *you*, Sir Robert?' Rennie, over him.

'In course you have deceived me. You have both of you deceived me and Their Lordships, the nation and the King!'

'In what way?'

'In what . . . ? By God, sir, you dare to ask me that?'

'I do dare, certainly. Further, I say that it is *you* that has deceived.' Before Sir Robert could reply Rennie raised his voice to fierce, carrying quarterdeck: 'In everything of this affair, from the very beginning, ye've contrived to blackguard me, and all of my endeavour – endeavour honourably undertook!'

'Be quiet, sir!'

'I will not be quiet! *You* be quiet, damn your blood! Your whole design has been deception, and hoodwink, and commanding others to do your dark deeds, while you *skulk* behind! Aye, *skulk*, sir, like a rat in a sewer!'

James stared at Rennie in beginning comprehension, as Sir Robert:

'Rennie, I warn you – '

'Nay, I warn you! Mr Scott! Mr Smuggler Scott! Mr underhand, sticky-fingered, creep-in-the-dark and fill-your-pockets bloody Scott! You wish to malign me and Mr Hayter? You wish to bring charges of treason against us? Hey! Then y'must wait your turn, sir. Y'must wait in line. Because we are there before you. We'll bring a charge against you! Aye, and ram it home double-shotted, too!'

Sir Robert was silent a moment under this onslaught, and Rennie went on:

'Major Braithwaite, of the Board of Customs, will be eager to hear the charge, I think. And Colonel Macklin of the Marines, that is Lieutenant Hayter's intimate and colleague. We will make detailed statements to both of these officers. We will in addition write out despatches to Their Lordships at the Admiralty, and send a fair copy to Sir Garfield Kemp, at the Admiralty Court. We shall call a great many witnesses – '

'To what?' Sir Robert interjected. He was now almost preternaturally calm, and his voice was calm.

'To what! To your conduct, sir! We will smash, burn, and sink you!'

'My *conduct*, gentlemen, has been exemplary, in the nation's interest.' With quiet, unruffled emphasis.

'We will not send a boat, neither!' Rennie stood squarely, his back straight, but he was beginning to bluster. 'We will let you drown!'

'Ahh. Will you? When all of these charges are false, as you know very well, and your threats empty? Even if you go to Major Braithwaite, or Colonel – Macklin, is that his name? – what can you give to them? What facts have yet got, to put in your guns with your powder and shot? Hey?' He had not raised his voice, but spoke as if making a polite enquiry about Rennie's health.

'You will find out!' Rennie, stoutly.

'Hm. Your counter-attack has failed, Rennie, I think.' Sir

Robert calmly took a pinch of snuff. 'But you know . . .
gentlemen . . .' He snuffed, and employed his handkerchief.
'. . . I think I can help you, after all.'

'Help us?'

'Hm. Hm. Yes, I think so. We are – after all – on the same
side in all of this. Are not we?' An enquiring glance, tucking
away his handkerchief. 'I am therefore prepared to say
nothing of what happened at sea, to put aside all of our
differences, and allow you this . . . final opportunity.'

'Final – '

'To find Aidan Faulk and bring him back!'

Not long after, Rennie and James walked away from
Kingshill House, and climbed into their waiting gig. As they
took their seats, Rennie blew out his cheeks in relief:

'I was obliged to call the fellow's bluff, James – else we'd
have been skinned alive.'

'Did not he call yours, sir?' James took up the reins.

'He thought he did, by God. We got what we wanted by
allowing him to think so.'

'Yes, he gave us a damned near impossible task, and only a
week to achieve it.'

'In least we have saved our skins, James.' Reproachfully.

'I do not think they are saved quite yet, are they?'

'Well well, I don't know about you, James, but I have no
intention of losing mine. I am very attached to it.'

'Aye, well said, sir.' A grim little smile. 'Let us crack on,
then! There ain't a moment to lose!' He clicked his tongue,
slapped the horse's rump with the reins, and sent them
clattering towards the gates.

*

There are mornings in the English summer when heat comes
slowly streaming through the trees like a fine haze of dust on
the wind, and distance is given added depth by the

shimmering air, like a glimpse into the future. It was on just
such a morning that Lieutenant Hayter and Captain Rennie
drove away from Kingshill towards Portsmouth, with their
whole lives dependent on the following seven days. Aidan
Faulk must be captured, but was he still alive?

'Still alive, James? In course the fellow is alive. How could
Lark have been sailed away, else?'

'She was not dismasted entire, sir. His crew could have
jury-rigged her and sailed away, simple enough, even when
their master lay dead.'

'Frankly I do not think that probable, James. The cutter is
his, and only a man of great determination and strong
leadership could have managed to spirit her away so quick,
when she was so gravely damaged.'

'You had not considered that she may have sunk?'

'I don't think she foundered. Nay, she limped away to
France.'

'Then we can never hope to find him, leave aside take him
a prisoner.' Shaking his head.

'We must try, whatsoever the odds against us, James.'

'Yes, sir, we must.' James clicked his tongue to encourage
the horse, and tapped its rump with the reins as it trotted on,
its tail lazily swishing. James was silent a moment, then: 'But
why France? Why not – England?'

'England! Don't be a bloody fool, James.'

'I hope that I am not, sir. Will not you hear me out? I can
make my case right well, I think.'

'Go on.' Dubiously.

'By the time we came to the bearing where we had left the
Lark, the wind had veered to the south. You remember? This
would have aided her to make for England, not France. In
truth, her only hope would have been to run north, run
before the wind, in her reduced condition.'

'Well . . .'

'Now then, smuggling vessels oftentimes creep along the
coast to evade 'cise cutters, do not they? And then lie low, hid

in coves or little bays? Why should not the *Lark* be hid in just such a place, at this moment? To carry out repair?'

Rennie looked at him, then looked away.

'Even Revenue officers themselves, wishing to disguise smuggling vessels they have took as unofficial prizes, use these little coves to hide them – eh?'

'Perhaps, perhaps. I think it unlikely *Lark* is hid in English waters. She would have made for France, even with the wind against her.'

'Why don't we put my speculation to the test, sir? D'y'recall Major Braithwaite, of the Board of Customs? We could enlist his help.'

'Braithwaite? Why? How?'

'He has a large force of men, and many informants, up and down the coast. If we told him that we wished to apprehend a certain person, whose cutter we believed to be lying along the coast, a person perhaps connected to a fellow called Scott – would he not at once wish to aid us?'

Rennie sniffed, glanced again at his companion, and conceded:

'Well well, that is a possibility, I expect.'

'We could ask him to instruct his men, and his informants – all of them – to keep a sharp eye open for such a cutter, and to inform us immediate if they should sight her.'

'We could, aye. However, James, we may be wasting valuable time – if *Lark* has gone to France.'

'Ain't it worth the attempt, though, sir? If she has gone to France, then very probably we are lost. If she has not, and is lying in an English cove, then in least we have a chance of finding her.'

'Very well, James.' A nod. 'Very well. We'll go to Major Braithwaite, and put it to him.'

'Very good, sir.' Gladly, and he urged the horse again with the reins, and shouted: 'Come on, my beauty!'

*

'I have come to this meeting, gentlemen, against my better judgement.' Major Braithwaite paused, his gaze moving from Captain Rennie to Lieutenant Hayter and back. All three stood in the narrow little parlour of the Pheasant, an inn on the outskirts of Portsmouth, toward Bosham. 'Your message to me, I must say to you, struck me as fanciful in tone, not to say puerile.'

Again he opened the seal-broken fold, glanced at it, and read:

As brothers in arms we can aid each other. If you desire a favourable and fruitful outcome in the question of Mr Scott, pray meet us at the Pheasant Inn at three o'clock. Come alone, do not wear your uniform, and certainly tell no one of your destination.

The Hawk

'Which of you is the Hawk?'

'Lieutenant Hayter,' said Rennie. 'That is his command, d'y'see, but it was my notion. It was meant to add a distinctly dramatic touch, to whet your interest.'

James nodded, glancing briefly at Rennie, then:

'At any rate, Major, you have come. You will like to help us?' Indicating chairs. They all sat down at the cramped little table.

'I do not yet know your proposal.' Looking about him. 'You might have chosen a more comfortable place to make it, though.'

'It is small and out of the way. Here we will not be overheard, nor overseen.'

'Indeed. There is no room for anyone else. Barely enough for us.' Twisting in his chair, and peering behind. 'Is there a servant girl, or a potboy, away at the rear?'

'We gave instruction that we was not to be disturbed,' said Rennie. 'I have a flask, if you will like – '

'Nay, nay, let us proceed, if y'please.' Tapping the note. 'I am here about Mr Scott. What do you propose?'

'We think that we may know his smuggling partners, and how to apprehend them – the entire crew, and their vessel.'

'Yes?' The major's face was carefully neutral.

'Yes. However, we need to enlist your support.'

'In what way?'

'We need to discover exactly where the vessel lies, and – '

'Where it lies? Do not you know? I thought y'said – '

'Please, Major.' Rennie held up a hand. 'Hear us out, will you? Their cutter – as we have direct reason to know – has been badly damaged. It lies somewhere along the coast of England, we believe not very far, either east or west of Portsmouth.'

'Either east or west! Good heaven, this is nonsense!' Angrily, making to rise.

'Nay, it ain't.' James, leaning forward. 'The cutter is called the *Lark*. She has eluded all her pursuers over many months. Perhaps you may have heard of her?'

'I have heard the name.'

'We think, we believe, the *Lark* is how Mr Scott gets his brandy and tobacco into England. She is a big, fast cutter, with many guns. But now she is damaged, and in need of much repair. Your large force of men, and your many informants along the coast, can help us discover where she lies repairing and vulnerable, and then . . .'

'You will allow me to take her? Allow me my moment of triumph? Hey?' The hint of a sardonic smile.

'Something like, something like, Major.' Rennie, nodding. 'However, there is a proviso.'

'Ah, yes. I thought that perhaps there would be a proviso.' Pushing out his lips.

'We must be entirely certain that when she is took, her master is aboard.'

'Well, I hope so, certainly. He is the connection to Scott, ain't he?' Looking from one to the other.

'Exact. Exact.' Rennie nodded again. James took his cue and nodded vigorously to himself.

'What is his name?'

'His name?' said Rennie.

'He is called Aidan Faulk.' James, over him, taking a decision. 'And before we can tell you anything else, you must give your solemn oath that you will not reveal that name outside of this room.'

'Eh? Why?'

'It is a matter of the gravest consequence to the nation.' James glanced at Rennie for support, but Rennie – shocked that James had said the name at all – could only frown.

Major Braithwaite looked from one to the other. 'And I am to help you – on your own assertion alone?'

'We are not alone, sir. The whole of England is behind us.'

'Hah, is it? Then why all this secrecy, and remote inns, and damned foolish notes in the name of Hawk?'

Rennie now felt himself obliged to aid his friend, even if he thought him wrong to have revealed the name.

'Major, you will like to apprehend Mr Scott, I think? Yes?'

'Yes.' A curd nod.

'It need not trouble you who the other fellow is, that we seek, nor what he has done, if he will lead us to Scott? Ain't that so?'

'If he does. If he can. Or would.' Dubiously. 'How? That is the question. We at the Board have sought Scott high and low, and cannot discover him. He made use of Sir Robert Greer's property, or the property contiguous, but since we found that store of spirits and tobacco he has vanished. How d'you propose to connect Scott to this cutter you seek, and this other man – Aidan Faulk, is it? – when Scott himself has vanished?'

'We believe that Scott will seek to escape with Faulk in the cutter when the repair is completed,' said James. 'England has become too hot for him, as it has for Faulk. Our design is to take them both, and the cutter, at the moment they attempt their escape.'

'And now I must ask – what is your real interest in Faulk? Smuggling ain't your concern.'

'He is a spy.'

'What?'

'He is an agent of France, that comes in and out of England in the guise of a smuggler, and the government wishes him took. It is our job to take him.'

Major Braithwaite looked at James, then at Captain Rennie. Then he sat quiet a moment, everything in his expression and the set of his body suggesting doubt, anxiety, disbelief. At last he drew a deep breath, and his expression changed to one of determination.

'Very well, gentlemen, in spite of my doubts – and they are many – I am prepared to take you at your word. If it will lead me to Scott, then I will help you.'

'Good, good!' James smiled, and shook his hand. 'You will not regret it.'

'Thank you, I hope that I will not. I have a proviso of my own.'

'Yes?' James exchanged a look with Rennie, who asked the major:

'What is it, Major?'

'It's this. If all this should prove to be a wild goose chase, if what you have told me about Faulk, and Scott, was no better than a concocted story, for your own ends, that you have not revealed to me, and if I now put my men to work for you, to help you in all particulars, and then we do *not* find Scott, nor the cutter, nor Faulk neither – I propose to arrest you.'

'Arrest us!' Rennie was astonished.

'On what charge?' demanded James.

'That you must wait to discover, gentlemen – if you fail me. And now, Rennie, I will like a drop from your flask after all.'

*

Now on the day following the two sea officers were going to Bucklers Hard, where *Hawk* had again been taken to undergo repairs, these to be swiftly done. Rennie and James between them had defrayed the cost, saying to Mr Blewitt that time was of the essence, there was not a moment of it to be lost. Those members of *Hawk*'s complement that were hale were again at the Marine Barracks, this time under the eye – at James's request – of Colonel Macklin, to whom James had promised 'keen action soon, if you are willing'. Colonel Macklin had said that in course he was. The wounded Hawks had been taken to the Haslar by Dr Wing, by arrangement with his old and good friend Dr Stroud.

The port admiral at Portsmouth, Admiral Hapgood, had been kept in ignorance of the two sea officers' plans, but they both knew that sooner or later – probably sooner – the admiral would hear of the returned *Hawk*, and her officers and people, and that he would then demand to know all particulars of their recent activity.

For the present, however, Rennie and James were in buoyant spirits in their hired wherry. At Bucklers Hard they instructed the wherryman to wait for them, and proceeded to Mr Blewitt's small office – little more than a shed – by the larger slip, where a brig was repairing. The *Hawk* lay in an adjoining slip, shored up, with a large crew of artificers at work. Redway Blewitt emerged from his shed, his pipe clenched in his large yellow teeth. He raised his tricorne to his visitors.

'Good day, gen'men. I will say candid that I had not wished nor expected to see your cutter again so soon. I would ask that you please be more careful of her when she is made whole this time. Will you?' Looking from one to the other. His tone amiable, but with an underlying seriousness. 'I should hate to see her lost altogether – not to say those who sail in her.'

'I will do my best, Mr Blewitt,' said James. 'However, I fear I cannot promise that she will never again suffer damage. How goes the repair?'

'As you see . . .' Mr Blewitt pointed with the stem of his pipe '. . . the repair proceeds well. The damage to her wales was quite severe – at first glance. When we came to examine her close, though, we found she had not suffered so terrible severe as we'd thought. She is stout-built, your cutter. Dover-built, I b'lieve.'

'Dover-built, aye.' James, nodding.

Redway Blewitt nodded in turn. 'No finer cutter ever passed through my hands. Stout-built, sturdy, a lovely weatherly sea boat, aye.' His pipe back between his teeth. A puff of smoke. Another. 'Three days more, and you may have her.'

'Three days?' James, anxiously. 'Could not you let us have her in two, Mr Blewitt?'

'I could, yes.' A puff. 'But she would not be ready for sea.'

'I am willing – we are willing – to pay whatever you ask, if that will – '

'Ain't a question of moneys, Mr Hayter.' Over him, firmly. 'It is a question of my artificers doing their work right well. Wales scarfed and butted, a quantity of caulking, a coat of paint. Cable-laid rigging. Three days, at full effort.'

'Very well, Mr Blewitt. Thank you.' They shook hands, and James and Rennie walked across to the slip to look at *Hawk* close to. Mr Blewitt returned to his hut, puffing clouds of blue smoke.

'D'y'think I offended him?' James wondered aloud.

'No, no, James. Blewitt is a sensible fellow. He knows you want the *Hawk* back right quick, and is sympathetic. We are damned fortunate in this yard, I reckon. Had we wanted a quick repair at Portsmouth we should have been waiting a month.'

Presently, having made their brief inspection, and been satisfied, the two sea officers returned to their wherry. As they climbed into the boat, and the wherryman shoved off, James: 'By the time we get her to sea it will leave us scarcely two days to find and capture Faulk.'

As if to give emphasis to his anxiety a herring gull swooped

low overhead and gave its urgent, echoing cry: kee-ow . . .
kee-ow.

Rennie glanced up at the heeling bird, set his hat firmer on
his head, and said nothing.

*

When they returned to the Marine Barracks – Rennie with
his hat pulled low on his head and his shoulders hunched, for
he was yet in Portsmouth a despised figure, he thought, that
had better not be seen – there was a message for James from
Mr Hope at the Haslar. Would the lieutenant come there
forthwith, if it pleased him? It did not please him, but James
went. His plan to take the *Lark* and capture Aidan Faulk was
all-important to him, but he was a junior officer and Mr
Hope his senior, who should be kept informed in a matter
that was in course common to them both.

James came to Gosport by a hoy, went in at the Haslar
gates, and was directed to a private upper room where he
found Mr Hope reclining on his cot in his nightshirt. He
looked thinner, James noted. He was immersed in papers
that James saw – as he came close by the bed – were ship
draughts. The room was stuffy, with the distinct odour of
stale urine.

'Ah, Mr Hayter.' Looking up. 'You have come. I am glad.'

James had shifted into his dress coat and hat, and the hat
was now correctly and neatly held under his arm. A brief
formal bow.

'And I am glad to see you better, sir.'

'I am better, certainly.' A wink, slightly disconcerting to
James. 'In truth, when I woke this morning, my life's
companion was at full alert.'

'Sir?' Politely, puzzled.

'Christ's blood – hhhhh – you young fellows are slow on
the take-up. My strumpet trumpet! Hey? What?'

'Ohh. Yes, I see.'

'The surest sign that I was beginning recovered was that! Hhh-hhh-hhh!'

'Indeed, sir. – You wished to see me?'

'I did, Mr Hayter, I do.' Sobering, thrusting aside the ship draughts. 'To business.'

James waited, his expression attentive. There was no chair in the room, so that he was obliged to remain standing. The air was very close, and he began to sweat under his coat.

'I have received a despatch, Mr Hayter.' Mr Hope took from under his pillow a folded letter, the seal broken. He opened it, perused it a moment, and:

'It is from a very high source. You will understand that I am not at liberty to reveal, and so forth – but the very highest source.'

'I understand you, sir.'

'That source enquires what progress we have made.' Looking up. 'What progress have we made, Mr Hayter?'

'Considerable progress, sir.' Not allowing himself to hesitate. 'We are nearly at our destination.'

'Are we?'

'That is so, sir.'

'When shall we reach it?'

'Within the week.' With a confidence he did not feel.

'That is well, excellent well. I'll come with you.' Swinging his legs to the floor, and attempting to stand up straight, pulling back his shoulders. At once he faltered, lurched, and would have fallen had not James stepped quickly forward and supported him. James held him up a moment, then Mr Hope sat down shakily on the edge of the cot, the stale smell of his nightshirt in James's nostrils.

'Thankee, Mr Hayter. Not quite restored, I fear. Not yet quite hale. Have ye a drop of something in your flask?' Holding out a hand.

'I – I did not bring my flask, sir.'

'What, no flask?' Querulously.

'Shall I ring the bell, sir, and ask for brandy?'

'Nay, Mr Hayter. You could ring that bloody bell all day, and all night too, and never get any brandy here.'

'I am sure that if I were to ask Dr Stroud himself – '

'Stroud is the worst of them! And that bloody little Wing is his echo. "You may not take alcohol until you are improved." Busybodies, sir, damned vexing busybodies! – Whhhh . . .' Putting a hand to his head, and lying back against his pillow.

'Should I leave you, sir?'

'What?'

'Should not you rest now, sir? I do not wish – '

'You are certain you've forgot your flask?'

'I am, sir.'

'Will y'not go through your coat pockets, hey? Just to be certain, absolute?'

James made a show of checking all of his pockets. An apologetic grimace. 'Alas . . .'

'Damnation. Y'cannot have the least notion what it is like to lie here, day in and day out, and all the night long, without comfort of any kind.'

'Well, sir – I do know what you are suffering, in fact. I have been confined in the Haslar myself – '

'Yes yes, but you are young.' Testily. 'I am a man that is accustomed to a regularity of refreshment. I must have my comforts.'

'Perhaps I could arrange – '

'D'y'think that has not been attempted, good heaven? That I have not exercised all manner of deception? But that damned fellow Stroud has got athwart my hawse every bloody time! Did he make you give up your flask before you came in? Hey? I'll wager ten guineas he did!'

'No, sir, he did not.'

'Yes, well, in course he would oblige you to conceal it from me. That is his nature. Doubt, and suspicion!'

'I assure you, sir – '

'Yes yes, Mr Hayter, in course you do. Thank you for coming to me.'

'Very good, sir.'

'Pray keep me informed of all you accomplish. Will you?'

'I will, sir.' Another little bow, and James quit the room. Mr Hope's fingers strayed to the ship draughts, and without enthusiasm he pulled them before him and began again to peruse them.

*

'I do not think Mr Hope will likely fall aboard us immediate, sir,' James said to Rennie, as soon as he returned to their quarters at the Marine Barracks. 'He is not yet himself, but I fear he may be inclined to interfere when Dr Stroud lets him go. He feels himself neglected.'

'Do not trouble yourself about Mr Hope, James. We have had news.'

'Oh, Colonel Macklin.' James, noticing the Marine officer. 'I beg your pardon, I did not see you when I first came in.'

'Lieutenant Hayter.' A nod, a brief smile.

'What news, sir?' James gave his full attention to Rennie.

'We have had word from a place called Wyrefall Cove. You have heard of it?'

'No, sir.'

'It is a very small, concealed cove, a few miles beyond Bucklers Hard on a lonely part of the coast. A cutter is lying there, repairing.'

'Is it the *Lark*?'

'Perhaps. The informant – '

'Only perhaps?'

'The informant is a local man, paid by Major Braithwaite to bring news of smuggling activity along that line of coast. The cutter he reports is painted blue, and a new mast has been got into her from a raft alongside. She lies behind a ledge of rock, which shields the small natural mooring.'

'Painted blue?' A frown. 'That don't sound like *Lark*. She is black.'

'Was black, at any rate. Now she may be blue, in disguise.'

'How many crew there?'

'The man could not be certain. Naturally he had to conceal himself some little distance away.'

'We must go there.' James, going to the chest of drawers beside his cot, and opening his pistol case.

'I am willing to provide a dozen men,' said Colonel Macklin.

'Thank you, Colonel, but I will not need your men tonight. Captain Rennie and I must go there alone.'

'Alone! How in heaven's name d'y'intend to attack them, alone?'

'We will not attack them, you know. We will do nothing except observe.' Thrusting pistols into his coat, and taking up his long glass.

'Would not it be more sensible to mount a heavy attack at once? I can give you more men, if you wish me to.'

'I do not, Colonel. I must be certain of the cutter herself, her crew, and her master. This may not be the vessel we seek, nor the man.'

'Very good.' Clearly disappointed.

'I am very grateful to you for your offer, and in course I will call on you when we are certain of our facts. Your assistance then will be invaluable to me – to us.' A glance towards Rennie, who nodded.

'I am ready to give it whenever you ask.' Colonel Macklin. A polite bow, and he went to the door.

'Thank you, Colonel.' To Rennie: 'You are armed, sir?'

'Nay, I am not.'

'Colonel, may I call on your assistance, after all? Captain Rennie will like a pair of pistols.'

'Certainly.' Pausing in the doorway. 'But – if you do not intend to attack, why d'y'need firearms?'

'I do not intend to attack. That don't mean we may not

need to defend ourselves, on that part of the coast, and I would never wish to be without the means.'

*

They went in a commandeered ship's jollyboat, with a single mast and a lugsail. Because of James's more recent experience in handling a small boat, he took charge of sail, sheets and tiller, and Rennie was his obedient crew. They made the journey to the cove by midnight, close-hauled on a lifting swell, tack on tack under a gibbous moon, occasionally darkened by drifting cloud. They were guided by glimpses of lights ashore, and by Rennie's knowledge of the coastline. They beached the boat to the east of the cove, and climbed across a broad rise to the cove itself. They were careful, keeping to a low crouch, and very quiet. When they were immediately above the cove, hiding behind a clump of buckthorn on the humped eminence, James lifted his head and peered down.

A steep shingle beach gave on to a spoon-shaped bay with a narrow entrance. A ledge of rock running east to west made a natural breakwater. The place was just wide and deep enough to accommodate a small ship or a brig. Within the breakwater tonight lay a large cutter. Her mainmast had been stepped, but not yet her topmast, and her shrouds and other rigging were only part-rove up. There were lights in her, and about her, and activity in the dull glow. James could juts make out the shape of a raft alongside, and there was a boat tethered astern. James nudged Rennie, who moved forward and looked down for himself. On the shingle beach lay casks, yards, rope, and under canvas the humped shapes of her guns.

'Is it the *Lark*?' Rennie, whispering.

'If she ain't then she is her twin, I recognize the lines.' James peered through his glass at the men working on the vessel.

'Can you see him, James?'

'No, sir. The light ain't enough for me to see faces clear. I do not think he will be here, though, when she is repairing still, and her guns remain out of her. He will likely come only when she is ready for sea – don't you think so?' Whispering, then peering down again through the glass.

'I think we'd better wait here a while, hey? In case he should come?'

James nodded, and lowered his glass. 'Very well, sir.'

They settled themselves as best they could on the uneven stony ground, concealed by the buckthorn, but they were not comfortable. They were tired and damp from the long trip in the boat, and the night air was chill.

'Did ye bring a flask, James?' Rennie, presently.

'I did, sir.' Handing it to Rennie, who took a long, grateful pull.

'Rum, hey?' Handing the flask back.

'Aye, rum.' Sucking down a mouthful of neat spirit. 'There is nothing quite like it for keeping out the cold, and lifting a man to his duty.'

Within a few minutes both men were asleep.

They woke in the small hours to the sound of raised voices below. Both felt ashamed in having allowed sleep to overtake them, but neither said so. James lifted his head and peered down, and saw that a second boat had entered the little bay. The moonlight was brighter now, unimpeded by cloud, and James noticed a figure in the second boat as it beached on the shingle. The others crowded round the man as he stepped ashore, and appeared to defer to him as he pointed at the cutter, asked questions, and made comments. James handed his glass to Rennie.

'Is that the man?' Whispering. 'Is that Aidan Faulk? I have never seen him.'

'If I can only see his face . . .' Taking the glass, and pointing it downward.

'Well, sir?' Impatiently.

Rennie focused the glass, and peered. After a minute or two
he sighed in exasperation, and:

'I cannot see his face clearly, even in the moonlight. He
wears a hat.'

'We must discover if it is him – or not. Also whether or no
the vessel is the *Lark*.'

'Y'said you recognized her, James.'

'I thought so . . .'

'I am fairly certain of her myself.'

'. . . but we must be certain, absolute. There is too much
hanging on this to allow of any doubt.'

'Yes – yes, you are right, in course. I will go down
there.'

'You, sir?'

'Why shouldn't I go down?' Curtly.

'Well – it is a very great risk. It will require a certain . . .
agility of movement.'

'I am not a decrepit old man, James. I am healthy and
strong – and agile. I will go down and look at the fellow close,
and at the vessel.'

'How will you do it, sir?'

'Eh?'

'How will you contrive to get close enough on the
beach. It is a shingle beach, impossible to walk over silent,
and – '

'*Lark*, I recall, had particular furniture at her tafferel, that
I would know at once.' Ignoring James's protests. 'We cannot
hope to see it from this height, but from the beach I should
certainly be able to make it out.'

'Furniture?' James, doubtfully.

'Aye, it is the stepping for a ringtail mast. I have never seen
it before on a cutter.'

'I did not notice it.'

'It ain't something you would likely have remarked,
perhaps. I remember it distinct from the first encounter, after

Lark had bested us. She delivered a final broadside, and ran to the north, and I saw her tafferel then as we wallowed on the swell, crippled and half-drowned, and you lay near death upon the deck – '

'Yes, yes, thank you, sir.' James, over him. 'You saw her tafferel. However, I do not think you should climb down there.'

'One of us must. I have proposed myself, and I fully intend – '

'You forget, sir, that at present you hold no commission, and therefore cannot be in command, cannot give orders.'

'Eh? What the devil d'y'mean, James?'

'I am in command, and I do not permit it.'

Both men were now growing angry, and the necessity to limit their speech to furious whispers did not improve their temper.

Rennie drew in a deep sniffing breath, and bit his tongue. Then without another word he crawled rapidly away from James along the top of the little eminence, and disappeared down the slope to the west.

'Sir! Captain Rennie!' A hoarse, dismayed, furious whisper.

But Rennie was gone.

*

Rennie came down to the beach from the steep slope on the western side of the cove, and wished that he was wearing Lieutenant Hayter's working rig. In the past he had deplored these clothes – old shirt, jerkin, and breeches, and a blue kerchief tied rakishly on the head – as unbecoming to an officer, altogether too much of the lower deck, and likely to lead to familiarity and indiscipline among the people. Now he would have welcomed any and all of these faults. James's working clothes would have allowed him to appear on the beach as a natural member of the throng there. He crept along the top of the beach, discarded his coat, waistcoat and hat, tore off his stock, rolled up his sleeves and tied his pocket handkerchief loosely round his neck. He took a handful of earth and rubbed it on his face and forehead, then smeared it to a smooth patina of unwashed skin. Then he took a deep breath, another, turned and walked swiftly down to the pile of casks and other gear, and caught up a length of rope. Coiled and slung it on his shoulder, and strode steadily down the shingles to the water's edge, joining the large group of men there. All were at work, some carrying gear aboard the raft, others preparing it ashore. A forge had been set up, and fired. There was a ring of lanterns on the shingles, and others aboard the cutter and the raft. The rumble of voices, the clinking of metal on metal at the forge.

Rennie edged closer, cleared his throat and spat, and settled the rope on his shoulder. He peered at the tafferel of the cutter, and at once saw the stepping for the ringtail mast. He noted that although the vessel had been painted blue, traces of black showed underneath the blue paint along her port strake. Here was the *Lark*, without question. Rennie looked for the man who had come in the boat. Was he still on the beach, or had he gone aboard the cutter?

'Clap on to t'other end of this, mate.' A voice behind Rennie. He turned cautiously, keeping his head lowered a little, as if he had a natural stoop. Took hold of the length of planking thrust at him, shouldered it and found himself stepping in unison with the other man, in line ahead, across a short gangway to the raft.

'Heave!'

And they heaved the timber on the pile of planking already there with a thwacking thud. Keeping his head down Rennie pretended to push the plank better into position on the pile, and looked across the *Lark*'s deck. There was no sign of the man he sought.

'Is you going to stand there fartin' into y'breeches all the night long, mate? Bear a hand lighting along the rest.'

Rennie straightened up, nodded, and in an assumed

seaman's blur: 'Aye, go on. I am wiv you.' And followed his
companion ashore.

'Come in the uvva boat, has you, from along the coast?
Wiv the master?'

'Eh? Oh, aye, in the boat. Got a painful feerce head on me,
from the drink.' He spat again.

'A-going back theer t'night, is it? On the tide?'

'I am to stop 'eer. Lend a hand, like.'

'Bofe 'ands, then. Cheerly, too. She must be made ready by
t'morrer night.'

'I shall pull my weight – but I must piss away some of that
drink, first.'

He stepped up the shingles, unslinging the rope from
his shoulder, and pretending to unfasten the front of his
breeches. As soon as he was safely beyond the glow of
the lanterns he ducked down and ran doubled-up away to the
place where he had left his hat and coat, gathered them up,
pulled them on, and began to make the climb to the top of the
steep slope. Presently he reached the top, and made his way
cautiously along to the clump of buckthorn bushes, and
James.

'Christ Jesu, I had given you up for lost, sir – or took!' Half
angry, half delighted.

'Hhh – never think that, James – hhh.' Short of breath
from the climb. 'Hhh – I am here, as you see. Whhh . . . I am
not as young as I was.'

'What did you discover – if anything?'

'There can be no doubt. None at all. She is the *Lark*.'

'Very good, excellent.' James, nodding. 'You saw Faulk?
You recognized Faulk?'

'I did not.'

'Ah! Damnation!'

'However, I spoke to a man who referred to the fellow that
came in the boat as the master. That can only be Faulk, I
reckon. And I discovered another valuable piece of
information. She is to be made ready by tomorrow night.'

'Tomorrow night! Hell on fire, then we cannot lose a single moment.'

*

'I am sorry to wake you so confounded early, Colonel, but we must assemble and depart by nine o'clock.'

Colonel Macklin was not yet wholly awake in his cot. He stared blearily at James, sat up and rubbed his face, yawned, and scratched the back of his head. Then: 'Nine in the forenoon?'

'Aye, today, if y'please.' James, briskly. 'We have found our quarry, and if we are to best him we must take him by surprise. A dozen men, I think you said?'

'I did, Lieutenant.' The colonel sat up, and swung himself out of his cot. He shrugged off his nightshirt, and tipped water from ewer into basin. 'Allow me five minutes, and I shall join you.' Dashing water into his face, and sluicing himself from head to foot with a dripping sponge. The bare floorboards round his cot were soon liberally splashed. James stepped back to avoid getting wet, and went out.

True to his word Colonel Macklin appeared fully dressed in the corridor five minutes after, strapping on his sword and gorget.

'We need a larger boat, Colonel.' As they walked along the narrow corridor towards the stairs. 'A thirty-two-foot pinnace. Can you request one at the yard?'

'I expect so, yes.'

'Very good. Extra powder and ball for musket. And several brace of spare pistols, if you can get them.'

'I will get them.' As they clattered down the narrow stone stairs. As they came out into the open air, the colonel saw James's drawn unshaven face in the harsh glare of daylight, and: 'By God, Hayter, you look all in.'

'We've been at work all the night,' admitted James. 'Many hours in the boat, and watching ashore.'

'You must get some rest, if we are to fight an action.'

'I'll snatch a wink or two in the boat on the way to Bucklers Hard. Captain Rennie is waiting for us. I must rouse and assemble my people, and – '

'Have you ate breakfast?'

'Nay, there ain't time. It is already past seven o'clock.' Striding away across the barrack square.

Colonel Macklin hurried after him, gripped James by the shoulder and made him pause. 'Now then, don't be altogether a damned fool. No sleep, and no victuals neither, will not answer. You and Captain Rennie will eat breakfast with me, if y'please, and my sergeant of marines will assemble the men and equipment.'

'I tell you, there ain't – '

'That will take forty-five minutes at the very least.' Over him. 'During which time, eggs, bacon, toast and coffee for you, m'dear fellow, and for Captain Rennie and me. – You there, Corporal!'

*

At Bucklers Hard Lieutenant Hayter said to Redway Blewitt that he must have the *Hawk* today, as a matter of extreme urgency.

'She will not be ready until the morrow, Mr Hayter, as I told you very specific last time you was here.' Jamming his pipe into his mouth.

'I do not care about that, thank you. I must have her *today*.'

'And I cannot do it.'

Below them the contingent of Marines, and the Hawks, waited at the boat under a cloudless, gull-tilting sky.

James drew a determined breath, but Captain Rennie had now stepped forward, and he took James's elbow and murmured something in his ear. James frowned, and then moved away to stand at the side of the slip. The smell of adzed timber floated on the air, and tar, and tide.

'Mr Blewitt.' Rennie smiled at him.

'I am here.' Puff.

'I am willing to pay you a handsome bonus.'

An exasperated sigh, pulling the pipe from his mouth. 'And I have said, repeated, it ain't a question of money!'

Rennie smiled again, nodded, moved a step closer. 'An hundred guineas over the agreed sum, as a boon. Gold guineas.'

'One hundred . . . ?' In astonishment. 'Ye'd pay that?'

'I would. I will.'

'But . . . but that is half as much again as we agreed.'

'Aye, it is. – Well?'

'I don't know . . . my artificers are working at full speed, and – '

'Was they working at midnight last night?'

'Eh? Midnight? Nay, in course they was not.'

'I was. So was Mr Hayter. And we was being paid nothing. Nothing, sir. While you are being paid handsome. With an hundred guineas offered, extra and above, if you will only grant us this small favour.'

'Well . . . you put it very persuasive . . . but I do not think it can be managed. No. No. I think it cannot.' Shaking his head. 'My artificers – '

'Oh, very well.' Rennie shook his head in turn, with a wry, downturning mouth. 'Stop the work. Stop it at once.'

'Eh?' The pipe poised halfway to his mouth.

'If we cannot have our cutter by this evening then we will not need her at all. Our duty must be abandoned, and our task go by the board.' He turned away, paused as if on an after-thought, and: 'In course, there may then be a dispute as to moneys owed.'

'Dispute!'

'Indeed, dispute, Mr Blewitt. Perhaps Mr Hayter and I will like to call down a quarterman from Portsmouth Yard to examine the work in all particulars, at some later time. In a month, say, or six weeks. It may then become a matter for the

Admiralty Court – who can say? Well well, good day to you.'
A few steps down the side of the slip, and he called: 'Stop the
work, at any rate. Stop the work, Mr Blewitt.'

'Wait! Wait a moment!'

*

'What in the name of Christ our Saviour and Comfort did
y'say to him, sir?' James had asked, chuckling and shaking his
head in admiration as they walked together down to the boat.
'What made him change his mind?'

'Well well . . . I showed him where his best interests lay.'

'Yes, but how?' Still chuckling.

'By calling his bluff, James.' And he would say no more
than that.

They had sailed at dusk, not heading toward Wyrefall
Cove direct, but south-west in a long sweep, then west, then
at length north, then east, until they stood off the coast half a
league, immediately to the west of the cove, having described
nearly a full circle in several hours of sailing. Now, standing
off a little, the wind in the west, they had the wind gauge.
When *Lark* made her run into the open sea she would be at a
disadvantage.

James had ordered *Hawk* darkened. No lights of any kind
were to be shown on deck, or aloft. Every man aboard had
been obliged to blacken his face, and to wear the darkest coat,
jacket or jerkin he possessed. The Marines had not made the
trip from Portsmouth in their scarlet coats, but in blue jackets
found for them at James's request. Even Colonel Macklin, in
usual very smart in his appearance, had been persuaded to
shed his scarlet and don a plain blue frock coat lent him by
James. There was absolute silence on deck, fore and aft.
Orders were to be conveyed by relayed hand signals, or in
whispers, until battle was joined.

Hawk's carronades were loaded with roundshot for the first
broadsides, and were to be reloaded with more roundshot.

'Not grape, James?' Rennie had asked. 'I thought you had a preference for grape as a man-killer, did not y'tell me?'

'I do not want to kill men, sir, this action – for fear of killing Aidan Faulk. I want to disable *Lark* and take her, and him. We must produce the fellow alive.'

'Yes, in course you are right . . . only, will not eighteen-pound roundshot smash *Lark* so heavy that she will likely sink? Surely it will be better to cut across her stern and rake her with – '

'Sir, if you please.' Firmly, over him. 'Allow me to know best how to handle my ship and fight my guns. Will you?'

'Indeed, indeed – forgive me.' And Rennie had then shut his mouth, contrite.

The *Lark* made her run in the first faint glimmers of dawn.

*

And at first, *Hawk*'s lookout did not see her. James had insisted that *Hawk* should not remain hove-to or lying at anchor during the hours of darkness, but should continue to tack by the wind, go about and run before, &c., in order to keep the watches on their toes, since *Lark* could appear at any time. He had not, however, insisted that his guncrews should stand by their guns. He wanted them fresh and eager when the time came.

When the lookout did see *Lark* she was already slipped clear of the cove and begun to head south-east on the starboard tack. She was in disguise. She was again painted black, and her canvas was also very dark. Against the dark line of the coast she was nearly invisible. *Hawk* had been sailing west, and was coming off the wind to go about, and the lookout – forgetting all notions of silence – bellowed:

'D-e-e-e-e-ck! Cutter standing away to the east!'

James raised his glass, saw the *Lark* and recognized her, and:

'Mr Love! We will beat to quarters! Mr Dumbleton! Set me a course to intercept!'

The calls, thudding feet, and the deck heeling as *Hawk* came round on the new heading, the heavy mainsail boom swinging over the heads of James, Rennie and the afterguard at the falls. The urgent sighing and creaking of a weatherly sea boat answering the helm. A glitter of spray like liquid fire against the dawn. The hissing, seething rush of the sea. The shouts of guncrews, and powderboys with cartridge. The clatter and fury as tompions came out, and:

'Larboard battery ready, sir!' Midshipman Wallace.

'Starboard battery ready, sir!' Midshipman Abey.

'Has she seen us, d'y'think?' James, his glass to his eye.

'Certainly.' Rennie, at his side. 'That is why she is running.'

'Then we will run, too. Run right at her, by God.'

Hawk closed the other cutter, running on the port tack with the westerly wind on her quarter. *Lark* ran steadily sou'-east on the starboard tack, the wind on her beam. She could not run due east to make her escape, because if she did she would wreck herself on the Needles. Although *Lark* was a fast, weatherly cutter, *Hawk* was faster running before, and as she came within range the *Lark*'s starboard battery spoke, a stutter of orange flashes and ballooning smoke preceding the deep concussive thuds of her guns over the sea.

Roundshot ploughed into the swell just astern of *Hawk* in multiple eruptions of spray. All the shots had missed, but James was not in any way relieved.

'By God, he has got carronades! Twelve-pounder carronades!'

'Aye, the guns hid under the canvas on the shingle in the cove,' nodded Rennie. 'I should have looked under that canvas, but I did not.'

'He has sixteen carronades to my ten! Eight twelve-pounders in each broadside!' James was aghast. 'Christ Jesu, we cannot best him now.'

'We must try, James.'

'Aye, we must. Mr Abey!'

'Sir?' The whites of his eyes in his blackened face.

'Stand by your guns until we cross his stern.' A long, heeling, sea-hissing moment, and:

'Fire as they bear!' James.

'Starboard battery! Fire! Fire! Fire!' Richard Abey.

BOOM   BOOM-BOOM   BOOM   BOOM

Hawk trembled her whole length. Gritty smoke boiled out and wafted away on the wind, and James saw that only one of his shots had struck home. The *Lark*'s stern was damaged, but not shattered, and her helm and rudder were intact.

Hawk came about on the starboard tack in order to chase her quarry south-east. As she tacked, *Lark*'s guns spoke again – her larboard battery.

THUMP   THUMP   THUMP-THUD
THUMP-THUD   THUD   THUD

Twelve-pound roundshot struck the *Hawk* in four places. She shook horribly, and there was the sound of splintering timber. Then moans, and a harsh, agonized scream. Repeated. And repeated.

Half the forrard rail on the starboard side had been smashed away, and hammocks hung trailing in tatters in the sea. Two of the starboard carronades had been hit, and torn off their carriages. There were dying men, and dead men. There was blood streaming along the deck, and spattered across the reef points of the mainsail.

The scream came again.

James picked himself up, staggered on the tilting deck, and lurched aft to the tafferel. Peered over and down in an effort to examine his rudder. It appeared to be intact. But the helmsman was absent, the tiller beginning to swing free.

'Mr Dumbleton! . . . Mr Dumbleton!' Taking the tiller himself until a new helmsman could be found – or the missing one.

The red-gleaming, yellow-glittering sun seemed to pierce his head when he glanced east. The low-sitting, fiery light burned across the swell, across the restless, living sea. He looked south and saw that *Lark* had altered course to run sou'-sou'-east, and was already nearly half a league distant, making good her escape. How long had he lain there on deck, James wondered.

'Mr Dumbleton! We must give chase!'

But Garvey Dumbleton did not attend him. The scream came again, fierce and piteous in the same moment.

'Mr Abey!'

'Sir . . . ?' The youth came aft, pale with shock.

'Who is hurt? Who is that screaming?'

'It is Mr Dumbleton, sir. He . . . he has been very horribly injured . . .'

'Find Dr Wing, and ask him to come on deck at once.'

Thomas Wing was already on deck, kneeling far forrard, tending to the wounded there. James gave the helm to Richard Abey, went forrard himself, and found Garvey Dumbleton trapped in a splintered shot-hole in the decking and side. He was hanging head down over the side, one arm half submerged in the rising and falling sea. One of his legs was caught deep in the hole, and the other lay useless beside it, with a dreadful injury below the knee. The injuries to his legs were not the most severe he had sustained. At his midriff was a mass of blood and bloodily pulped tissue soaking under and through his shirt. He screamed again, his eyes staring, his mouth gaping in a savage desperate grimace. James looked at him, turned his head away a moment, looked at him again.

'Ohh . . . ohh . . . ohh, God . . .' pleaded the wounded man.

James reached and tried to free the trapped leg. But this made him scream again, and then again came the helpless, panting 'ohh . . . ohh . . . ohh, Christ . . .'

'Doctor! Dr Wing!' shouted James, half-standing, half-kneeling. The sea sucked and lifted along the damaged wales, and submerged Dumbleton's dangling arm up to the shoulder.

And now Thomas Wing was at James's side, a bloody saw in his hand.

'We must release him, Thomas, and get him below.'

Dr Wing took it all in with the careful, detached gaze of a man who cannot allow emotion or delicate feeling to dictate. A swift intake of breath, and leaning close to James:

'There is nothing can be done for him. We must end his suffering.'

'What? We must get him free, and – '

'No, sir. No. We must end his suffering.'

'But how? How, if we don't release his leg?'

Quietly: 'Have you a pistol?'

'What?'

'I cannot reach down to give him a lethal quantity of physic. Your pistol must answer.'

'Good God, Thomas . . . Good God, I cannot . . .'

'Then give the pistol to me.' Calm and grim.

'Nay – nay, if you are entirely certain it must be done . . .?'

'Yes.' With finality. 'I am.'

'Then I will do it.'

He took his pistol from his coat, cocked it, and as Garvey Dumbleton moaned 'Ohh . . . ohh . . . ohh, Christ . . .'

crack

James ended it, and threw the pistol far out into the sea. Felt Thomas Wing's hand grip his arm, a brief, strong, heartfelt squeeze, and then the doctor was gone, hurrying forrard.

James stood still a moment, steadied himself with a deep breath, and was about to turn aft when he became aware of a seaman staring at him in shocked disbelief. James briefly met the seaman's gaze, then the man turned away. However,

James had seen the accusation in the man's eyes, and opened his mouth to speak, to say some quick word of explication and reassurance. No words would come. He stood irresolute a moment longer, then swung round and strode aft. Another breath, as if to cleanse his breast, and:

'Mr Abey! We will get under way, if you please! Let us clear all wreckage and put it over the side, and reload our guns! We are in a chase!'

'Hands to make sail!'

The calls, and renewed bustling activity. Captain Rennie appeared.

'There you are, sir.'

'I helped to carry some of the wounded people below, James. What is my duty?'

'Eh? Duty?'

'Give me a task.'

'Very well, sir, I will. Y'may help put Mr Dumbleton over the side, that has been killed, forrard. And then y'may captain a carronade.'

*

Hawk had been damaged and had lost men, but she was no worse injured than *Lark*, and was as swift – swifter – so that soon she began to gain on *Lark*. The dawn light had become full morning, broad and clear, the Needles and the Isle of Wight to the east.

When after a further glass it became apparent that *Hawk* would likely run *Lark* down, the black-painted, dark-sailed cutter came about and prepared to meet the challenge. She would not run any more, she would stand and fight.

James tacked and ran sou'-west close-hauled, as if sailing away from the *Lark*. Then as *Lark* herself began to run sou'-west, briefly the predator, James brought his cutter about once more, and flew on the starboard tack, with the wind on his quarter, straight at *Lark*. He had kept the wind gauge, and now was very close, well within range before *Lark* could counter. On James's instruction, as *Hawk* now abruptly swung to starboard, the larboard battery was brought to bear as one gun. In giving this instruction earlier, he had added:

'We will aim to dismast him again, Mr Abey. We cannot allow him first fire, else he will likely smash us altogether. We must dismast him, throw his people into desperate confusion, and lay alongside before he can recover. Every man to have a cutlass and a pair of pistols as we board. Colonel Macklin?'

'I am here.'

'I will lead the first group, boarding at the bow. Will you lead the second, boarding aft with your marines?'

'Very good.'

'And remember – we must take her master alive.'

'What will you like me to do, James?' Rennie, anxious to be of active use.

'Take command of *Hawk*, sir, if y'please, as soon as I am out of her.'

'You will not like me to board *Lark* with you?'

'No, sir.'

'Well well, very good, as you wish.' Disappointed.

And now they ran at the *Lark* in a tight curve, Mr Love acting as sailing master in Garvey Dumbleton's place. A creaking, heeling moment, then:

Richard Abey: 'Larboard battery . . . on the lift . . . fire, fire, fire!'

BOOM BOOM BOOM BOOM-BOOM

Belching orange fire, the hiss of roundshot, a storm of sulphurous smoke.

Lark faltered. Even as her own guns thudded, she faltered. Her mainsail shivered, and slumped. Shrouds, stays, foresails, yards, all tipped tangling and tumbling from the great stick of her mast, and with a rending, splintering, quivering crash the mast fell away over her starboard side into the sea.

A ragged cheer from the Hawks. *Lark*'s broadside had gone wide. She was at their mercy.

'Lay me alongside her, Mr Love!' James bellowed. 'Prepare to board!'

Resistance at first was fierce on *Lark*'s tangled deck. There was hand-to-hand fighting, bloody, yelling, and hard. Attempts were made by the defenders to fire canister-loaded swivels into the advancing boarders. Both attempts were thwarted by quick action and the swivels thrown overboard. As the two boarding parties fought towards each other, faces blacked, pistols cracking, cutlasses hacking and thrusting, the hapless crew of the boarded vessel, caught between them, saw that the position would soon become hopeless, and rather than surrender their lives they surrendered their weapons instead, and capitulated.

'Now then, where is he?' James strode through the kneeling men, and went aft. 'Where is her master?'

He went below, and found only wounded seamen, and much bloody confusion. The great cabin was empty. James came again on deck, and stood by the binnacle, surveying the damage. Richard Abey came to him, his hat off.

'If you please, sir. There is a man lying under the broken mainsail boom, part covered by canvas. I think he is dead.'

'I will look at him, Richard.' And he followed the boy across the deck. At the place James pulled away blood-soaked canvas and a tangle of cable-laid rope, and gazed down at the motionless figure. A heavy splinter protruded from his throat in a welter of blood. His eyes were open, staring sightless.

'Yes, he is dead. – Jump aboard *Hawk*, Richard, if y'please, and say to Captain Rennie with my compliments that I will like to see him here.' Sheathing his sword.

'Aye, sir.'

A few minutes after, Rennie came aboard, stepping over debris, and stood beside James. 'Why did not you allow me to board and fight, James? We have always – '

'Because this was my fight, sir.' Over him. 'I did not wish to see you risk your life untoward.'

'Untoward! Surely we are – '

'Is that the man, sir?' Again over him, pushing aside bloody canvas with his foot.

Rennie looked, sniffed in a breath, and let it out as a sigh: 'Yes, that is Aidan Faulk.'

'So it has all been for nothing, has it not?' And he covered the dead man's face.

'Never say that, James.'

'What, then? What should I say? That we have won?'

And he stepped away to the rail, and stared out over the lifting sea.

NINE

'Escaped!' Major Braithwaite was both furiously dismayed and extremely sceptical, and his face said so. '*Both* of them escaped?'

'No, sir.' James, very correct, his back straight. 'Mr Scott has escaped. Faulk – was killed.'

'Damnation and hellfire! You gave me your word that Scott would be took! And now you bring me this wretched intelligence!'

'You may imagine our very considerable regret that Aidan Faulk – '

'Candidly, Mr Hayter, candidly I do not much care about Mr Bloody Faulk, now! You have allowed Scott to give you the slip, that is the – '

'Major Braithwaite. Sir.' Rennie took a step forward with a polite but firm little smile, and a brief nod to James. 'We have suffered very heavy losses in the action we fought earlier today. Men are dead, and gravely injured. Mr Hayter and I was lucky to escape death ourselves. We did not know Scott had escaped until half a glass after, and then it was too late altogether. *Hawk* lay near crippled in the sea, there was hand-to-hand fighting, and – '

'Christ in tears, Rennie, could not your damned lookouts have kept a better watch? Was not the entire purpose of this battle at sea to capture Scott?'

'In course it was, Major, in course it was. Scott and Faulk both. And as sea officers we did our utmost to achieve that end. However, Scott and several others had escaped in a boat, and –'

'You failed! Failed, sir! When I had put at your disposal all my resource, and you gave me your solemn oath!'

'Our solemn oath that we would do everything in our power. But anything may happen – '

'I warned you what I would do if you failed me, did not I? That I would place you under arrest!'

'Anything may happen at sea, as I was about to say.' Rennie, very firmly, over him in turn. 'We are only human men, not gods, and men may only do their best.'

'You call this dismal outcome your best?'

'Honourably do their best, as we have done today, at great cost.'

'Hah!'

'You scoff, sir?' Rennie, his eyes narrowed. 'You question my honour?'

'A man of your reputation, Rennie, had better not talk about honour.' Glaring at him.

James now took his cue, and re-entered the fray: 'I do not think it wise in you, Major Braithwaite, to question Captain Rennie's honourable intent, and his best efforts in your behalf, since that would be to question his courage.'

'I have only said – '

'To do so would mean, in course – that you doubted my own courage.' A hint of menace.

'What damned nonsense is this?' Major Braithwaite was now less sure of himself. 'What I said was that I – '

'Sea officers that have just fought a bitter, bloody action will not like to hear their courage questioned ashore, nor their honour maligned.' James placed a hand on the hilt of his sword. 'They will likely take that very hard, you know.'

'Do you presume to threaten me, sir?' His anger reasserting itself.

'Will you look out of the window, Major? The officer you see standing under the tree is Colonel Macklin of the Corps of Marines. Should I have cause to signal for his assistance, he will summon his men, and come in. I hope that will not be necessary?' Raising his eyebrows.

'Good God, sir. You do threaten me!'

'No, sir. I merely point out – that you had better not threaten me.'

'I have not threatened you.' Very stiff, containing his anger. 'I have done nothing of the kind.'

'Did not you say something about arresting us both . . . ?' Including Rennie with a glance.

'Perhaps I did. I may have been hasty.'

'Hasty . . . ?'

'I did not mean it.'

James looked at him a long moment, then he smiled, and removed his hand from his sword.

'Very well, Major, thank you. I am glad that we understand each other.' A polite bow. 'And now I must look to my wounded people, and see to their comfort. Your servant, sir.'

'Servant.' Major Braithwaite gave him the briefest of nods.

Rennie glanced at James, bowed in turn to the major, and the two sea officers retired.

All of Major Braithwaite's dreams of making an important arrest, and perhaps being party to even greater events – events of national significance – had been dashed. He was dissatisfied, agitated, angry, suspicious, almost certain that he had been lied to and used, was nearly consumed by a desire to be vengeful – and knew in his heart that he could do nothing.

'God damn and blast them to the burning fires of hell!'

*

'What was that dishwater about Colonel Macklin, James?' As they came away in their gig.

'I knew Braithwaite would not go to the window to look out. He was too proud. He attempted to bluster and intimidate. I was obliged to respond in kind.'

'Hhh-hhh, he did not like it.'

'Nay, he did not. D'y'think he will stir up trouble for us?'

'About Scott? Hhh-hhh, nay. Even if he felt that he'd been hoodwinked, he is too vain to say so. Nay, he is not the fellow we must fear now.'

'Hm. Greer, d'y'mean? About Faulk?'

A glance. 'I do, James.'

'We had better go there, I expect, and get everything settled.' They drove on through the evening a moment or two, then: 'D'y'think he will ask to look at the body, to be certain?'

'Faulk's corpse?'

'Very probably he will insist on seeing it, will not he? I should not have allowed them to put him over the side. I should have insisted that his body was brought into *Hawk*. There was such damned confusion after the action. And I should not have put poor Garvey Dumbleton over the side, neither . . .'

'Now then, James, y'must not allow y'self to sink into a condition of gloom and guilt. We fought a bloody action, and there was not room in our vessel for all of our wounded, and theirs, and – '

'I should have insisted, though, insisted. I was lamentably at fault. It is all a wretched mess.'

'Now, James, this will not do – '

'Garvey Dumbleton was a married man. His widow will wish that she could visit her husband's grave.'

'Well well.' A shrug, and a reluctant, sighing sniff. 'She cannot, and there it is. You must not – '

'She will feel that it was a very heartless, cruel thing to have put him over the side. I will write to her. That is the least thing I can do.'

'It is always a good thing to write to the bereaved.' A nod.

'And to young Wallace's family, that was injured.'

'He will recover, though, will not he? He is at the Haslar?'

'Aye, under Thomas Wing. But many others will likely . . . not recover.' A deep sigh, and when Rennie glanced at his companion he saw that James had tears in his eyes. For a moment he thought of saying something encouraging or consoling – and then he did not. A commanding officer who has lost men in battle will always grieve, thought Rennie, and that is fitting, that is right; if he did not he would not be worth anything as a commander, nor as a man.

They drove on in silence, and after half an hour came to Kingshill, in gathering darkness.

'A great many bluffs have been called, sir, in this affair.' As they reached the urn-flanked stone entrance. 'We have exhausted the supply between us. There can be no attempt to do anything, inside, other than to tell the plain facts. Hey?'

'I reckon that is true, James.'

'You need not go in with me, you know. I am able to – '

'Not go in by your side?'

'You are not attached to me official, sir. You have already suffered much at Sir Robert's hands. I am willing to bear all of his – '

'We was in this together, James.' Rennie, shaking his head. 'We are in it together yet. Let us walk in, heads held high – together.'

'Very good, sir.'

They went in.

Sir Robert turned from his fireplace.

'I had half expected it. Half expected that he would elude us. You brought the body ashore?'

'No, Sir Robert. His people disposed of the corpse at sea.'

'Ah. – So there is not even the possibility of verifying his death?'

'I can vouch for it, Sir Robert.' Rennie had been silent until now, allowing Lieutenant Hayter to make his report in full. 'The man I saw lying dead upon the cutter's deck was Faulk.'

Sir Robert's black gaze. 'You are certain?'

'Yes.'

'Very well.' He walked to his desk, a little stiffly, thought Rennie. There he tied a sheaf of papers into a leather fold, and placed the fold in a drawer, which he locked.

'This is a dark day, gentlemen.'

'It has certainly been a dark day for me, Sir Robert.' James. 'I have lost several men killed.'

'I do not mean this one trivial battle, Lieutenant Hayter.' He turned and walked from the desk to the window, stared out a moment at the night, then drew the curtains there. 'I meant that it is a dark day for us all.'

James did not like the word 'trivial', and would have said so, but Sir Robert continued:

'The Prime Minister, Their Lordships at the Admiralty, the Secret Service Fund – all of us wished Aidan Faulk took, in order that he might be converted.'

'Converted, Sir Robert?'

'Aye, his mind turned again into that of an Englishman, rejecting his radical foreign beliefs, returning to the truth known by his father, and his father's father, and all his antecedents. That if England is lost – so is the world.'

Rennie and James exchanged a glance.

'Aidan Faulk has brought into this country several and many spies. An whole secret clan of alien men, working against our interests, sending intelligence back to France. It was our hope that we could return him to his original beliefs, so that he would betray these men to us. Betray them, and then begin to act in turn as our own spy in France. And now he is dead, and we will never discover these evil creatures that hide among us.'

'Surely – was you to capture only one, might not he lead you to the others?' Rennie enquired.

'Faulk was the key. Without him our task is infinitely harder.' Sir Robert returned to the desk, and leaned on it. 'We needed such a man in France – several men – else place everyone in these islands, from His Majesty himself down to the humblest yeoman, at risk from dark, vile, poisonous tribulation. It is not too much to say that all of Europe faces a new Dark Age.'

'Really, Sir Robert – ' began James.

'You think I exaggerate, gentlemen? You think I overstate my case?' Over him. 'I assure you, I do not.'

'In least if we cannot persuade Faulk now, Sir Robert – since he is dead – then he cannot bring any more of these fellows into England,' said Rennie. 'And ain't it probable that without his guiding hand, those that are here will now find themselves at a loss – and thus of very little use to their masters in France.'

'You are an optimist, hey?' Sourly.

Rennie was about to say that he was not, that in usual he was the opposite, but Sir Robert:

'You may wish to brighten this black circumstance, Rennie, and you, Lieutenant Hayter, but it cannot be done.'

'Surely all is not quite lost as yet, Sir Robert?' said James. 'England is strong. And there are many of us to defend her, was she to be attacked.'

'She is already under attack.' Grimly. 'And I have failed. Failed altogether.'

'Does that mean you think I have failed altogether? As a sea officer?'

'Nay . . . nay . . . I placed too much upon your shoulders. I should have known you was not up to the task, Lieutenant. Neither you nor Rennie, that are merely pawns in the game.'

James began to bristle. 'I think perhaps you have forgotten, Sir Robert, that the task – as you call it – was not given me by yourself, but by Their Lordships. I will place myself at their disposal, if blame is to be apportioned in this.'

'Yes, yes, yes, Lieutenant, you are aggrieved.' A black glance. 'You do not like to be called a little man. We are all little men now. We have failed, and must face the consequence.'

*

A week passed, and Rennie and James were still at Portsmouth, at the Marine Barracks. A message had come to them from London, requiring both men to remain where they were until otherwise advised.

Admiral Hapgood had sought out Lieutenant Hayter there, and James had been obliged to endure a very uncomfortable interview with the Port Admiral at his office:

'You have took a prize, I hear?'

'I have not, sir.'

'What? You deny y'took a cutter out of the Channel? The *Lark* cutter?'

'I was obliged to defend my own cutter against attack by smugglers, sir. We towed the smuggler in, dismasted.'

'Where is that cutter now?'

'I believe she lies at Bucklers Hard, sir.'

'By whose authority?'

'She was turned over to the Board of Customs, sir. To a Major Braithwaite, I believe, that requested it – and since the Board is the proper – '

'Yes, yes, very well. I was not informed, in course. Where is your own cutter, now?'

'At the Dockyard, sir.'

'Why? Why have not ye rejoined the fleet?' &c., &c.

Then, on the eighth morning, another message came from London, addressed to James. When he broke the seal and unfolded it, he read:

Whereas the Lords Commissioners of the Admiralty, having determined, at Board, that the undernamed officers shall attend on them in the matter of the *Lark* cutter, and all associated Questions pertaining to that vessel, Their Lordships require that Lieutenant James Rondo Hayter RN, commanding HM *Hawk* cutter, 10; and William Rennie (late Post Captain RN); shall present themselves upon the date hereunder named, to answer for their Actions in all Particulars related to & concerning the said cutter *Lark*.

'Well, sir, there it is.' Showing the letter to Rennie. 'Our death-warrant.'

*

On the due date the two sea officers duly presented themselves at the Admiralty in Whitehall, having travelled from Portsmouth by express coach overnight.

James was in dress coat, with tasselled dress sword and cockaded hat. Rennie had deliberated long about his own clothes, and had repeatedly asked his friend's advice.

'What shall I wear, James, d'y'think? Should I attend in civilian dress – in Mr Birch's coat? Or should I wear my uniform?'

'I should wear my dress coat, sir, if I was you.'

'Ah, uniform. You think so?'

'Yes, sir.'

'I am not entitled to it, you know, since my court martial. I am no longer a post, official. I am nothing.'

'Then why have they wrote the word "officers" in their letter?'

'I was to've been reinstated, in course, but now . . .'

'Certainly they must regard you as an officer, if they wrote that.'

'Yes, but lower on that same page you will see me called plain "William Rennie" – "*late* Post Captain". Nay, I had better dress in civilian clothes.'

'Very well, sir, as you think best. It don't matter much, as things stand.'

'On t'other hand, though, perhaps they will take it as an insult – if I do *not* wear a dress coat.'

At length, quarter of an hour before their time of

departure, Rennie had shifted into his dress coat, pulled on his hat, searched frantically for his sword – until he remembered that he no longer possessed it – and rushed to the crowded High, where the coach stood waiting outside the Marine Hotel. He had clambered aboard with barely half a minute to spare.

And now they turned in under the arched stone entrance of the Admiralty, removed their hats at the door, and were asked to wait.

They waited in a side room, not very large, with a window but no view, only a modicum of stone wall and filtering light. They waited long, and began to fret. Rennie fidgeted, sitting on the single chair; James paced the floorboards, one of which creaked each time he trod over it. At last Rennie:

'James, James, for Christ's sake stop making that damned nail squeak, will ye?'

'What? Does it squeak? I did not hear it.' He stood briefly at the window, staring at nothing, then resumed pacing.

An hour passed. Rennie stood up, and James sat on the chair, and tapped the summoning letter against his thigh, until:

'James, for God's sake, dear fellow – will y'stop that bloody tap-tap-tap?'

Presently they were released from their misery, and summoned.

The clerk who took them upstairs showed them into the Board Room, with its tell-tale on the end wall, its wall of furled charts above the fireplace, its long table at the centre. All members of the Board were today absent, save one. Vice-Admiral Lord Hood came forward to greet the two officers.

'Gentlemen, come in.' Deep-set eyes, and a face that might have been forbidding in a less sympathetic man. 'Mr Hayter.' Shaking James's hand. 'And Captain Rennie.' He shook Rennie's hand. 'Let us sit down, and be comfortable.'

They sat down, James and Rennie on each side of one end of the great table, Lord Hood at the head.

'A glass of sherry, gentlemen?'

'No, thank you, sir.'

'Thankee, sir, no.'

'No? Well, perhaps not, just at present. I am today representing the First Lord, the Earl of Chatham, who is indisposed.' He opened a leather fold that lay on the table, and turned over several pages. He nodded. 'Hm. Yes. It is all quite straightforward, I think.' And closed the fold. 'The position is this. You are to be reinstated as post captain, Rennie, with immediate effect. Your warrant of commission is being wrote out in another room.'

'My . . . warrant of commission . . . ?' Staring at the admiral.

'Indeed. You are to have the *Expedient* frigate once again, as your command. That is – if you want her?'

'Want her? Good God. I beg your pardon, sir. Yes, yes, I want her.'

'Very good.' Turning to his other side. 'Mr Hayter, now we come to you.'

'Sir?'

'You are to be offered the ship-sloop *Eglantine*, twenty-two, with the rank of master and commander.'

James sat with his mouth open in astonishment, became aware, and closed it.

'However, you must make a choice.'

'Choice . . . ?'

'Yes. We have decided – the Board has decided – that should you wish to return to duty under Captain Rennie, as his first lieutenant in *Expedient*, we should not object. It would in no way reflect on your character and standing as a sea officer. But I should make clear that if you do decide to return to *Expedient*, the *Eglantine* would in course be given to another officer. We could not hold that commission open indefinite, you apprehend me?'

'I – I do, sir, thank you.'

'In course you need not decide immediate. We are disposed to allow you a week or two to make up your mind. That is right, that is fitting.' Turning back to Rennie again: 'You will not object, Captain Rennie, to a short delay?'

'Eh? No, no, in course I will not object, sir.'

James sat quiet a moment, trying to come to terms with all that had happened in the past few minutes. Tried, and could not.

'Sir, with your permission, I should like to understand . . . are we to be asked nothing about the *Lark*, today?'

'No.'

'The letter I received . . .' James took the letter from his coat '. . . said that we should – '

'It was merely a formal summons, wrote out in formal language. It don't signify in this room.'

'Ah. Oh.' James put the letter away, then: 'Sir, again with your indulgence, may I know – '

Lord Hood raised a hand, and over him: 'We have decided – the Board – that given your very courageous conduct in fighting several actions at sea, in the nation's interest – albeit without the result desired by all parties concerned – we have decided that you should be suitably rewarded. What better, what greater reward can there be, Mr Hayter, than the offer of his own ship to a sea officer?'

'None, sir.'

'Exact. And there you have your explanation.' A glance at both of them, now. 'A condition attaches, gentlemen, to both of these offers.'

'Condition, sir?' Rennie.

'Aye, a proviso. You are, neither of ye, to discuss in any distinction, with any person, any of the matters pertaining to the *Lark*, nor the man Faulk, now or at any future time. Your lips must be sealed, gentlemen, sealed absolute and for ever. Is that quite clear to y'both?'

'Yes, sir.'

'Yes, sir.'

'Very good. I will say in passing that large effort is being made to discover the spies that Faulk smuggled into England – but that need not trouble us as sea officers, gentlemen. It is not our duty, nor our concern, thank God. And now, I think, we will drink that glass of wine. Yes?'

'Thank you, sir.'

'Thank you, sir.'

Heartfelt.

*

Lieutenant Hayter had returned to Birch Cottage, his home at Winterborne in Dorsetshire, to be once more with his beloved wife Catherine, and his son, and to decide upon his future; neither did Captain Rennie remain in London. He returned to his own home, Southcroft House, at Middingham in Norfolk.

The passage of many weeks had not altered the appearance of his house, but Rennie noticed that the garden was not as well kept as he would have liked, that there was a slight air of neglect. His housemaid Jenny was not quite her usual cheerful self.

'The gardener has took hisself off to the farther side of Fakenham, sir. He has got more reg'lar work there, he says. I asked him what was more reg'lar than his work here at Southcroft, and he says – '

'Yes, well well, thank you, Jenny. We will engage another man presently, I am in no doubt.' He walked from room to room, and saw that everything was in good order, but with the same slight air of stale neglect he had seen outside. His maid – should not he call her his housekeeper? – came bustling downstairs, having taken up his valise, as Rennie emerged from his library.

'All bills and accounts have been settled in my absence?'

'Yes, sir, as you required of me. You wish to see my book?'

'Nay, nay, later will do. We are provisioned in the house? If I wished to invite guests?'

'Guests, sir? If you will tell me what to get in I shall order it in the village, in the forenoon tomorrow.'

'Yes, very good.'

'Will you like tea now, sir? Or hot water and vinegar?'

'What, vinegar? Ugh. Tea, by all means. Thank you.' Distracted, walking again to the entrance and looking out.

Since his return to Portsmouth from the sea action in the Channel, Rennie had not seen Mrs Townend. During the week he and Lieutenant Hayter had spent at the Marine Barracks, Rennie had gone to the Cambridge Road house where Mrs Townend was living with her sister, and had found it empty. Puzzled and dismayed, he had enquired at a neighbouring house about the two ladies who had lived at number fifty-four. He was their friend, he said, and had been at sea. The elderly occupant of the neighbouring house, who let rooms, had told him:

'They have gone away, sir. Mrs Rodgers desired to return to London, and her sister went home to Norfolk, as I understand.'

'Ah. Ah. This was very sudden?'

'As I understand, Mrs Rodgers found the house intolerable damp, sir. She complained that her health would suffer if she did not go away at once.'

'Damp? I did not know it was damp.'

'Between you and me, I do not believe it was damp. There was . . . I do not like to say anything harsh . . . but there was words said between the two ladies. There was disagreement. Damp was not the reason, but damp was proposed as the means to break the lease.'

'Ah. You have been very kind.'

'I hope that I am kind, sir.'

And he had given her a gold sovereign.

Rennie stood now at his door in Norfolk, and looked out at the familiar landscape. He had known Mrs Townend only a short time, and they had been lovers only very briefly, but now he was determined to take things further. He had deliberated on the journey from London whether to call on her at Norwich, and had then decided that he would not. Instead he would return to Southcroft and send word to her as a man in possession of his own house, a man of substance, a post captain RN, newly commissioned. He would ask her to be his wife.

'Speaking of guests, sir,' said Jenny, 'there has been a caller at Southcroft, only recent, enquiring when you was to come home.'

'Caller?' Turning from the door. 'When?'

'A lady, sir. She came the day before yesterday. A Mrs Townend.'

'Mrs Townend! She came here? Why did not y'tell me at once, good heaven? When did she come, did y'say?'

'The day before yesterday, sir.'

'Well? Well? What did she say? Is she staying in the village?'

'I – I do not know that, sir. I said – '

'You did not ask her where she was staying, good God?'

'It ain't my place to ask a lady such questions, sir.'

'No, no, you are quite right. Forgive me, I did not mean to bite off your head. Perhaps she left a card, or a note?'

'Yes, sir. She did leave a note. I had forgot. I left it on your desk, sir, in the library.'

'Very well, thank you, Jenny.' And he smiled at her so that she would not think him an ogre, hurried into his library and retrieved the note. It read:

My darling William,

I am staying with my cousins at Redland House, a mile beyond the village. Your housekeeper has told me that you will soon come home – that you had sent word. I was so very fearful that you would think I had deserted you at Portsmouth. My sister and I have become estranged after a very bitter dispute. I will call again on Thursday, and pray that you will be at home then, dearest.

Sylvia

Rennie folded the note, opened it and reread it, and:
'Jenny! Jenny!'
'Sir?' At the library door.
'I do not want tea, after all. I am going out.'
'Now, sir?'
'Aye, now. I must call on the lady who came here, and ask her a question, right quick. There ain't a moment to lose!'

*

At Birch Cottage, reunited with his wife, James told her at once of the Admiralty's offer of a new command.

'My darling, you are rightly valued,' said Catherine, looking into James's eyes. 'You are favoured.'

'Yes.' Holding her hands in his, and feeling that nothing mattered but this moment. He brought her hands up and kissed them, then held her to him, and kissed her mouth, her eyes, her neck. 'Yes.'

Presently: 'In course, I will not like it.' Catherine, softly.

'Not like it?' Murmuring, her hair on his cheek.

'No, I will not. It will take you away from me again.'

'Then I will not accept.'

'Not accept?' Drawing back her head to look into his face.

'Perhaps I will not.' Looking at her, and giving her a half-smile.

'But surely you have always wanted this, have not you? Preferment?'

'The thing that every sea officer wishes for, hey? That he cannot wait to get?'

'Is it not so? My darling, you look as if you did not wish it, after all.' Searching his face, seeing doubt in his eyes.

He drew her to him again, held her, then broke the embrace. 'The truth is – I am not sure.'

'But, why? Surely you have earned it? It is yours by right.'

'Yes, yes, I have earned it. Am fortunate and more to be offered it . . .'

'James, my dearest, I hope that you will not refuse your new command because of anything I have said. I was being foolish just now. I did not mean – '

'I know it. I know you will only wish for my advancement and satisfaction in the service.'

'Then . . . ?'

'I . . . I was obliged to do something at sea, lately, that was very painful to me. It has been much in my thoughts. In truth I have thought of little else since.'

'You had to punish one of your men?'

'No, it was not punishment. It could not be called punishment.'

'Will you tell me?'

'I do not think I can.' Shaking his head.

'James, I am your wife.' Softly, earnestly. 'I can bear anything you tell me.'

'I was . . . I was obliged to shoot a man that was horribly injured, so that he should not suffer any more.' He turned away a moment, and sat down, holding in a breath. Catherine came to him and took his head in her hands, and turned it gently to her.

'Oh, James. Oh, my poor darling, it hurt you so.'

After a moment, when he was again able to speak: 'I don't know that I can ever return to the service. I don't think I am able to command men, now, after that.'

'You must rest, my darling, and try to put it from your mind.'

'I wish I could.'

'Come and see your son. He is so eager to see you, James.'

'Is he? Is he? I will like to see him very much, dear little

boy. Forgive me for being so melancholy a fellow, will you?'
He stood up.

'I would not love you if you did not feel as you do.' Taking
his arm as they moved to the door.

*

Sir Robert Greer looked up from his desk in his library at
Kingshill House.

'What is it, Fender?'

'There is a gentleman wishes to see you, Sir Robert.' His
servant, at the door.

'Gentleman? At this hour? Tell him to go away.'

'I do not think he will go away, sir, as I may have cause to
know.' Touching his cheek.

'What? Who is he?'

'It is the same gentleman that came here before, sir.'

The door now swung fully open, and the servant was
pushed aside.

'Good evening, Sir Robert. Or should I say more accurate
– Mr Scott? You remember me, I think. I am Major
Braithwaite, of the Board of Customs.'

He beckoned in his men, and as Sir Robert rose angrily:

'Do not think of summoning the marines, sir. Do not think
of that. They have had instruction from elsewhere, and they
will not come.'

'You damned impudent wretch, I will – '

'No, sir. No. You will do nothing. Because, at long last, you
are took.'

ALSO AVAILABLE IN ARROW BOOKS

Mr Midshipman Fury

Peter Smalley

1792. HMS *Amazon* a 32 gun frigate arrives in Bombay where she discovers that a number of ships of the East India Company have disappeared somewhere in the Indian Ocean. There are reports of a very powerful privateer at work and the Governor despatches *Amazon* to find and destroy her. Soon afterwards *Amazon* is in a fight for her life against a much stronger foe, resulting in many of her officers killed. Midshipman John Fury finds himself, in his first ever combat, in charge of the gun deck.

In such crucibles of fire are the officers in His Majesty's Service forged. Showing exceptional courage and coolness, the shadows of the past are forever banished and Fury's naval career begins in glory as he becomes a leader of men.

'A rollicking adventure, real Boy's Own stuff, which will stir into life the most sluggish blood of the even the most pacific of readers. Among the most engrossing scenes is the forcefully described battle. Towering above all the action is Fury himself, a teenager with the skill and cunning of a superhero . . . Fury promises to go far' Peter Burton, *Daily Express*

arrow books

ALSO AVAILABLE IN ARROW BOOKS

HMS Expedient

Peter Smalley

1786: Captain William Rennie and Lieutenant James Hayter are on the beach and on half pay when they are given a prime commission: *HMS Expedient* is a 36 gun frigate which is to be sent to the South Seas on a scientific expedition.

But there is something odd and disturbing about the nature of their task. They sense that they are not being told the whole truth about the forthcoming expedition? Why is their voyage through the Atlantic dogged by sabotage and why are they followed by a mysterious man of war? And what are the secret orders which may only be opened once they round the Cape of Good Horn?

The answers lies on a beautiful uncharted island, in the remotest corner of the Pacific immensity, to which the storm-battered Expedient limps for desperately needed repairs. Soon the dangers of the voyage will pale in comparison with what the crew discover there, across the limpid waters of the lagoon.

'Smalley has written a real page-turner, engrossing and enthralling, stuffed with memorable characters. Highly recommended.' *Daily Express*

'Following in the wake of Hornblower and Patrick O Brian . . . there is enough to satisfy the most belligerent armchair warrior: cutlasses, cannibals, as well as a hunt for buried treasure. All this plus good taut writing gets Peter Smalley's series off to a flying start' *Sunday Telegraph*

arrow books

ALSO AVAILABLE IN ARROW BOOKS

Colours Aloft!

Alexander Kent

SEPTEMBER 1803

Vice-Admiral Sir Richard Bolitho finds himself the new master of the *Argonaute*, a French flagship taken in battle. With the Peace of Armiens in ruins, he must leave the safety of Falmouth.

What lies ahead is the grim reality of war at close quarters - where Bolitho who will be called upon to anticipate the overall intention of the French fleet. But the battle has also become a personal vendetta between himself and the French admiral who formerly sailed the *Argonaute*.

Bolitho and his men are driven to a final rendezvous where no quarter is asked or given.

—

arrow books

THE POWER OF READING

Visit the Random House website and get connected with
information on all our books and authors

EXTRACTS from our recently
published books and selected
backlist titles

**COMPETITIONS AND PRIZE
DRAWS** Win signed books,
audiobooks and more

AUTHOR EVENTS Find out which
of our authors are on tour and
where you can meet them

LATEST NEWS on bestsellers,
awards and new publications

MINISITES with exclusive
special features dedicated to our
authors and their titles

READING GROUPS Reading
guides, special features and all
the information you need for
your reading group

LISTEN to extracts from the
latest audiobook publications

WATCH video clips of
interviews and readings with
our authors

RANDOM HOUSE INFORMATION
including advice for writers,
job vacancies and all your
general queries answered

Come home to Random House
www.rbooks.co.uk